Wanderlust

Wanderlust

A
Wartime
Search
for
Hope
and
Home

KATHLEEN L. MARTENS

BYZANTIUM
Sky Press

Byzantium Sky Press
Ellendale, DE, 19941

ISBN 978-1-955872-00-3 (hardcover)
ISBN 978-1-955872-01-0 (paperback)
ISBN 978-1-955872-02-7 (ebook)

Library of Congress Control Number: 2021912040

First Byzantium Sky Press hardcover edition, July 2021

Interior design by Crystal Heidel, Byzantium Sky Press

Manufactured in the United States of America

Body of book is typeset in Sabon LT Pro
Dotunder font is typeset in Minion 3
Decorative fonts are typeset in Liza Display, Liza Text, Liza Caps

Wanderlust

Wanderlust is dedicated to my daughter and author, Kristen Janine Sollée. Her creativity abounds, and her wisdom and insights into people, life, and the written word are invaluable to me.

Thank you for your inspiration—you are treasured.

In memory of my loving mother Bernice Cecelia
Coyne Langmaack who inspired me with her gorgeous
singing voice, abiding faith, Irish-style humor, and
passion for a good read.

Acknowledgements

Maribeth Fischer, my irreplaceable, patient editor, and superb novel class teacher who guided and inspired me in my rough ride from short story writer to novelist.

Judy Catterton, my story editor, who dedicated endless hours sharing her incisive insights, logic, and uncanny ability to understand a character's inner drive.

Nancy Powichroski Sherman, my eagle-eyed copyeditor, for her invaluable feedback and guidance.

Rehoboth Beach Writers Guild, for providing unparalleled support, encouragement, and writing opportunities to those fortunate enough to be members.

Seaside Scribes, the sisterhood of women writers who have been so generous and loving as I pursued my later-in-life venture into writing.

My friends and readers, who tirelessly read my chapters, giving me honest, on-target feedback and advice:

Jean Aziz
Christy Briedis
Jane Klein
Fran Mossberg
Kristen Janine Sollée
Judy Wood

Steuart Martens, my husband, for cheering me on in the pursuit of my passion for writing.

Crystal Heidel, my publisher, for her faith in my work and her outstanding creativity in capturing the drama and feel of *Wanderlust* in its cover and interior design. Being in the hands of a dedicated publisher who is also a gifted designer and writer is a blessing to an author. She gets it!

CHAPTER 1

LEAVING LEATHER

KATE'S ESCAPE PLAN was no longer some remote fantasy; it was here; it was real. Wedging her foot against the crumbling brick wall, she tugged open the heavy gray door. The gunshot boom of it slamming behind her drew no attention from the sea of workers on the basement level below. Rebounding off the century-old factory walls, the deafening din of the shoe-making machinery and the cordwainers at work set her nerves on edge. Those syncopating sounds had filled Kate's life and threatened to swallow her future. Until now.

She read the creased correspondence in her shaking hand and tucked it into the pocket of her black leather miniskirt. Scanning the massive buzzing room for the family and friends she loved, the familiar scent of dyed leather wrapped around her. Kate wouldn't miss the odor that followed them home from work each day, sat in their parlors, and clung to the Ketchum clan's hair.

Mid-way down the stairs, Kate felt for the letter again. Acceptance. She smiled. Hadn't it seemed crazy applying to

UConn? Coming from a fourth-generation family of shoe craftsmen from a declining factory town in Massachusetts? And then to put her name in the running for a scholarship?

The notice had lived in her dresser drawer for six torturous weeks—no money, no way. Why even mention it if there were no funds to pay for it? Then the scholarship letter for her two-year free-ride had arrived, and Kate's way out of town had materialized.

For years, she'd endured her six siblings' teasing and jealousy about her foolish ambitions—dreamer, brainiac, prude, bookworm. Enough to make her doubt herself. Enough to make her feel selfish, even ungrateful at times for indulging herself in dreams of a life outside of Glynn.

She should be celebrating her good luck, swirling in circles with her arms out, Kate thought. Isn't this what she'd worked for? Prayed for? Then why was she holding her breath? Why did she feel like a heavy wool blanket had dropped over her? Kate wrapped her arms around herself. Not everyone in her Irish tribe would be overjoyed with Kate's departure, she thought. In her head, Kate could hear her Grandma Kendall quoting the old Irish saying, *Now don't be talkin' about yourself while you're here; we'll surely be doin' that after you leave.* Sharing good news about yourself would invariably be read as bragging in her Irish clan; Kate understood that. "Too big for her britches, that one," her grandmother would say.

Spotting her mother amid the scores of employees in the handmade shoe section, Kate continued down the metal stairs. At least her mom would be elated. Tension traveled to Kate's stomach. There were layers of reasons that pulled at her to leave Glynn, the most powerful one she didn't even understand herself. The minute Kate had taped the world map onto her bedroom wall in the fifth grade, her mother said she'd recognized Great-grandmother Katherine's unmistakable trait in Kate—wanderlust.

For years, Kate had devoured geography and travel books that seemed to jump off the library shelf into her arms. Stabbing pushpin after pushpin into exotic places on her map— foreign countries, too foreign to imagine—she'd shaped her dreams.

Kate sought the serenity of the yellowed-walled town library since she could first read. It had been her haven, her only escape from the clatter and chaos and resounding ruckus in Kate's life. Even today, at twenty-one, on her day off from her two jobs, she'd sat there in the corner all afternoon, waiting to make her announcement. She'd re-read the scholarship letter and admired a book with photos of the bucolic Connecticut countryside. *A college nestled in farmland*, she laughed. She'd never even seen a pig or a cow or a horse in real life until her campus visit.

Kate moved down the ridged metal steps to the factory floor. A line of hot moisture ran down her spine. The truth struck her; if it weren't for all that clatter and commotion in her life, would she have taken refuge in a world of books? Would she be here making her announcement today? After three years of working to pay tuition for community college, she'd desperately wanted to finish her degree at a good university.

Inhaling the pungent odors, Kate imagined breathing fresh air outside the factory neighborhood—a quiet place that held no acrid scent of shoe-making and tanning in its every corner. The rhythmic sounds of crickets and the occasional spray of sparrows overhead had captivated her when she'd secretly visited the lovely campus last year. A place where the sunlight filtered through vibrant fall maple leaves, not a place where it pushed through dusty windows of endless rows of yard-less houses.

Kate's redhaired Ketchum clan stood out like a dozen red roses scattered among the hundred dark-haired domes—a distinction she shared. Half of the brunettes were related to her too. In her periphery, the shop foreman, Mr. Donohue, stood with his vigilant eye looking down from his pint-sized glass loft. Hands on his hips, he forced a smile—a swift pull of the corners of his mouth that could have been read as no more than a twitch. Kate had always counted him among the villains in the stories she'd read on Saturdays at the library as a child—evil pirates, slave drivers, or cruel stepfathers. Too much imagination, Kate.

News of her scholarship would flash fast through the streets of a small town, she thought as her elation began to seep in. But the happiest part was about to happen—telling her mom.

Descending the stairs to the factory floor, Kate imagined someday seeing her mother tending her small garden instead of bowed over a half-made shoe. She wanted to help with Dad's medical bills when his back finally gave out. Working in Glynn would never pay enough to buy Kate the life she wanted or an exciting career that she loved. Maybe she'd find a job that would take her on business trips to those exotic countries she'd fantasized about. Maybe she'd have extra money to travel on vacation. She saw herself sipping coffee at a café in Paris, kneeling in the Duomo in Florence, visiting the temples of Thailand, or riding horseback in the Australian outback, and of course, singing on the side in some cozy café. Always singing.

The angle of the light slashing through the tall, dusty windows meant her mom's shift was almost over. Taking in the factory in a way she never had before, Kate observed the scene as though it were for the last time. The production lines and employee numbers had dwindled these past few years as the American shoe industry had declined and moved to China. No longer the size of half a football field, the building expansion that had accommodated five long lines of equipment for machine-made shoes had been sold off along with the machinery. The operation had diminished to two lines in 1968. Half of the workstations were now empty.

In the far corner of the factory, Kate scanned the dozens of craftsman who still made the custom handmade shoes the Owl & Shamrock label was famous for—mostly her family and neighbors. Back in the golden age of handmade footwear, Kate's clan was known for their exquisite handiwork.

Two of her sisters, Kelly and Karen, sat at the sewing station with heads dropped low, focused on the line of stitches they ran down the toe box of men's black wingtips.

Across the high-ceilinged room, her twin cousins, Uncle Jack's girls, nestled the pairs of shoes into tissue paper in boxes imprinted with the famous winking-owl and kelly green shamrock label and snugly closed the lids. Kate's Ketchum kinfolk were among the few remaining craftsmen skilled at hand shoemaking who still had jobs in one of the lingering factories in Glynn—one of the shoemaking capitals of the world back in the day. *Souls for soles, get it?*—her grandfather liked to joke about her family's legacy.

Not *my* soul, Kate pleaded.

"Kev." Kate squeezed her brother's shoulders from behind.

"Hey, Sis. Came to see the peasants?"

That stung. No jokes today, please, Kate thought.

"Hang on, almost got this," he yelled. Kevin remained stooped over a stubborn, hundred-year-old antique shoemaking machine, applying grease to coax it back to life. Each of her brothers worked one of the three ancient machines that cut and prepared the oak-tanned leather soles. Kevin was at the first machine that cut the top channel; Keith, the second that cut the bottom channel; and Karl, the third machine that punched holes along the channel for stitching. Even after a century of use, this equipment was the best to get the job done. The final tasks were done by hand.

Her brother could have been her father, her grandfather, or great-grandfather—ruddy-faced, muscled, good-natured Irishmen with a distended belly pushing up against his leather belt. Like all the men in the family, he swallowed his fate like the foaming beers that followed work each night at O'Leary's Pub. A man who dutifully brought a paycheck home to an equally overworked wife. A good man, Kate thought. Proud to be a cordwainer—a maker of new handmade shoes—not a cobbler doing repairs.

"Hey, you singing at O'Leary's tonight? I could use it."

"Yeah, I'll sing your favorites for you, Kev."

Singing on the makeshift stage at O'Leary's was a gig Kate adored. Applause and tinkling tips in a mason jar had lit her up night after night for three years, but as her father said, it didn't pay the bills.

Kate waved to her mother who sat across the room stationed

under the Daughters of St. Christopher's Union plaque, the only decoration on the worn, cathedral-high walls. Sliding through the row of relatives and friends, Kate smiled and nodded to each one.

Resting her hands on her mother's shoulders, Kate kissed the top of her head and watched her burnish a russet, box-toe oxford. The color perfectly matched her mother's auburn hair before the dull silver tint had taken hold. Her mom's hands looked rough and aged as she worked.

Imagining her own hands raw from the tedious, repetitive assembling of sole to upper, Kate had a twinge of sadness for her mother. Those stained fingertips had inspired Kate to attend community college, studying toward some unknown destination. Liberal arts, anything to be educated and escape the family trade.

"Katie-girl. Are you sick? Aren't you supposed to be at the restaurant?" Her mother yelled over the noise.

"No, Mom, I'm fine. No shift today."

"Just a second, sweetheart." She worked on finishing the final details on the shoe.

In front of her mother, Grandpa Ketchum winked and continued fastening a cordovan leather upper to a large-sized sole at the lasting table. Kate would miss his habit of sitting on the porch telling tales of the old days when their ancestors had cut and shaped the leather by hand before shoemaking was mechanized. The old times when those interminable tasks were done by the clever hands of her relatives.

The work that had filled every inch of the factory floor had fascinated Kate as a child. Grandpa especially loved to talk about the one crucial step that remained a human's job to make a fine, handmade shoe—"the lasting." Perfectly-forming the leather, stretching it onto a custom wooden mold last, was done by "hand lasting."

Lasting, Kate thought—lifelong, eternal, undying, unending—not for her. But didn't her mother and father's labor bring her to where she was today? Their suffering, her salvation, she thought. Kate was grateful to them.

Luckily, the handmade-shoe had returned, a backlash against modern mechanization. Kate imagined the massive wall of shelves in the fitting room that held the fine, hand-crafted lasts—generations of custom wood molds lined up on the walls alphabetically—Adams, Bentley, Galloway, James, Hunt, Lowell, Washington. Sons and daughters were still brought in annually to make their molds until their feet stopped growing. Of course, those shoes and boots were hugely expensive now, something only the well-off could afford. But profits didn't trickle down to the factory floor.

Her family knew many of the well-to-do customers. Owl & Shamrock shoes were a family tradition for the *well-heeled* of Massachusetts and beyond. Her grandfather loved that play on words, "*well-heeled*, get it?" he'd said a hundred times.

Her mother put the shoe down on the long, metal table. The women around her glanced up, turned their eyes to the upper-level glass window where old Mr. Donohue stood, hands on hips, as usual. They rolled their eyes, smiled, waved at Kate, and went back to work.

Uncle Jack beckoned Kate over and yelled over the machinery noise into her ear, "How'd the finals go?"

She signaled a thumbs-up and smiled.

He went back to hole-punching with his stack of books

nearby and his usual mystery novel flattened out under a shoe-maker's hammer on the table beside him. Kate knew he was the one who most regretted not getting a college education. You'd never catch him without a book opened next to his station, sneaking a sentence or two as he worked, or waiting for his breaks when he'd stand in the corner by the window reading. She wouldn't forget his words, "Katie, don't give up until you get what you want. Hear me?"

Kate leaned over her mother and spoke into her ear over the chaos. "Mom, you can keep the burnishing going; I just want to read you something that you...well, just listen." Her moist fingers had left four oval imprints where she'd gripped the letter. Kate felt a tremble in her stomach that found its way up her backbone and quivered on her bottom lip. She hesitated, worried that jealousy or resentment might accompany the news when it came to the rest of her family. But, God, she was excited.

With her right arm draped around her mother's shoulder, Kate bent over and began to read the paper vibrating in her hand.

Dear Miss Ketchum: Congratulations on your two-year, full scholarship from the Daughters of St. Christopher Century Fund to attend the University of Connecticut to complete your baccalaureate. Based on your outstanding academic achievement—"

"A *scholarship*? I didn't even know you applied... why didn't you say something?" The chair clattered to the floor as her mother pushed back and threw her arms around Kate. "Dear God, Katie-girl, you've earned it." She pulled Kate close and yelled in her ear, "You're out, darling; you're out."

"Mom...don't..." She'd never heard her mother sob for a happy thing before; Kate felt it rise up in her throat too. It caught her by surprise—her un-Irish emotional eruption.

Kate's mother shook off her crying, blessed herself, making the sign of the cross over and over, and burst out laughing. Taking the letter from Kate, she righted her chair, stood on it, then bellowed loud enough for her Uncle Jack to hear. "On scholarship, our Katie-girl; she's going to university." Her mother waved the good news over her head like a flag. "Two years and she'll be a UConn graduate. Imagine, Class of 1970."

Uncle Jack spread the word, and the worse-for-wear machines stopped their plunkety-plunk, ka-chunk, shhhhh, and came to a halt. A buzz moved through the handmade section of the factory floor, and the applause began, first a few hands, then an unbridled standing ovation from Kate's three dozen aunts and uncles, cousins, three sisters and three brothers, along with her father, and nearly the entire crew of cordwainers, bonded for generations together.

Kate couldn't breathe. Who would have guessed the mere thought of her good fortune would excite them so? She'd taken such teasing about her dreams. Now she knew her family and even her life-long neighbors were secretly rooting for her, dreaming through her, hoping for her. Well, everyone but grumpy Grandma Kendall, who stood by her workplace with her arms on her hips, gazing through the discolored window.

Watching her family and friends hug and slap each other's backs as though they'd each won the lottery was not the response she'd imagined.

"Congrats, Kate." Her twin cousins, like sisters and best friends since childhood, jumped up and down, hugging her. "God, we'll miss you."

"We still have the summer."

As the applause and hoots quieted, Kate's mother announced through joyful tears. "Everyone, we'll be celebrating at O'Leary's tonight."

Kate watched the swoop-swoop of the paddle fans above that distributed the stale air around the colorless room as the cacophony of machines started up again.

CHAPTER 2

Michael

ANVIL OF ANGER

HOW COULD HE kill again? How had Michael ever enjoyed watching the iridescent ducks drop into the lake—feathers scattering, the family retrievers rocketing off into the water? Since his return from Vietnam, memories seemed to have a will of their own—pulsing in and out of Michael's mind.

Crouching in the duck blind yesterday on the first day of hunting season, he'd made the squawking, perfectly-timed duck call to attract his prize. The late summer sun penetrating his camouflage jacket couldn't squelch his chills or silence the taunting thoughts. The excitement of his exquisite timing, the sweep of his rifle, and the squeeze of his trigger finger would never thrill him again. Michael knew he would forever see the world through a different lens after he'd taken-aim, fired his standard Marine issue, and brought down his first faceless man.

During the seventy-two hours since he'd returned from Vietnam to his parents' Nantucket home, the pressure had built inside Michael. Sure, he was alive, but he didn't feel like himself—detached, floating above, spying on his privileged life. The present in Nantucket and his past in Nam fought a continuous battle for his attention.

"You going to putt that ball, son?" His father tucked one foot behind the other and leaned on his club.

"Sorry, Dad." Duck hunting yesterday, golf today, always games, Michael thought. He lined up and swept his putter back and forth across the scissor-trimmed green of the 18th hole. The soft brushing sound connected him to the past—like the rhythmic whisper of the straw broom Ha̕ng had used to clear her parents' walkway after a monsoon. Michael swung the club, and his custom, monogramed ball came up short.

The noise in his head was getting louder and louder, like the whine of an incoming bomb. He couldn't get the musty scent of the rice fields out of his nostrils. Or was it the suffocating, age-old smell of his father's prestigious Nantucket Bluff Golf and Country Club? Michael knew that was harsh. Not like him. The anvil of anger that had sat on his chest hadn't lifted since his return.

His father and the two colleagues handed their putters to their caddies.

Why did it seem wrong to Michael, now? Strange to have an aging man carry his clubs in the oppressive heat wave—like Michael had carried his combat gear, trudging through the unbearable steamy rice paddies. He could see himself taking over for Ha̕ng's mother, shifting her bamboo carrying pole onto his own shoulders. He could hear Ha̕ng's warm laugh as he tried to slip into the proper rhythm, balancing the two sloshing buckets of water.

Her name was Ha̕ng.

"It's *Hahng*, not Hang." She'd corrected his mispronunciation of her name and laughed behind her hand. "I don't want to hang."

Michael looked at his father and then at the perspiring caddy. "Thank you, sir. I'll take it from here. It's hot; you must be tired."

"No, no, really, sir. I'm fine."

"I insist. Great job today. Thank you." Michael reached out, delivered a generous tip, and relieved the caddie of his heavy golf bag.

"You sure?" The caddie took off his cap, wiped his deeply-grooved forehead with his sleeve, and nodded gratitude to Michael. "Thank *you*, sir."

The sun played on the roof of the stone clubhouse off in the distance, ready to summon-in the late-afternoon shadows onto the rolling hills of green. His father and friends exchanged looks.

His father's business partner broke the silence. "You must have missed these fabulous, fescue-framed fairways of ours, Michael."

Mr. Galloway, the country club president, patted Michael's shoulder. "Good to have you back, son."

Back? Was he? Really? Michael knew they meant well. They just didn't know what to say. The few grisly truths about his war experiences Michael had shared with his father were enough to prevent any further questions from him. That was intentional. There were other stories, the personal ones, the heart-breaking ones, Michael couldn't bear to tell anyone.

"Join us for a drink at the gentlemen's bar, son?"

Michael didn't know how to carry on the familiar country

club banter anymore. Like he'd landed on another planet, he thought. "Thank you, I think I'll pass. See you all at the party." He ground his polite words out between his teeth. Michael's country club twenty-fourth birthday and going away party promised to be another horror show. Wouldn't formal be fun, his dad had said, as though replacing his fatigues with a tuxedo would fix everything.

"Fabulous, fescue-framed fairways," Michael muttered on his way to the locker room. What guy says that? Fescues, just scruffy grasses, weeds, he thought. Not like the sunlit, swaying, lime-green rice fields where he'd met Ha`ng.

He kicked off his golf shoes with flying clumps of turf into the oak locker marked by the brass plate—*Michael Edward James*. Three first names. Even that bugged him. Another family legacy. But then he'd returned, his father's hero, hadn't he? Michael's sarcasm bit. Believe me, Dad, he thought, you don't want to see all the horrors hidden behind my pretty, shiny military medals you've displayed in your library.

Too much of *everything* here at home. Why hadn't he ever noticed that before? The absurdity. Time spent with so little means in the simple village had seemed so rich to Michael; now time spent with so much affluence at home felt like so little.

Michael had heard his father's words, spoken under his breath to his buddies as he left the golf course. "Two more years at Harvard, the kid could have had his degree and been set for life at James & Son. Instead, four fucking years wasted in that 'hell hole.'"

Dad, you don't know shit about it. The war *was* a hell-hole, but not the country, not the people. Enlisting had been Michael's choice. No way he would work for his father. His second tour was Michael's choice too. He'd met his true love. Was it worth the abysmal loss that hung heavy on him every day to have had those two years of joy, to have felt that depth of love? Would he forever waver between gratitude and regret?

CHAPTER 3

LUNAR LAUNCH

THE LATE-AUGUST night sky was dark with clouds, and the flickering streetlight cast a pulsing glow around Kate. Deep breaths of heavy air did nothing to calm her on her break before singing her last set. Despite the oppressive heat, a chill swept through her. Kate's last set on her last night before leaving for college. Where had the summer gone?

A cloud of smoke and the familiar aromas of beer and corned beef and cabbage burst through the entrance to O'Leary's Pub as Kate pulled open the green door. Clustered three-deep around the bar in the wide-open, converted Victorian house, the boisterous crowd of family and friends, eating, drinking, and laughing made her throat tighten.

O'Leary's was like a second home. As the locals' old joke went—you could be baptized, educated, married, raise kids, eke out a living, celebrate your milestones, die, and be buried, all within three blocks of your house—no car necessary. With his usual Irish humor, Kate's father, Kevin Sr., had dubbed the three hallowed places central to the Ketchum's family life, *The*

Holy Trinity—their Sacred Heart parish, the Owl & Shamrock shoe factory, and O'Leary's Pub.

With a weak smile, Kate hugged, kissed, and collected congratulations and farewells as she made her way along the glossy, mahogany bar. The local hangout was over-capacity for her farewell performance. Flattering, yet the turn-out added a touch of sadness to her leaving. The one-hundred-fifty-plus patrons spilled out over the bar area and filled every table in the open dining room. It was eighteen-hundred-square-feet of buzzing fun in the old, gutted house.

The sixteen patrons, who'd been lucky enough to snag a stool at the forty-foot bar, sat with eyes riveted on the pub's TV with people packed three layers behind. Kate paused to watch the documentary—alternating clips of President Nixon, NASA, and a replay of the 1968 Christmas Eve broadcast of the Apollo 8 launch—the sixth month anniversary of America's first men-in-space mission to orbit the Moon.

Sitting at the bar, Kate's brother Kevin put out his muscled arm to stop her progress.

Kate bent in to hear him.

"Hey, stargazer, still can't believe it. Space travel. And soon to the *moon*?" His eyes followed the clips of the lunar launch on the screen above him. "Ten times around the moon in twenty-four hours. Damn. Check out the launch." His eyes didn't leave the screen. "Can't see it too many times."

"Unreal." She patted his shoulder. *Launch*, Kate thought, glancing up at the mysterious moon and the blazing rocket on the TV. *Yes, you and me, Apollo 8.*

The clunk-clunk of her platform shoes was lost in the din of conversation and music from the jukebox. Uncle Jack's barrel-chested laugh boomed from behind the bar, and a glass of Kate's favorite beer appeared in her hand. "Here you go, darlin'—proud of you."

"Thanks, Uncle Jack."

He cleared two plates and swirled a cloth around in circles on the shiny bar surface, long after it was clean, as though some words of importance were forming in his mind. "You did it, Kate. I can't say I'm not a bit jealous. You all packed?" His watery eyes touched her.

"Almost. Oh, Uncle Jack, you and Mom were the ones who told me to follow my college dreams. I'll always love you for that."

"We know the Ketchum brains when we see them." He winked.

From the one-step-down, open dining area next to bar, more patrons at tables-for-four viewed the TV behind the bar with arched necks. Not a seat was available at the eight-tops that encircled the well-worn dance floor. Some couples leaned in, trying to hear each other at the booths-for-two that hugged the walls. Kate closed her eyes. There were nights, she and a date had held hands talking at one of those booths. She hadn't dared let those boys become anything more than dates. Was there something wrong with her?

Just last night, Kate had made the mistake of having a few too many and nearly followed in the footsteps of her sisters— pregnant, married, and back to working in leather by twenty. Out of wedlock, no thanks; out of town would be better. Kate had almost succumbed last night when an attractive guy she'd been dancing with at a bar outside her community college kissed her and ran his hands down her body. God, she was only human. As always, her passion for her future overrode her passion for an alluring guy. Well, at least she wouldn't see him again. She hadn't come this far to be trapped in a life that wasn't for her. She couldn't leave too soon.

Moving through the crowd toward the open dining room, Kate found her younger sister, Kelly.

Already "showing," Kelly unwrapped her arms from around her newlywed husband's neck. "Damn, who made your leather skirt?" She called out to Kate over the clamor.

Kate cupped her hand over her sister's ear, "Grandpa K, on the sly, at the factory after hours with leftover ends."

"Well, there's one advantage to having your family working in leather." Kelly looked down and pointed to Kate's lustrous, black platform shoes. "OK. Maybe, two."

Kate laughed. "Look at him now." Wistfully, Kate took in the happy scene and spotted her grandfather nudging through the crowd with an unfamiliar, down-on-his-luck, disheveled man—Grandpa K's classic act of kindness. No matter how tight things were at home, no homeless man on the streets of Glynn went without a meal if the head of the Ketchum clan was around. Something she loved about him.

Kate had exhibited a bit of Grandpa in herself as a child, too, her mother had said. Known in the family for dragging home an unending series of stray dogs on a rope to feed them, her brothers and sisters had laughed at her. That's Kate, always trying to save the world, they'd say.

Kelly nudged Kate and jabbed her finger toward a table by the stage in the back of the room. "Check out the stud."

Oh, God, you're kidding. It was him. Kate shook her head.

Tilting back on the legs of his chair, the twenty-something

guy sat leaning against the knotty pine paneling. Smoke from his cigarette spiraled up like an entrancing cobra. His warm, attentive look unnerved Kate. He hadn't been there for her first two sets. Of course, some good-looking, sexy guy would show up right before she leaves town, Kate thought. She laughed to herself.

He was smiling at her, as though he knew Kate in ways she didn't know herself. God, look at him. The heat from the night before flushed across her face and down her neck. His black hair and those flirty, electric blues that studied her. He'd positioned himself for a perfect view of Kate where she would sing her final songs on the one-step-up, wooden stage her carpenter cousin had made.

Lowering the beer glass from her lips, she managed a wave and a faint smile. Someone new in a town where people rarely came to live and old-timers never left was so intriguing. How much longer could she hold out?

"Interested, Kate? Come on, one last chance. You can't be a virgin forever, sister." Kelly elbowed Kate and began to sing the local ditty, swaying her glass of ginger ale.

Glynn, Glynn, the city of sin,
You never come out the way you came in,
You ask for water, but they give you gin.
The girls say no, yet they always give in.

Kelly had a good laugh.

The silly, but true, tune evoked Kate's inner voice. Not this girl, Kate thought. No guy would stop her from following her own path. Kate smiled at her sister. "No, thanks; I'm not in the market."

"What's with you? Check him out, sister." Kelly put her

hand on her growing belly. "Never mind, better pickin's at UConn. Guess you've come too far to settle for a townie." Kelly called a truce.

In the bar mirror, Kate could see that the attractive customer's eyes were on her. "When or *if* it comes time to pick, I'll do the picking."

Karl, the youngest of her three brothers, called out from the end of the bar. "Hey, Kate. Don't forget my request." He owed his wife an apology for coming home a little lit last night, he'd told Kate earlier that day.

"Ten minutes. It's coming up."

Kate's two older sisters, Karen and Kendra, and their husbands, and babies were at their usual table at O'Leary's. Watching Kendra woozy with love over her infant daughter's face made Kate sigh. She didn't quite understand that love; as sweet as it seemed, and as much as she adored her nieces and nephews, somehow it wasn't for her. That maternal instinct her mother and sisters talked about hadn't been passed down to her, she thought. Kate was different.

The dreamy look on her sister's face—wasn't that the same feeling Kate had when she'd spun her globe around or read about an exotic, faraway place? Or when she'd looked up at her handmade, celestial, paper universe rotating from her ceiling in the fan's breeze? And the euphoria that electrified her when she'd hit the last note of a song to resounding applause—that was the ultimate. Was it foolish to think her *dreams* were like her children? Shouldn't she raise them up, feed them too?

Turning away, Kate caught her reflection in the mirror behind the bar again—her red hair gleamed in the spotlight, excitement ignited her eyes. *You can do this.* Kate stepped onto the small stage at the opposite side of the dining room, picked up the mic, and hitched one hip up on the wooden stool. Had she really been performing there for three years? She'd still been a teenager when she'd started. O'Leary's was her sanctuary where she'd perched, night after night, crooning and rocking tunes amidst the clamoring audience of neighbors, friends, and three generations of Ketchums, Kings, and Callahans. Singing on stage made her feel real, free to be herself. She felt the transformation the minute she took her place and cradled the mic in her hand.

Swiveling back and forth on her stool, she thought of her departure and pretended to study her song sheets. God, she would miss this stage.

Her brother Keith limped across the worn, wooden dance floor, grabbed an empty chair, spun it around, and sat backwards on it like a cowboy. He started an animated chat with the handsome new guy. Some war story from his Vietnam tour she assumed from the slant of her brother's body and his explosive hand gestures.

Kate scanned the crowd. Her last performance. She wouldn't just miss the old place, no, she would ache for it— its mirrored wall that caught the smiling faces of the crowd packed into the long, narrow bar area. The dining room where she'd propped in the corner to sing, with the stray peanut shells scattered on the floor, was packed, waiting for her voice to ring out again.

Lights flickered. Uncle Jack yelled, "Last call; drinks are half-price," and most were takers.

Kate clutched the mic. If she could just release the tightness in her chest, get through the final set, and sing her last number of the night for her brother, she could go home and pack and get ready for the rest of her life, she thought.

Tonight Kate felt the usual high when she stepped into the spotlight. Tonight she was ecstatic. But on this night, her exciting news had a flip side—not like the favorite songs they played on the jukebox during her break—but the B-side, the side of the record no one wanted to hear—she would never be a regular at O'Leary's again. Sure, Uncle Jack would welcome her anytime to sing a set or two, but the next time Kate's family and friends walked through that green door, some other young wannabe would have taken her place. The "Singer Wanted" sign by the front door had made it real. An ache twisted inside her; Kate was envious of the stranger, whoever she might be.

Nodding at her brother, Keith, and cousin, Matt, they took their places. Their little band had gotten by with drums and keyboards since their guitarist, Cousin Danny was killed in the Vietnam war. The family hero. It was too soon, too tender a time to replace him. They'd left his flag draped on the wall above his unplugged bass guitar, along with a star for every friend and neighbor's son who had lost his life in the war.

Nettie, Ethel and Edie, O'Leary's aging waitresses, hurried to gather foam-edged mugs and crumpled green and white Leprechaun logo napkins. They half-filled empty peanut bowls and delivered final drinks.

Without a word, Uncle Jack handed Kate's grandfather two more mugs of Irish red ale. On the house, no doubt. Pushing through the bar crowd to the dining tables, her grandfather palmed Kate's brother's shoulder. Karl stood and pulled up extra chairs at his table for the two elderly men.

Grandpa K spoke to the homeless gentleman above the clamor in his distinctive, deep voice and pointed at her. "That's our singer, my granddaughter, Kate—had pipes since she could talk. Just like her mother."

The words touched her. Grandpa K was the sort of man you had to search the corner of his mouth to read a smile. The kind of man who showed his love with action and a wink at most. A man who never said much, but in an odd moment of intimacy had told young Kate, someday he'd buy her a blue pony. How did her five-year-old self connect so powerfully with that fantasy?

It was a family joke now, but somehow in that senseless blue-pony-promise, Kate realized he'd planted hope. The hope that she might have something different. Not a regular-colored pony, but a blue pony, a rare dream. Even as a child, she believed that something different was out there somewhere, and she was going to find it.

Signaling with a nod to her Uncle Jack, the TV sound went off, and the jukebox went quiet. He made his way from behind the bar to the stage.

Tossing her fiery red hair over one shoulder, Kate balanced on the stool and crossed her legs.

The new guy sat back, lowered his chair to the floor, crossed his arms, and winked.

Heat rushed to Kate's face.

Uncle Jack bent over her brother Keith's mic. "Hey, every-body, listen up. Let's give Kate and the guys a warm welcome back for the last set. And send our Kate off to college with a round of applause. She's leaving tomorrow. We'll miss you, Kate. Thanks for coming, everybody."

The crowd hooted and clapped. "We'll miss you, Kate." "Good Luck!"

Wiping her hands on her cocktail napkin, Kate test-tapped the mic. "Testing. Thank you so much, really." Her words squeezed through her throat. "Welcome back, everyone. Let's celebrate. Soon, we'll be walking on the moon, people!"

Cheers rose up from the audience seated at the old oak tables and gathered around the bar. Those neighbors' faces, those Ketchum family's glinting eyes she loved. Kate knew the power of lyrics. She started with "The Sound of Silence," then moved to a love song that predictably brought lips together in a darkened corner and instantly lured couples onto the dance-floor. Not a single beam of light leaked between those loving couples, hungry for comfort after a long day working in leather. When she'd switched to an old favorite, eager voices raised in a sing-along. With the right lyrics, she thought. With the right words, you can change someone's world.

The final set had gone well. The audience seemed pleased.

"OK, guys, let's do this. Last song." When Kate shifted legs to get comfortable, several guys in the audience shifted to the front of their seats. Yes, she had to admit, she liked the power to move people, the high and the joy that being in the spotlight gave her.

Her musicians shuffled through the pieces on their music stands. Signaling to wrap it up, they played the lead-in for her last song.

Closing her eyes, Kate took a breath, cleared her throat, and searched for the first note. "I'm sorry, so sorry," she put an ache in every word of Brenda Lee's hit song. When Kate drew out the last suspended note, the lean of the crowd and

the warm applause told her they felt it too. "Love you all."
She winked at her brother, Karl, whose wife sat with her head
on his shoulder. Kate was grateful for her power to touch
someone with her voice.

As she looked out over the attentive crowd, she realized she
would always be off somewhere in her fantasies. She'd always
be seeking faraway places, impassioned by things beyond their
world in Glynn—a cross-country drive to San Francisco, a visit
to Stonehenge, a gondola ride through the canals of Venice. Or
maybe a visit to her family's homeland in Ireland. Kate could
see her untraveled mother's face lit up from the tales her Aunt
Edie had told of her trip home to County Cork years ago.

She glanced at the silent moon floating across the TV screen.
Why was the unknown so alluring? That disease of desire she
suffered from had pulled her toward some unknown place out
there, as though she were in a trance. Like the desire for a
higher education, when she had no clue about what she wanted
to be.

Kate glanced at the stranger she'd kissed the night before.
He winked back and headed her way as she slipped out the
back door and locked it behind her.

Sweeping her eyes across the darkened sky, she found the
slim sliver of the moon etched above her, slicing through shifting clouds. Kate opened her arms to the sky. Tomorrow she
would launch too—chasing the places that had enticed her
since she'd stabbed the first wishful pin into her childhood
map.

CHAPTER 4

Michael

A BETTER GRIP

MICHAEL PACED IN the men's locker room. Get ahold of yourself, Sargent Major James, he said to himself in the mirror. Ripping off his sweaty golf shirt, he cranked on the shower and waited for the chill of the water to pass.

He'd almost decided to remain in Nam. Michael pictured himself as one of those guys who went missing, wandering back into Hà ng's family village and staying. MIA. He wanted to live alongside Hà ng's people, eating simple bowls of shimmering rice noodles with bits of vegetables. He wanted to snuggle close to Hà ng's younger siblings and soothe the pain of her loss reflected in their innocent eyes.

Coming home meant facing the searing wounds no one could see. Coming home meant arguing against adding his name to the forty-foot sign that hung on his father's towering Boston building—James & Son. Managing wealthy people's money had never been Michael's dream. Only thoughts of his mother's face, that had consoled him through his combat years, had persuaded him to return to the States. Michael couldn't let her lose her only son. He needed the comfort of sitting side-by-side on the piano bench with her, escaping into their music.

Michael tested the shower water, still not hot enough.

The sound of his father's hunting rifle off in the distance yesterday morning and the scent of smoke had triggered it— Michael's first full-on flashback. Not the usual agitating buzz of memories that had inhabited his head, but his complete, quivering collapse at the sound of the gunshot. He could hear the artillery, smell the acrid smoke. He was there, again. So real, he'd dove for cover. Later, Michael had made up excuses to conceal his shell shock when he was with his father. Tripped. Tired.

"Don't forget daily bag limit's six ducks, Michael," his father had called out from the duck blind across from his. "No more than four mallards and remember female limit's two."

Female limit's two. Michael had felt his breakfast rumbling up into his throat as his father outlined the rules.

"Maximum three wood ducks, two redheads, three scaup, one pintail, two canvasbacks, one mottled duck, and two black ducks. Got it, son?"

Michael had no voice to answer.

When his son had no prize to show for the day in the duck blind on their lake, his father said he'd written it off to Michael's lack of shooting practice. Lack of *shooting practice?* Really, Dad?

Running his hands through his short, silver-blonde hair, Michael gripped his skull to keep a hundred memories of killing from spilling red onto the locker room tile floor. He needed to keep busy; silence invited the memories—some sweet, some unbearable. Touching Ha`ng's beautiful face, his hand soothing her forehead; Ha`ng, running from the foxhole in her muddy blue split tunic and tattered white flowing trousers, her *ái dào*. He would never forget the word for the traditional outfit the Vietnamese village women wore. The one she'd folded carefully when they'd made love. He'd never forget her sweet voice. My name means, *angel in the full moon*, she'd said. Angel, yes, she was, he thought.

Steam rose from the locker room shower, and he stepped in. Michael's hands searched out his scars through the slip of soap. The divot on his shoulder from the shrapnel. The thick, raised, knife-wound scar that encircled his neck—a wound inflicted from behind just two days before his tour was up. When he'd lost his focus. Too close. Another millimeter and he'd have been gone, the surgeon had said. Michael hadn't said what he was thinking—he'd have welcomed that extra millimeter, back then.

His fingers traced their names, inked permanently on his upper arms—*Ha`ng*, imprinted on his left arm in curling Vietnamese characters—*Hy Vọng*, tattooed on his right arm. It was the only way he could bring them home.

Stop, Michael told himself, as his emotions rose. He started to sing out loud, "From the halls of Montezu-u-ma..." Manly Marine stuff. Singing—the best way he knew to block out the memories. He turned off the water and stepped from the shower.

The soft Egyptian cotton towel felt good on his weathered skin. How many times would he have killed for a shower— something to ease the aches that wracked his entire body, the itching, the red-hot rash of insect bites, the peeling of his skin. He pulled on his starched formal shirt and struggled to fasten his grandfather's antique pearl studs through the holes and the gold, initialed cufflinks through the slits in the cuffs. Damn. Too small for his fighting hands. Rugged good looks, he'd heard his father's golfing buddies say. Michael looked in the mirror and stroked his angular jaw. Rugged? They had no idea.

The socks didn't slip easily over his rough, peeling feet. He applied a salve and put on the high-gloss formal shoes he hadn't worn in years—the custom ones his mother had bought for him on their annual factory trip to Glynn. Sliding his foot into the shoe, the familiar Owl & Shamrock logo caught his eye. Everything had to be the best. He had disdain for the excesses of his family's life.

Michael pulled on the perfectly creased pants, slipped on the black tails, rocked his bow tie into place, and left the locker room. As he walked toward the clubhouse door, his father caught up with him.

"Write that golf score off as just four years out of practice, son. You'll get back to your old swing." He thumped Michael's back with support.

A golf handicap was the last thing on Michael's list of things he needed to fix, he thought.

"I think the problem's in your grip."

"You're right, Dad; it's my grip. I need to get a better grip." He could tell from his reaction, the meaning went right over his father's head. A privileged man who had never served.

"See you at your going away party. I've got a... a call to make." His father slapped Michael's back again and rushed away.

31

Who is she this time, Dad? Passing the wall of glass trophy cases just outside the locker room, Michael spotted them—his All-American medals for Crew: First Place for the single scull; silver, on the eight-man boat. His trophy for the all-time Harvard record for pole vaulting—higher than anyone had rocketed themselves up and over the bar before. And Michael had only been a sophomore, his dad had always remarked to his friends. Who cares. It wasn't the trophies that drove him.

At the *Club*, Dad? *Really?* His father had no right to display those, Michael thought. What else had he misappropriated from Michael's room to stroke his own ego? It was bad enough Michael's pain had already been reduced down to a military medal display in a gilded-edged, glass case in his family's Georgian mansion. He imagined his grandmother touring the collectibles with guests to show how patriotic the family could be.

Needing some air before the party, Michael stuffed his trembling hands in his tux pockets and walked toward the ink-blue water. It still didn't feel right without his weapon. Didn't feel safe. And yet Michael was sick at the sight of his father's gun collection.

His eyes followed the line of shadows that moved toward him across the shimmering chop as the sun dropped behind the clubhouse. The water and being outside calmed him a bit—outside—like in Nam with Ha`ng.

Balmy August breezes blew in hot across Nantucket Island. The sound of the snap of his tails flapping was like the flag on the pole at boot camp outside his barracks. Before it all happened. Before he'd been made the designated family hero. Before he'd become the winner who'd lost everything.

CHAPTER 5

CARAMEL-COLORED CLOUDS

THE KETCHUMS AND their in-laws and *outlaws*—as her grandfather called those crazy enough to marry into the family—filled the street with Kate's going-away, end-of-summer celebration. Their sweaty, happy bodies drifted from O'Leary's into the front door to continue the party at the Kate's family home.

"A toast to our Katie." Her father, Kevin, stood in the kitchen by the old, avocado green refrigerator. "Sing me 'Danny Boy' like an angel, and we might let you go finish packing and get some sleep."

Kate stood by her burly father and sang the words that brought him to tears. "For I'll be here in sunshine or in shadow." For her close-to-the-vest family, words could never touch a heart like lyrics in a song well-sung. Looking at the weak smiles of her two best girlfriends, her cousins Carlie and Carol, Kate choked on the lyrics.

"What are we all upset about? I'll be home at Thanksgiving. I'm less than two hours away." Kate hadn't thought much about how she would feel when she would actually have to leave her family and hometown.

The night ended the same as always—a *whistle*, a *yoo-hoo* or a *hey babe* from the front porch split the women's chatter. A chair scraped back on the linoleum as each of Kate's aunts recognized their husband's signature call, said their goodbyes, and gathered their children from upstairs where they were jumping on beds or taking part in other hooligan activities.

Leaning against the oak stairway, Kate thought about how much she loved her family's laughter, joking, carrying-on, and the round of cheers and hugs that accompanied their departures.

"I guess we'll all have to start carrying dictionaries like Uncle Jack, then we'll know what our *College Kate* is saying, right, Kate?" her brother Karl laughed.

"No, I'm thinking you'll need the entire set of encyclopedias." Kate flipped her hair back over her shoulder.

The family burst out laughing.

"Thanks, everyone." Kate's final laugh was swallowed by her unexpected tears when she closed the front door behind the last of her relatives.

She could hear her father flip on the TV in the parlor and her mother clattering the last of the dishes in the kitchen as she climbed the stairs.

"Mom, you need help?" Kate yelled from the landing.

"I'm fine; you finish packing."

The letter outlining the steps for matriculating to UConn sat on her bed. How many times had she stared at the news? Tuition scholarship and a Resident Advisor position provided a private room and all her food, even on weekends, plus a cash stipend for pocket money and books. Being older, and just going into her junior year at twenty-one had felt embarrassing, a liability. But Kate's maturity was an asset when it came to being selected as an RA, the interviewer had said. There was only one hitch. At the bottom of her registration packet was a notice—*music audition for voice performance major, at 3:00 p.m., August 27, 1968*. Kate had to pass the audition to major in music. And she had to study a second instrument to accompany herself in a solo performance in front of a jury. That had come as a shock. Second? She'd played around with the guitar, knew a few chords. Would that work? Majoring in music was no crooning to a crowd, she realized.

Kate wrapped her arms around herself. She had one night before leaving home. Could she figure out anything without looking up at the hidden messages on the familiar cracked ceiling— those caramel-colored stains she'd followed since she was a little girl after the boys' bathroom in the attic dormer had flooded overhead? Could she even *think* in a strange dorm room with a clean white ceiling above her and a hallway filled with sleeping strangers?

One more night under the coffee-spilled-clouds on her childhood bedroom ceiling. One more steamy night with the white cotton curtains her Mom had made from sheets, pulling away from the screens. One sleepless night with the big attic fan sucking the circulating late August air through her room, her door propped open with her mother's old iron.

The neighbor's noisy, drunken arguments floated across the narrow alley delivered on muggy air. It would be impossible to sleep. She'd always wished they would move away. Pushing aside her open luggage, Kate plopped on her twin bed, her fingers laced behind her head. How could the good news that had elated her also make her feel so sad now?

Draping her Navy peacoat over the chair, Kate stuffed the final blouse, three pairs of jeans, and her favorite rust-colored corduroy bell-bottoms into her green vinyl, musty suitcase, and sat on top of it. Pushing the tarnished brass-plated latches in—one clicked in, the other wouldn't catch. She wrapped a stretch belt around the bulging girth of the bag. It had to hold through the bus trips to Boston, on to Hartford, then to Storrs, and across the Connecticut campus until she got into her dorm room.

She'd abandoned old Nellie, the blue and white 1955 Chevy that had taken her to each job since she was seventeen; or had Nellie abandoned Kate? Yesterday, the old girl had finally *given up the ghost*, her father had said. Old Nellie had just made it to the finish line and took her last gasp on the side of the road right in front of the payphone at the Carvel in town. Kate was down to buses and shoe leather—and she had plenty of that. Her duffle full of hand-made footwear was ready by her door.

Kneeling on the bed, Kate carefully pulled at the tape to remove the band posters from her plaster walls. Curling each poster up, tight, Kate watched the famous faces she admired disappear into the crease of the roll—Janis Joplin, Carole King, Judy Collins, Bonnie Raitt, Grace Slick, Aretha. She snapped a pink rubber band on each end and stuffed them in her brother's old Marine duffle bag. These and her silly, but beloved, pin-pricked map she couldn't leave behind.

The thirty-eight dollars her brother had gotten selling Nellie for parts had helped.

Kate counted the money on top of the lace doily on her oak dresser. She was set, flush for the moment.

How many times had she fantasized about that 4,400-acre campus? Only ninety minutes from Boston, but UConn might as well have been on Mars. When she visited, she'd fallen in love with the space between the buildings—space to spare for trees and flowers. It would only take five minutes to walk to the music department from her dorm.

Kate laughed at how she had chosen the university. Her Uncle Jack had suggested she locate no farther than a two-hour drive if she must go away, making visits to home drivable. She'd spread out a map, calculated the miles, stuck the sharp-end of her protractor on Glynn, expanded it, and spun the pencil around in a circle. On the absolute outside edge of the two-hour-away pencil line was UConn. Enough distance to make it feel like an adventure.

It was after 10:30, getting late. Kate went downstairs to the kitchen. She sat on the same red, plastic-padded kitchen chair with the metal trim where she'd always sought her mother's good counsel. Mom had always grounded Kate with no-nonsense words like *eat and wash up, you'll feel better; don't worry, it's a waste of energy; you always come out smelling like a rose; if you don't ask, you'll never get;* and finally, *Katie-girl, I have faith in you; you'll figure it out.* Never a word of exactly what to do, but Mom's words expressed confidence in her daughter. She wanted Kate to think for herself, she'd always said.

Diminishing most of life's worries into those not-to-worry words always made Kate think, *really, what am I worked up about? I can do this.*

In a powerful way, her mother's unwavering faith had given Kate faith in herself.

"Are you all set?"

Kate's worry over the audition, the solo, and majoring in music made her head buzz like a hornet in a jar. "Yes. I have the bus schedule, bags are packed, plenty of money, ready to go." Kate could hear her feigned optimism dripping from her tone.

Her mother moved about the kitchen humming. Back in the day, she was an Ann-Margaret look-alike, people said. Given a chance, her mother could have been famous with her auburn hair, green eyes, and her magnificent voice, Kate thought.

"Like looking in the mirror when I look at you, Katie-girl. Well, a magic mirror that reflects back in time." Her mother laughed.

Kate could see that resemblance—their matching green eyes, high cheek bones, and fair Irish skin that everyone had always talked about. "Mom, it's amazing—everything falling into place—scholarship, a private room, money."

"Proud of you." Her mother stopped to kiss the top of Kate's head.

The kettle's familiar cry made Kate smile, but the pressure behind her eyes caught her off guard.

"Tea, sweetheart?"

"Sure."

It was a rare moment to have her mother to herself. Her mom shuffled among the mugs on the shelf, finding just the right one for Kate. *Her* mug, Kate thought—the one with the blue letters *Katie* she'd painted at church camp. The one with the small chip on the lip.

Filling it, her mother dropped a Lipton teabag in the steaming water. "I'm *listening*." She threw the comment over her shoulder, turned, and delivered the mug to Kate.

Kate spun the mug around to the unchipped side and blew off the steam. "It's that obvious?"

"I know my Katie-girl."

Mom had always said she wanted her girls educated. With her sisters working in leather with a string of unplanned babies of their own, Mom's dreams hinged on Kate now. Just get out of leather, Mom would say, nothing about where to get to.

"Katie, what's that look?"

"What look?"

"That out-the-window look. Worried about leaving home? Something else?"

Mom had always had time to listen to her four daughters' concerns. But could she understand this situation, really? How could she help Kate to choose a back-up major or a second instrument? Talks about pregnancy, break ups, money worries, yes—college majors, future careers, no, she thought.

Kate delayed with a slurping sip of the hot tea. She hesitated to burden her mother. But she needed support. "Yes, and yes." She spread the letter out on the table. "And this." She'd throw it out there and see what Mom said.

The same baby blue terry robe and matching fuzzy slippers on her mom since Kate's childhood, in some way, made Kate feel safe. The familiar drip of the kitchen faucet marked time; the same plaid wallpaper from the fifties grounded her. There was comfort in being with someone who was comfortable being herself. Even if she couldn't understand what it felt like to be you.

Mom always had the sugary scent of hope on her. Did she carry her daughters' worries once they'd passed their cares on to her? If so, she'd never let it show. Her quiet strength in facing the challenges of raising a big family of small means was contagious.

Kate's fingers ran over the map of gray veins in the linoleum table. Usually, just saying something out loud to her mother, helped Kate figure out what was on her own mind. "Mom, I'm finally here and... I don't know what I want to do? After working three years to get through community college, it's embarrassing that I still don't know what I want to be. I want to get my degree. I love learning, but I don't have an academic direction, Mom.

"I thought you said you already had to choose a major when the acceptance came." Her mother put her hand on Kate's shoulder.

Kate blurted out her concerns. "I did. I signed up for music, but then I read you have to audition. Am I making a mistake? I don't have formal training. And I can't just run off with no plan and try to make it under the spotlights; I'm no Linda Ronstadt. Like Dad says, O'Leary's never paid the bills." Kate stopped only to take a breath and a sip of the tea, then launched into her concerns. "Where would I even start? And how would I support myself while I tried to get my start? There's no guarantee I'll get into the music department, either. Other students will have had lessons from professional instructors for years already. And what if I fail the audition? I'm not trying to be a downer. Am I making the right decision? I want it so bad."

Kate's mother looked over her shoulder. With the TV

blaring in the parlor, Kate followed her mother's line of sight to her father sitting in his lounge chair watching the Jack Paar show.

"Katie, I understand better than you think. I'll only say this once...and it's not to be repeated." She lowered her voice and shot another look toward the parlor.

Kate stood and closed the kitchen door. "I'm listening," She shuffled her chair closer. "Go ahead, Mom."

"I do know Glynn isn't for you—the factory, this small working world. And I know you don't see yourself in my shoes. No pun intended. There was a time I didn't see myself there, either."

"What do you mean?"

"Your father would tell you to major in something you can fall back on after your kids are in school. Teacher, nurse, secretary. That's dream enough. He'd say, never mind what you wake up every morning missing—that *something* you're passionate about. I say you've worked too damn hard not to do something that makes you truly happy, darling. Something that would haunt you if you didn't follow."

"Mom, you've always supported me." Kate touched her mother's arm.

"I had a dream once."

Kate could sense sadness as her mother gazed past her. "What's that out-the-window look, Mom?" Kate teased. It was what a Ketchum did when the emotion got too high—a gentle joke, a breath before a confession.

"Waking up to regret that you didn't do that *something* day after day is... when my friends pushed me up onto a stage at a club in Boston, well, I can't explain the feeling when the band started and I sang one song, and then another." Kate's mother looked out the open window into the dark alley, and the neighbors turned on their kitchen lights and lit up an argument in their kitchen. "I found something inside myself I didn't know was there." The darkness outside seemed to swallow her thoughts and words.

"You sang in a *club*? Why didn't you tell me?"

"A promoter wanted me. He made me an offer on the spot." Kate's mother closed her eyes. "Well, never mind, I'm foolish to think of the road not taken. But every time I see you on O'Leary's stage…"

Kate leaned across the table and took both of her mother's hands. "What happened with the offer?"

"I found out I was pregnant with Kendra. Shameful, not married and pregnant in those days, so shameful." Her mother stood and shut the window.

For the first time, Kate imagined her mother as a young woman in love with dreams of her own. Dashed. How sad, such a loss, Kate thought. She imagined her mother making the call to turn down the offer. "But, we all have Kendra now, Mom. And I wouldn't be here either, to be selfish about it. None of us would."

Her mother let out a small puff of laughter. "You always find the bright side of things. Yes, that's what took away the disappointment. But you're starting fresh, and you should find what lights you up, makes you happy."

Kate ticked through her card catalog of things that made her light-up. She liked learning and reading, but nothing she could think of translated into a direction, a career—besides music. What would Kate do if she didn't get into the music program?

She didn't dare go off to the city and try to make it on her own singing. More than anything she wanted to be educated, professional, not some untrained, struggling, raw talent. And the thought of crawling home having failed, haunted her.

Kate couldn't see how any of the things she loved or made her happy would give her a step up to the life she wanted without a college degree to fall back on. She had no fantasy that someone with no connections and no formal training could make it big as a singer. She didn't want to be some shooting star, fizzling out, or losing her voice. To not worry every month about how to pay the bills was the dream. To have money to travel. To use her mind. But how to make music pay?

"Where are you, Katie-girl?"

"Just thinking." What her mother said rang true in one way, but shouldn't Kate go for a career that was a sure thing? She would not end up back in Glynn, no way.

"Well, if the singing doesn't work out full-time—you spend an awful lot of time tucked in a book in a library. Maybe that's a good back-up plan for you, Katie. Librarian."

"Librarian? Hmmm." Kate let that sink in. There was a librarian in every school, every town. "You might have something there, Mom." She imagined herself surrounded by books day after day. The idea gave her a warm feeling, introducing children to books. But would it be enough to read about the world out there? No, she wanted to be in it.

"One thing I do know, I want to try out for the church choir there. St. Thomas Aquinas Choir took a National gold medal last year under some famous choirmaster, Father Sullivan."

"Wonderful, a good start. Will you sing with me at Mass tomorrow for good luck before you go?"

Honestly, Kate had lost any connection to Mass and her family's religion. It wasn't something they ever discussed when Kate slept-in after her late Saturday night waitressing job. But when asked, she'd never refused the chance to sing with her mother.

"I only need to be at the bus stop by eleven." A shudder ran down Kate's arms. Was she excited or petrified? Kate put her hands over her face. "Mom, I never thought I'd be a twenty-one-year-old going into my junior year at a good university and not knowing what I wanted." She laughed.

"Katie, the university part, I knew it when you said your first word."

"What was my first word? You never told me."

"Book."

"Ha. Seriously?"

"Well, after Mama and Dada. And you living in those books before you could even read. Who would be surprised?" Her mother rinsed her cup out in the sink. "Wish someone could drive you to campus, Katie, but with overtime, and Daddy is—"

"No problem. So, let's do the 9:00 Mass, then."

"I'll let the others know. They'll want to say goodbye." She put her hand over Kate's on the familiar background of the aluminum-trimmed table where so many decisions of Kate's had been made. "Everything will work out if you make it right for you. And I can bear you being gone to live somewhere else *if* I know you're happy." She leaned in again and kissed Kate's forehead. Her mother rose, moved toward the doorway with Kate behind her. Then stopping, with her hand on the light switch, she spoke with her back to Kate. "Katie-girl...you deserve love, you know."

"What do you mean?"

Her mother turned. "What happened to your sisters and me and you wanting to escape the leather, I know it weighs heavy. Don't forget to let yourself have love too. And don't stop singing. It's who you are, darling. I wish I'd …well, that's water under the bridge, or is it over the dam?" Her mother laughed— but just a small laugh that had an edge of melancholy.

Touching Kate's face, she hesitated and looked deep into her eyes before flipping off the light switch. Only the dim stairway night light was there to guide them upstairs, as though her mother's words could only be said in the dark. "A beautiful, smart girl like you should…" That's all she could get out.

It was cultural. Kate smiled and understood. Love wasn't anything they'd ever spoken of before; it was assumed. Words like *beautiful* never came out of any mouth in the Ketchum family either. It was a powerful first, receiving advice like that. In her mother's words, Kate heard some kind of permission to launch, to be herself.

CHAPTER 6

Michael

SECOND SKIN

STANDING NEAR THE cart path entrance to the first hole, Michael stared out at the candy-cane-colored lighthouse, he watched the sun drop over its glass top, sending shards of flashing light down on the golf links. Michael looked away—no triggers tonight, he thought. Everything seemed ludicrous in his country-club world, now. His cynicism seared his insides. He didn't feel like himself.

Just another uniform, this penguin suit; he was ready to celebrate his departure for college. Maybe he could burn off some of his sadness by rowing or pole vaulting when he got to UConn. When it came to the flashbacks, that didn't ring true. Sports were only a temporary distraction from his pain. He knew he needed professional help, but a fresh start in a new place might be the key to start healing.

Following his Uncle John's footsteps by finishing up his degree at UConn was a kind of rebellion against his father's family tradition—Harvard, fifth generation. But his mother's only brother was his role model, former ambassador to

Thailand, now CEO of a non-profit. International work called to Michael.

"No thanks," he'd said to his father when he mentioned Michael's returning to Harvard as they stood on the first tee the first day he'd arrived home. "I've transferred to UConn, instead."

"*UConn?* But I thought—"

"I changed my mind. Dad, I've tried to tell you, finance isn't right for me. I'm majoring in International Relations. And I want to...well, to start over."

"Whatever for? You have a job waiting for you with me. I thought you would change your mind once you..."

"I want to work overseas, make a difference, like Uncle John. The Foreign Service, maybe, or a non-profit." Michael knew the very words *non-profit* would raise his father's hackles.

"Non-profit!"

"Helping people." Michael caught his father's glance at the still-red scar on Michael's neck that rode the edge of his collar.

"Sounds good, son." His father's arm around him was rare, and comforting.

Walking back to the clubhouse, Michael realized his dad hadn't dared to argue with him since he'd returned from the war and told his terrorizing war stories. Did his father see him as a hero or an emotional time bomb?

From the hallway, Michael could see the ballroom was full. He took a deep breath. Checking himself in the full-length mirror, he knew his formal wear had worked. He'd found a way to pull the façade around him tight, like a second skin he would molt as soon as he was alone.

Michael brushed a bit of lint from his jacket. Showtime.

He spotted his mother across the room through the clusters of guests in conversation. How could she have understood when all he'd shared were some general stories about fighting in the war? His tales of the beauty of the countryside, the tender Vietnamese people, the antics of his pet monkey who'd kept him company would never convey the horrors. He'd almost begun to believe it himself. He couldn't burden his mother with the details of the damage he'd suffered or even an ounce of the weight he was carrying. She'd carried enough worry dealing with his father. Then again, who was Michael protecting, his mother or himself? He wasn't sure.

Could Michael ever share those terrible things that clattered inside him with anyone? The secrets from his days in dank marine fatigues, delivering their baby in that filthy fox hole, near *Con Thien* along the DMZ, or the enemy artillery, or seeing Ha'ng and their newborn slip off into the threatening sounds of the night.

He was well-practiced after years of proper country club behavior drilled into him from birth by his father and grandmother. The Grand Dame James would surely deliver the most appropriate dance partners for him from among the most suitable club member families, some descendant of multi-millionaire Mr. Matthew Murphy, who started the club in 1913. Probably Gayle Galloway, or some society girl whose family had been around since the days of hickory sticks and feathered golf balls.

Michael clenched his teeth. He would be charming, as always, wipe his palm before he placed it on his dance partner's silk covered back, avoid stepping on her pink or purple custom-made shoes, float gracefully through the waltz, be cool when the music turned upbeat, but not too cool. He would play the game for one more day, keep it together for one more night—for his mother, for himself.

He stepped into the party to a round of "Happy Birthday" and applause. "Mrs. Smithson, how nice to see you." He kissed the Chairman of the Board's wife on the cheek.

"You look wonderful—tall and handsome, as always. Good to have you home. You're well?"

"Never better, Ma'am." Michael worked his way through the crowd toward his mother, kissing, smiling, saying his *never betters*. His eyes took in the thick oriental carpets and the grand piano. Waiters wove in and out of the guests serving small bits of elegantly-plated, fancy food that wafted sweet and savory aromas. Delicate fingers plucked at Devils on Horseback—bacon-wrapped oysters—a traditional Victorian treat, jumbo shrimp cocktail, and mini crab cakes on rolls. Hands grasped the stemmed glasses etched with the club logo from silver trays lined with square linen cloths spaced just right so goblets wouldn't skid, drip, or clink. And shoes—all the fancy handmade shoes, made in USA, Massachusetts, of course— shiny shoes all moving to the beat of the fifteen-piece live orchestra, perched on gold velvet seats in front of the burgundy wall of curtains.

A lovely woman in wine-colored, alligator high-heels swayed at the mic on the elevated stage singing, "Fly Me to the Moon." Spinning couples circled the satin, striped-wallpapered, formal ballroom.

"Doesn't your mother look lovely in that lavender lace dress? Love the matching pumps." Michael's Chanel-scented neighbor whispered as she swept by.

Michael's mother stood under the wall of oil portraits of bearded men set in massive, gold-encrusted frames. Michael scanned the faces of his own family greats among the great-greats who had founded the club. At forty-two, his mother still had the same blonde hair as Michael. His home base, he thought.

She smiled at him, that loving smile he'd held in his mind when things had gotten tough in Vietnam. Pointing her eyes at the imminent ambush by Mrs. Galloway and her bleached-blonde daughter Gayle Marie, Michael's mother swept between the two generations of Galloways. "Cutting them off at the pass," she whispered in his ear and laughed while dancing in Michael's arms.

"Saved by the bell, Mother. The belle of the ball." Michael kissed her cheek, and the warmth of their closeness cut through the turmoil in his mind. They were bonded as always—in an enemy camp within their family where they felt like outsiders. Michael, the uncooperative, love-child heir to the family business and his unworthy mother, pregnant at eighteen—not Grandmother's first choice, not her second, nor third. A classically-trained pianist from a middle-class family wasn't good enough. Would anyone be good enough? But his mother was superior to his spoiled, arrogant father in every way, Michael thought. She was loving, genuine, accepting, and sincere. He knew her only dream for him was for Michael to be happy.

"Gayle Marie—tonight's delight—compliments of Grandmother." His mother laughed. "I know those girls are not your type, especially after you were in that war. It's changed you, somehow. Hasn't it?"

They waltzed away from the crowd.

"You're quieter, more...I don't know...more serious. Maybe troubled?"

His mother could always tune into his moods, Michael thought. But she would never be able to read the thoughts he was having now.

She hugged him as the song trailed off and the orchestra took a break. "Play for me? Something happy. Because I'm happy you're home safe and sound."

Safe, yes; *sound*, not so much, he thought. Michael took his mother's hand, sat her down next to him at the piano, and began to play Scott Joplin's "Easy Winner." Ragtime and that Joplin's song seemed appropriate—a syncopation, a complex coming together of military beats and blues, like him.

His mother leaned her head against his shoulder. Playing had always been something he could do to soothe her when Dad was up to his duplicities, he thought. Gayle Galloway's disappointed face glared at him through the triangular space between the propped-up lid and the glossy body of the Grand Steinway.

He wanted to tell his mother to remove the shard of memories that were still so raw. To tell her about his baby girl and the woman he'd loved—the mother of his child whose absence still crushed him. The music kept him from the silence, the space in which to confess his tortures. As his pinkie finger hit the last note, the loud applause suited his needs.

"Are you OK, sweetheart? I know there are things you can't bear to tell me." She shifted her head, leaned around to connect with Michael's eyes and placed her hand on his arm. Her touch was so close to the tattooed symbols she'd never seen that held his secrets. "I could see it in your eyes when you arrived home.

Maybe it would help to talk, darling?" She brushed her fingers over his forehead. "We're all proud of you."

His father bent over Michael at the piano and handed him a thick envelope. "Should hold you over until Thanksgiving vacation, son. Although we might be in Paris."

For once, Michael was glad for his father's rude interruption. It stopped the temptation to spill all his pain in the middle of the party his mother had planned for him.

Michael slid the envelope into the inside pocket of his tux. "Thanks, Dad."

"And what about a car? Take your pick. If you don't want a car, take the driver, he can drop you."

"Think I'll need wheels."

"Oh, the *girls*, right? I get it, son. Take the Ferrari Daytona, easy to *park*. He winked, enjoying his own play on the word *park*.

Girls, the last thing on Michael's mind. "I'll take the Jaguar. Thanks." The Ferrari was too much, let alone an XKE.

"Be selective, Michael; you'll find a nice girl from a good family and make your mother and me happy."

There could never have been a little brown grandbaby in their James lineage, Michael thought. And Ha`ng would never be accepted by his father and grandmother.

Don't worry, Dad, she's dead.

CHAPTER 7

Kate

NANA K

DAD AND THE boys had gone to the early Mass, and Kate and her Mom got up early to do what they loved—sing together from the high choir loft at the Sacred Heart of Jesus Church.

Kate scanned the church pews that were already full. Dye-tinted hands of her relatives were pressed together heavenward. Each Ketchum was ready to receive the body of Christ at the communion rail to sustain them through another week of labor. Some men wore those seeped-in colors proudly as a sign of honest hard work, even joy for having something creative for their hands to do; for some, it signaled stalwart resignation; some folded fingers inward with shame. But every woman wore her white gloves at Sunday Mass. One day of purity.

Standing beside her mother, Kate was ready to feel the musical magic. Why some people were compelled to warble or perform music, she didn't know. At twelve-years-old, Kate had first felt it. Singing with her mother in the choir—her mom's soprano, Kate's alto. Her mom's melody, Kate's harmony.

When the notes left their mouths, it seemed they rushed to cling to each other like long-lost relatives—immigrants who ached to belong. Like calling out in a secret cave, the sound echoed back bigger than its source—a harmony that electrified Kate's body with a wave of chills when her own voice took on another life—no longer hers alone, but *theirs.*

Studying her Mom's profile, Kate tried to imagine being away at UConn without her. As if her Mom could hear what Kate was thinking, she reached down and squeezed Kate's hand.

Last night, Mom had complained about losing some of the power in her voice lately, through aging and the early onset of emphysema. "Like losing one of my senses, the love of my life," her mother had whispered in the kitchen.

As the organist played the first few notes, Kate held her breath. But, when her mother's voice hit the high note in the "Ave Maria," the note came out clear, bounced off the beams striking like lightning into the congregation. Kate's harmony joined her. As one in two parts, singing together Kate felt their powerful connection, a kind of love.

Heads twisted back to find the source of the duet in the choir loft. The vibration sizzled down Kate's back, traveled to her throat, and closed it off. The clarity of their voices pushed tears into Kate's eyes. Maybe it made no sense for the financial security she wanted for her future, but Kate knew what she loved, what she *wanted* to do, *had* to do. A foolish dream? Her mother's face was filled with the joy of her musical prayer—a going away gift, Kate thought, as the coils of heavy incense wrapped her in a cozy cocoon.

Kate invited the images to live permanently in her

memory—her family and neighbors seated below with the searing sun illuminating the vibrant collage of colors in the stained glass windows; the kaleidoscope of light highlighting the profile of her mother's smiling face.

They exited the church into the parking lot. It was the kind of late summer day when even the leaves on the old oaks go limp. The August heat sucked the moisture from the street after a passing sun shower. Mist rose from the tacky tar like escaping radiator steam, and the strip of dampness instantly ran down Kate's cleavage.

What was going on? Kate's wilted cousins and siblings all suspiciously stood, two-deep, in two tight rows leading to the curb. Dozens of them, all lined up like a curved receiving line at a wedding, including the joking and punching among the younger boys. At the end of the aisle of relatives, Kate could see just the edge of an open car door.

"Your chariot awaits, Princess Kate." Her brother Kevin offered his arm and directed her down the human funnel of family. Her father stepped out and jangled a set of keys on a ring decorated with a miniature high heel shoe. He hung it above Kate's head, like tempting a puppy with a treat. "Madame, your keys to your new chariot." He wiped his forehead with his handkerchief and took Kate's arm and tucked it under his, closing his rough paw over her soft hand.

"*Chariot?*" Kate looked back at her mother, who stood with her hands over her face, eyes peeking out. A dead giveaway. Mom had known the surprise all along.

"Well, not a *new* chariot—new *keys* maybe," a cousin called out from behind her.

Kate's two best friends stood in front of the car on the curb waving. The male family members pushed closer and gathered around laughing, anxious to put in their two cents. Her bewilderment whirred inside, as all the voices blended into a confusing chatter.

"1963 Chevrolet Corvair Monza Spyder. Your favorite color, blue."

"Yeah, iridescent, silver blue."

"We fixed it up for you. Karl, Keith, and me," Kevin said.

"But *I* helped; I buffed the tires," her sister's four-year-old son chimed in.

"Only 52,222 miles on it. A beauty, huh?"

Kate felt her knees go out, but she was moving. Her Dad put his arm around her and walked Kate to the driver's side, her feet floating over the ground. Then he ran to the other side and got in.

She held the warm steering wheel while her two brothers and one cousin stuck their heads through the open windows rattling off the facts with pride in their voices. The hot seat was burning through her skirt but she was too thrilled to care.

"This baby's got bucket seats, and we handstitched the slice on the passenger seat like a shoe."

"Yeah, looks like she's got a great scar from winnin' a schoolyard catfight." As always, the boys competed for the best wisecrack.

"Yeah, Patrick, you should have seen the *other* girl, right?" Kate drew a round of laughs.

"Check it out, a 4-speed transmission with manual floor shift."

"We added the eight ball shift handle for good luck."

"They call it a Poor Man's Porsche," Keith got a comment in.

"Nah, this beauty's a *Town Car.*" Kevin patted the red-hot hood of the car, snapped his hand back, and shook it. "Like, nearly the whole damn *town* bought this car for you. Let Mom through, you bunch of ruffians." Kevin stepped aside from the open window and shooed away the guys, still laughing from his joke.

"Mom, you *knew* this last night?"

"Couldn't miss seeing the look on your face." Her mother bent closer, brushed a stray damp clump of faded, red hair behind her ear, and handed a gift through the window. The wrapping made Kate smile—a carefully cut A&P brown grocery bag with a handmade bow from scraps of gingham fabric. The scotch tape gave way easily to expose the framed antique photo of her great-grandmother Katherine on the local Glynn newspaper's front page, July 28, 1868, with a protest placard in her hand. *Equal Day, Equal Pay!* Kate grasped the photo to her chest. She'd heard the stories of Nana Ketchum's outrageous courage as a woman picketing for fair pay and starting the first women's union, but she'd never seen the picture. "Mom, thank you, but where did you get this?"

"Grandpa K found it in his basement when he was clearing it out for Cousin Kenny to move in."

"I love it." Kate ran her hand over the tiger-striped maple frame.

Her mother leaned in, avoiding the hot car door and kissed Kate. The same kind of hands-off kiss that had put her to sleep each night as a child, the same kind of Ketchum kiss she would miss. "Luggage's in the trunk, Katie-girl."

"Oh, Mom, I can't tell you…" Kate slumped over the warm, black steering wheel. The truth sunk in; it was *her* car, a gift from the entire family. When she lifted her head, Kate caught a glimpse of Grandma Kendall on the edge of the crowd. She wished her mother's mother wasn't always so cynical and critical. What had soured her?

"You can't win them all, Kate," her father said, nodding toward his mother-in-law.

Kate turned on the tuned-up engine.

"Hey, what are you gonna call her? How 'bout Nellie II?"

"No time for that, Kev; this girl's got to get herself to college. She can think about a name later." Her father stepped out of the car and closed the door with an insistent push.

Kate looked at the photo of her great grandmother Katherine on her lap, "I'm calling her Nana K." She blew a kiss to her mother and the entire crowd, and put Nana K in gear.

CHAPTER 8

Michael

CURSING THE MOON

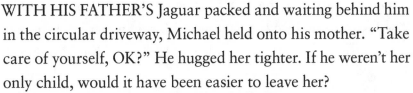

WITH HIS FATHER'S Jaguar packed and waiting behind him in the circular driveway, Michael held onto his mother. "Take care of yourself, OK?" He hugged her tighter. If he weren't her only child, would it have been easier to leave her?

For Michael, his departure was bitter-sweet. He knew it was the last time he would live at home close to his mother, playing bodyguard in his parents' dysfunctional marriage. Summers he would spend alone at their Berkshire cabin on the lake. His respite.

After college, he'd be off to grad school or whatever overseas job he could find. His eye-opening time in Vietnam made him want to make a difference.

As Michael left for a summer abroad after sophomore year at Harvard, his mother had hinted at the possibility that he had a choice about living out his family business legacy. Maybe you don't have to work for J.E. James & Son, she'd said. Michael knew she didn't expect him to run off into the military as his escape. Now, with more maturity than he wished he had, he knew there were easier ways to have avoided the James family legacy.

His father said his goodbyes at breakfast and went golfing. That was good; Michael wanted to be alone with his mother, yet he didn't. He was afraid she would read his pain in his eyes, and she did.

"Michael, four years in that terrible war; I know there's more than you've told me." She brushed her hand through the short swath of his hair. "I worry about you. You're so...different now, reserved. Maybe those memories are best left to fade. But, when you're ready to talk... I'm here."

The heavy August air creeping in off the gray water sparked a memory—the day he'd met Ha`ng by the tree along the river. The loss pressed in. "It was tough, Mom; I won't lie. Just need a little time. Sorry I have to leave. I know being alone with Dad is..."

"Never mind him, sweetheart. I always knew you'd go away to college; I confess I never thought I'd lose you to four years in that horrible war on the other side of the world. But I'm proud of you." She put her hands on his shoulders.

Her blue eyes had a mist of sadness forming on the edges, and he kissed her cheek. He owed her so much, but Michael had to get away to see if he could find some kind of happiness again, to find something to revive the part of him that had been crushed.

"I hope Dad behaves, Mom."

"Oh, Michael, he's a victim of his ego and his family pressures. He's not altogether bad at heart."

Leaving her with his father felt like abandonment, as always. But it was his mother's choice to stay in her marriage after his long history of betrayal—his "wanderings." Always her euphemisms and excuses, Michael thought. That was something he could never understand. At times he blamed his mother for much of her own suffering. He wanted to confront his father about his affairs. Call him out—fucking cheater. But, then his father's temper would only be directed at his mother in Michael's absence. All was well when you did whatever the goddam, manipulating narcissist wanted. And she always did.

Was it some kind of fear or some flawed dedication that kept his mother in her mock marriage? It made Michael think, was he also keeping himself in his own misery? Was his self-torture a way of keeping Ha`ng near?

"Mom..." The truth was pushing at his lips, wanted to explode from his mouth. Holding back his reality about his time in Vietnam was getting too big for him. Fortunately, his mother was still left back on the tracks in their previous conversation about her unhappiness with his father.

She squeezed his shoulder. "I'll be fine, sweetheart; I always am. I know how to deal with your father. I have my friends, my charity work, and my faith." She cupped his face again. "And I have you."

"Just know I love you, Mom, and I'm not far."

"Promise me you'll go to Mass, Michael. And you'll write? And call?" Her eyes filled. "Now go, before I get selfish and give you a good dose of mom's guilt." She laughed.

He got in the low-slung, silver car and looked up at his mother. The three-story family manor loomed behind her. Too much room; too much emptiness, he thought. "I promise I'll write and call."

"Call when you arrive, please? About five hours with the ferry ride and stops, I'm guessing."

"Yup, call you about 5:00 then." The guilt of leaving his mother after four years away in the war rose up in his throat. A familiar feeling. He'd found such peace being with her before the Marines. They'd always found something in their skewed world to laugh about. She was so strong. He needed to find that strength in himself to punch his way out of the horrific memories that wrapped around him, constricting his breath. If he could only filter out and keep just the good memories with Ha`ng—their laughter, their tender moments.

"Be safe." The rearview mirror framed his mother waving goodbye.

Michael pulled around the private driveway, and tore out, leaving the grinding, spitting sounds of gravel behind him. At the edge of town, the familiar sight of the massive old pin oak tree sparked memories—the way it bent, the missing branches on one side, and the charred scar from a lightning strike.

The daylight sliver of a moon riding in the sky overhead along with the sun made him shiver. Lining the road to UConn, the sunlit morning grasses flickered Michael's thoughts back to the first time he'd seen Ha`ng. Her slender shape as she leaned against the old tamarind tree—its branches dripping with long, copper-colored seed pods. Its wide arc shaded her from the blazing sun like the umbrellas the women held overhead as they padded by him on the path to the market.

He could picture the small herd of baby goats huddled under the tree's cool protection near the young woman. The traditional village woman had a book spread open in her hands. As he approached, he saw the title, *The Great Gatsby*. No way. *In*

English. Fascinating. He was sure she didn't fail to feel the heat of his riveted stare as he passed her.

She glanced over her shoulder. "Hi. You like to read?"

Her smile like a wild jungle vine snaked around him and squeezed his heart. A new feeling, not like any other response he'd had to a girl before. "Oh, uh, yes. But how is it that you…?"

"You are surprised a village girl reads English novels?" She leaned her head back against the tree and laughed. "Oh, it's the clothes that fooled you. Am I correct?"

"Well, yes…and speaking English."

She shared her name, Ha`ng, and pronounced it for him, "*Hahng.*" She was no village woman. While visiting at home, she liked to wear traditional garb, not wanting to forget her roots, she'd told him. For her family. She'd only been visiting her parents on break from her job as a professor at the university in the city.

Her timing was so perfect, and so poor, Michael thought, sliding his hands along the arc of the steering wheel. The moments he stole with her over the summer months he'd spent assigned to her village area had made him never want to leave. Her classroom English was no barrier. They'd felt the same way about so many things. He remembered talking while watching a young child in the distance riding on the neck of a water buffalo beside the rice fields. Strange a small boy could tame such a beast, they'd said in harmony.

Michael remembered *not* talking too—their instant, electric attraction had bridged their cultural divide. Her touch still felt real on his taut shoulders as Michael shifted gears and took a turn toward the UConn campus.

In his mind, he was there, again—sipping tea with her parents and five siblings in their small cottage—translating, laughing, as Hà'ng dropped her head against his shoulder. After two years, his Vietnamese was good enough to communicate and bad enough to cause a lot of good-hearted laughter. It was those damn six tones he screwed up regularly.

"Wrong tone, darling." She'd smiled. "GI, you said *butter* instead of *walk*."

Those special times, before he returned to his unit each night, were the most *family* he'd ever felt.

How had he found such peace in the chaos of war? How hard it had been to leave her when his company pulled out after such a long time together. She'd wanted to follow him. It had made no sense. They both finally agreed she would wait and continue her teaching. With his discharge date only ten months away, Michael would return to get her, and they'd be married and return to the States. He'd slipped a crude ring on her finger Michael had twisted from lime-green grass.

"Stop the memories," Michael said out loud, as he accelerated the sleek convertible up the two-lane highway. As though the speed could distract him from seeing it again, or blur the memory, or make the images pass. Hà'ng dropping into the mucky hole where he'd hidden. Not a village woman, *his* woman, disguised, dressed in her country woman's attire. Hà'ng, his lover, bursting from her clothes with their child about to come. How had she found him nine months later? Why had she risked it? He could hear her words—*it's crazy, I know, but I had to be with you.* They'd embraced and kissed and couldn't let go. His arms wrapped around her trembling body.

He'd dreamed of their life in Vietnam; she'd dreamed of their life in the U.S. There could be no dreams of living near his family, he'd told her. It was something she couldn't understand.

"But, they are your family, Michael."

His mother would love Ha̐ng, he explained to her, and accept her as her own, the daughter she had never had, but his father wouldn't have such open arms. And Michael wouldn't subject her to that. As different as Ha̐ng and his mother looked, they were a lot alike. Strong, with a loving nature, and that laugh. They would share that laugh.

Michael tightened his moist grip on the steering wheel, shivered, and took a deep breath. Memories of comforting Ha̐ng rushed back—whispering soothing words, making promises he couldn't keep as her breaths of childbirth came faster. "We have to have hope," he'd said. "Breathe, darling, breathe!"

Echoes of Ha̐ng's screams in the foxhole when the fire came down on them were splitting his skull. Trying to stay focused on the road ahead of him, Michael accelerated down in the farmland roads, imagining her running through the flashes of the unexpected conflict. He'd cursed the cruel moonlight that had escaped the shadow of a cloud, spotlighting her against the dense green. Every detail was still alive: Ha̐ng's muffled screams when he'd guided their newborn daughter from between her legs; Ha̐ng running from the cross-fire in slow motion, one arm bolting upward, shrapnel pummeling her arching back, the other arm desperately gripping their child; lifting his true love's lifeless arms from around their baby girl. Would he re-live his loss in living color, the red on Ha̐ng's blue and white clothes, forever?

Michael pulled over and screeched this sportscar to stop by a pond on the country road as he entered the campus. He'd failed to protect her, he thought. Failed their little girl too. Failed the Marine's pledge—honor, courage, commitment, always faithful...*Semper Fidelis.*

Would it be a betrayal to let Hàng's and Hy Vọng's memories fade? Would it insult his lover to stop suffering over her?

CHAPTER 9

CAMPUS A CAPELLA

KATE CRANKED UP the radio and took her Nana K Corvair into the final curve. She took it well. The smooth vibration of the rumbling engine Kate felt in her leather bucket seat made Kate smile. She pictured her brothers huddled around the car in front of church vying for credit for their generous going-away present. So touching a farewell.

With the red needle pointing to full, the temperature gauge normal, windows down, her bright auburn hair twisted up and held in place by her signature crisscross of two number 2 pencils, all was well. Except she was aching from separating from her clan for the first time.

The framed article on the passenger seat slid into the turn, and she grabbed it just in time. Nana Katherine was a legend within the family, but they'd never talked about her much. It was a source of awkwardness when it came to the owners of the factory. They certainly didn't honor the rebellious woman whose protests against their ancestors had cost them. A married woman trapped in a factory making shoes with pittance wages had risen up against all odds—a founder of the first women's union in America, the Daughters of St. Christopher. It was hard for Kate to fathom a woman being so bold in 1868, a century ago.

Her Nana Katherine had left her eight children at the kitchen table to lead her fellow women workers in a strike that had won them fair and equal wages. Those were times when feminism wasn't even a word. Great-grandmother's actions, working her way on a ship from Ireland to America to seek her dreams, then helping others to seek theirs, inspired Kate.

Kate had always known she'd be the first one to leave home. But she didn't have as noble a goal as Nana Katherine—fighting for the good of others. Kate's was just fighting to be herself. She glanced down at the folded map beside her. "OK, Nana Katherine, let's do this."

The single-lane road from the highway to campus was beautiful—small, white-steeple churches and rolling hills dotted with dappled cows taking refuge under scattered arching trees. Through the window, the humid breeze brought little relief from the August heat, but Kate was too enthralled to care.

At the campus proper, she impulsively turned down the first street, a church row: the modern Unitarian Universalist on the corner; the traditional United Methodist, white wood with green trim; and the brick St. Thomas Aquinas Catholic Church with its stained-glass window. She knew the afternoon Mass would likely be over, but maybe the choirmaster would still be there? Kate parked on the street in front of the church, got out, and took in the scenery.

St. Thomas overlooked a quiet little lake surrounded by weeping willows with reflections of the sloping, grassy green banks. It was lovely and peaceful with wooden garden benches. Two students sat reading like bookends, legs propped up with feet touching. Across the small clear lake, a couple enfolded in a lingering embrace. Kate lingered with her gaze too. "You deserve to be loved." Her mother's words came back as Kate pulled at the heavy, stubborn door.

Kate's snake-tooled leather platform shoes echoed in the empty church as she walked down the tiled aisle past the empty oak pews toward the altar.

"May I help you, Miss? I'm afraid you've just missed the last Mass." The baritone voice rebounded off the arches above.

Kate spun around. "Oh, I've just arrived on campus and..." She spotted a tall, lean man with dark hair standing above her at the choir loft railing, hands clasped behind him, dressed in a long black cassock with a white-collar. Through the circular stained glass window, the late afternoon sun cast colorful beams around him. "I just hoped to meet..." The sight made her smile. "Father, you're all lit up. Or, I should say, illuminated."

He looked at his hands, splashed in the rainbow of light through the collage of colored glass. "I'll take that to mean 'lit up' from sunlight, not alcohol."

Kate laughed. "I just wanted to see the choir loft. I was thinking I might try out for—"

"Seek, and you shall find. You sing?"

"Yes, well, I try."

"Come up here, young lady, and try. We need good voices."

She froze; it was *the* Father Sullivan. "*Now?* But I..." She wasn't prepared to audition for the gold-medal-winning St. Thomas Aquinas Student choir.

"Now is good; now is always good."

Her stomach quivered as she climbed the spiral stairs along the caramel-colored wood panels and arrived in the loft under the flashing, round, stained-glass window of St. Thomas Aquinas.

"The things that we love tell us who we are," the priest said.

Kate looked up at the figure in the window above her. "So, that's a St. Thomas Aquinas quote, right?"

"That's right. Let's have you stand right here; acoustics are perfect. I'm Father Sullivan. Choirmaster at your service. And you are?"

"Kate Ketchum, Father. I hadn't expected to audition with you; I got here just now and wanted to—"

"I'm guessing if the first stop a young coed makes on campus is a choir loft, she's got what it takes."

She envisioned the photo of her great-grandmother on the front seat of her "town car" and put down her pocketbook. "I'm ready."

"So, Kate Ketchum, might you want to wrap your cords around the 'Ave Maria'?"

"Ave Maria?" Kate's eyes widened, thinking of her mother that morning in church, chilling everyone with those same notes. Of all hymns, he would pick that one. Could she sing it alone?

"You know it, I assume. The Shubert version?" The priest smiled, sat at the old pipe organ, the silver tubes rising to the ceiling, flipped on a series of levers, and began to play.

Kate missed the lead-in.

"Too challenging? You prefer something else?"

She shook her head, no.

"We must start by believing; then afterward we may be led on to master the evidence for ourselves," he said.

"St. Thomas, again?"

He twisted on the organ bench and smiled at her.

Come with me, Mom, Kate thought. "Can you play the intro again, Father, please."

Father Sullivan bobbed his head to the slow beat, his long slender fingers moving masterfully over the three levels of keys.

Kate jumped into the Latin lyrics on the second pass. It was the first time she wasn't standing beside her mother singing any hymn, she realized. No one to bounce off of; no one to sing the melody to her harmony. She felt strange taking over her mother's part.

One, two, three, four, five, six—she kept the beat, tapping on the side of her leg with her left hand, and released the notes, "Ave Mari-i-a." And when that high note came, she channeled her mother's crystal voice and prayed for her to come through her. And she did. Kate hung on to the note until it rebounded off the rafters and came back to her. It filled the church wall to wall.

She sang on for two more notes, acapella. Kate could see his eyes were closed.

"Miss Ketchum, I've heard enough."

Kate held her breath.

Father Sullivan turned to face her, and then he rubbed his arms. "Chills."

She was thrilled. Her vocal cords had released, echoing her mother's beautiful bellows.

"Choir robes are downstairs in the first room on the right behind the sacristy."

"I'm *in?*"

"Let's just say I know where to go for our 'Oh, Holy Night' solo this year. Practices Tuesday and Thursday evenings, 5 p.m. sharp."

CHAPTER 10

Michael

LOSING HOPE

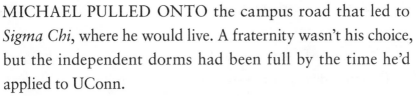

MICHAEL PULLED ONTO the campus road that led to *Sigma Chi*, where he would live. A fraternity wasn't his choice, but the independent dorms had been full by the time he'd applied to UConn.

He'd accepted his Uncle John's help to join *Sigma Chi*. The prestigious fraternity was happy to oblige their biggest benefactor's request, especially for an All-American crew and pole vaulter from Harvard, and a hero just in from Vietnam. Bunking with the offspring of Uncle John's brotherhood at the state university would be fine. No one would know him. He wanted anonymity.

Maneuvering the Jaguar into the parking lot, Michael found a shady spot to park near the north end of campus. At the edge of fraternity row, he nestled his car between a green Ford pickup and a blue Camaro with a fender missing. With his Marine duffle over his shoulder, a bag in each hand, and his satchel of music sheets under his arm, Michael approached the fraternity house. Halfway down Fraternity

Quadrangle—a horseshoe-shaped lineup of a dozen brick houses with brass Greek letters affixed on each front door—he found Sigma Chi.

Two bare-chested guys were popping a soccer ball around each other on the well-worn center of the grassy courtyard edged with shade trees. Michael was relieved; he liked the casual feel of the place.

A short, muscled student was exiting the door. He held it open for Michael and his one-man-caravan of belongings.

The scent of charring meat from inside the fraternity house immediately turned Michael off, and acid rose in his throat.

"Hey, Man. Welcome... Nam? Marines, right?"

Michael flinched and looked down at himself. No buzz cut, no more uniform.

"The gear. Michael Edward James, right?"

Looking down at the stenciled letters on his bag, Michael laughed.

"Oh, damn, Senator Edward's kid, right?"

"His nephew, Michael."

The guy started to offer the secret brotherhood handshake Michael's uncle had mentioned he would learn at the initiation ceremony. "Oh, sorry."

Burdened by his baggage, Michael nodded to substitute for the official greeting. "Check-in?"

"Oh yeah, down the hall on your left. I'm Nugget. Nickname. Long story." He tapped Michael on the shoulder. "Crew, right? That's the word around here about you. I'm the coxie." He talked and walked beside Michael. "You do both the eight and single, right? Read about your All-American record breakers. Damn."

"I'm out of practice now." Michael lifted the Marine duffle.

"We practice on Coventry Lake, not far. Not on a river like Harvard, but...you've seen our new black hulls and navy checkered blades? Really cool."

"So, you're the coxswain. I'll be listening to you in the eight-man race a lot then." Michael smiled, shifted the heavy load across his shoulder. He couldn't wait to burn off his stress in a single scull again. Alone. Being on the water kept him calm.

"Yeah. We lucked out when you decided on UConn. Hey, see you at dinner? Follow your nose, dining hall's on the right. Always steak to celebrate the new semester."

"Thanks, Nugget." Michael caught his short but sturdy frat brother staring at his neck scar.

"Need anything; I'm your man. Room 3, third floor."

No monogrammed dress shirts, Michael thought. And Nugget, well, his name alone made Michael's shoulders release, *right?* One first name; he liked the guy.

In contrast to the simpler main area, halfway down the hallway, a door was ajar; it opened to an elegant room. Over the faux stone fireplace was a portrait of the fraternity chapter founder no doubt. On the wall was a portrait of his Uncle John among a line-up of former fraternity leaders, the Worthy Grand Masters.

He'd lucked out. Only a single room with its own bath on the top floor was available. No roommate. Was his uncle at work here, again? Fine with him. This was a favor he would gladly take. Michael dropped his duffle on the floor and unpacked his things. He filled each drawer with the tightly rolled rows of stark white undershirts, socks, and ironed, blue pinstriped boxers. Snapping his shirts and pants to shake out the wrinkles, he flipped up the mattress, neatly flattened the clothes out in the shape of a surrendering soldier and lowered it—the perfect ironing system. He felt better with things all lined up.

Hands behind his head, Michael stretched out on the bed. Her sweet face was always there in front of him. "Please call her Hope," he'd said to the old village woman. Although he'd had little hope, himself. The woman had struggled to repeat the English name. Would she remember? Would she keep his daughter's name? He'd pulled out his tattered two-way dictionary and found the baby's name in Vietnamese. Hopeful, trust, *Hy Vọng*. Pointing to the newborn, he'd pushed his meaning into the old woman's wrinkled eyes.

"*Hy Vọng*." She'd repeated and nodded.

Then he'd flipped through pages to find the meaning of the name of his, his *what*—girlfriend? Lover? Soulmate? War bride? Wife? Had they only had the chance. He'd found the right spelling, Hàng—*angel in the full moon*. Too much irony to handle.

Michael pulled his green canvas Dopp kit from his monogrammed leather luggage and headed into his bathroom. So far, so good.

CHAPTER 11

STRIPPED NAKED

IT TOOK SOME time for Kate to follow the map through the sprawling campus. Most of the brick buildings were three stories high with walkways, gardens, and longstanding trees woven in between them. She passed the men's gymnasium with its arced aluminum, rippled roof across from the block-long brick Student Union. Kate took it all in. Expansive lawns and landscaping were everywhere.

On the outskirts of the south end of campus, Watson Hall cast a shadow across the acre of front lawn—five floors of new gleaming windows. The first all-girls high-rise on campus towered above the other nearby dorms. A second-floor glass walkway connected Watson to another dormitory of equal size.

Checking into her room was easy; there were no cars in the loading zone, and there was no line at 5:45 p.m., fifteen minutes before dorm check-in closed. Mrs. Weinstein, the house mother, introduced herself and gave Kate the keys to her fifth-floor single room.

"Everyone is at dinner—through that first floor connector—the other tower beyond the cafeteria is a boys' dorm. Don't get turned around on your way back."

Even the hum of the elevator was thrilling on her trip to the fifth floor. She'd rarely ridden one. Kate held the key to her own place in her hand—a first. Turning the brass key in the lock, she opened the shiny oak door to her room and felt a waterfall of tingles down her spine. Her view was an apple orchard on a hill and a blue sky filled with cottony clouds. Kate checked the ceiling next—it was snow-white with no water stains, and she laughed. Turning full circle, she took in the small but well-appointed room—a twin bed, which she bounced off of very nicely, a solid oak desk and chair, and a large built-in closet along one wall and a wall phone.

Across the street, she spotted the perfect place tucked under a graceful tree where she would go to read, practice singing, or write the daydreamed lyrics for future hit songs. Sitting at the very top of the hill nestled in a field of unmowed wildflowers and grasses, the oak spread open its arms like the celebration of a great performance. A bump-out, halfway up the trunk, looked like one hip thrust out as if the tree were taking a bow. Kate took one last look out the window before heading to the cafeteria. Her hand went to her chest, and she smiled. It was stunning, up high—a private room with a delicious view.

The cafeteria was clattering with students reuniting. Familiar aromas of salty Salisbury steak and cinnamon buns brought Kate home to her kitchen with her mom. Walking into the crowded room and not knowing almost every person had only happened once before when she'd first arrived at community college. Even there, Kate had only known a few students from high school. A small hollow ache passed through her. Strange to be on her own for the first time. The din of chatter surrounded her and a touch of loneliness joined her elation. Two emotions were at odds inside—the thrill of the new and the fear of having left the familiar, making her both excited and exhausted.

Kate balanced her tray with one hand and wiped the moisture from her forehead onto her embroidered, gauze blouse. Following the girl ahead of her, she slid the plastic tray along the silver runners. Kate was hungry. Taking anything she wanted, as much as she wanted, was delightful. She still couldn't believe there would be no cashier at the end of the line. Everything was included in her RA package. Should she slip a few extra soft Parker house rolls into her patent leather satchel for later? Kate resisted.

"Love your boots." The girl ahead of Kate stopped. Her blue and white paisley head bandana imprisoned an explosion of black corkscrew curls. A treasure chest of silver spangles and bangles danced from her ears and her fingers, wrists, and neck. Like Cher, dressed for a gypsy skit. "Where'd you get those boots, Italy? Really cool."

"Ha, actually, my mom made them." There was a sudden pride Kate felt at the thought of her family's skills. Who else could say their mother made their fine leather boots?

"Funny. Did your mother make that incredible leather bag too?" The student gave Kate a smile with a teasing pop of her shoulders, took a plate of salad, and pushed her tray ahead.

"My grandfather made the satchel." Kate laughed in

response to the look on the girl's face. "Oh, you think I'm kidding. No, they're both cordwainers."

"Cord-who?" The girl put a cinnamon bun on her tray.

"Cordwainers. Shoemakers." Kate cringed at using the wrong word, but she knew it would convey. "My family works in handmade leather shoes, five generations. I'm the first factory escapee."

"OK, I've got to hear more about this; sit with me? I'm Shiloh. 4th floor RA."

Her invitation gave Kate a sigh of relief. She was grateful to not sit alone. "Kate, 5th floor RA. Shiloh, such a beautiful name."

"It's from a famous fight in the Civil War, Battle of Shiloh."

"Now, *I* want to hear more." Kate spied two seats at an empty table on the far side of the room.

Shiloh plopped her tray down and slid into her seat across from Kate. She began to openly share her story. She'd been raised in a nearby commune; both parents were Political Science professors at UConn, her father, a Cherokee Indian.

No wonder, those high cheekbones and shiny black hair, Kate thought. Shiloh planned to go to law school and wanted to represent foster children. It was hard for Kate to concentrate with the hypnotizing jingling that accompanied Shiloh's every word. Not a finger was free of handmade silver rings. Hoop earrings that nearly reached her shoulders swayed with her every gesture.

Kate could scarcely eat, taking in Shiloh's history, family life, liberal politics, even her belief in "free love." That made Kate squirm. Who would even admit it? They had a word for girls like that where Kate came from. But Shiloh seemed different, not ashamed. It was natural to have desires, she'd said. True, but what you did about it was another thing, Kate thought.

"We eat rebellion for breakfast, my grandmother likes to say." Shiloh laughed. "It's in our blood. I'm a member of the SDS. You know, Students for a Democratic Society." She put her elbows on the table and her chin in her hands.

Rebellion in her blood? Had that thread broken in Kate's ancestral line? Kate ate a few green beans and tore off a piece of a roll. "My great-grandmother started the first women's union in the U.S. at the same shoe factory where my family works. *Equal day: Equal pay* was her slogan. But that was the last rebellion for the women in my family."

"What about *you*? You're the first one to leave the factory, you said."

"I never thought that I was meant to carry my great-grand-mother's placard forward."

"Maybe you are. Just different times, you know. Pretty cool. I'm going to get a coffee. I like to have it with my meal. Want some?"

"No, thanks." Kate thought about her legacy and her great-grandmother. Kate wasn't quite like Shiloh, but in her own way, maybe going to college, not wanting to marry and have children was a kind of rebellion, she thought. Why was she telling a stranger all of this? How often had Kate ever needed to summarize her life in a world of relatives and old friends at home? And when had she ever had a girlfriend who wasn't a cousin or a sister?

The entrancing sound of Shiloh's bangles and all of those distinctive silver rings seemed to announce her self-confidence, her history, a girl with her own style. Did Shiloh see beyond the fancy boots to the inexperienced small-town girl Kate was? She'd always felt a certain confidence at school, singing in church with her Mom, and especially on stage at O'Leary's with the applause ringing, and Uncle Jack behind the bar. She'd distinguished herself in the family as smart and talented. Shiloh's well-defined-self immediately made Kate aware she'd been a big fish in a little pond. She was unworldly with no real pins on her map. Just dreams.

Shiloh returned and resumed the interrogation, sipping her coffee. "How about you?" She lifted a piece of lettuce to her mouth.

"Well, my story's pretty short and sweet compared to yours. OK. I'm the daughter of five generations of Irish Catholic shoemakers in a factory town not far from Boston. My six siblings, their spouses, my parents, aunts and uncles and grandparents are all in the cordwainer trade. Our lives were... school, church, library, and a local Irish pub where I sang. I just finished working my way through community college. Singing is my passion."

"So, you lived in a commune too."

"Ha. True. I guess you could call it that. Lots of love in our Ketchum commune."

"Speaking of love? Do you have a boyfriend?" Shiloh tilted her head.

"Um...there's no boyfriend." Kate took a bite of Salisbury steak. Shiloh's question had crossed a line somehow. Her sparkling eyes and warm smile and the way she leaned forward made it seem that Shiloh was sincerely interested in what Kate had to say. Still, the subject agitated Kate. At some level, lack of interest in a permanent guy, marriage, and children wasn't something Kate had meant to reveal; sometimes, that worried her about herself. Her sisters hadn't understood that Kate's passions were her children. How could she put books and school and singing over love?

It had made her an outsider, a little strange to them. Even her mother had said, don't forget to let yourself be loved. Kate was not going to share all that with a stranger she'd just met in a cafeteria.

The light was dimming, Kate watched students drift out of the room. A dropped plate crashed by the tray return area made Kate jump. Conversations stopped, then roared to a pitch again. It seemed like everyone knew everyone.

"Well, forget about boyfriends, then, how about just 'romantic interests'." Shiloh fluttered her eyebrows and smiled. "I've got a few of those."

"Not me. Even free love costs." Kate kept her tone light, not allowing a tinge of judgment in her voice that might insult Shiloh.

"True. But my mother says, always taste the batter for sweetness before you bake the cake. A girl has needs, right?"

Not exactly what any mother, Kate knew, would say. "You and your mother talk about that stuff?"

"I tell my mom everything. And she probably tells my dad everything I tell her too." Shiloh laughed.

Kate realized that was an unspoken rule among the Ketchum women, don't tell your dad or husband.

"We're talking about two beatniks turned hippies married in the early fifties. You know, black-clad, poetry-reading set."

"No, I don't know; I only know apron-wearing, go-take-that-make-up-off-and-make-your-bed set."

Shiloh's laugh was loud and free, like her. Kate was seeing herself through a new lens. Was she unique or one of many girls in college who felt this way?

Kate slid her chair back a bit and crossed her fork and knife on her plate. The conversation was nearing a cliff that she didn't want to jump off. She wanted to get off the sex subject.

"Yeah, I guess I had a somewhat odd upbringing. My parents were both...how would I describe them? Intellectuals. Dad's also a musician; Mom writes."

Kate's ears perked up at the word, musician.

"They did spontaneous political theatre all over the country when I was a kid. To quote my mom, their whole thing was encouraging people to freely express individual beliefs and desires. They took my brother and me along in a VW van."

A flicker of sadness crossed Shiloh's face at the mention of her brother. She stared off at a young boy who was cleaning up a shattered, broken plate from the floor. Was she feeling as homesick as Kate was?

"Kate? Oh, I'm so sorry. Maybe all that was too much. I've been told I do that." Shiloh reached out and touched Kate's hand. "I hope I didn't offend you by all this. Let's change the subject."

"It's OK. You mentioned a membership. What's the SDS?"

"Students for a Democratic Society? Student activists, anti-war, anti-racism. What's your take on the war, Kate?"

"It killed my cousin, so not so good, obviously."

"Oh, I'm so sorry."

"Me too; we were close. Danny played in my band." Kate nearly stopped, then looked into Shiloh's compassionate eyes,

"And my brother served; he came home injured. Never really the same after that." Kate saw another hint of darkness pass over Shiloh's face.

"I just lost my only brother, Tim, my twin. We were home-schooled; we were close...it left a pretty big scar on my family.

"I'm so sorry about your brother; your only brother." Kate looked down, stabbed another green bean, and swirled it in gravy. "But the protests...don't they kind of say they died for nothing? I hate to think that don't you?"

"No, the opposite. I have to do something...you know, keep someone else's cousin or brother from getting killed."

"I haven't really had time to even think about my political stance." She wondered why it had never occurred to her that anything could be done about her cousin's death. Her family seemed to just mourn him, accept it, and move on. "I guess I'm against the war now, but I've never been an activist." An idea formed. "Do you have music at those protests? I'm a singer. I've never done protest songs, but..."

"Woah! Cool. I'll enlist you for our next rally. Messages go over bigger if they're in the lyrics to a good song. I'd love to hear you sing. If you made the St. Thomas Choir, you must be amazing."

"I hope I'm amazing on Tuesday. I'm a little nervous. I'm auditioning for a Voice Performance music major at 3:00. It means everything."

Shiloh looked over Kate's shoulder and waved. "Listen, I need a minute to speak to a friend; I've been looking for him all day. If you can wait just a minute, we can walk back together."

"Sure. I'll take your tray." Kate took a breath, then finished the last few bites of her cinnamon dessert, and stacked the trays and dishes. It was as if she'd just spent thirty minutes stripping naked in front of a stranger.

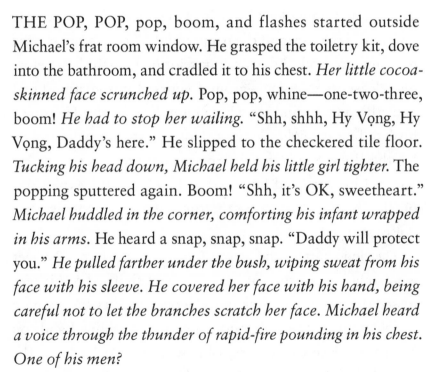

CHAPTER 12

Michael

SENSELESS SOUNDS

THE POP, POP, pop, boom, and flashes started outside
Michael's frat room window. He grasped the toiletry kit, dove
into the bathroom, and cradled it to his chest. *Her little cocoa-
skinned face scrunched up.* Pop, pop, whine—one-two-three,
boom! *He had to stop her wailing.* "Shh, shhh, Hy Vọng, Hy
Vọng, Daddy's here." He slipped to the checkered tile floor.
Tucking his head down, Michael held his little girl tighter. The
popping sputtered again. Boom! "Shh, it's OK, sweetheart."
*Michael huddled in the corner, comforting his infant wrapped
in his arms.* He heard a snap, snap, snap. "Daddy will protect
you." *He pulled farther under the bush, wiping sweat from his
face with his sleeve. He covered her face with his hand, being
careful not to let the branches scratch her face. Michael heard
a voice through the thunder of rapid-fire pounding in his chest.
One of his men?*

"*Michael?* Hey, I knocked, but...man, when I heard you...
well, are you OK?"

Michael shuffled farther undercover.

"Hey, buddy, it's me, Nugget. *Shit*."

"Take cover, Private," Michael said in a throaty voice. The sounds stopped.

"It's just fireworks, man. Opening day. Oh, shit…"

The voice invaded. Michael pushed through the sounds, rubbed his arm to stop the shakes, and his trembling fingers struggled with the zipper on his Dopp kit. *It isn't real*, Michael told himself. *Find something to smell, bring yourself back. Do it!*

"What do I do, buddy? Jesus…"

It's not Hy Vọng, it's not Hy Vọng, Michael chanted to himself, staring at the kit. He took out the toothpaste. Smell it, smell it, he commanded himself. You're in the bathroom. He unscrewed the cap, and the peppermint Colgate scent started to bring him back. Like his counselor had taught him before his release to go home—ground yourself in something real. Something to remind me where I am, he thought. He placed his hand on the cold tile floor. Not a bush, not palm fronds, it's the floor. See it; feel it. Focus on a scent, a sound. He covered his ears and hummed to block out the explosions outside his window to soothe the pop, pop, popping. The noises stopped.

The cloud parted, and he was focused on the face of Nugget, who squatted in front of him. Michael shuffled to his feet, tossed the toothpaste back into the open toiletry kit, set it on the shelf above the sink, and wiped his trembling hands on his jeans. "Fireworks, sure, I knew that." Michael saw the horrified look on Nugget's face. He breathed in deeply ten times. "You know, the fireworks—the artillery? Just a little flashback."

Nugget put his arm on Michael's shoulder. "*Little?* Shit, man."

"Thanks, I've got this."

"Not my business but...don't you think you need some—"

"What? Help?" Michael glanced at the toiletry kit, shook his head. "I know." Michael felt a blanket of shame fall down around him. "This is the first time anyone's been around for it." His shaking slowed, but the grip in his chest remained.

"Father Sullivan, a former Marine chaplain. He's at St. Thomas Aquinas. I've heard good things about him. He's Catholic but...I don't know what you...?"

"Me too. I'm Catholic."

"You know, he works with guys who... like you. So...you think it would help to eat? How about dinner?"

Michael thought of the bloody steak. He'd pass. "I'm good, thanks. Just ate before I arrived."

"OK. See ya...hey, sorry if I...came at a bad time; the door was unlocked and when I heard you..."

Michael had to laugh. "Perfect timing." He pulled his shirt up and wiped the sweat from his face. "Hey, keep this to yourself, OK?"

"Sure. But you'll get help, right?"

Michael looked down at the short, muscled guy. "Yeah, for sure. Got it. Father Sullivan."

Nugget closed the door behind him. Michael dropped on the bed and stared out the window at the moon's arc that hung in daylight above the building across the quadrangle. What the hell had just happened?

His face was red hot with shame. He was horrified that Nugget had seen that. He'd hoped the chilling, uncontrollable flashback that his father's rifle shot had triggered on the lake at his home was a one-time anomaly for him.

Even now, the thoughts wouldn't leave him. Always, Ha`ng's arms in his mind—slow motion, her arms releasing their baby girl to him. He'd spun the aching memory around a thousand times. Michael comforting their child for days, breathing in her innocence deeply, feeling her buttery skin. Her sweet scent. His infant's little mouth accepting the sweet, warm coconut water. It was all he had to feed her. He could still feel her fragile chest rising and falling, her tiny fingers grasping his thumb, and pressing his lips on her silky forehead. He could still feel the grip of his desperation until he'd stumbled upon that goat. The life-saving goat's milk. More hope than he had ever felt before.

Handing over his little girl to a stranger, a village woman, had cut a deep wound in Michael. No way he could get the child back to her own family hours away. That was the moment he'd felt his hate turn on himself when his hands let go of his daughter's bundled body swaddled in his marine T-shirt.

He'd cringed inside every time his buddies told the tale about him delivering a village woman's baby in a bunker. How could they have known it was a torturous tale about his own child and her mother, his true love?

No more of this shit. Michael couldn't live with the flash-backs. Memories were one thing—this craziness, another.

Sullivan. He wrote the priest's name on his wrist with a pen from his desk.

Remembering his promise to call his mother, Michael picked up the phone. Her voice would help.

He breathed deeply ten times again. It brought down the

shakes. His finger was still vibrating slightly when he dialed the wall phone. "Hey, Mom. Yup, here safe and sound."

CHAPTER 13

Kate

RAGING RIVER

CARRYING BOTH DINNER trays, Kate went to the kitchen service window. The sound of clinking dishes and the splash of dishwashing was familiar with her waitressing job not far behind her. No cooking, no serving; no dishes; how wonderful. For that alone, she would study into the wee hours.

A young boy with a shaft of red hair covering one eye stood behind the counter dramatically sweeping the dishwashing sprayer in his hand across the food-encrusted dishes. He turned it off. "Hi." The greeting was delivered with barely enough volume to reach Kate. He pulled a shank of his hair, then pointed at hers, then he dropped his head, rounded his shoulders, and rocked back and forth in shyness. He could have been a Ketchum with that scarlet hair, she thought. He must have thought they were connected by that hair tone too.

Kate stuck her head inside the oversized service window, and she imagined he saw her as a member of his tribe. "Thanks for doing the dishes."

The boy was awkward, she thought, from the way he smiled too long, too wide, and the self-conscious way he moved his body.

"You are welcome," he said into his chest.

It brought back a memory for Kate of teaching her eight-year-old physically disabled cousin Patrick to swim when Kate was a summer lifeguard. She could picture Patrick, isolated, arms wrapped around his knees on the grass by the rusted chain-link fence around their community swimming pool. Every aspect of his face and body said, *lonely*. His fear of the water was extreme. Not even a toe dipped in all summer.

Her aunt and uncle had asked Kate for help with their fearful son. "You're good with kids. Do you think you can get Patrick to just put his feet in? It breaks our hearts."

At sixteen, Kate had worked with eight-year-old Patrick for six weeks in secret each morning before the pool opened. He went from holding his knees on the grass fifty yards away from the pool, step by painfully slow step, to sitting on the edge, putting his face in, and finally, reaching the goal Kate had set for him.

On the morning of the grand reveal, Kate's stomach had been queasy; Patrick was ready, but she worried he would revert to his old fears. His parents were thrilled to see him approach the pool. He sat on the edge, dangling his feet in the water. They clapped as if that alone was beyond their dreams.

Overcoming his fear of being near the water would have been exciting enough. Kate remembered his parents' faces as Patrick surprised them. He stood on the edge and dove into the pool. His splashing lap of freestyle looked like a flopping fish being reeled in behind a boat. Not a pretty sight, his form, but beautiful to everyone who'd witnessed the miracle. Kate was proud; she'd found herself crying right along with them. Patrick had jumped up and down and hugged her, leaving his soaking wet imprint on her clothes.

Kate engaged the dishwasher boy. "What's your name?" Leaning in again, she pushed a few of the plates down the rollers closer to him.

He hung his head down and sprayed another plate free of leftover gravy and mashed potatoes. There was an awkwardness to his movements, yet a kind of grace to the way he swayed his arm to clean the dishes. Talking to the young man was more in Kate's comfort zone than her discussions with Shiloh had been. An element of fear and intrigue followed everything Shiloh had talked about.

"See you tomorrow." Kate knew the dishwasher had reached the limits of his social courage.

"Bye," was all he could muster.

Shiloh caught up with Kate. "He's from Rolling Hills, you know." Shiloh waved at the dishwasher as they left the cafeteria.

"What's Rolling Hills?"

"A state institution for disabled people near here. I think they mostly live there their whole lives. Some of them get out for jobs during the day, like our dishwasher guy. And there's a really cool candle factory there. They're really inexpensive."

"You're kidding? Where is it?"

"It's close by. I'll show you on the map if you ever want to go." Shiloh headed down the stairs to the dorm's front door. "See you later. I'm going out to stalk the wild hickory nut."

"The, *what?*"

"I'll explain later." Shiloh's warm laugh echoed in the entryway. "Good meeting you, Kate."

"You, too." Wild hickory nut? Left with the strange expression to ponder, Kate followed the glass hallway connector back to the women's side of the complex and took the elevator to the 5th floor. She had a slight tightness in her chest. UConn and living away from home was very different from her community college. She'd jumped in the raging river of life, as Shiloh had described her activism, and Kate felt a little in over her head.

In her room, Kate sang as she unpacked her things and lined up her shoes and boots on the top shelf of her double-door closet. She was excited to be majoring in music and confident about the audition. She would sing the "Ave Maria." That performance had already been reviewed by Father Sullivan. What about the second instrument of choice? Was guitar a good qualifying instrument? She'd only played chords to accompany her singing. What would she wear? She flipped through her clothes in the closet. Kate had to be on time on Tuesday. She'd check the campus map to locate the registrar's office. She would have to go right from the audition to sign up for her music classes before choir practice.

This was where she'd always dreamed she would be—on a college campus. Her first adventure. But she hadn't imagined feeling this unsettled. Kate couldn't take her eyes off the moon that road in the clear sky. One little sliver, tonight. She imagined how glorious it would look hanging full over the apple orchard centered in her dorm window.

CHAPTER 14

Michael

RHYTHM AND FLOW

IT FELT GOOD to be back in school; it had been the right decision. Funny, how he'd felt pretty calm all day, going from his World History to U.S. Government classes. Even the statistics class Michael needed to graduate didn't faze him. When his mind was focused on learning, Michael felt more in control. But the whole thing with the fireworks and Nugget made him realize his disturbance was leaking through. When it was all in his head, that was one thing, but curled up in a ball under a sink cradling a toiletry kit and seeing that look on Nugget's face was another.

He could still see Nugget's wide eyes, his shock and dismay. Would he tell all the guys in the frat that Michael was crazy? Nugget didn't seem like that kind of guy. Hard to explain to someone who hadn't served in Vietnam. It turns off and on like a light switch; doesn't mean you're crazy, Michael thought.

He set up an appointment at 4:00 p.m. at the Catholic church before Father Sullivan's choir practice. The former chaplain in the Marines had created miracles for some returning vets, Nugget had said. Michael had a small flicker of hope now that he had a plan. Just taking action had brought his inner noise down.

Since he was an hour early, he decided to stop at the Student Union for something to eat, then head over to the church. The chants of dozens of students outside the Administration building, protesting the recruiting on campus by some American weapons manufacturer made Michael shudder. He picked up his pace. It was a war he no longer believed in—just a damn cash cow for the military-industrial complex, he muttered.

Michael didn't want his past to swallow the sweetness of the sunny afternoon. The campus outskirts where soft hills ensconced the churches would be more peaceful. Breathing in early fall scents, he stopped to admire the flowers nestled in shredded bark chips that ran a ring around the oak trees. His steps brought him past the lake, the long route to the Student Union.

Craving serenity, Michael sat by Mirror Lake and watched the innocent things, a duck skimming across the campus lake, a splash-landing by one of the trumpet swans. It was soothing, the quiet split only by the occasional conversation of students passing by on the sidewalk, and the squawk and splash of a duck departing, webbed feet dragging, casting its passing shadow on the shimmering surface of the lake. How had he ever taken them down? How had it ever seemed like fun?

There was a fragile seed of hope in his mind. A certain logic he clung to. If he'd found joy with Hàng in the chaos of the war blaring around him once, couldn't he somehow find some peace in the routine of his safe life back home?

The central gathering place at the Student Union was quiet.

Michael ordered fries and a salad. Across the room was a piano against a white wall with the blue and white UConn logo over it, a trident of oak leaves with two acorns, and an Alaskan Husky dog. No reminders there. Michael ate, watching angles of sunlight reach out across the linoleum floor. He slid his foot out into the light and watched it play on his old loafer. Stabbing the last tasteless tomato slice, he dredged it through the puddle of Italian dressing, ate it whole, and scraped the folding chair back. The piano was calling.

He rested his fingers on the buttery keys of the beautiful new keyboard, deciding what to play. The feel of the cool, smooth ivory calmed him. Tender memories came: Hàng's soft hand running over his chest, cocoa on cream, Hy Vọng's chest rising and falling as she slept in his arms. He wanted to linger on those loving thoughts.

Stretching his fingers, he remembered holding his tense finger poised tight on a warm steel trigger. He lengthened them, flexed again, and began to play a quick warm-up run of Joplin's "The Entertainer." No lyrics to activate his violent memories. The rhythms broke up the haunting patterns. He sheltered himself in the tune. Wrapping his sore soul in the soft volume of the song, he was aware that his playing was just loud enough to draw attention from the students who'd wandered in. They settled into the chairs scattered around the student lounge to listen. Their applause encouraged him, calmed him, and he played several more tunes. Then he stood, saluted his thanks, and left.

Michael crossed the quadrangle and wound his way on the sidewalk toward the north end of campus to St. Thomas Aquinas Church. Summer flowers were giving up hope, drooping along the path's edge in the late afternoon sun. A breeze peeled back the day's suffocating blanket of humid air, and the temperature was finally dropping. In the beds that flanked the entryway to the brick church, only the vibrant purple and pink petunias seemed to be holding on through the last burn of August hoping for autumn. He bent over to touch a blossom.

Could *he* hold on, hold it together, and find the courage to explain to the priest? Where should he start the conversation? Which pain should he share? He hoped this guy was as good as Nugget had reported. The only help Michael ever had was a general session with his unit about adapting to life at home, and a single session with the Marine counselor as he was discharged, and he'd swallowed everything Michael had said. "No, Sir, no disturbances. Yes, Sir, I'm fine, sleeping well, Sir."

Grasping the warm brass handle to the church door, he pulled and hesitated. Why did every big heavy church door creak? Michael closed it softly. The click of the latch ricocheted off the brick walls, waning until it was silent again. A young altar boy snuffed out the last candle from the afternoon Mass and disappeared through the side door. The residue of the extinguished tapers reminded Michael of the acrid scent of an explosion. He'd stored mints in his pocket, tucked there for emergencies. Michael opened the wrapper and breathed in the coolness; the peppermint blast of cold jolted his brain.

He smoothed back his hair and marched up the tiled, center aisle of the empty church. Michael's worn-in, handmade penny loafers announced his hesitant arrival.

How long before he could talk about the bunker? His

beautiful Hàng? Their baby? He stopped, turned his hands over, and stared down. Empty. Where his daughter had once been.

The tall dark-haired, priest sat in the first pew. It was surreal to see the splashes of color on him cast from the stained glass window over the choir loft behind them. Michael pushed his fingers through his newly grown hair. So quiet. He moved forward up the aisle under the tracking gaze of Mary's statue-eyes.

At the sound of the approaching rhythm of footsteps on tile, the priest turned.

The thunder of pulsing blood in Michael's head was begging for him to retreat, but if nothing else, he was not a coward. Familiar sweating began. Beads of moisture erupted along the hairline on the back of his neck, responding to some uncontrollable signal. Why was he so afraid the let out the truth? Would it become so real that it would uncoil, slither around him, and finally crush him? Or would it bring a release? He put his hand on his chest and breathed.

The priest reached out. "Michael? Father Sullivan. Let's move into the back room. We won't be disturbed."

"Sure." All he had to do was imagine Nugget's face when he'd found Michael under the sink, and he knew coming to the priest was the right thing. Wiping his forehead with his shirtsleeve, Michael wondered where to start. He wanted to tell the priest how he couldn't imagine himself holding a military weapon when he'd enlisted. Now, he couldn't imagine not having some kind of protection. He felt naked being unarmed. Unsafe. He knew it was ridiculous. Protection from what? Wilting flowers on a college campus? An old brick church? Fireworks and a charred steak? He was afraid it sounded crazy.

"You take the *comfortable* chair with the cushion."

Was the burgundy velvet cushion worn paper-thin with divots from the weight of other troubled students?

"Well, I guess that chair won't offer much comfort." Father Sullivan plucked at the flimsy padding. "That's *my* job."

Michael sat in the shiny wooden swivel chair. He already liked the guy's style. He tried to guess the priest's age. Old enough to be wise but young enough to relate, smile lines that accentuated his kind eyes. Late thirties, forty, maybe? Hands that had labored, a former career, or a tough childhood?

Hands. The old village woman's withered hands. Had she been judging the soldier who would relinquish such a treasure to a stranger? What the hell could anyone do to cool Michael's scorching guilt? He had to try. OK, he'd just give the guy a chance. Nothing to lose. Was there?

Father Sullivan pulled up a straight-back chair from behind his old oak desk, took off his black jacket. He set it on the credenza behind him, rolled up his sleeves, loosened his collar, as though he were ready to get down to work. "So, what do you love?" His smile was warm, and his tone so matter-of-fact.

"You mean...what exactly do you mean?" Michael twisted in the chair, rotating it a few inches back and forth, and perused the sterile room. There was nothing to distract him from the task at hand—just ivory-colored walls, and a single cross with a stack of dried-out sprigs of palms from former Palm Sundays arched over it. What *did* he love? He massaged the back of his neck.

"'The things that we love, tell us who we are.' A St. Thomas Aquinas quote. He was a very prolific writer, our St. Thomas; I'm afraid you'll find I lean on his wisdom quite a bit."

There was such calm, a peace emanating from the guy. Like they were two friends chatting about sports scores over a beer.

Michael tilted his head and took a breath. So what *do* I love? His mind ticked through times when he'd been happy. Something he loved? "Rowing...alone, in a single scull...um... early morning on glassy water." The priest's nod pushed Michael forward. "Sun sucking up the fog, my blade in the slipstream, you know, that gurgling sound of the wake..."

"Leaving everything behind." Father Sullivan leaned forward.

"Right." Michael thought. He liked the metaphor. Hadn't really thought of it that way before. He just knew with the pull of his flexing arms when the angle of his oar was just right and the rhythm perfect, when his body obeyed the unheard commands of his instincts, he felt like his old self. Michael relaxed and shared more of the images. He loved his scull skimming over gleaming water, the vibrating trees reflecting upside down, ducks scattering with his approach, their fluttering wings waking the morning silence. Just moving forward. "That kind of love?"

"Exactly. And by the way, poetically put." The priest laced his hands behind his head, leaned back, and smiled, seeming satisfied.

"My mother's trinity of lessons—music, poetry, and nature." Michael let out a short laugh accented with a touch of embarrassment, rolled his shoulders, and rocked his neck. Staying in those memories for a moment felt good. Michael wasn't ready to leave them. It was easier to talk about what he loved, harder to talk about who he loved.

"And? Another?" Father Sullivan's voice came into focus, urging Michael to share his thoughts.

Michael stayed away from hard subjects. He thought he was ready to share his truth, but he remained in the demilitarized zone. Avoided the triggers. "Playing the piano."

"Can you describe, please?"

"You know...fingers moving just right over the smooth keys." Michael fluttered his fingers over the old oak desk. "And turning the page of the music score without losing a beat." He pictured his mother sitting next to him teaching him and her elegant fingers, her arm reaching across his face to turn the page, the scent of her perfume, that familiar feeling, having her attention.

"More rhythm, more flow. Interesting."

"Interesting *good* or interesting I-see-how-fucked-up-you-are? Sorry, Father, bad habits from the field."

The priest smiled. "Not a new word for me; I was a Marine, too...well a Marine chaplain. "So, take me to a scent you love."

It took a split second for Michael to have the answer to that one. His baby daughter, Hy Vọng's skin. Deep breaths of... what was it? Not a scent. Maybe too pure to be a scent. He wouldn't open that door.

"You have one, but you're not ready to share. That's fine."

"Yes, Father." The priest was beginning to earn his reputation.

"Do you have flashbacks? Panic attacks?"

"Yes, and yes." There was no point in holding back, at least on the easy parts, if he wanted to get anywhere.

"Have you had any counseling, help from the service?"

"Some general counseling. I wasn't exhibiting the...I didn't have any problems until I got home and my father..." Michael put both hands up. He didn't want to go there, either.

"We'll get to that when you're ready. Enough for today." Father Sullivan unrolled his sleeves. "So in helping veterans to move forward through counseling and some tricks of the trade, I find it's best to keep things simple at first and focus on the good. So, here's the trinity—do the things you love more often, learn something new, and help someone else. Oh, and above all, have hope."

Hope. Hy Vọng, he thought, but he'd lost Hope in the most real way. He automatically reached in his pocket for a mint at the thought of his daughter. He liked the calm he had with the priest, couldn't let his mind go there and ruin it. "So, I get it. Piano and rowing are the things I love. Oh, and I left out pole vaulting. There's a high there too. No pun intended. I'm in classes for the *learning something new* part—but *help someone else?* I'll have to think about that."

As Father Sullivan walked Michael out, he gestured to the first pew. "If you have a little time, and since you love music, you might want to sit here a while and listen to the choir practice. Keep in mind it's the first day. I'll see you Thursday, Michael, same time. I hope you feel you're on your way."

"Thanks, really, thanks, Father." As Michael settled into the pew, he heard the door open, and the shaft of late sun sliced up the center aisle. A female figure with a flow of red hair swept up the choir loft steps and disappeared. Michael pulled the kneeler down and knelt to process his conversation with the priest.

He felt a bit lighter like the uplift of a slight welcome breeze on a wet blanket day in Nam.

CHAPTER 15

ARM OF ACCEPTANCE

THE MUSIC DEPARTMENT building was like a candy store for Kate. Passing the long line of rehearsal rooms, she stopped and closed her eyes, listening. The battling dissonant sounds of the students practicing paralleled her state of mind—the whines of violins, heavy moans of the bass, piano fingers following warmup patterns—all comingled and escaped under practice cubby doors. The chaotic notes, like the sounds of excited kids at recess, filled the hallway and electrified her. Kate could camp out in the music building forever if they would feed her, she thought.

What should she choose as her accompanying instrument? Maybe not the guitar. Why not something she'd never tried before, knew nothing about?

Kate found she was fickle—fell in love with every instrument's call as she absorbed each unique sound walking down the music-filled hallway. She'd never been in marching band; she'd been working after school. There was no orchestra in her small Catholic high school, and by the time she was in community college, Kate was riveted on earning tuition through extra jobs.

She wanted to study every one of them—breathe life into a clarinet; how did they purse their lips to vibrate those reed instruments? Could she bear the weight of a hefty tuba throughout an entire symphony? She looked at her lean arms and laughed, imagining it's hot brass body like a boa snaking around her. Did she want to slide the sleek brass arm of a trombone? No, she couldn't see herself playing that, but she loved the elastic sound of it. Wrap her arms around a cello, or an Irish harp, maybe? She looked through the small window of the seventh room. Just watching the woman's position reaching to caress the strings of her harp hurt Kate's back.

She wanted to embrace them all, make them come alive, but Kate was distracted; she was there to choose an instrument that she could sing with—no wind instruments, no violin. Her performance instrument couldn't steal her wind or constrict her throat, she thought.

Piano made the most sense, Kate thought, like Carole King. *She* played and sang.

At the end of the hall, Kate found the performance room where she was to audition. Pushing open the heavy door, she stepped in, took the center aisle, and sat down near the stage. The small concert hall, a semi-circle of two hundred red seats with an elevated stage draped with burgundy velvet, seemed to be waiting for her.

Kate sat up straight and smiled at the thought of her audition at the church. Yes, "Ave Maria" was tested and true. It would get her the major in music. But where would the music major get her? How could she earn a good solid living on her voice alone? She would figure it out. You can't wake up every morning, missing the things that light you up.

As Kate turned around and looked over her shoulder, a woman and a younger man entered. The glow of the morning sun illuminated them from behind, blinding her from seeing their faces. Closing her eyes, Kate clung to her confidence and that perfect note she'd sent rafter-high singing "Ave Maria" for Father Sullivan.

Tall and elegant, the woman was simply dressed in a blue and white A-line shift and navy blue and white spectators. Kate knew the Irish origin of those two-toned low heels—those Brogues. They felt like a message of good luck. She watched the shoes walk the woman down the steps—sturdy leather uppers with decorative perforations.

It wasn't something Kate had control over—the shoe thing. Kate's classmates at community college had made fun of her insufferable habit—her entire family shared it like a genetic tic. Shoes were the first thing she noticed about someone. It was just something she couldn't help noticing—the color, the perfection of the stitching, the thickness of the soles. Kate wondered if that was what gave people the impression that she was a little shy—those downcast eyes when they met as she checked out their footwear.

The man beside the woman was a true-blue hippie wearing raggedy, cracked, brown Birkenstocks that had been taped with duct tape. His faded, tissue-thin, floral, long-sleeve shirt looked like it had been hung out to dry in the sun, too many times. His tattered jeans had seen better days too. The duo took a seat in the center of the tenth row and introduced themselves, Ms. Jane Hawley and Phillip Monroe.

Kate heard the concert hall double-door snap open at the top of the steps of the center aisle in front of her. She hadn't expected an audience for her audition. From the empty stage, Kate stared at the outline of the girl in a long, flowing skirt. The student closed the door and sat in the shadows of the back row.

Must be here for the next audition, Kate assumed.

"Ms. Ketchum? Are you ready? What would you like to sing for your warmup?"

"I can do something religious, if that's OK?" Kate was ready for mic or not, acapella or accompanied—Church and O'Leary's had prepared her for either.

"Whatever shows off your range, *sans* amplification." The woman shifted the clipboard on her lap.

Sans? Kate began to sing "Ave Maria." She trusted Father Sullivan's opinion. When she hit the lyrics, "Ave Mari-i-a," the wonderful acoustics in the concert hall tossed her notes to the ceiling, splashing like cymbals, and Kate knew she was pitch-perfect.

"Brava." They nodded to each other.

Kate wanted to think it meant we have a winner here, or she'll work nicely. She was confident when the person in the back of the hall clapped enthusiastically. Kate let out a long sigh of relief. "Thank you."

She stood with her hands clasped behind her, smiling. The two professors had their heads together, mumbling and shifting sheets of music.

At a loss, Kate headed toward the steps to descend from the stage.

"Just a minute. Here is our compulsory selection for you."

Ms. Hawley rose, stepped forward, handed Kate a sheet of music, then walked back up the aisle to her seat.

The little black marks marching across the lines on the page were familiar but might as well have been Chinese.

"Problem?"

She must have read Kate's horrified face or heard her breath catch, Kate thought. Sometimes Kate could follow the hymns having sung them so often. They'd became embedded in her memory, and she could read the guitar chords in her song books for O'Leary's but sight read music, *cold?*

"Is there a problem?" A touch of impatience was clear in Professor Hawley's voice.

Kate rolled the sheet music in her moist hand, tapped her thigh, and faced the department head and the professor. She searched for the right words. "I memorized my parts in the choir by ear. I've never learned to...actually, *read* music."

Her two-person panel of judges looked at each other, then stared at her. "Ms. Ketchum, we appreciate your candor but—"

"Excuse me?" Kate was lost in a blur of thoughts, then focused on what the woman was saying.

Ms. Hawley signaled for Kate to come forward to the front of the stage. "I asked, did you truly have no idea that as a voice performance major, you would need to sight read, at least at a basic level, Miss Ketchum?" The department head's voice had a tone of disbelief, but it was delivered with sympathy, making Kate feel even more pathetic.

A wave of homesickness passed over her—a humiliation that the girl in the back of the hall had witnessed her failure settled into her stomach. Kate lowered her voice. "I...hadn't planned…I've never had any formal training. I learned all my songs by ear…in choir from my mother, and I sang in a local pub for three years. Yesterday, I got into the St. Thomas Choir, and I just thought…well, I just took a chance. I'm sorry for taking your time." Her awkward answer spilled out, and Kate kept talking without a breath as though her long string of words could forestall the inevitable, crushing rejection.

"Oh, it isn't your voice, dear. Not at all. It's quite stellar. It's simply our requirement. Besides sight-reading for singing, you'll have to be able to read music to dive right into an accompanying instrument for your solo performance next term, you see?"

Kate stepped off the stage, and moved a few steps up the aisle closer to the professors.

"I'm so sorry, Miss Ketchum. Get a good teacher, a coach— perhaps a fellow choir singer. You have talent. The registrar will help you change your schedule so you can stay up. Music History, perhaps. I'm afraid we…we regret we won't be offering you a major in voice performance, dear."

A dense cloud fell over Kate. "Thank you… so much." There was no avoiding the judges in the tenth row, nor the girl at the top of the stairs.

The hippie professor flashed a quick look at Ms. Hawley, as Kate approached. The two judges titled their heads to confer in whispers. Kate was mortified. What were they saying about her? Slowing her steps to eavesdrop, she tried to make out their words. The pleading look on Mr. Monroe's face made it seem as though he were asking for some agreement from Ms. Hawley. For what? The music director turned both palms up, shrugged and nodded, seemingly in surrender.

"Wait, Ms. Ketchum." Kate turned to see Mr. Monroe smiling. "We don't usually do this, but we will give you until the end of this semester to come back and audition again."

"Excuse me? Really?" What did that entail, Kate didn't care; she just wanted to get out of the auditorium. "Thank you so much." Kate dropped her head and climbed the stairs, not wanting to meet the eyes of the person who'd slipped in during her audition. As she passed the girl on the darkened stairs, an arm wrapped around her shoulders. Kate pulled back and looked into Shiloh's eyes. "What are you doing here?"

"I came to hear you sing and show support. I'm glad I did. That 'Ave Maria' was amazing. Those idiots' rules. I'll walk you to choir practice where they know how to appreciate you."

Kate was shocked Shiloh had remembered the time and place of her audition. She didn't think she was paying attention to her chatter in the cafeteria. It was a touching gesture of sisterhood; something her best-friend cousins would do. "Thanks." She managed to push the single word out of her tight throat, then squeezed her eyes to prevent her tears.

Where would she find someone willing to teach her to sight read. Mortifying, like Kate was about to be sick. She'd failed, and in front of the only person she knew on campus. Failure was a stranger to her when it came to singing. Shiloh leaned into Kate, as they took each step together.

CHAPTER 16

LOSE TO WIN

THE CHURCH WAS empty except for one blonde guy in the front row who was kneeling with his head in his hands praying. Kate was still trembling from her audition failure as she climbed the steps to the choir loft, the first to arrive. Her new life had all started so wonderfully—then the most essential thing had gone wrong. She'd been crazy to think she could compete in music just on raw talent and desire. Shiloh had said Kate should find another way to pursue her singing. What way?

It was comforting to see Father Sullivan. Paging through his sheet music at his organ, the usual afternoon blotches of colored lights flickered through the stained-glass window as clouds passed overhead.

"Father Sullivan?"

He swiveled around on the lustrous Mahogany bench, the organ pipes reaching to the rafters behind him. "Ms. Ketchum, good to have you join us. You're a tad early. I admire that."

Why she immediately choked-up at the sound of his voice,

she didn't know. Yes, she did know—she'd been among strangers all day. No sister, mother, or cousins to bounce things off of. "Father, can I ask your advice?"

"That tends to be what happens." He smiled.

That touch of humor, that hint of home, made Kate relax a bit and smile. She told him about the sight-reading and the failed audition. How desperately Kate had wanted a college degree in music. How confused she was. She let it all spill out.

"Quite the first day. Very brave." He tapped his index finger on the book of hymns, fanned through the pages, then glanced up at her.

She could almost see the thoughts rolling over in his mind. "Do I sense a St. Thomas quote coming?"

"Observant. You don't miss much, do you?"

Kate smiled. She liked how the words of wisdom had a flavor of long ago, yet the advice made sense and had meaning for today. "I need one right now."

He laughed and played a flourish of fanfare on the organ that sounded like the bugle start to a horse race. "So here is one for you that applies, 'If the highest aim of a captain were to preserve his ship, he would keep it in port forever.' Or, in your case, *she*."

"Oh. That one's perfect. Still, it seems I'm stuck in port right now."

"So, perhaps I can give you a hand to cast off." Father Sullivan glanced at the young man in the front of the church, then back at Kate. "It would be important for you to read music for the choir's sake too."

"I have to sight-read to be in the choir?" Kate drew in her breath and held it.

"No, no, no. You could learn your parts by ear, no doubt, but without reading music, you couldn't lead."

She let out a long breath of relief like steadily blowing out a cake full of candles.

"I think I can do you and me a favor...and do a favor for someone else in return. Come with me. A win-win in the making."

He led her down the stairs to the front of the church. The young man was just rising to leave. Kate couldn't help but notice his chiseled profile, his biceps fighting to burst out of the sleeves of his blue cotton dress shirt, and his strong hands with slender long fingers jutting from his rolled-up sleeves. Then his shoes, circa 1960, penny loafers. They were definitely Owl & Shamrock. There was a faded spot on the right side below the overstitches where the tiny logo had once been. She smiled and saw her father taking the custom wooden mold from the wall, her mother's hands working the shape, her sisters working the stitches, and her Uncle Jack putting a shine on them. Imagine where those shoes had walked that young guy in those eight years—dances, parties, movies. Imagine, they'd started in the hands of a Ketchum.

Father Sullivan introduced the blonde student as Michael Edward James. "Excuse us for a moment, will you, Kate? Michael, may I speak with you?"

They stepped aside, speaking in low tones. Michael glanced at Kate, then smiled, and nodded as he listened to the priest.

Kate found herself tapping a four-beat with her fingers against her leg. The confident way Michael stood there talking—his formal posture, attentive to Father Sullivan, yet humble, his hands folded in front of him—was nothing like her unpolished hometown guys. Michael had a respectful, sophisticated way about him. It seemed to speak of quiet class and a privileged upbringing. His demeanor, dress shirt, blonde hair and cornflower blue eyes, the whole look of him, said class.

She studied him as he approached with Father Sullivan. So familiar. Kate had seen guys like Michael before, arriving at the factory with his well-heeled parents on a family outing. Pressing his feet into the mold, his custom wooden foot last would be placed on the shelf alongside his gentry generations.

"Kate, Michael is a classically trained pianist, and he'd be happy to volunteer."

"Sure, I can teach you to sight-read music...no problem." Michael smiled, kept his eyes on Father Sullivan, but made no eye contact with Kate.

"Really?" Confident yet shy, she thought. "That would be so great. I'd pay you, of course."

"No payment necessary."

"Something Michael wants to do for a program he's working on." Father Sullivan looked satisfied with himself. The clouds overhead moved away, and the unavoidable splash of colors from the stained-glass window lit them up. "The Lord has answered," Father Sullivan said, turning his hands over in the flashing lights.

They all laughed.

"It seems you have an angel, Ms. Ketchum." Father Sullivan clasped his hands behind his back.

"Oh, I wouldn't say I'm an *angel*," Michael said, shuffling from one foot to the other.

"Oh, no, I was referring to *myself*." Father Sullivan smiled.

The priest's sense of humor made Kate feel more at home.

"Well, I see the choir loft is buzzing, shall we, Ms. Ketchum?"

"So, two-thirty tomorrow at the Student Union piano?" Michael squeezed the back of his neck for the second time.

"Sure, that's perfect." Kate looked over her shoulder at him as she followed the priest to mount the stairs to choir practice. She stopped and turned. "Michael, thank you so, so much. You have no idea what it means to me." She connected with his arresting blue eyes for the first time. He cast them downward. It seemed he wasn't there. What had just happened? Like a light went out in his eyes, like a wall had dropped between them. It was better that way. She would keep her mind off that square jaw and alluring smile, keep her eye on the ball like she always had.

In forty-eight hours she'd been accepted, rejected, saved, and left with a big challenge on her hands. What else was new, she thought. By the time Kate arrived at dinner, there were only two other students in the cafeteria. Her buddy, the dishwasher, was barely visible under the stacks of plates decorated with half-eaten pepperoni pizza crusts, curled lettuce leaves, tomato slices, and green beans drenched in slick rivers of oil.

Kate stuck her head behind the end of the counter and waved. She wondered how old he was—eighteen, maybe. He had to be to work here. His face lit up, and he gave a vigorous wave back but said nothing.

"If I knew your name, I could say, 'Hi,' so much better." She walked away with her tray. When Kate was three paces away, the name came from behind her.

"Bobby."

Kate smiled. Her only success today. "See you, Bobby."

CHAPTER 17

Michael

LYRICAL LESSONS

THE THOUGHT OF teaching Kate made Michael nervous. There was her beautiful face he'd watched as she clunked up the church aisle in those Owl & Shamrock platform boots, a privileged girl. The famous label told him that. Was she another clone of Grandmother James' fix-up dates? Yet, she seemed sweet, not full of herself. Father Sullivan was right—*doing what he loved* and *learning something new* had worked so far, so Michael would add the third tenet of the priest's healing trinity—*help someone else*. Besides, he trusted the priest, and Father knew Kate from choir, and when Michael was playing or thinking of music, all the noise inside stopped; and she did seem sincere.

A cloudburst ran sheets of water down the floor-to-ceiling windows at 2:30 on-the-dot. Michael saw Kate enter the Student Union using a folded newspaper as an umbrella. The heads of the three guys who were seated by the door rotated in sync. There was no missing how beautiful she was, the sheen of her hair—that gorgeous shade—not carrot, not rust, an easy-on-the-eye red, and those high cheekbones and green eyes. She cut an incredible figure walking in the room. Not a care in the world on that face, Michael thought. In seconds, the switch happened, and there was nothing but Ha`ng's face in his mind and a dull ache in his chest.

"Hi, am I late?" She snapped the wet paper on her thigh and tossed it in the trash.

"Nope, exactly on time. Let's do this." Michael spread a blank music composition sheet next to a song book on the upright's narrow shelf and lined up a few number 2 pencils. "So, how much do you know?"

"First, can I borrow one of these?" Kate nodded toward his row of pencils.

"Uh, sure." Was there any option? Michael watched the magic happen, she swirled her damp hair up, twisted and twirled it, and it settled into a neat pile on the crown of her head. Smiling, apologetically for the delay, she deftly drove the pencil through her creation. The entire sculpture defied gravity and stayed in place. Another Michael from the past would have found himself looking forward to watching her reverse the process. He would have watched the shiny, ruddy nest fall around her shoulders at the end of the piano lesson as he reclaimed his number 2, makeshift hair skewers.

Now he had no reaction. Couldn't feel it. He even dared to let himself try, but no emotion. Like a petrified piece of wood had permanently lodged inside his chest, blocking any feelings for anyone else.

Michael began to play. Watching his hands, he could see them as they ran over his lover's supple skin. He pushed the image of Ha`ng into its hiding place. Watching his fingers light down on the slick keys, he grounded himself back in the Student Union. Focus on the scent of pizza, the greasy burgers and fries, he instructed himself. The memory of Ha`ng retreated, and the torment passed. He was relieved to have Kate's voice interrupt.

"Well, I know what those little black marks are—from pretending to read them for years in choir, and if the dot goes up a line, I sing a note higher, right?" She laughed.

Down to earth, a pleasant surprise, Michael thought. "OK, we'll start at the beginning, then. There are two sets of lines, treble clef and bass clef." He pointed to the blank, lined sheet music. "Sorry, am I being too basic?"

"No, no, it's all good. You can't insult me."

"The treble clef consists of five lines and four spaces. Michael pointed to the empty lines on the page. The way to remember them is, "Every Good Boy Does Fine—see, EGBDF are the notes on the lines."

"So, music is kind of sexist then? Only the good *boys* do fine?"

He caught her smile and laughed—the joyful sound he emitted had been dormant, a remote stranger from his past, he realized. "As my mother's only child and a boy, I never thought twice about that; kind of sends a message to girls, huh? So, then FACE is the trick to remembering the notes in the spaces on the treble clef." Face, yes, she had one you could lose yourself in. Open and almost glowing with that smile and sassy sense of humor.

Michael taught Kate whole notes, half, quarter—and the hour passed quickly. She picked it up fast, but she was a long way away from sight-reading cold for singing, he thought. He could see it would take weeks, months maybe before she could audition. He liked that. She was easy to be with; he enjoyed her company.

Flipping open one of the song books, he began to play, talk along, and identify the notes, one by one. He tested her knowledge by having her sing a few bars. She stumbled once; then, she got it.

"Do you sing, Michael?"

"I try. A little harmony with my mother. I generally lean on my piano playing to make up for my howling."

"I have to sign up for a second instrument…besides voice. I'm thinking the piano?"

"Well, you can't carry it around with you like you can your voice.

"I can't lose it either."

She was funny. Michael needed that.

"And if it goes off-key, you can blame the piano." Kate laughed.

"And you can pay a tuner to make it perfect." Michael smiled at their banter.

Kate nodded and smiled. "My mother could sight-sing anything; she led the choir. I just memorized everything I heard coming out of her mouth. Never thought to learn how. And singing with the guitar—easy, it's just chords."

"You only need to achieve a basic level of sight-singing, right?"

"Yes, and so much hangs in the balance, and I won't know which piece of music until they hand it to me. But it won't be a super sophisticated piece, they said."

"You'll do great." Michael flipped open the songbook and

played a little Carole King. From the corner of his eye, he watched Kate silently move her lips to the lyrics, her head drifting left and right like rice in a breeze.

Afternoon classes had let out, and the dripping crowd invaded, snapping umbrellas. Shaking off like dogs, they entered and gravitated to the area around the piano. They slumped into chairs with coffees or cokes, and their clamor of chatter and bursts of laughter interrupted the lesson. Michael noticed the few dozen occupied chairs had shifted in the piano's direction. He played louder, and the crowd quieted. When the second verse came around, Michael could see Kate holding back like she was ready to explode with the song, "You've Got a Friend." He nodded at her. "Go ahead; might as well make a little concert out of this; we've got the audience." Michael let out a quiet sigh. No hauntings in his head for the moment.

The sound that came out of Kate shot down his spine. Velvet? A bell? No, a smooth swallow of fine wine. He couldn't find the words—she did.

"When you're down and troubled..."

CHAPTER 18

Kate

CITY OF SIN

"THAT WAS SO mind-blowing, Kate." Shiloh emerged from the applauding audience, snapping her fingers after Kate's last song. "I've been dying to get here for weeks. My SDS meeting was canceled today, so here I am, finally. And thanks for singing at the protests. Keeps them peaceful." Shiloh hugged Kate.

"You're welcome; wish I could have done more. Thanks for coming, Shi."

The crowd lingered, now that Kate and Michael had become a regular thing at the Student Union. Conversations filled the room; the jukebox blared.

"Listen, can we talk?" Kate stuffed her music sheets in her satchel.

"Sure." Shiloh pointed to the hallway. "Let's get out of the noise."

Her new college friend had become Kate's self-appointed scout and guide through the first weeks on campus. Shiloh encouraged her to play the field, start dating, and find ways to plug-in, but without success. You can't just study, eat, and sleep, she'd said to Kate. She knew Shiloh was right. She'd spent every day studying at the library, attending classes and singing. Kate deserved a little fun, Shiloh had said. To Kate music and classes *were* fun. "I'll never forget you showing up at that horrible music audition. You're a good friend, Shi." Kate took Shiloh's arm and they moved toward the door.

"The audition wasn't horrible; the rules were. They missed out. Look what you've done for yourself."

"I have a surprise. I did the second audition today and passed. I'm officially a performance voice major."

"Oh! Congratulations. And you're already performing, so there. Are you going back to the dorm? I'll walk with you."

"No, I've got to return a book to the library, then choir practice."

"So how does it feel to be singing again? I'm impressed. You were amazing at the protests."

Kate felt her face flush at the compliment. "I should be thanking you, Shi. Singing in front of hundreds of passionate protestors is good for the ego. You couldn't find a more appreciative crowd."

"And so cool you snagged a gig here at the Student Union."

"I just took your advice. I found a different way. I would never have found the courage to convince the manager to hire Michael and me without your encouragement. I just pretended I was you and asked when there was a big crowd listening."

"Now that's a job interview. Glad I could inspire. I bet Michael was impressed."

And now Kate had an excuse to be with him every afternoon, she thought. "What did I have to lose?"

"Exactly, and everything to gain." Shiloh looked over her shoulder. "So tell me about your good-looking piano player. Do you like him?" With tilted head, she begged for the truth.

"You know Michael taught me to sight-read; I owe him. We kind of fell into the performing part."

"For kind of falling into it, I'm impressed. It works."

"Seriously, we're just friends."

"You're sure there isn't a spark?" Shiloh adjusted her turquoise, paisley bandana.

Kate smiled at Shiloh's signature gesture, and hugged her file of sheet music to her chest. "Nothing. Believe me."

"That's not how I read it, but I'll take your word for it. Maybe it's just part of the music act."

"Seriously, there hasn't been anything personal about it." Kate laughed at Shiloh's sheepish grin. "Funny, he never talks about himself, for the weeks now since he started teaching me."

"Why do you think he's like that?"

"Ha. Some girlfriend at home, probably. I don't want to push and jeopardize our lesson arrangement. Maybe the only way for him to feel right about spending so much time with me is to keep it strictly business."

Kate loved her budding friendship with Michael and the special music thing that was growing between them. She was thrilled he'd finally harmonized with her; it really worked. The audience loved it, and his soulful playing put her somewhere else. She'd seen him close his eyes when she sang today. Their music must have transported him, too. To where? To whom?

"OK, but I want to be the first to know if something happens between you two."

They both stood staring at Michael.

"Don't look now, but your 'friend' is waving at you."

What was it she felt? A tingle. Kate waved back and smiled. "He's definitely taken, Shi. A girlfriend at home. That's how I read it."

"A shame. Either that or the boy is blind."

"Ha. See you back at the dorm."

Shiloh carved a path between the two girls and Michael, turned over her shoulder, winked at Kate and left through the double doors.

What *was* Michael's taste in girls? Kate was curious to see which of the flirting duo would peel him off.

"Kate, wait." Michael caught her eye, waved again, and wedged his way through the two swooning girls toward her.

By the time Michael reached Kate, he looked panicked. Sweat beaded on his forehead. More confirmation, he had someone out there somewhere. So loyal. So hard to find a guy like that, she thought—a class act.

"Going to choir practice at 5:00?"

"I am. But first a stop at the library."

"I have my usual appointment with Father Sullivan. Can I walk with you?"

"Sure. You played really well today. I liked the new pace on our last song."

"Yeah, I think it fits your style better."

"Hey, I wanted to tell you when I arrived today, but not in front of the whole world. I passed the sight-reading audition this morning." She observed his reaction carefully.

"That's so great; you earned it; now on to fame and fortune." He seemed distracted.

"I don't know about that, but I'm really grateful to you. You didn't have to give me lessons." Kate watched him tuck the letter he was carrying into his back pocket.

"Mail today?"

"News from home." The way the late sun hit Michael's face, his scar shone on his neck. Kate hadn't meant to stare. She'd already guessed that scar must be what he was meeting Father Sullivan about. The war. It made her shiver to see how close he must have come to dying. Her brother never talked much after he returned from Vietnam with his leg injuries. Said he needed time.

"I guess you've figured out I've... got to work some things out about Nam."

Students folded around them on the sidewalk, returning to their dorms. "Sullivan's a great guy. He's really helping."

"I'm glad."

He shifted his Government textbook to his other side. "You could be a pro, you know. Your voice is out-of-sight." Changing the subject was an art form for Michael.

"Look who's talking."

Today Kate noticed he wore a dark look on his face. Not his usual calm when he was into their music. "Something wrong?"

A flock of ducks took off from Mirror Lake behind him. They both turned to watch, shading their eyes with their hands until the broken vee disappeared over the trees, electrified with orange and red tints of fall.

She searched his eyes, and he let her gaze linger for the first time. He cast them down and looked pensive as he nudged a cluster of leaves with his toe.

"You know some of my frat brothers think we're together."

He scanned the sky and put his hands in his pockets, his eyes following a trailing duck.

"They *do*?" Kate made light of it, covered up her surprise. "Yeah, Shiloh insists we're just in denial."

They laughed. There was a long silence.

"You seem distracted?" What was rolling around in that head of his?

He let it out. "I got this letter today. He patted his pocket. My parents are having Thanksgiving in Paris."

"You're going to *Paris*? That's why you're...what are you? Sad?"

"No. I'm not going. Something about an event with my father's old WWII buddies. Last- minute change in plans."

"Where will you go? Relatives? Crazy, I don't even know— do you have brothers and sisters?"

"No. Thanksgiving with my grandmother and her friends isn't my idea of a good time either. I'll probably stay here."

"Here? Not as long as the hinges on the Ketchum's front door work, you won't."

"What?"

Her invitation was as surprising to Kate as it was to Michael. "Come have Thanksgiving with us. They'll be thirty-seven maybe more, packed into our house for dinner—what's one more?"

"I couldn't impose on your family?"

"Ha, wrong family. There are always a few strangers that I've never met at every holiday—siblings' friends, fiancés, you name it. Seriously, they'll welcome the friend who taught me to read music; you'll just melt into the insanity and have fun. What do you say?"

He shrugged, nodded, and smiled. "You know...sure, I'd love to go. Wait, where do you live? You never mentioned. I know it's a small town in Massachusetts, but..."

"*Glynn, Glynn, the City of Sin.*" Kate laughed.

"Really, Glynn? I know it well."

"You do, really?"

Michael looked down at her feet. "I've been to the Owl and Shamrock shoe factory. Well, you have too, I guess." He glanced at her shoes.

Kate laughed inside. "Yes, I've been there a time or two."

CHAPTER 19

Michael

CRAFTING COMMANDMENTS

THE CLOUDLESS AFTERNOON had all the beauty of his beloved New England. Bronze and gilded leaves dropped onto the glass finish of the lake. Kate's invitation two weeks ago had sparked a mild panic in Michael. What did it really mean? It had seemed straightforward and friendly. He needed to talk to Father Sullivan.

As he walked across campus, Michael thought of the weeks since he'd started teaching Kate. They were filled with Father Sullivan's trinity plan, plus a bonus. Something happened when they performed together after their lessons—the recurrence of his painful memories subsided with the sounds of his piano and her voice. Those hours before his session with Father Sullivan and Kate's choir practice had become a rhythm in his days. Those two days, Tuesdays and Thursdays, Michael lived for them. And when he stepped out of his comfort zone and threw in a little harmony in response to much urging on Kate's part, the full-house crowd's applause at the Student Union had drowned out his repetitive thoughts.

Their friendship grounded Michael. Yet, since the invitation, their connection had made him a little uneasy about meeting her family. Would they get the wrong idea? She was nothing like the other girls he'd dated in his hometown or at Harvard; she was more like Hàng—funny, easy-going, and a true nature girl. He'd made sure the only thing they'd talked about was music and nature. He was addicted to that peace, their friendship, and he crawled inside those moments and hid out, safe and sound. He didn't want that to change.

His athletics were going so well—making the team for the eight-man race in the spring. Nugget had set the perfect rhythm as though his calls and Michael's arms were connected. All eight of the guys had been in a groove together. The crisp Connecticut air had seemed to separate with a welcome as they sliced through it. His muscles burned with the last stroke that slid them over the finish line a full boat-length ahead in the intra-mural race. In the single scull, Michael had taken gold to the sounds of his teammates' cheers. It gave them all great hope for the UConn spring season. His old skill had clicked in, channeling his anger into the ripples of the water. An unexpected and small compensation for his suffering. He was at his athletic best, boosted by his pain.

They planned to leave for the holiday on Wednesday. Kate had mentioned something about traditional family plans for the night before Thanksgiving. He'd found himself getting nervous. Was something changing in their relationship? Michael reviewed the call he'd made last night. "Hey, Kate. You sure about me coming home with you tomorrow for Thanksgiving?"

"What?" Silence. "Of course. But if you rather not…"

"No, not at all. I just wanted to give you an out if you'd changed your mind. I'm happy to drive."

"Great. I'll be outside the dorm tomorrow at 9:00 after breakfast. How's that?" Yes, he needed Father Sullivan's advice. He didn't want to blow it.

It seemed like only days since the warm sun had baked Michael walking across campus for his first session with Father Sullivan. Still, the chilling promise of winter was whispering in the fall air now. Pulling his jacket up around his neck, Michael bent into the wind. He was relieved that the priest could fit him in before a holiday break—he really needed help before going to Kate's home.

What a strange coincidence, Kate lived in Glynn. He imagined his annual trip to get measured for his new school and church shoes with his mother. The sounds of the old brick factory were so exciting when he was young. Like Santa's workshop, his mother had said. Seeing a shoe come together had always amazed him.

He found himself holding his breath at the thought of Kate with anyone else, but it couldn't be him, Michael thought. Ha`ng still inhabited his heart.

The church was empty. Michael stopped and listened to the silence. He hadn't told the whole truth, but he *had* told the priest nothing but the truth about the horrors of the war, his murder missions tracking down targeted Viet Cong leaders. Thou shalt not kill. Michael knew his kind counselor wouldn't judge him, so he'd asked the question. How do you justify it, Father? Taking a life had all made such sense when he was in the war; none of it made sense sitting in Father's therapy chair.

Michael was still terrified that even the mention of his love and his child would eviscerate him completely. Wouldn't releasing the past make all of the domino pieces he had lined up to keep him in balance come crashing down, one after another, his ultimate breakdown. He still wasn't ready to talk about them; he might never be.

"Michael, glad you felt free to call." Father sat down across from Michael with that welcoming smile that had such a calming effect on him.

The thin, ruddy cushion and the squeaking wheels of the old chair that welcomed Michael had become a familiar place for over two-and-a-half months. He'd settled into the trinity of rules Father had first discussed with him—*doing what he loved* and *learning something new* had helped him keep his flashbacks and anger pretty well in check. So had *helping someone else*. Michael's mind drifted to the hillside under Kate's favorite tree where they practiced together when the Student Union was too crowded for lessons. Staring skyward, hands behind his head, he'd listen to her practice notes, weaving between the sounds of small birds in the branches above him. The way her singing voice wrapped around lyrics mesmerized him.

But, when girls stopped to flirt with him at the Student Union, he'd felt agitated. A kind of betrayal of Hàng. Her beautiful cocoa skin and her delicate features were beginning to fade. First, her eyes had blurred; then he could only conjure their deep chocolate color; now only the shape of her face remained. No clear memory. He couldn't see her, but he could still *feel* Hàng—*that* he couldn't forget. The silky feel of her.

"Michael? Do you need time, or shall we talk?"

"Father, I almost asked Kate to last week's Fall Fling dance."

"I didn't realize you two were...so go on. Problem?"

"No, just as a friend. She's new, and I thought she'd want to meet people...oh hell, I'm lying. That's not the only reason; I needed a cover. Pressure from my frat brothers, you know, them wondering why I never have a date. I couldn't use her that way. I don't want to mislead her or ruin the friendship, Father. We're getting close, and now she's invited me to her house for Thanksgiving.

"So, you think she's interested in you other than as a friend?"

"No, no, my family will be out of town; I think she's just being nice."

"I see."

Michael shuddered. He should have left things alone. He could feel himself getting sucked down into that hole, that wretched hole of memories. "It's complicated; I had second thoughts. I didn't want to give the wrong impression to Kate by accepting. To jeopardize our friendship. And maybe I'm not exactly sure of her intentions. But I'm pretty sure it's just friendship. Kindness."

"I have an idea for the short term. Rules seem to work for you so far. Makes life clear and simpler to deal with. Am I correct?"

"Yes. Your trinity was my first breakthrough. I haven't had a flashback since. Unreal. Are there more?"

"You must tire of this, but I can't do it without the words of our good St. Thomas."

"I'm dying here."

"There is nothing on this earth more to be prized than true friendship." That's the St. T. quote. "You and Kate are friends, correct? What rules will help you to best be that *friend?* Think of that, Michael. Make the rules—you have the character to keep them. I'm off to prepare for Mass for those proactive parishioners praying to avoid a guilt-ridden hangover this weekend. Father Sullivan laughed. "There's no quote from St. Thomas for that one." The priest moved toward the door. "Will that help get you through the holiday, Michael? Maybe you need a start. Here are the first two. Rule 1: No drinking. Rule Two: No mixed messages. How do those two work?"

"Thank you, Father, I can do this." Michael crossed the road from the church and sat by the reflecting lake on the chilled bench. Orange-red and dried leaves crunched beneath his feet and swept up in little eddies around him in the late afternoon breeze—like the chaos and confusion in his head.

Here he was like Moses writing his own ten commandments on his tablet. Michael laughed. He would be embarrassed if Kate knew he was like a little kid needing rules for being a good friend to her. But he knew Father's rule system worked. Michael took a breath, pondered each statute, then jotted them in his notebook.

Rule 1. *No beer; no booze*, period. He needed to stay in control.

Rule 2. *No mixed signals.* It wouldn't be fair to Kate if he, in any way, showed her that his emotions were wavering between staying friends and exploring what they might have together. Not with Ha`ng still lingering in his heart.

Rule 3. *No silence. Play music.* Silence was the enemy, space for his memories to return. Michael shivered. He would play her family's piano with Kate singing as soon as they arrived at her home—something upbeat and loud to fill the silence and delight the family. He would submerge himself in music to stop the stuttering memories. He'd be safe in a song without the silence.

Rule 4. *Have Kate's back.* He couldn't imagine how that would play out, but he was ready to be there for her.

Rule 5. *No touching.* Clear and simple. There were moments when he'd fantasized lately—touching her face, pulling those pencils from her hair. This was important. No electrical connections to trigger some circuit he hadn't intended. Or one he had.

The rules for the weekend were set. Michael felt more in control, and he repeated them in a marching chant on the way back to the fraternity house.

CHAPTER 20

MELODIOUS METAMORPHOSIS

KATE'S KNOCK WAS tentative and soft. "Shiloh?

"Come in."

The red lava lamp lit the room aglow. Kate squinted and pushed through the beaded curtain that jingled behind her like the sound of a magic spell.

Shiloh sat cross-legged on the bed outfitted in a long, turquoise, cotton skirt with a white top accented with multi-color embroidery of vines and birds. A matching bandana and the ever-flashing, silver accessories of bangles and rings finished her signature style.

"Are you busy or meditating?"

"No, just getting ready to go out and meet up with a guy."

Kate smiled and shook her head. "You mean, stalking the wild hickory nut?" Kate sat down on the desk chair under the woven hemp plant hanger suspended from the ceiling. "That's from Euell Gibbons and his outdoor hunt for unusual things to cook. I looked it up. Very clever."

She reached up and touched the wild, writhing vine that

twisted around the ropes above her. "So, you're seeing who? Lark or Theo?"

"We'll see."

Kate knew her face had said it all. She didn't judge Shiloh, but her friend's "free love" lifestyle always caught Kate off guard, made her blush sometimes.

"You know I'm teasing. I'm not a total whore. Well, maybe I am." Shiloh threw her head back, and a laugh escaped her raspberry-red lips. "Seriously, I'm going to attend a rally with Theo. And maybe an afternoon delight. Do you have any idea how much I love to tease you?"

"Yes, I *do*. You're my daily blush, Shi. No make-up necessary." An array of candles flickered around a dark polished Buddha statue on a shelf across the room. "Are these the candles you bought at Rolling Hills?"

Shiloh tilted her head up. "Aren't they great?"

"I think my mom would love some for Thanksgiving. Can you give me directions? I'm going to head over now. By the way, Michael is going home with me for Thanksgiving. His parents will be in Paris; I didn't want him to be alone."

"I bet you didn't. Thus the interest in candles... and birth control, maybe? Is Shiloh maybe just a little right about your piano guy?"

"Stop, teasing. No, strictly as a friend. After all, he taught me to—"

"Yes, I know, the old sight-reading excuse." Shiloh shot Kate a coy smile. "But like, *your* kind of friendly or *my* kind of friendly?"

"Smarty, just give me the directions."

The souped-up Corvair blasted through the autumn leaves, straining to take the curves on the winding back road to the Rolling Hills campus. Crisp breezes from the open car window wreaked havoc on her hair. As Kate accelerated, the cutting edge of an early New England winter chilled her. She rolled up the windows, and the escapees from her French twist stopped dancing around her face.

Turning up the radio, Kate sang along with "Mustang Sally." Her Student Union singing gig with Michael, being a part of the choir, the sight-reading lessons and music history classes had made her life at UConn so full of music. Kate loved their lessons on the hill, fall dappled sun on the turning leaves, and trusting Michael enough to sing acapella outside with no one else around. With Michael's eyes closed, lying back in the tall grass, smiling, he was so easy to be with after classes.

Kate entered the long tree-lined driveway that led to the main buildings. The sprawling Rolling Hills facility did have a haunted atmosphere like Shiloh had said. Ivy-covered, historic Greek Revival and Victorian buildings dotted the expansive acres of wooded beauty.

A couple stood close to each other talking on the side of the road, leaning against a tree. They kissed as Kate passed them. The intimacy between them evoked a yearning. The new feeling surprised her. Kate wanted someone special in her life. Maybe now that she was in college and had her singing going, she could make room for someone for her personal happiness— not as a substitute for her dreams.

Being with Michael singing and feeling their connection grow had only made her more aware of that missing piece. There was one problem; guys who came to hear them at the

Student Union had the impression she and Michael were an item. They'd even said so. And in some ways, it felt that way to Kate too.

How would dating someone affect her daily time with Michael? She hadn't thought of that. Hanging out together with him before and after their lessons and their performances had become a pattern. He'd sit alone in the first pew and listen to choir practice and walk her home, talking about each piece. He was so mannerly and kind.

At the end of the driveway, Kate caught sight of the Rolling Hills gift shop's old, wooden sign. She followed the route and parked. When she entered the front doors of the main brick three-story building, the bayberry and vanilla scents drifting down the hallway connected her with the holidays. Kate could smell the little, brown, bottomless bottle of Vanilla extract, cinnamon sticks, and her mother's baking. She couldn't wait to be home and see everyone for Thanksgiving.

But as she took in the candle fragrances, they failed to fully cover-up the untold odors—an astringent cleanser, mildew, and the subtle underlying trace of urine. If not for that brilliant idea to have those homespun candle aromas greet outsiders at the door, how would customers have tolerated being in that place?

Kate followed a small group of candle shoppers down a windowless, concrete block hallway, painted a dreary green. At the door to the shop, a petite woman with the features of Down Syndrome, handed her a brochure. Waiting in line in the hall for the crowd of holiday customers to clear out, Kate skimmed the material.

The Rolling Hills Training School and Hospital is a residential state facility celebrating its Centennial anniversary. Beginning in 1868 as the Rolling Hills Training School for Imbeciles, the school upgraded its title to the Rolling Hills Training School for the Feebleminded in 1918.

Outrageous, they had used those words back then, Kate thought. Terms and labels certainly had changed over time, not something she'd thought about before. What words were they using now that would be dispelled with time?

Leaning against the door jamb of the twenty-foot square shop crammed with colorful candles, she finished reading the history. Long before Kate stood at the door to the institution in 1968, its name had morphed into Rolling Hills Training School with nearly nine hundred staff and faculty and over sixteen hundred residents, and a farm, she read. Kate had no idea the facility was so large.

Once inside the shop, she picked up candle after candle and breathed in their aromas. The selection of candles, tapers, towers, all sizes and scents, was impressive. She chose two bayberry pillars and six vanilla votive candles.

At the check-out counter, a young man grinned and made delightful little chuckling sounds while twisting a ring of keys. "It's my first day. See my keys?" He rocked his head and jingled a ring of keys.

He might have been in his early twenties, like her, Kate guessed. He wore a white shirt, yellowing at the armpits, with a name tag, Jimmy, and a brown leather belt that desperately held onto his cliff of a stomach. An uneven crewcut finished the look.

Flipping each key around the silver ring with reverence, he chanted, "1. Laundry room, 2. Candle shop, 3. My room, 4. Mailbox. Four keys. See?" Jimmy grinned at Kate.

His joy over his keys touched her. How much we had in our lives that passed by our eyes without notice, Kate thought.

"Wow! Really cool to have *four* keys, Jimmy, huh?" Kate said.

"How did you know my name?"

Kate pointed to his nametag.

"Oh yeah." Jimmy laughed too hard, too long; she joined him.

"Why are you buying these candles?" he asked, eyes cast down.

"We're...uh...having a family party." She decided on a simple answer.

"Family party? Oh! Can I come, *please?*"

Jimmy's unabashed question caught her off guard. She smiled. He was so honest, sharing his desires like that. Kate realized she was drawn to people who could be open and upfront, like Shiloh, and this young man, Jimmy, even though they were different from her, or maybe because they were. She wished she and Michael could be so candid about their feelings. Imbued with their Irish culture, they'd struggled with that openness she craved.

A man entered the shop from a side door and stopped at the counter. "Everything OK here, Jimmy?" He introduced himself as Brent Bradford, operations manager and director of the institution's training programs.

He was a thirty-plus hippie type, lean, long ponytail, with wire-rimmed glasses.

Kate introduced herself.

Jimmy interrupted. "Mr. Brent, I want to go to her family party."

"Please count the young lady's change carefully, OK?" He tried to distract Jimmy from disappointment about the party, Kate thought.

"But I think I like parties. She might say *yes*." He pointed at Kate.

His plea was so pure and innocent. Kate bit her lip and regretted mentioning a party.

Jimmy counted the change into Kate's hand. "Five minus two is three. One, two, three." On the last count, he folded her fingers over the bills, "Don't drop it, OK?"

"Thanks, Jimmy. Your math is good." Kate smiled.

Jimmy tucked his fists under his chin, squeezed his eyes shut, and grinned.

How did Mr. Bradford get into this kind of work; what was his background? Kate took her candles and stepped aside for the next customer, just far enough to be out of earshot.

The director joined her.

"Why is Jimmy so proud of his keys?"

"It's a status kind of thing, shows he can tell time and count and read a bit, requirements for getting a campus job to earn pocket money."

Kate looked across the room at Jimmy. "Director Bradford, what do the people here do for fun? Do you have parties?"

"We try. And it's Brent. No way to be formal here, right? This is...well, humbling work. Will you excuse me? I'm on my way to check in on things in the Music Room."

"Music?"

"Jimmy, you better go now, you have orchestra rehearsal; let Susie take over the register, OK?" Brent headed for the door, as a cheerful blonde girl in a simple cotton dress and horn-rimmed eyeglasses took over at the counter and began to ring up the next customer.

"Wait, you have an *orchestra*?" Kate turned to Brent.

"You like music? I'm headed over there now."

Kate laughed. "I love music, but…" She checked her watch, 5 o'clock. She was singing at seven and had to have dinner, but she was intrigued. Imagining Jimmy with his uncontrollable hand and body movements, pushing a note out of any instrument was impossible.

"Can you come to hear me play? I'm good, I think."

"Sure, I'll come for a bit." His enthusiasm sealed the deal for Kate.

Jimmy left the shop, snapping his fingers.

A gangly young girl squatted in an alcove, just inside the door as Brent and Kate left the main building. Kate said, hello.

No response. The girl sent an empty glance up at Kate.

"Hello, Mary." Brent took a second to squat down. "Chilly here, let's take you back to your classroom, Ok?"

Mary pulled away and shrunk into a tighter ball. The young girl's straight, platinum hair hung over one eye like a curtain. She stood and ran down the hallway, limbs flailing like a duckling paddling on the surface of the water, struggling to take off.

"Will she be OK, alone?"

"Let me get her some help." Brent signaled her teacher in the hallway.

A chill met them at the door, as the New England evening began to settle in over them. The sun's last shards flashed over the undulating hills of the verdant campus, and Kate pulled her fringed suede cape tighter around her.

"The music room is that third building over there." Brent turned his jacket collar up. "Let's cut through the inside route."

Kate crisscrossed the lawn with Brent and entered the first of a chain of crumbling structures. Each building was dedicated to a specialized level of care. Rolling Hills provided a home for every child and adult who couldn't fit in; for every child who wouldn't survive the hazing and the rigors of public school or who had no family to care for them; for every adult who had come as a child and had no option but to stay, Brent told her.

Classrooms were filled with children whose limbs and lips refused to be in their command. Kate saw things that closed her throat, like the dull-eyed, microcephalic, pre-teen boy sitting in a crib whose body was normal but his head was tragically undersized. She saw things that made her smile, as well, like the excitement the residents all showed when Kate said "Hi" and waved.

"They're always happy to see a new face." Brent pushed open a double swinging door to show her more.

Happy younger children were playing basketball, despite missing nearly every shot. Attentive teachers gathered the winners into their arms.

Brent opened the door with a sign that read, Rolling Hills Music Hall. Inside, an unlikely line-up of musicians, instruments in hand, residents of all ages were ready to practice against the green tile backdrop of the all-purpose room.

Jimmy stood by the wall, holding a saxophone.

Are you kidding, Kate thought.

"I'm over-scheduled today, but I can't resist." Brent scraped two metal folding chairs over from the front row, and they waited for the first piece to begin.

Brent was so wonderfully compassionate, taking time from his busy schedule to hear them, Kate thought.

"It's OK; I can't stay long, either." She'd only meant to grab a few candles.

Even at their ready position, the dozens of musicians moved like rows of waving dune grass undulating in a brisk ocean breeze before a storm—shifting, convulsing, one way and the other, promising a kind of chaos in their music. Kate lifted her shoulders thinking of the likely off-key screeching pain she was about to endure.

As the bushy gray-haired conductor lifted both hands high, a baton in his right hand, Kate prepared to prevent her reactions from coloring her facial expressions.

Jimmy shook like a dog after a heavy downpour. Placing his fingers on the keys, they twitched in anticipation. A young, tall boy sat at a drum set nodding his head to some unseen beat with drumsticks poised beside his head like antennae. The orchestra began—a familiar John Phillips Souza march Kate's dad used to play on their old console stereo to march her and her siblings up to bed.

Startled, Kate's eyes flew open. She sat at attention. Impossible. The transformation stunned her. Was it a recording? She scanned the people who were creating the harmonious sounds. No, it was clearly live music. Kate focused on Jimmy's deft, deliberate fingers, his concentration, the melodious tune floating from the mouth of his sax, a miraculous makeover from the shaking staccato of his norm.

In the second row, she spotted Bobby from her cafeteria

playing a violin, snaking his body side to side, eyes closed. She recognized his signature rhythm he'd used to sweep the gravy and stuck food from the cafeteria plates with the sprayer. Kate was aware that her mouth was open in surprise. She put her hand to her face.

Her mystified glance at Brent, brought a grin, and he leaned over and whispered, "I know, right? They're called *idiot savants*. A number of them in residence here; they carry the entire orchestra.

Idiots? Savant? She'd never heard the term; the words certainly didn't fit.

"They're mentally disabled and 'genius-ly' abled when it comes to music. A few, like Jimmy, just pick up an instrument they like, hear a song, and soon they're playing."

Kate wished she could pick up sheet music and just sing. She could envision being at the Boston Symphony with a center section ticket stub in her hand. But different. Even better. She couldn't swallow the lump of emotion in her throat. Beautiful— the strings, the brass section, all in perfect pace. They switched smoothly to a sensitive waltz—from *Doctor Zhivago*. Kate felt the sizzle of chills flow over her arms. "Somewhere my Love." Would she ever be able to play an instrument like that even after years of practice?

When the music ended, the players had all resumed their gawkiness, breaking out in a cacophony of vocalizations, like the warmup in the orchestra pit before a symphony—except in this case, Kate thought, the chaos was at the end of the performance—from a smooth, symphonic harmony of music to a dissonance of human instruments.

Kate approached Jimmy. He surrendered his confidence

like a costume and returned to the artless young man she'd seen in the candle store. Her words got stuck at first, she was so emotional to hear the beauty of the performance delivered from the awkward hodge-podge of people.

Jimmy stood there, hands folded under his chin, eyes shifting from left to right avoiding contact—as though he were afraid to hear her bad review.

"Wow, Jimmy, that was so cool. You're *really* good." She reached out her hand.

"Hello, two bayberry pillars, six vanilla votives." He dropped his head. "I liked it too."

What a keen memory. Kate smiled. So refreshing to hear his candid truth; he liked it. No false humility, and she knew exactly how he felt. Like her feelings leaving O'Leary's or choir practice or singing the Student Union, she liked it too.

Jimmy stuck out his hand without looking up and shook Kate's like he was pumping water from a well. Then he slinked away into the crowd.

"Kate!"

She turned to see Bobby waving as he exited the door. Kate waved back in disbelief, overwhelmed by the superb music and fascinated to be entering this new world of *different*.

"You're a hit, Kate." Brent approached smiling. "That's the second time Jimmy's made contact with you. A little breakthrough for him, today. Be careful, though. He's triggered by touch. Let him call the shots."

"Oh, of course, sure. Um…what would happen, exactly?"

"He would have a meltdown, a fit, I guess you would call it, shaking, yelling. Doesn't happen often; people know not to touch here, part of the training."

"I'll be careful. Do residents like Jimmy ever get to leave, spend time in the community?" She imagined him rocking the crowd and playing with her and Michael at the Student Union. She wanted to sing along with his mind-blowing sax.

"They would if they had the chance, and under the right circumstances." Brent opened the exit door for Kate. "They don't get too many invitations."

Jimmy and his musical comrades' transformations remained with Kate as she left the music room. Uplifted, she clung to the echo of the last note they'd played. A glow of joy from the experience stirred her own love of performance. Jimmy knew who he was; and so did she.

CHAPTER 21

Michael

JUST FRIENDS

MICHAEL FELT CONFLICTED—happy to have somewhere to go for the holiday break, but nervous about being in a house full of strangers. Holidays were sometimes spent with housekeepers or babysitters when he was young, while his parents cruised or explored foreign countries. He could hear them arguing—father in favor of leaving, mother against it. Dad had grown up in a world of nannies and traveling parents. Young children stayed at home.

Michael ate breakfast in the dining hall, looking out the windows across the quadrangle. It was a perfect fall day. The guys in the grassy yard were raking up piles of multicolored leaves, laughing, and goofing off. He didn't belong in so many ways. It was his age, but also his wall that kept him in his friendly but distant prison, and he couldn't seem to take it down.

Back in his room, he changed his clothes, then drove to the crew's dock at Coventry Lake. He needed to be on the water in a single skull to think. How would Hà ng present herself while he was with Kate? What if he had one of his crazy flash-back episodes in front of her family at the sound of a plate dropping, a door slamming, or a baby crying? Flashing back to those memories wasn't something he'd learned to control. He had Father Sullivan's rules in place. He'd be OK, Michael counseled himself, as he slipped the boat into the water and paddled from the shore.

His questions continued with the swish of water and the gurgle of eddies around the hull. What would it be like with her big family vs. his only-child home life? Certainly, not like his family dinners—one son, one silent father, one hopeful mother, everything perfect, fourth-generation Limoges water pitcher passed by his mother's maid. And the expectation from his parents—fill us up, Michael; make us happy; make this marriage make sense.

He wouldn't miss the country club affairs over the Thanks-giving weekend with too many members in attendance to have a real conversation. There were some nice neighbors, but too many questions about success and possessions and travel and golf scores. Doing and going. What did you do about your stock buy-back? Where did you go for the winter? What was your golf score? Oh, I adore Venice. And the topic he could never avoid—I hear you're not joining your father in the business.

Kate hadn't hesitated to invite him to a holiday dinner. No call home to explain. No permission necessary. It would have caused a major catastrophe in his household if he had done the same for one of his grandmother's dinners. Not on his mother's behalf; she would have welcomed a guest, but grandmother's plans were inflexible and perfect. Seating plans thought out well in advance—who went to what school, what

were their hobbies? No room for a stranger. A stranger. He'd
felt like one, himself, at the Grande Dame's home.

Michael dragged the boat up onto the shore and set it back
on the rack.

"Hey, what are you doing, sneaking in an extra practice?"

Nugget caught Michael off-guard.

"Hey, Nugget. No, just taking in the sunny day before the
lake freezes over."

"I just came to check on everything before I leave for the
holiday. When are you leaving for home?" Nugget checked to
ensure the locks and straps were in place on the boats.

Michael hesitated. It was embarrassing that his family would
go away without him. Even more unusual, that he was going
home with Kate. It played right into what everyone already
thought. It was awkward having to say it out loud to someone.

"A friend of mine invited me home with her."

"*Her*? You holding back on me, buddy?"

"No. My father has a special event for the WWII Veterans
in Paris. He and my mother will be away." Michael opened
the car door.

Nugget, who measured up, physically, to tall Michael's
shoulder, really measured up where it counted. He was sincere
and always looking out for Michael; he liked the guy. Like a
personal pit bull, he was protective, keeping Michael's secret
about his shell shock. He owed Nugget the truth.

"OK. It's Kate. She invited me so I wouldn't be alone."
Michael spun his keys around his finger.

Nugget clapped. "Yes! I knew it. Good going, buddy. She's
something else."

"No, she's…I'm giving her lessons."

"Lessons? Yeah, I bet you are."

Michael rocked his shoulders to release the tension as if to loosen them after the row. He felt the heat reach his face. Not a flashback coming, but the feeling as if Ha`ng had caught him betraying her. Guilt. It wasn't the first time Nugget had questioned his relationship with Kate. Michael knew what the buzz was about him at the frat house—wondering what was wrong with this new, older guy, or whether he even liked girls. He'd never attended a single frat event; never had a date. Before every dance, someone had asked him if he was bringing a girl. "What about your gorgeous red-head?" they'd ask.

The pressure was on. To find a girl like Kate, so real, so kind, who shared what he loved, and then to realize he couldn't be there in the present with her, or with any woman, sent a pain into his chest. He'd trade everything to be normal again.

He managed a measured answer. "We're just good friends and music partners." Michael could hear that his tone had an edge to it; blood rushed in his ears.

"Sorry, I just thought you two were...I didn't mean to pry."

Michael popped a mint in his mouth. He took a deep breath and let it out through a smile.

Nugget looked out over the lake. "How's uh, you know, Father Sullivan?"

"He's really helping. Honestly, I didn't have much faith, but so far so good. Thanks, man." Michael patted Nugget's shoulder and got into his car. What was he feeling? Exactly what was his relationship with Kate? Was he in denial? It was hard to get a clear picture with the flash of memories waiting in the background, ready to devour his feelings. Time with Kate was an elixir. He didn't want that to change.

CHAPTER 22

PRODIGAL STRANGER

LINES OF FROST like shattered spider webs filled the lower corners of Kate's dorm window. The morning sun crept over the hill illuminating the chilly etchings. Briefly sliding open the window, Kate felt winter in the November air.

She pulled her leather bag from under the bed. Needing space to bring back the winter things she'd left behind, Kate stuffed only a few essentials inside. Who wouldn't love the holidays with her siblings and crazy cousins all piled into her family's row house? She laughed, thinking of her family members trying to outdo each other's wisecracks, making clever comebacks, guessing the movie titles in a game of charades, and mostly, their evenings at O'Leary's. She hoped she and Michael would have the chance to perform there.

After Michael had accepted her Thanksgiving invitation, Kate finally had asked him the question that had lurked inside her. While walking her from the lake to choir practice, she couldn't stand it any longer. "What about your girlfriend?" had just flown out of Kate's mouth.

She could handle it either way, but she had to know before taking any risks with their friendship.

With Kate's question, Michael had looked like he'd been punched.

"Oh, sorry, did I overstep?"

"No, no. There's no one. Used to be, but no more." Then that look.

Kate was tempted to press for an explanation, but she'd left it for another day. Getting Michael to open up, chiseling away at his aloofness, one question at a time without jeopardizing his comfort level with her, was tricky. What would they talk about since he'd headed her off at the pass every time she'd asked about his life, his past? The Vietnam subject that had come up briefly when Kate discovered Michael was seeing Father Sullivan for counseling was never re-visited. Kate respected Michael's privacy, having watched her brother Keith hold everyone at arm's length. Patience. But there was so much she wanted to know. She assumed relations with his family might be strained. And what *was* that enigmatic, faraway look, if not longing for someone he loved? There was something else.

Kate checked outside the window for Michael's car. She could hear the family teasing, *sure, sure* when she invoked the "he's just a friend" phrase. She'd called ahead to ask her mom to tell everyone. Had Kate imagined that little crack in the friendship wall when they'd danced at the Student Union to the jukebox? She'd shivered when he'd stepped in closer.

Kate pulled on her jacket and grabbed her satchel and luggage. She was so curious to see how Michael would respond to her basic abode and down-to-earth family. She knew from a girl in the dorm from his hometown that Michael was from a prominent, affluent family. His car, his clothes, and his demeanor said it all—opening doors for her, pulling out her chair, standing when she stood to take breaks at their gigs—gentlemanly behavior. She liked it. It made her feel feminine and a little less like his buddy.

Imagining Michael's home and his typical holiday celebration was a string of clichés; she knew that. With no family chaos, and Kate perched on a Louis the Fourteenth settee sipping a crystal glass of mulled wine. Michael, leaning against the mantle of the toasty fireplace—wearing Owl & Shamrock wingtips, one hand in the pocket of his gray flannel slacks, classical music in the background.

Kate laughed and clicked the one working latch and strapped her luggage with the belt. It was too late to change her mind; he was picking her up in fifteen minutes.

The sound of the crunch of silver crust underfoot on the chilled morning grass made Kate cheerful; she loved fall and winter. Michael's low-slung sports car headed up the road toward the dorm as Kate arrived on the sidewalk with her old beat-up bag. A little pulse of electricity shot its way down her spine when she saw Michael's blonde head tucked down inside the sleek car as he pulled up to the curb. Kate pulled her Navy peacoat up around her neck.

"Hey, Good morning." He emerged out of the car in gray flannel slacks, a baby blue dress shirt, and a navy blue mono-grammed sport coat.

"Hi." She bent over to get her luggage.

"No, no. I'll get that." He rushed over and tucked the bag in the trunk. It barely fit beside his own leather suitcase and his golf shoes with little clumps of grass and dirt still clinging to the spikes.

Kate watched Michael close her door, hop around the back of the car, and get in the driver's side. "I'll pay the tolls since you're paying the gas. Or I can give you gas money? I don't know what's right here." Kate opened her pocketbook.

"No way." He reached over and put his hand out to stop her from taking out the cash. His hand hesitated on hers. She felt that spine-fizzle repeat. "Tank's full, and I've got the toll money ready. It's enough you've invited me." He pulled a small pile of bills from his jacket pocket.

Kate was relieved; money was tight. She had to watch her small savings. What was it like to never worry about gas money or phone bills? Would she ever find out, majoring in music? She changed the subject. "Nice car. What is it?"

"Thanks, it's a Jaguar." He turned the key, and the shiny vehicle purred. The windshield wipers continued clearing fan shapes in the film of morning moisture on the glass.

"Michael, do you ever notice we hardly talk about family or our lives at home?" She saw his grip tighten around the steering wheel.

He glanced at her. "Funny, Kate, do you ever notice, you always say what's on your mind?"

"Not always." She loosened her boots from the hem of her long rust suede skirt Shiloh had insisted she borrow. "Listen, just so you know, I'd better give you the low-down. I'm from a huge family—Dad's from a family of eight, and Mom's one of nine—all sisters—very fertile sisters. And my three sisters too. Having lots of babies is the tradition. Although...I...well, I won't fit in when it comes to that custom." Kate took a quick peek at Michael. He was still smiling. He didn't seem fazed by her statement about not wanting children. Didn't seem to judge her. That was good. "Anyway, we're all Irish and Catholic to varying degrees. So, do you know what that means?"

"I have a feeling you're going to tell me." He dropped the visor to block the bright morning sun as they turned east and drove past the row of churches to exit the campus.

"Dozens of cousins, three sisters, three brothers, Mom and Dad and a hoard of aunts and uncles. Grandparents on both sides still alive, and they'll all be buzzing around you asking endless questions and making conversation to make you feel at home." Would he be OK with the chaos? Kate plucked at Michael's jacket. "And they won't let you off the hook like I do."

Michael laughed out loud. "I didn't know you were going so easy on me."

"Oh, and stories about the factory and our ancestors—you'll know the whole kit and caboodle from Grandpa Ketchum and Grandma Kendall before you go." Kate glanced sideways at Michael. She loved the comfort of being with him.

"Factory?"

"You'll see, and all my siblings have first names that start with a K. That makes us all K-squared. Double trouble. In my case, triple Ks."

"Sounds like three times the fun."

Was he flirting? "We live a block from the factory, and a block from the family's favorite hangout, O'Leary's Pub, and two blocks from the church, school, and the cemetery. They say you can be baptized, go to school, work, party, and die, all within three blocks—no car necessary." That got her another puff of a laugh. "What about...you?"

"Well, you know, I'm an only child, and no double K's."

"But three first names. Michael Edward James. Is that a family tradition?"

"You noticed. Yes, but I only have two girl cousins; they live in Connecticut. My mother's only brother's kids."

"You never mentioned, are your grandparents still living?"

"Only Grandmother. Well, she's a doozie. The Grande Dame is always trying to fix me up with appropriate partners."

"Grande Dame, huh? Ah, and what might she consider appropriate for young Mr. James?"

Michael stopped, readjusted the rearview mirror and flashed a smile at Kate.

She found herself holding her breath, not wanting their conversation to stop.

"Oh, she likes girls in purple Pappagalos."

Kate dropped her head back against the seat and laughed. "What, no Owl & Shamrocks? Shame on her."

"I'll tell her you said so." He put the radio on. *Kind of a drag when your baby don't love you.* "Feel free to search stations."

Wrong song. Kate rotated the knob. "Come on, baby, light my fire." She sang along, swaying side to side, bumping up against his shoulder at the end. She watched the corners of his mouth turn up.

The tree-lined, country road blurred by with an occasional ruddy barn surrounded by maple trees sprinkled with crimson, yellow, and browning leaves hanging on for their last hurrah. "Don't you just love fall?" She'd never felt so happy; she could ride forever with him, singing and talking. The morning sun peaked over flat farms and lit up the frosted grass across fallow fields peppered with retired, rusted farm trucks and plows. Kate imagined the old equipment giving up one day and remaining right where it was. She never wanted to just rust in one place; she had dreams. "Do you have a dream?" Kate blurted out the question.

He flashed an enigmatic look.

"I mean for your career."

A suspended silence. "I'm thinking the foreign service or an international non-profit. Some overseas assignment. My uncle's in the Foreign Service. I summer interned with him in Bangkok after my freshman year at Harvard. It's a beautiful country."

His answer made Kate's stomach flutter. Travel, dreams of life overseas. "You lived in Thailand?"

"Yes, it was great. How about your dreams? Singing, I assume."

"It would be wonderful if it involved singing, but...I'm working on it."

"Kate, you're too good not to."

"I just don't want to be a starving artist." She shared her story of the old childhood map and the pins in the places that lured her.

"I love that story." He engaged her eyes, then went silent again.

The music and occasional comments about the changing scenery made the time pass.

"Here we are, our home state." Michael's only comment.

When they approached the exit for Glynn, Kate started to give Michael directions to her town.

"I've got this." Michael came out of his faraway stare. "Tell you what, I bet I can find your house by psychic intuition."

Kate studied his profile. "OK, you're on." What kind of joke was he pulling?

He turned onto the Glynn exit and negotiated the turns to the downtown. The factory town had already awakened with delivery trucks and people off to work on the last day before the holiday. The sun was finally high enough to push its way over the brick factory walls, casting dappled light on the narrow tree-shaded streets.

He pulled up along the front of the factory, past the church, and slowed, turning to watch Kate's face.

"How did you do that?" Kate was dumb-founded.

Winking, Michael stopped only one house away from hers. "Am I getting close?"

"101, next one down. OK, you're a man of many talents."

"I told you—psychic."

Michael got out and opened her car door. "Welcome home, Ms. Ketchum. We'll get the luggage later. You'll want to see your parents first, right?"

What was going on? Kate hoped the initial meeting would go well. She'd told her brothers to take it easy on her friend. No joking about a wedding, first thing. She knew they would love to tease, embarrass, or chase Michael away if they didn't like him. Kate was the only sister left to protect and taunt.

They went up the steps, and Kate saw her home through Michael's eyes. The end unit of the row of four houses with faded wood siding and peeling frames around the big windows. They took the stairs to the covered porch and passed the four unraveling rattan rockers they'd bought when she was a kid. The creaking sound of the door opening made her smile. Sneaking in late from work, her siblings' arrivals were announced one after the other by that familiar sound—the music of their lives. How many times had their mom stopped her brother Kevin, Keith or Karl from greasing the hinge to avoid detection on his tipsy returns from O'Leary's? That squeak was the key to knowing all her kids were home safely.

"Our family security guard, that squeak."

"Funny." Michael opened the door for her. The scent of meat roasting and onions caramelizing, and the sounds of TV and distant laughter filled the entryway.

Kate hung Michael's jacket and her navy peacoat on the walnut coat rack in the narrow hallway and called out, "Yoo-hoo, Mom? Dad? I'm home."

Her mother came around the corner, wiping her hands on her flour-dusted apron.

"Katie-girl."

"Mom, this is— "

Michael stopped. "Mrs. *K*?"

"Michael James! *Where* have you been?" Cecelia rushed forward and hugged Michael.

"Wait, Mom...you *know* Michael?" Kate made the connection. She pictured Michael walking toward her up the campus church aisle the first time she'd met him. Once she'd torn her eyes away from his handsome face, she'd seen them. His old beat-up, black Owl & Shamrock penny loafers. His surprised look told Kate he knew Mrs. K. as the woman who waited on him over the years, and he'd never known her last name was Ketchum.

Kate's mother stood with her hands on Michael's shoulders. "How's your mother, Michael? She's well, I hope; she's such a dear."

Michael's mother, a *dear*? Of course, Mom knew Michael's mother too. Her mother knew more than Kate did about her mystery man. Kate wanted to punch the guy in the arm, but she was too incredulous.

"Big Kevin, come see who's here." Her mother took Michael's arm.

Kate's father shuffled in wearing his usual brown corduroy slippers, after-work sweatpants, and a plaid shirt. "Michael Edward James. I'll be damned." He shook Michael's hand. "Good to see you, young man. Twenty years of measuring your feet, and then poof, we didn't see you. Come in. Come in. You look well. Four years and not a new last on the wall." Her father scratched his head. "Although, I doubt your foot is still growing. Hard to believe you're a grown man."

"Kevin, Michael is Katie's guest from college, can you believe?"

Ha, yes, Kate thought, one of their *well-heeled* regulars. A well-loved one, at that. It made her want to laugh. Who would have guessed someday she would randomly bring one of those exotic boys home for a holiday.

Michael winked at her and shrugged, signaling a swearing of his innocence. She squinted at him. All of her angst over him meeting her family; all of her worries, hoping he would see beyond their humble life to their loving hearts, for nothing. She loved the way he settled right in chatting with her parents. OK, now to stop the runaway horse before her parents and brothers had her married off to Michael.

"Katie, invite the young man into the parlor for goodness sake."

Leading Michael down the hallway, she nudged him with her elbow. "I told you we should've talked more."

Michael laughed and answered under his breath. "I swear, I had no idea that Mrs. K stood for Ketchum. You said, a block from the factory, so I guessed where the house was. I only knew where the town and the factory were."

"What's your pleasure, son? Beer, Irish whiskey?"

"Beer's good, sir."

"Katie, get the young man a beer, please." Her father kissed her forehead and huffed down into his favorite chair, waiting to continue their chat.

Son? He called him, *son.* Kate shook her head. Was this some dream?

"Sounds good." Michael shrugged at Kate; the message was clear; he hadn't put it all together either until he'd seen her mother's face.

"Katie's brothers will be here soon. You haven't tasted pot roast until you've had Cecelia's recipe. It's her tradition, the night before Thanksgiving."

"I can't wait. The aroma's got me already."

"After dinner, we'll all hit O'Leary's for a few beers and some fun, and you'll meet everybody." Her father continued peppering Michael with questions. "So, tell me what's been happening that kept our long-*lasting* customer away? We wondered where you'd gone. We had a record going from the time you were two. How's your mother? Your rowing success at Harvard? But now UConn? Tell us everything."

"Mom's fine; she's in Paris with my father. Vietnam, two

tours, Mr. K.; it's not a good story." Michael settled into the sagging, tan corduroy chair.

Kate eavesdropped from the kitchen, picturing Michael growing up before her parents' eyes. She could see them measuring him for his custom shoes, taking the mold of his foot each year—baby shoes, child, teen, man. He would have charmed her parents with that platinum hair and sincere blue eyes, Kate thought. Like he did her, she had to admit. Letting out a little staccato of laughter under her breath, she filled the iced mug. The beer foam sizzled up and over the rim, down her wrist, and onto the floor. She cleaned up quickly, returned to the parlor, and handed Michael the frosty one.

Sitting on the arm of the old overstuffed chair, she put her arm around her father's shoulder.

He patted her hand. "Kate, what a shocker, huh? Your Michael is *our* Michael. Small world."

CHAPTER 23

Michael

FIRST LAST

THE USUAL CLOUD of beer and corned beef and cabbage aromas exploded through the entrance when Michael opened the door to O'Leary's. The typical boisterous crowd had already gathered. Laughter drowned out any chance of conversation.

Kate's father waved from a table by the stage he'd snagged. Excusing themselves, Kate and Michael pressed through the smoky crowd along the polished, wooden bar. Kate quickly yelled an introduction to a cluster of family members as they passed. "This is Michael, my friend from college."

A chorus of greetings rose above the noise. Guys and girls at the bar threw comments over their shoulders as she passed.

"Hey, Kate."

"You're back! Singing tonight?"

"She'd better damned be singing, or I'm leaving."

"Nice work, Kate." Her cousin, Carol, flashed a look at Michael.

Kate embraced the chorus of "welcome homes," and tears settled around the edges of her eyes.

Uncle Jack leaned over the bar. "Kate, I cleared the slate for a set for you tonight. Hope that's OK? God, we've missed you. And you must be Michael, welcome. I must have made dozens of your shoes over the years."

"Then I owe you thanks."

"Is there anyone who doesn't know you, *Katie-girl?*" Michael pulled out her chair at her family's oak double-eight-top. He stood beside her, taking it all in.

"You mean, is there anyone here not related to me? And by the way, that nickname, Katie-girl, is reserved for my mother, Mr. James."

"How can you sing in this din?" He had to yell to be heard.

"You'll see. You'll play with me, won't you? The piano may not be in perfect tune."

He didn't answer.

Keith signaled Kate's other two brothers. The infamous "K-squared, Ketchum Brothers," Kevin, Keith, and Karl surrounded Michael.

Kate sipped her beer and watched over the rim of her glass. She liked seeing the guys laughing and getting along together.

They weren't at O'Leary's fifteen minutes and had only taken a few swallows of their beers when barkeep, Uncle Jack, turned on the mic. "Everybody!" He had to whistle twice to get the mob's attention.

Michael took his seat next to Kate.

"Now everyone, we've got Kate here back from college, so give her a big warm welcome back. All of you behave yourselves. We've missed you, sweetheart."

Kate shrugged one shoulder flirtatiously, and Michael helped her to step up on the stage, then sat back down.

Kate loved how Michael's mouth formed that familiar crooked smile whenever he learned something new about her. Everything was just too easy on this trip home. Barriers she'd feared had just melted. Standing on the familiar stage was another kind of homecoming that tempted her tears. She pulled it together and took the mic. "Thank you, Uncle Jack. Please welcome my good friend, Michael, on the piano, a nice, Irish Catholic boy from Nantucket. And I'll have no obscene limericks rhyming with Nantucket in front of Michael, you hear."

The hoots and whistles made it impossible for him to refuse. Michael made his way up onto the stage. He waved thanks, sat at the piano, ran his fingers over the chipped and yellowed keys, and Kate slid a song list in front of him. Their regulars. He knew them cold.

Kate's brother Keith jumped on the drum set, Matt on guitar, and the ruckus evaporated with the first note. Kate could see Michael was surprised. Most bar crowds wouldn't stop for performers, quiet their voices a little maybe, but Kate had long ago trained the O'Leary's gang.

She sang the songs on the list alone for the first set as Michael played. During the break, Michael jumped up, dropped a coin in the jukebox, shrugged his shoulders, and extended his hand to Kate. She slid off her stool and Michael wrapped his arms loosely around her in a slow dance. His charming move elicited hoots and cheers from her family and made her romantic sisters fall in love with him. Even her brothers thought it was a smooth move.

She'd almost thought he'd been using her for a joke, but that was her own insecurity, she realized. Back on stage, she took a chance. "Sing the last one with me...please? It needs harmony."

They alternated verses in the duet, and when they hit the harmony section, "There's no, no looking back for us," Kate felt a wave of arousal through her body. That something that happens when voices blend. Some kind of enchantment came from singing together, a physical connection as Michael's deep, bright tones wrapped around her velvet, soulful sounds. Tight harmonies; two as one. Leaning toward her on the piano bench, he crooned the line about her being his destiny and connected with her eyes. It nearly knocked her off the stool. Singing together was thrilling—a bond beyond their voices.

The cold gray door scraped open, and Kate flipped on the lights. Michael held the door to prevent the boom.

She'd never been to the factory when it was so tranquil. Kate could still hear the boisterous machinery in the quiet of her mind. The clunk of her heels on the metal stairs echoed in the ceiling. They crossed the grimy, manufacturing rooms to the sales office. Another world. Fit for well-to-do customers.

The aging, mahogany chairs were upholstered in gold brocade. There was an elegant but ancient wood desk with a leather blotter. A hallway led to the fitting room where the *lasts* were made. Along the massive wall was the alphabetical line of every customer's wooden lasts—families' stories captured, generation after generation.

Finding the "J's," Michael scanned the wooden feet until he found his own. *Michael Edward James*, from tiny to teen to twenty. He took the smallest one down and turned it over in his hands. "1948? I was only four."

Kate saw that look on Michael's face—faraway, pained. His secret must have surfaced. She touched his arm and almost asked. *Please, tell me.*

Michael cradled the little wooden foot, then put it back.

"Too sentimental for you?"

He turned and looked into Kate's eyes for longer than anyone ever had. Too long, uncomfortably long, but she held his gaze. It burned through her.

"You, OK?"

"I will be." He pushed her hair behind her ear, reached his arm around her back, nearly lifted her off the floor, and kissed her. Tucking his head in the crook of her neck, he breathed in and kissed her behind her ear. He stayed nuzzled there, his lips against her skin sending little shivers through her. When he stepped back, Kate felt an awkwardness descend, clearly, both his and hers, as they ventured beyond the realm of friendship.

"Had I known you would react to your *lasts* that way, I would've brought you here *first*." A joke was the only weapon Kate had to cut through the flood of new emotions that consumed her.

"Kate." His tones became low and alluring. "I think we need another rehearsal."

"Music?"

"Corny, but you could call it that." He hesitated just before his mouth pressed against hers again.

He didn't devour her, didn't swallow her whole, like some guys had. He wasn't greedy; he met her on equal terms, his tongue tenderly exploring hers, waiting for her response. They lingered, gripped each other tighter, sighed at the same time, and laughed to release the tension.

CHAPTER 24

Michael

SAFE AND SOUND

EVERY PART OF him was caught up in the joy of feeling something for someone again. He'd never thought it could happen; he'd given himself over to it, let it consume him. Her beautiful face, their connection while singing, being with her family, their history, the laughter—all of it was what he'd craved.

He'd moved in for the second kiss, hoping to keep the sensation from slipping away, the softness, the ache to belong, the comfort of her arms. Then he crashed from the high of their intimacy. Guilt stole everything the moment his lips left her soft neck.

Michael had sunk into a dark self-loathing for his selfishness. So much guilt. For Hà`ng? It made no sense, but as always, it felt like a betrayal. And lies by omission to Kate. Where was his loyalty? The ever-perplexing question. Did it make sense to be loyal to a woman who was no more? And what about fairness to Kate. Was he kissing Kate or Hà`ng? Yes, it was Kate he'd kissed and held tight. Her scent of citrus and honey perfume, not Hàng's coconut sweetness. OK, so that's good, right? He counseled himself. He felt guilty that Kate had no idea he was taken. A kind of lie. Would he ever be able to love Kate the way he loved Hàng? Was it unfair, selfish, dishonorable? He wanted it back, that fleeting passion and joy that had flashed through him when he'd kissed Kate. He wanted it again. Wasn't he allowed?

"Wow, Michael. What just happened? Where did you go?" Kate had kept her hand on his cheek.

The walls of the factory fitting room came back into focus. He'd broken every one of Father Sullivan's rules. Kate was no longer a friend. "I'm here with you. I'm here."

Falling asleep didn't come easily, alone in the twin bed in Kate's room with the memories of the day buzzing in his mind and a raging heat in his face at the thought of their first kisses. He'd settled into the family like he'd belonged—like a brother or a son. Still, what they had together now was no longer just a friendship. Had he ruined everything?

He imagined them together, Kate casually walking through the bedroom door from the bathroom, toweling her hair, sleek and naked from the shower. That long, lean waist and shape he'd seen silhouetted under her gauze embroidered blouses. Honey? Shall we go see the family this weekend, he imagined her saying. He'd never fantasized about her before. It felt wrong.

Why was everything so easy here with her family? No ricocheting emotions until that kiss. He stared up at the stains on the ceiling, like amber clouds. Imperfections. Would his own imperfections fade away? Could these emotions sustain? But it was clear, he had strong feelings for Kate. Perfect for him—independent, caring, smart, and so beautiful with that tone of red flowing down her back or twisted and propped up with two pencils. That made him smile. Made him want to go out to a five and dime and buy ten dozen more yellow number 2s.

Michael looked around the bedroom. The sides of the pull-down shade had the glow of daylight. He'd slept peacefully. A radio show drifted from the house next door, and the sounds of the day started in the house below him. Dishes clinking and laughter, always that Ketchum laughter. Not a sound he'd often heard at home. The kind of home life he'd always wanted, ever since he'd sat encircled on straw mats with Ha`ng and her loving clan.

He heard a soft tap at his door and Kate's voice. "Michael? Are you awake?"

He'd never been so awake, he thought. He bolted up and drew on his jeans, struggling with the zipper. "Just a sec." He reached for his shirt. "Come on in." He heard his own rapid words and took in and released a deep breath to slow his heart. Caught in the act. Of thinking of her. That way.

Kate pushed against the door to unstick it, and it popped open. "Hey, sleepyhead." She stepped in and closed the door and stood waiting. "You, OK? Did you sleep well?"

He caught her eyes flickering between his scars and the tattoos on his shoulders as he pulled his shirt on. He hadn't been thinking right. Her tilted head and look of concern told him she had questions. The way her bellbottom jeans hung below her hips—lower on one side—almost held a promise.

And barefoot, wearing a tight Janis Joplin T-shirt tucked in. Damn. He stuffed his hands in his pockets.

What if the daylight had brought clarity to her and she'd decided he wasn't right? Then what? Could he sing with her, teach her, still be friends? Oh, what the hell. "Good morning, K-cubed." He crossed the little room in two steps, rested his hands on her shoulders, and kissed her forehead as he'd seen her family do over and over the night before. Safe enough. "Happy Thanksgiving. I'm fine, better than fine. You sleep well?"

"I...did. Once I fell asleep. I had a lot to think about, frankly."

Michael studied Kate's response. Unreadable. He dropped his arms from her shoulders, anticipating the worst. He'd spent so much time assessing how he felt about her and hoping he could open up to Kate that he hadn't considered she might back away once he did let her in.

She tugged twice on his earlobe.

"What's that mean, a Ketchum signal for something I don't want to hear?"

"No, a Kate signal making sure you're real."

"You're so unpredictable."

"Ha! Look who's talking, Mr. I-bet-I-can-find-your-house -psychic!"

He laughed. "Yes, I keep it close to the vest, I guess." She had no idea how close, he thought.

"Do you mind? What do those tattoos mean? They're Vietnamese, I assume?"

Michael felt a chill as she ran her fingers over the memories, his lover, his child. The gesture was invasive, somehow. He could almost see the veins in his biceps swell as his muscles tensed. Why hadn't he put on his shirt before he'd let her in? He kept his voice steady and found the words he'd practiced for just such a time. "Oh, *Hy Vọng* means hope. We all really needed that over there. *Hằng* means"… he wanted to be honest without admitting it was also a woman's name…"Hằng means angel—angel in the full moon." He choked a bit. "Like, a guardian angel on my shoulder."

Michael let out a breath; he'd made it through the explanation. Hằng's face appeared with that same yearning look she had the day his unit moved out, and he'd left her standing beneath the tamarind tree.

"It's over, Michael."

The tone of Kate's whisper in his ear made him woozy and brought him back to the room. He held on. It's *over*? Their friendship, their music? He stiffened. His heart pounded.

Kate went up on her toes and kissed the scar on his neck. "It's over. Your angel on your shoulder…she did her work." Kate ran her hand over his shoulder, and he shuddered.

Hằng, I'm sorry.

"You're back, safe and sound."

Michael closed his eyes and sighed. Safe. Sound. Was he? Sound enough to be with Kate? "My mother said that phrase once too."

Michael felt the presence of Hằng through the entire Thanksgiving dinner at 101. But something had changed. It was as though she'd stood behind him, hands on his shoulders, supporting him. Hằng wanted him to be happy. He felt it.

How could he let her go so soon? Yet how could she stay with him now, watching him with Kate?

With a beer in hand, engulfed in aromas that held the promise of a luscious meal, Michael observed the family from the corner of the parlor. Thankfully, Michael had avoided the pot roast the night before by piling on the vegetables. He would be fine with the turkey.

Kate was away delivering food baskets for the church. Still, he felt content surrounded by her relatives and the hum of their banter. A big family suited him. You could lose yourself in the chaos of conversation and laughter, yet still feel connected, close. A kind of undemanding love.

An unkempt man entered the Ketchum's front door across from him. "Look who's here. It's Don," Kate's father announced. Scents of cinnamon and nutmeg in the house nearly covered over the incoming waft of stale booze and cigarettes. "Hey, Don, good to see you." They treated the down-on-his-luck homeless man as though he were a dear friend of the family.

Kate's youngest sister Kelly swept by Michael with a hello. She scanned the many wobbly card tables and folding chairs set up in every corner of the house, smiled at him, and dropped a napkin over the back of two chairs at the main table. "For you and Kate, she just arrived home."

They all sat, and Kate conducted introductions around the table with her arm tucked in his for support, no doubt. "There *will* be a quiz, Michael. Only thirty-seven names today." She leaned into him.

He laughed, put his napkin in his lap, and tried to memorize the faces with the names.

Seated next to Kate, her father clinked his fork against his glass, and everyone said grace. The meal began, and Michael enjoyed the lively conversation around him, while catching glimpses of Kate's happy face. It was contagious. Cousin Christine and her husband Jake sat to his right with a baby girl, Anna, bobbing on her lap. Next to Kate was a young cousin named Patrick, who kept leaning his head against Kate's shoulder, telling anyone who would listen, "Kate taught me to swim."

Cecelia brought a platter to Michael's side. She whispered, "I'm guessing meat isn't your thing." She winked and spoke up. "Those petite portions won't do, Michael. You don't want to insult the cook, do you?" She squeezed his shoulders and served him a mountain of hand-made cranberry and orange relish and her signature sage and oyster stuffing. "A way to a man's heart, you know."

"Thank you, Cecelia; I think you found the way to mine with that last scoop." He took Kate's hand under the table and squeezed.

The scent of Kate was all around him when he returned to Kate's bedroom. He found the source on the dresser, a half-empty bottle of Shalimar perfume. That citrus-sweet scent. Michael slept peacefully again, only awakening when the kitchen came alive again below him.

Departing was surprisingly difficult. Michael's chest felt heavy, as all the K's lined up to hug them and see them off. How do you leave a family like this? More affection than he had felt in twenty-four years from his own father. A room filled with people like his mother, open-hearted, yet a bit emotionally close-to-the-vest. That hands-off Ketchum kiss left to glow on his forehead. He felt, what? Accepted? Or was it loved? In love?

CHAPTER 25

ENCHANTING CANDLES

PUSHING THE THUMBTACK into the wall, Kate positioned the Polaroid family photo above her dorm room desk next to her map. Just off-center, Michael's honey hair glowed amidst the sea of redheads and brunettes. Propped-up on the wide windowsill next to her bed, she looked out at her favorite tree on the hillside where she and Michael had often stretched out in the grass practicing. It had taken on a different meaning. Their tree.

Tap, pause, tap-tap. Shiloh's signature knock interrupted Kate's thoughts.

"Entrée, Shi."

"Welcome back." Shiloh blew a kiss and perched herself on the end of the bed facing Kate and tucked her long skirt around her legs. She wasn't her usual, vivacious self. The flourish of sound from her silver bangles that habitually accompanied her presence was noticeably absent. Redness around Shiloh's eyes reminded Kate it had been a tough first holiday without her twin.

Kate stretched over and put a hand on Shiloh's shoulder. "Thanksgiving without Tim must have been so hard."

"It was strange and sad. My brother's empty chair screamed our loss at us through the whole the meal." Shiloh adjusted her orange print headband. "We all talked to fill the emptiness for a while, then just the sound of silverware clinking on plates, you know?"

Kate sat back in the window alcove in silence. "Saying *I'm sorry* is never enough. Cousin Danny wasn't my brother, but he was close and our band's guitarist. I remember that hollow feeling. I still have it every time I see his flag over our stage at the pub."

"I feel so empty without him, Kate—like half of me is missing."

"Well, it is." Kate hugged Shiloh.

"Thanks for understanding, though. But tell me, what happened with Michael? Was I right? I could use some good news."

"Good news? Let's see." Kate delayed and crossed her arms. What *was* her relationship with Michael now? Had it just been a fun and spontaneous, sentimental journey for Michael from his childhood trips to Glynn or the start of something more serious? It was so confusing. The shift from friend to whatever they were now was too new, too hard to explain, even to Shiloh. Kate could feel Shiloh's expectant stare.

"Well? Your favorite confidant is waiting here." Shiloh turned her palms up.

"I haven't really processed it all myself. I'm just thinking how to…"

It wasn't just a few little kisses… they were deep and

passionate and so unexpected. Yet it seemed so natural for them to slip into that closeness. Kate had wanted it; she was afraid to believe it. And that was no *friend* who lifted her off the stool on the stage and slow danced with her to the family's applause.

Saying it out loud made it more real. "Well, he did kiss me. Twice. Well, three times."

Clapping like a kid, Shiloh broke out in her usual engaging smile. "You were holding back. I knew it. Tell me everything."

Shuffling down off the windowsill, Kate sat across from Shiloh, mimicking her cross-legged position. She relayed the romantic details of the weekend to Shiloh's big, brown, enraptured eyes.

"How did he get along with your family? Was he his quiet self?"

"Quite the opposite of quiet." Kate related the bizarre coincidence of her parents' connection to their third-generation customer.

"Hysterical. I can just picture your shocked face."

It *had* felt like fate when her mother ran into Michael's arms. Magical and comical after she'd worried all the way there about how it would all go. Kate could see Michael standing in her childhood bedroom, struggling to put his shirt on. When she'd kissed the scar on his neck, brushed her hands over his exotic tattoos, and breathed in the faint scent of his English Leather, she'd experienced such a new level of intimacy and caring, like falling in love. It was wonderful; it was threatening to cross the threshold from the known of their friendship to the unknown of a potential future together.

Shiloh examined the family photo on the wall like Sherlock

Holmes. "I can't imagine a family this big. Look how his head is tilted toward yours. That angle screams, *couple*. And his hand on your shoulder." She hugged Kate. "I'm so excited for you two."

"Thanks, me too, but there's still his strange, distracted look. He definitely had it on the drive back to campus." Kate was afraid Shiloh's enthusiasm would cloud her judgment.

"He's a war vet; it's common to have memories of the war that need pushing away. I wouldn't see that as a threat. He'll tell you, eventually."

"True. I just don't want to get ahead of myself." In one way, Kate had come to see Michael's classic faraway look as her ally. Wouldn't a little distance keep him from breaking her heart? She could easily lose her mind over this enigmatic guy. "Michael says he wants to live overseas."

Shiloh arched one eye. "Overseas? Did he say that before or after the kisses?"

"Before, on the drive there. I asked what his dreams were for the future. I felt threatened by his overseas dreams, somehow. I can't imagine not being with him every day and singing."

"Let's not jump ahead; graduation's three semesters from now." Shiloh put both hands over Kate's as if to prevent both of them from getting too eager.

"Shi, you know me and world travel…since childhood. I admit; I'm a little envious of being able to just decide you're going to live overseas. What a dream. And isn't it crazy to get close to a guy who was already planning to leave?" Kate glanced at the map with the red and blue pushpins scattered throughout the continents. Either way, she realized what Michael chose to do now would affect her future. If his dream was to move overseas, would that include her? What if she had an opportunity already in place here? She'd hope it would work out. It felt too soon to even think about their plans together. The future changes made her feel unsettled.

Shiloh sat back down on the end of the bed and looked out the window. A few dark clouds were clustering over the hilltop. "Maybe go easy on things with Michael. It's so new."

"Listen to Miss 'jump right in; life's too short.' Seriously, you're right. I'm more concerned that I don't have a solid idea about my own career yet." Kate wasn't ready to share her thoughts about Rolling Hills. She knew so little about how it would work. Was her path right in front of her? There was an irresistible pull. Maybe she did have a gift for getting through to people who were differently abled, as her aunt had said. Had the Rolling Hills Orchestra and Jimmy put it all together for Kate? Why was she nervous about asking Shiloh to the concert? Would she think Kate was crazy giving up on her singing hopes?

"What's going on in that head of yours. These long silences?"

"Sorry. Are you busy Saturday night? There's a concert at Rolling Hills."

The look of disbelief on Shiloh's face added to Kate's reluctance to share her fascination with the institution.

"I didn't have a chance to tell you what happened when I went to buy candles just before Thanksgiving." Kate described her experience with the orchestra—the captivating sound and the way the people had astonishingly come together in concert. "You need to hear them. There's a young guy named Jimmy who plays the saxophone. He's a natural; well, it's so amazing, no lessons, he just started to play." She struggled to explain the term, *idiot savant*, hating to use that word *idiot* for such talented musicians. Waiting for Shiloh's response made Kate uncomfortable, almost embarrassed about her interest in the dilapidated place for her career.

"If I didn't know you, I would think you were joking." Shiloh put her hand to her chest. "But I'm intrigued. You have to admit, it does sound hard to believe. I'm in for the concert."

"Oh, and Bobby at the cafeteria plays the violin."

"Bobby? *Dishwasher* Bobby?" Shiloh tilted her head and squinted her eyes.

Noting the bluster of the November evening rattling the trees across the road, Kate snaked her vibrant, turquoise scarf around her neck, put on her peacoat, and took the elevator.

In the dorm lobby, Michael embraced her in a bear hug and kissed her. "I've missed you," he whispered and lingered with his lips pressed against her ear.

Again she was flooded with an electrifying sensation in his arms. Kate didn't say much during the ten-minute walk. She caught Michael's questioning glance, but she was lost in thought. Serious thoughts. She was falling hard for him—a first for Kate, and she needed to know if this was fun, convenient, or just a fling for him. Things were different with Michael. It wasn't like they'd just met. The two of them had spent a part of nearly every day together building a close friendship since she'd first come to UConn. And there was so much at stake if things didn't work out. What would happen to their singing?

It began to drizzle, and Michael opened the blue and white

UConn umbrella. "You're awfully quiet. What are you cooking up? My goose?"

"Ha. No, just thinking about my future."

"I can't believe the year is half over; one more semester and we're seniors." The rain started to thwack the sidewalk; she took his arm, and they rushed up the steps and tucked in under the canopy.

Keeping it in anymore was impossible. She stopped him from opening the door. "Michael..." Was Kate foolish to ask so soon? No, she had to. They had enough history; she should be able to be honest. "You know how you say I always speak my mind?"

"What an opening line. Let me have it."

"What did those kisses in the factory mean?" She thrust the words out in a single stream. "Was it just a spontaneous thing, a sentimental moment? Because if it was, it's OK but..." Taking a calming breath, she pushed on, "...we're both trying to figure out our lives, and we're not kids; I think we need to be brave enough to be open, don't you?"

Staring into his eyes, Kate tried to read the changing looks on his face. She tapped her hand on her thigh and waited for his answer. Any answer, just so she knew where they were headed.

"We *should* be open. I need to learn to do that more, Kate." He dug the point of the umbrella into the porch floor. "I don't know where we're headed...exactly."

She closed her eyes, and regret caught her breath. Michael was backing away. Better to know now, she counseled herself as disappointment washed through her.

Michael pushed her hair behind her ear and leaned over and

kissed her cheek. "But wherever that is, I can't imagine not going there together."

She tried to dampen her reaction, the joy, the thrill of the door opening to their relationship, their new love. "I...feel that way too." Every part of her said yes. It surprised her how easy it was for her to go from friend to lover with this perplexing guy.

In the past, Michael would have taken advantage of the rain's rhythmic noise to avoid the conversation, Kate thought. But something had changed. Some channels had opened since their visit to her family.

Michael put his arm around her. "I'm so happy. With you. With us." He crushed her in his arms and kissed her forehead. "Better get close, or you'll get chilled."

"Very cute, Mr. James, using my family signature kiss to seal the deal."

"You say you can read me like a book, remember? I'm reading *your* book now." He laughed.

Luigi and Sophia's was nearly empty when they arrived. They sat in the little Italian hole-in-the-wall on a side street on the edge of campus. Kate loved the charming, bare-bones spot they'd share after their afternoon gigs at the Student Union. The owner took their order. "The usual?"

Matching plates of Kate's favorite eggplant parmigiana sat in front of them in the flickering candlelight on the red checkered, plastic tablecloth. She flipped the layer of luscious homemade buffalo mozzarella from the top of her dish. The spicy aroma rose, as she folded the cheese on the side of her plate.

Michael forked it over to his dish in their unspoken ritual.

"I hate to break the spell. Tell me; what else is going on?" He took her hand across the table.

"You *are* getting good at reading me. I must be slipping."

He spun his glass on the tablecloth and smiled. "Well, it is a mystery book though, Kate. Like Nancy Drew."

"You're funny."

Michael filled her jelly glass with a too-purple wine.

Cutting a bite of the oily veal, Kate ate it and swirled a crust of bread in the bright sauce, buying time. "I want to talk about a concert." It took the entire meal to explain how she felt— what she'd seen at Rolling Hills, the uplifting music, and Jimmy's transformation. Why did it touch her so deeply?

CHAPTER 26

CAPTIVATING CONCERT

AS MICHAEL PULLED up the winding Rolling Hills campus road, the excitement started inside Kate. "You two are going to be amazed." She looked over her shoulder at Shiloh in the back seat. "Seriously, this is not a charity event. Prepare to be astonished. Just pull up to the main building here and drop me; I'll get the tickets from the school director and meet you over at the music hall, third building over." She pointed.

Inside the main building, Kate found Brent in his office.

"Oh, thanks for coming. I have your tickets. It's not quite a sellout, but a good crowd tonight."

"Thank you." She tucked them in her pocketbook. I have a quick question; I know you're busy."

"Shoot."

She looked around the room painted a pretty azure blue, unlike the institutional-green walls in the hallways. The walls were decorated with Brent's Yale diploma, a few plaques recognizing contributions to the community, a photo of him with his arm around a woman, and a grouping of artwork Kate recognized. They were lovely landscape scenes of the lush campus. Through the Venetian blinds, a spotlight illuminated a garden withering in the chill of the turning season.

"Love the color." Kate ran her hand down the wall.

"My wife's touch." He blushed a bit.

Kate looked at the diploma. "Just curious, what kind of educational requirements do you need to work here?" She couldn't miss his look of surprise.

"Depends on what job. Teachers have at least a teaching certificate and a B.A., some a Masters in special ed. Are you interested?"

"I'm...not sure, but the orchestra really captivated me."

"I remember your amazed look. Very gratifying."

His unpretentious way made Kate feel unusually open. "I'd always hoped I would sing professionally. This work seems more...can I be bold enough to ask, do you like working here?"

"Here? Not for a minute."

His answer made Kate step back. "Really? I thought..."

Brent laughed and swept his arm around. "Here? No. But with these people? Absolutely. My wife works here too; she heads the art program." He put his hands on his hips, scanned the paintings, and smiled. But it's not for the faint-hearted. Still interested?"

"I might be."

"If you ever are, see Dr. Goodman. Director of the Ed. Psych department. She's a friend; she can tell you everything you need to know." He checked his watch, straightened his tie, and swept his navy sport coat up from the back of his chair. "Sorry, I have to go make sure the musicians are ready."

"Of course, thanks, sorry to have kept you."

"You know..." Brent turned around. "Since your into music, you might want to stick around for the jam session we have after the concert. Can't promise anything, but we have some local musicians who sit in with the group sometimes. It's fun. Very casual. There's a dance floor for the spontaneous ones."

"Really? That sounds like fun. My friend plays the piano, but he didn't bring his own."

"Oh, she's a comedian too." He laughed and saluted. "See you at the concert."

Brent had such a warmth and passion about him. Kate could almost imagine being a part of his team.

Cutting through the buildings to the Music Hall, Kate entered a hallway filled with residents and guests. She was elated. The whole thing was inspiring, and watching Michael and Shiloh's faces would be a highlight of the night. She hoped. Kate knew they were a bit skeptical. It was so important for them to get it and to have their support. She needed to test her theory about the place, to build her confidence in the idea. It was so different from anything she'd ever considered for her future.

She found Michael and Shiloh waiting at the door. Lined-up behind them was a handful of ticket holders with their own instruments in hand.

The trio relinquished their tickets, took their programs, and were seated in the front row on folding chairs.

Michael leaned over and scanned the front row sprinkled with the gray-haired people with leather music cases of all shapes and sizes. "I didn't know you were supposed to bring your own instrument." Michael shuttled his eyes from case to case.

"Local retired musicians, sometimes they jam at the end, Brent told me."

"Really?" Shiloh glanced at Kate skeptically. "Who knew this was here?"

"And there's a piano if you want to join in." Kate nudged Michael.

The orchestra streamed in and took their places on the three-level stage. A small boy, or was he a very short young man, hobbled onto the upper level with a set of cymbals nearly his size. The same drummer boy she'd seen before took his place, and dozens of musicians, young and old, wielding brass, woodwinds, and stringed instruments settled in.

"Oh my God, you weren't kidding. It's Bobby from the cafeteria." Shiloh waved to him.

He grinned and waved back, then cocked his head and closed one eye to listen as he plucked a string on his violin to tune it.

"I'm finding this hard to believe. Bobby, our *dishwasher?*" Shiloh shifted to the front of her chair and scanned the musicians under Kate's studied gaze.

Jimmy's eyes went wide as he entered the Music Hall. He hugged the sax and stood frozen in place. Then, swaying to self-soothe, as Kate had seen him do before, he dropped his head and shuffled through the chatting crowd to take his place on stage.

"That's Jimmy. Watch this transformation." Kate leaned forward.

Players readied themselves, and the audience got seated. The usual warm-up with whining sounds like cars with bad brakes ensued. The metamorphosis took place as the first song began—a blues number—"The House of the Rising Sun." Brass instruments flashed under the spotlights, violins swayed, drums captured the soul of the dirge-like beat—an emotional, breathtaking performance complimented by the low hum of the audience singing along.

Kate watched Shiloh's boot and Michael's loafer tapping the slow beat as they exchanged astounded looks. Their upturned hands, open mouths and heads shaking, mouthing *no way*, was exactly the first response she'd had. Kate clapped and laughed silently at their reactions, then reached over and tapped each of their knees. "I told you."

The concert went on, lilting through jazz and blues numbers, exploding with movie theme songs, pop, and marching band pieces, all played skillfully.

"Kate, I'm loving this." Shiloh bobbed her head to the music.

With each song, Kate became more enchanted with the whole experience, and the reactions of her boyfriend and best friend drove it home.

After the last song and an appreciative round of applause, the musicians left through the back door. Most of the audience filed out to the parking lot humming and singing the lyrics of the final tune.

"OK, Kate, that was amazing; I'll give you that." Shiloh hugged her. "So glad you invited me."

"I've never seen anything like it. Thanks, sweetheart." Michael touched her face. "So now there's a jam session?"

A group of Rolling Hills musicians drifted back in after their break, and the guests in the front row pulled their chairs over to the stands, opened their leather cases, and began to tune their instruments.

Hugging his beloved sax, Jimmy dropped his head and approached Kate. "One bayberry tower, six vanilla votives, five-dollar bill, two dollars change." He pointed his chin toward his shoulder and cast his eyes aside.

Kate introduced Jimmy to Shiloh and Michael, warning them in a whisper not to shake his hand. They showered him with compliments.

Jimmy sighed and grinned. "Thank you. I like playing. I might be good."

"Michael plays the piano, and he is good too, maybe you'd like to play with him."

"OK."

Michael squeezed Kate's shoulder. "I'll play if you sing. What do you think, will you sing with Jimmy and me?"

Kate liked the change in Michael—flirtatious, and fun. "Deal."

She'd never sung with an orchestra. Kate wouldn't know the first thing about the signals the conductor gives to make the whole thing work in synch. But the idea of jamming, singing with Jimmy's sax, and crooning along with Michael on the piano was enticing.

"Only if Kate sings with us, right? How about "Summertime," do you know that one, Jimmy?"

"OK. Uh, yes."

"Ladies and gentleman, we'll begin our impromptu jam session. Let's keep it fun and spontaneous, as always." The conductor and Brent stood on the side and listened as the musicians kicked it off. "Feel free to dance. Whatever lights you up," Brent announced.

His words caught Kate's attention. Whatever lights you up.

Like her mother had said, something that lights you up. Only you will know, Kate. A chill flowed down her arms.

Does anyone have a request?"

"Mustang Sally." A voice called out from the other side of the room.

It was like a private party. Only a few dozen musicians and guests remained. Two older gentlemen danced with Rolling Hills women residents in their pleated skirts and pilled sweaters, housecoats, and limp hair pinned back with Bobbie pins.

A young red-headed woman with a ponytail, named Barbie, asked Michael to dance. Dressed in a flowered house dress and Keds, she bobbed her head, twisted left and right with shyness, walked pigeon-toed, and followed him to the dance floor. Michael seemed to enjoy seeing her happy.

Kate was touched by his kindness.

A young guy in green pants and an oversized dress shirt pointed, "Ooooh, Barbie likes that boy." The group laughed, then he stopped in front of Shiloh, his body shrinking in as his shyness took over.

Gyrating in her signature, free-spirited way, Shiloh started to dance with him. The boy copied her every move. Holding each end of his loosened tie, he slid it back and forth in his collar like drying himself after a shower.

"Mustang Sally, a huh, a huh..." The orchestra and local musicians rocked back and forth, grapevine steps left and right, brass horns swinging up and down, like elephant trunks.

At the next song, Michael demonstrated a dance and Barbie imitated, elbows held close-in, feet shifting side-to-side, her head nodding perfectly to the beat. Others, who'd chosen partners, folded in behind them and filled the dance floor. The joy was palpable.

At the next break in the music, Michael called out, "Summertime." He took his place at the piano. "Jimmy, come on, buddy, let's play for Kate."

Kate took the mic, and Jimmy approached.

"Kick us off, Jimmy." Michael played a few lead-in notes of the song to attract the audience's attention, and the room settled down.

Quivering, Jimmy brought the sax to his mouth. The room was silent, except for Michael's lead-in and, finally, Jimmy's perfect notes.

Kate cradled the mic and chimed in. The bluesy song flooded the room. She'd never blended her voice with the sensuous ache of a saxophone before. Other instruments joined in.

With his eyes closed, Jimmy's fingers skillfully skipped up and down the neck of the sax like fluttering butterflies landing on the final notes.

The enchanting fusion of human vocals and the woozy woodwind vibrated through Kate. Beyond description. Kate was transported to that place she'd always loved with Michael playing along beside her.

CHAPTER 27

ANALOGIES AND AUDACITY

AS KATE HURRIEDLY made her way to Dr. Goodman's office through the December chill, she could barely contain her excitement. The past semester had been a whirlwind of activity. Her relationship with Michael had taken off. After Thanksgiving with her family, they'd moved seamlessly from best of friends to best of lovers. He respected her need to find her own way. And he'd fit right in with her family. Even her brothers loved him. Was marriage somewhere off on the horizon? Every time she thought of that, she laughed at herself. Kate, the one who had no interest in commitment.

Making her way to the Educational Psychology building, Kate felt like she'd left her body. She was traveling somewhere out over a string of future moments, fantasizing—teaching and singing with an orchestra of young musicians, a farewell party for her and Michael after graduate school before leaving for... where? Maybe their first overseas assignment? It caught her in the chest. It could all work out so well, *if* she could get into Dr. Goodman's program.

Being a regular, singing at the Student Union with Michael and performing solo when he had classes, had been so gratifying. Stumbling onto the Rolling Hills opportunity when she'd simply gone to buy some candles for her mother for Thanksgiving made her laugh. You never know where the spark will come from that lights you up.

At the library, Kate researched the field of special education. Then she'd discovered the article on passion by Dr. Dorothy Goodman, the Head of the Educational Psychology Department. It was inspiring. Kate tucked her research under her arm, left the library, and headed for Goodman's office.

Crossing the quadrangle through the usual anti-war student sit-in, she reached the building. The images from the Rolling Hills concert had entirely inhabited Kate, leaving no room for other considerations. This had to be the spark her mother had talked about.

The mahogany chair was cold and slippery, the miniskirt, a big mistake. Waiting for an appointment with Dr. Goodman, Kate read the requirements for a Special Ed major. Her own nerve made Kate laugh inside. Was she crazy?

Shiloh hadn't blinked when Kate told her about her plan; she'd told her to go for it. After attending the concert, her friend understood. So would Michael, wouldn't he? Kate had held off talking to him until she'd done her research, but she'd discovered the deadline for class registration was today. Kate lost her nerve for a minute and imagined herself escaping the office. She rose to leave.

"Miss Ketchum, this way, please." The director's assistant shuffled her into the inner office before Kate could change her mind.

The last thing she saw on the wall by the door made her laugh—the framed magazine article Kate had just read with the heading "Follow Your Passion." You can't make this stuff up, Kate thought.

"Ms. Ketchum?"

"Yes, nice to meet you, Dr. Goodman." Kate found herself shaking hands with a fifty-something, attractive woman. They both sat, enshrined with diplomas, awards, and photos with illuminaries like JFK and Gloria Steinem. Impeccably dressed in a linen suit, her dark hair swept back, the department head was commanding.

Goodman removed her glasses and leaned back on her leather desk chair. "So, my good friend and colleague Brent sent you?" The director was confident and no-nonsense but with a warmth in her eyes. "I understand you're interested in changing majors to special education? And your current major is music?"

"Yes, Ma'am. Well, actually, if it's possible, I'd love to see if I could do a double major." Kate folded her hands to keep them from shaking.

"Double? Ambitious...well, there are certain requirements you're already missing. Nearly an entire semester behind, actually."

Kate conjured up her mother's words, *Kathryn Ketchum, you can do anything.* Did she want to work with special young musicians, like Jimmy, who brought that quiver of delight to her stomach and ache to her heart? Kate didn't even know how that all worked. She had a music background; she knew she needed the teaching credentials. Could she tolerate a place like Rolling Hills? Could she work overseas if she followed Michael on his path? She didn't know. Kate was spiraling down into a sea of unanswered questions. She didn't dare ask those questions and weaken her case or give the woman who held her fate a chance to see Kate's naiveté and say, no.

"Ms. Ketchum, you want to say something?"

"Yes." Kate took a chance mimicking a phrase her dad had used all the time—what would it take for you to... "Dr. Goodman, as a scholarship student, I don't have much going for me but my driving passion, and well, a 3.8 GPA, and a history of hard-working factory workers behind me..." Kate took a breath. "What would it take for you to let me into your program? Would you consider taking a chance on someone with a passion for music and kids who are... who are different? A person who needs a little boost to change her life?"

Goodman pushed her chair back as if to leave more space for Kate's oversized idea. She tapped an envelope on her desk. "Brent has a good feeling about you. He doesn't say that often."

Kate held her gaze. "I know this may seem audacious, but... my mother says you never get anything without *asking*." Kate leaned forward in her chair. "Dr. Goodman, I *want* this."

The feeling was there, like hanging her head back on her swing as a child, that sizzling thrill that made your stomach flip. A sure way to know the cliff you just leapt off of was the right one.

"I will admit you're passionate *and* convincing, and I love your mother's wisdom."

The words pushed at Kate's lips... "So maybe I can make up the missing requirements? I worked two jobs through community college; maybe I could...take a full load, or take the additional requirements over the summer to get a double major in music and special ed.?" Kate let out a clipped, embarrassed laugh. How would she handle the cost of summer school, and where would she live?

"Here are the problems. First, you need Early Childhood Development 101. You're missing a statistics course, an internship, and you haven't taken the Miller Analogies Test, an absolute requirement—it correlates with success in this field. And I assume you would consider our Human Learning Master's program with a focus on special education once you've graduated? The master's program is very competitive but the best way to secure the kind of job you want."

Goodman was testing her passion now. Kate only had a scholarship to finish college. She wanted to run from the office. Why hadn't she thought this through? Where would she get the funds? But it worked perfectly with Michael's future plans for grad school at UConn too.

Dr. Goodman picked up the phone.

Kate's first thought was, she's calling security to say, *get this maniac out of my office.*

Goodman asked her colleague to conduct a private test in the psychology department and hung up. "Ms. Ketchum, here's one step you'll have to take in any case. Go to Dr. Fletcher's office, room 302, in the Psychology Department. He's waiting for you. Come back here for the results after lunch. If you get in the 85th percentile, 85th, absolutely no less, you understand, *and* get into the two courses and ace them this spring, I'll arrange an internship with Brent this summer. According to your past performance, I have no doubt you will do well...then you will be positioned to apply to get your master's after you graduate. "No guarantees, you understand."

Kate melted into the chair with the news. Too much to take in. She stood and turned toward the door. "Thank you, Dr. Goodman; thank you for considering me."

Dr. Goodman stared at the outdated photo of herself leaning into her husband, surrounded by two young daughters on a white ski slope, then looked up at Kate. "Good luck."

The Miller Analogy Test was so strange, like no other test she'd ever taken—a car is to a frog as your mother is to a sled. Crazy comparisons that made Kate laugh. Nonetheless, puns and plays on words were at the core of the Ketchum family's humor.

Three hours later, Kate returned to Goodman's office for the results and to report she'd weaseled her way into the two closed classes in the Education Department. She'd left off the part that she'd used Goodman's name to get in. *Dr. Goodman has asked if you would make an exception and add me to your roster next semester. I know it's late,* she'd said to each professor... A slight twinge of guilt wasn't enough to stop Kate from her little hustle. The end swould justify it.

"So, I've registered for both classes, and..."

"Yes," Goodman had a smirk on her face. "Both professors called me to let me know that they had complied with my request."

The blush raged across Kate's cheeks.

Caught in her desperation, Kate said, "I...well, truthfully, I'm embarrassed as indicated by my sudden sunburned face in

December...I confess, I'd do it again. Anyway, thank you..."
Kate got up to leave.

"Don't you want your score?"

"What?"

"The Miller's, your test score?"

"But I thought..."

"98th percentile, Ms. Ketchum. A first for this department. I will see you next semester. We'll make things work." Goodman smiled and looked in Kate's eyes for an insufferably long time. "Impressive, albeit a bit shady—your passion, very impressive."

It gave Kate a bit of hope and a touch of embarrassment.

"Here's to you for doing your homework. You know, reading my *passion* article?"

"Was it that obvious?" Kate stopped at the door and resumed her red-faced hue—she was caught in the act. Her legs went weak. "Oh, Dr. Goodman, one more thing...regarding graduate school, just to be upfront, I...I don't have any money. I don't know why I thought I could go after I graduate."

Goodman laughed. "Oh, what a surprise; you mean all you brought was your *audacity*?" She flashed a quick look between her daughters in the photo and Kate. "I have a fellowship I just might make available to someone as passionate as you."

CHAPTER 28

Michael

PAYOFF FOR THE PAST

SOMETIMES MICHAEL MARVELED at the progress he had made since coming to UConn. Of course, he still thought of Hàng often, but things were good with Kate. Conversations were going in the direction of a lifetime together after dating for nearly two years. The summer weeks they'd spent at the lake house had been perfect. They both loved being in nature. And all the holidays he'd spent with the Ketchums since that first Thanksgiving made him feel like he belonged. When Michael had brought up his desire to live overseas someday, or Kate shared her future dreams of travel and singing, they both talked as if they'd be together.

Only a month before, in April, he and Kate had celebrated his acceptance to the UConn Graduate School of International Diplomacy. Honestly, he'd applied to grad school to be near Kate since she was so excited about her potential master's program with Dr. Goodman. Now as they approached graduation, they faced the unexpected. She hadn't receive an acceptance letter. Her disappointment over the grad school debacle was an understatement. It was so strange that after her 3.8 grades in both of the required classes and catching up on her requirements, Kate still hadn't gotten into the master's program. Senior year, spring semester almost over—now what, Kate had said. It had all gone so fast. Wouldn't she love to live overseas like she'd always dreamed?

Michael took the path around the rim of the lake to his fraternity house, where he'd agreed to meet Mr. Harrington for the interview. Skirting the center of the campus where the sit-ins and protests had always caught fire, he thought of his friend, Greg. Michael was surprised that his buddy from the war had talked to his father about Michael's talents and interests. Mr. Harrington's transfer from Washington, DC, to be Deputy Chief of Mission in Bangkok had been perfect timing.

What exactly was the job he'd mentioned on their brief call? Greg's father had given no specifics. He'd only mentioned it involved the arts. Ever since interning in Thailand with his uncle, Michael had always wanted to work in the foreign service, or for a non-profit far away from home. Still, he'd never imagined a job involving the performing arts. Who would have thought Michael's constant talk about missing playing the piano and singing with Greg through their war traumas would have resulted in a job offer to work at the American Embassy in Thailand?

Speaking Thai was a requirement for the opportunity, Greg's father had said on the phone. Michael's daily obsession with learning Thai during his summer internship in Bangkok was paying off. The musicality of the tonal languages, both Vietnamese and Thai, had captivated Michael. Five tones, like singing a song, each word had its assigned note. High, rising, low, mid, and falling—mistakes were easy if you couldn't carry a tune.

Would Kate think he was nuts turning down grad school and spontaneously accepting a job halfway around the world? An advanced degree on a politically-heated college campus had been a mistake for him, Michael realized.

Michael passed a group of students at the edge of the lake holding a sit-in, protesting the war. They tapped handmade signs on the grass, a rhythm of dull thuds like a tribal war call. He needed to get on with his life. After two tours in Vietnam, the constant reminders were hard to tolerate, and school just didn't suit him anymore at his age. Being at UConn made him feel he was stalling in his life.

There had been a constant far-off blare of chants lately. Always a hint of smoke in the air from bonfires, spontaneously lit by activist students in the quadrangle—burning books— anti-napalm, anti-war, anti-racism protests. The agitation and mimicking sounds of combat were unnerving. He needed to get away from all the conflict. He was ripe for the principles but wrong for the fray. And a job overseas was what he'd always wanted.

The scene in Vietnam repeated as Michael walked down the hallway to the meeting room. Memories of Greg's pleading face flashed—the scene broke open: Michael dragging his fellow Marine from under the toppled jeep with the deadly chaos around them; Greg lifted by the copter and swept away into the sooty sky. Michael had done it on instinct; he didn't feel like a hero. Greg was his friend, his crew buddy from Harvard.

Mr. Harrington looked so much like a seasoned version of Greg—tall, willowy, craggy face and kind blue eyes. "Michael, great to see you again."

They shook hands and sat on the burgundy upholstered chairs in front of the fireplace.

"I know this is sudden, but frankly, the position came up unexpectedly while I was on home leave, and Greg suggested you. Well, it seemed like a good idea. So, Michael. Here's the position. A junior officer in the United States Information Service office at the Bangkok embassy. You'll be helping with cultural exchanges—the arts, music, dance, that kind of thing—bringing American performers to Thailand. Interested?"

Michael could hardly hear the rest of what Harrington had to say; he'd almost laughed, it was so perfect. There was talk of needing to speak basic Thai, details of salary range, a required pre-departure program and language test in Washington, DC. Michael found himself shaking hands again and accepting the job.

As he left the formal room, Michael glanced at his uncle's portrait and turned. "Oh, and sir, if all goes well, I will be bringing my wife."

"Wonderful, I'll note that." The man in the blue suit and red tie smiled.

"Well, she doesn't know it yet. And Kate really isn't my wife yet, but..."

Michael didn't mind that Mr. Harrington laughed. "And she's a professional singer, an amazing singer."

"Then, I'll wish you and your bended-knee good luck. If your fiancé is as good as you say, we can always have her represent the U.S. singing at Bangkok's Thai American Club. There's a spot opening up. I'll arrange an audition as soon as you arrive. The Thai's can't get enough of our music, and the expatriate Americans love a slice of home."

"Really? Thank you. That's amazing. She would love that; it's a dream of hers."

"One more thing, Michael. If not for your bravery, well..." Mr. Harrington's words were thick with emotion. "Greg's mother and I want to thank you again...for what you did for our son. For us. We're grateful, and Greg says Semper Fi."

Michael shook Mr. Harrington's hand. "We got ourselves into that war together; we promised to get each other out." Michael could see the two of them standing outside the recruiting center in Boston, patting each other's backs—they'd had no idea what they were getting into. "Greg's a great guy. Please tell him when I come back from Bangkok on home leave, I'll come see him, and we'll catch up."

"And I'll see you and your new wife in Bangkok." He winked at Michael. "And I'm glad you can accommodate the short notice; as I said, the job opened unexpectedly, and we need you over there to plan the upcoming season."

"No problem. This will be amazing."

Michael's feet were light as he climbed the stairs two-at-a-time to return to his room. He had the skills to pass the basic language test in DC, and they'd be off to Bangkok in a few weeks after the State Department got his papers in order and he had his orientation and inoculations.

He wished there had been time to discuss the decision with Kate. She was in class when the call came, and then she had her show at the Student Union. He knew Kate was getting nervous without her plans in place since, surprisingly, she hadn't been accepted to Dr. Goodman's graduate program. She would love the chance to sing in Bangkok. How could she not? Kate's and Michael's goals would be achieved.

Doubts interrupted his joy. The realities of his situation became more apparent. They would leave in a few weeks. He hoped Kate would see this opportunity the same way he did. The new job had changed everything.

The wave of high from his good fortune was replaced by a sinking in his stomach. Did he just make a big mistake? Was accepting the position in Southeast Asia some twisted way of feeling closer to Ha`ng? That new thought threatened the stability he'd worked so hard to find. No, he wouldn't entertain that thought.

Back in his room, Michael called the administration building and withdrew his acceptance to grad school. It was freeing. The Bangkok position with the United States Information Service was a perfect fit for him, and singing in Bangkok was one of Kate's pins in her old map. Still, it made him nervous—guess what, Kate, we have two weeks to get married, then travel to Washington for a week, and then move to Bangkok. Now that he was out of school and had a source of income, he wouldn't worry about his grandmother pulling the purse strings tight on his trust fund if she disapproved of his "selection" as she would say. He'd make it on his own.

He was jumping the gun. First, he had to propose; Kate had to accept. They were good together, and as long as she was with him, in nature, singing, and talking, he was calm, no flashbacks; they were happy. And damn, she was gorgeous.

Reaching into the bottom of the desk drawer for some stationery, Michael found his only photo remaining of Ha`ng.

He would have to let it go. He stared at the discolored scene—Michael in uniform, gear on his back, helmet dangling from his hand, his arm around beautiful, smiling Hàng dressed in traditional clothes, her head resting on his chest. A circle of smiling family and villagers surrounded them. He tucked it back into his drawer. He would do away with it ceremoniously and with respect, let it drift off into the lake—a symbol of his moving on, a tribute to Kate. And yes, Hàng often came to mind with an ache, but he loved Kate. He wasn't drawn to Thailand to get closer to where he'd met Hàng. No, he'd been captivated by Bangkok before he was sent to Vietnam, and he loved Kate, everything about her.

Maybe Father Sullivan would marry them. There was little time to make plans. So much to figure out. Now what had seemed natural and wonderful seemed crazy.

Michael walked to the window. Flowers were popping up along the beds in the quadrangle. How did this all happen? He would be part of her Ketchum family. She wouldn't have to give up performing and singing. Michael pictured her singing on a stage overlooking the lights of the foreign capital.

He sat down and jiggled his leg as he tried to write a thank you note to his benefactor. It was impossible to express his gratitude. His words fell short. After several tries, Michael slid the thank you note into the envelope, addressed it, and affixed a stamp. Kate would be back any minute from her final performance at the Student Union. He felt he would explode with the news.

CHAPTER 29

Kate

LOST LETTER

KATE COULD ALWAYS remember the shoes she'd worn for the milestones in her life. Running from Sacred Heart school in brown leather Buster Brown's to tell her parents she'd gotten her first "A." Cutting across the alleys in black patent leather Mary Janes in the eighth grade, to tell her best friend that a boy had kissed her. And now, adding her purple suede platforms to her catalog of shoe memories. She ran from Goodman's office to the Student Lounge, dragging her guitar case, a blue satchel of music, and a letter with the good news.

Her acceptance had been lost in her dorm mailroom. Goodman's concerned call had cleared up the error. Could it be any better—Michael and Kate both on the same trajectory, grad school—and she had the fellowship to pay for it? Such fantastic prospects were in sight with her summer internship at Rolling Hills and grad school in the fall.

As soon as she told Michael, she would call her mother and father. Two emotions battled inside her. The joy of her future plans and the regret that sat in her stomach when she propped up on her stool to sing for the last time in the Student Union. Nearly two years. There would be no performing during finals or for the summer; she would be too busy with classes wrapping up and the Rolling Hills internship. It had been a tough decision; but it was the right one, and she would have the orchestra at Rolling Hills to satisfy her music cravings.

Pushing back the edge of her fringed suede cape, that worse-for-wear signature outfit of Kate's, she managed to get through the Judy Collins lyrics to "Both Sides Now" without breaking down. A challenge, but she'd made it, cracking only on the last note. Just like the song said, she really didn't know life at all. No one noticed her tears in the ring of the applause. A few of her regulars gathered around her.

"You're like a fixture here, Kate."

"I'll miss you, Kate."

She was touched by the words of her followers who had loyally hung around over coffee in the afternoon all semester, or napped on a stack of books, or slumped in a corner against the tile wall near the fireplace listening, nodding, smiling, and tapping their feet. She'd missed Michael at the piano on the two days he'd had classes in the afternoon, but singing daily at the Student Union had become her new O'Leary's. Another departure? Or maybe she would have time to sing again in grad school.

Without a doubt, she looked at her college life from both sides now—her dedicated and intense studying at community college, soon graduation from UConn and on to graduate school—Kate Ketchum, daughter of cordwainers. It had been over in a flash. Except for the campus riots, she'd loved it all.

Leaving her last solo show at the Student Union, she felt like a child whose beloved toy was being taken away just because she'd outgrown it. You're too old for that, Katie. Too old to be singing for tips at the Student Union, she thought.

Packing up her guitar, Kate ran to the Kappa Sig house. She needed Michael's arms around her—she was excited to tell him about grad school. For months they'd danced around discussions of marriage. They'd fantasized living together in the married graduate students' dorm and attending their master's programs. Then she hadn't received her expected acceptance.

There was one thing they needed to do. Kate had to meet his parents. She understood that Michael's mother was out-of-town most of the past year-and-a-half caring for her sister in Arizona. He'd wanted his mother to be there when Kate met his father and grandmother. His grandmother was always traveling, or Kate and Michael had schoolwork, or their performing commitments had gotten in the way. It was time.

The house was quiet, she thought. Not wanting to announce her arrival to the entire world, Kate removed her platform shoes when she reached Michael's hallway. Knowing everyone would recognize her thumping footfall, she didn't feel like stopping to chit chat with Michael's frat brothers. The news was ready to burst from her.

Kate tip-toed up the hallway and stopped. Michael's door was open. One thing Kate loved about the fraternity house was the wood. Beautiful wood desks with tooled legs. The rich dark trim around the window framed her handsome boyfriend and let in the glow of the day end's sunlight around his mahogany desk. It lit the remaining golden highlights of his platinum hair, leftover from last summer at his lake house. She'd watched the sheen fade week by week at the hands of the bitter New England winter days. How was it May and graduation time, already?

Kate imagined the stories that lived in every crack and ding of the paneled walls. Who else had stood there smiling in the doorway surrounded by that lovely wood when it first smelled new, Kate wondered? This room held the memories of her first real love. This was where they'd shared intimate conversations about their futures. Where they'd first made love. Where they'd faced each other crossed-legged on the twin bed writing songs, and where she'd discovered his crazy ironing system, his clothes pressed between the mattress and box spring under the second twin bed. Kate could see them holding their stomachs, laughing together.

Michael was addressing a letter. She watched him load more deep peacock blue ink into his Montblanc Meisterstück 149, the distinctive fountain pen his mother had given him to celebrate his admission to undergraduate school at Harvard. He placed it down on the shiny wood desk, put his hands behind his head, and stretched back, smiling.

Standing in the doorway, Kate watched Michael. The crazy, spontaneous decision she'd made last year to beg Goodman for a spot in her special ed. program had been the right thing. And now Kate had the double major that combined two passions. And they could be together in grad school. It was a fantasy to ever have thought she could carve out a life as a singer. Too risky for sure. It was as though some unknown force had made that choice for Kate. A gut feeling. How had an orchestra of disparate, young people from a state institution, who rocked their delighted bodies and laughed behind cupped hands, have been so alluring? How could singing with a young man named Jimmy, who could make a saxophone resonate with pure joy, have brought her to her future?

In two weeks, she would be interning with those young people and the orchestra that had ignited her life. The gold medal won by the choir this semester was a glorious achievement. But having a clear path with a solid paycheck was both calming and exhilarating.

She lingered at Michael's door and felt a deep affection for him as he concentrated on a letter he was writing. The way he pushed his lips forward and furrowed his brow to get the words just right. He was such a guy of substance, she thought. And kind. That was important to her.

She'd followed a passion and an instinct when it came to Michael and Rolling Hills. Impetuous, her family had more than once said that about Kate. The chance for love and a future filled with summers off for travel with the ideal guy? Yet, she'd found her own way too; she wasn't just following Michael's path, Kate thought, as she stepped into his room. That was so important to her.

CHAPTER 30

Michael

IN AND OUT

SCRAPING HIS CHAIR back on the shiny hardwood floor, Michael stood. "Come here, graduate." She loved the way his eyes lit up and body came to attention whenever he saw her. He always knew what she needed. Michael hugged her and breathed in. "You smell so good." His engaging eyes held a message.

"What are you up to?"

"I have the most fantastic news. It's big, and I'm so sorry to surprise you like this. I didn't know myself until today."

"Surprise me? What is it?"

"Kate, first, I'm not going to grad school."

"Wait, you're *not* going?" She stepped back.

"I... canceled grad school after my job interview today. I got the perfect job. It's at the Bangkok embassy, with the United-States Information Service."

Was this some kind of a joke, she'd gotten *in*, and he'd *quit*? She tried to process what it would be like to have Michael half-way around the world. The news was devastating.

He kept squeezing her shoulder. "Can you believe it, Kate? Babe, say something."

"I'm a little stunned." Kate's head began whirring. How could he have made such a decision without her? But hadn't she always insisted they each follow their own path and they would find their way together? "Seriously? Bangkok? Oh my God, congratulations." She tried to keep the quiver from her voice—too many feelings, too much confusion.

"Wait. It's great news for me *and...I hope* you. You remember the story I told you about my friend, Greg, and his injury?"

"Yes, but what's that got to do with quitting grad school and a job?" The thoughts thundered in her head. If they couldn't sustain two years apart, did they have what it took for a life together? She could visit him. Liquid gathered around her eyes. "I just thought we were both..." Kate stood, walked to the window, and folded her arms as if to shield herself from the news.

She couldn't picture decades of living as a piece of his life, a foreign service wife, not directing her own career. Yet, she couldn't imagine not being together and giving up a chance to live in exotic *Thailand.*

Michael slipped his arms around her from behind and joined her in gazing outside. "Greg's father became Deputy Chief of Mission in Bangkok and was home on leave. He wanted to thank me for... saving Greg. So he set me up with a job in Bangkok."

Through the open window, the spring breeze brought in lilting laughter and fragments of conversation from the students returning from late afternoon classes. Michael turned her around, lifted Kate's hand, and ran his thumb over her silver rings. "I always pictured us living somewhere exotic, hearing a string of foreign words just outside our apartment window. I think you did too."

"We did fantasize that kind of life." She pictured Brent's face if Kate announced she'd changed her mind. And oh, God, Dr. Goodman…and Jimmy. She kept the news of her acceptance letter to herself.

"It is the perfect job, Kate. I'll be arranging cultural exchanges. Imagine booking all the best of American ballet, bands, orchestras, and operas to share with the Thai people. It's too good to be true. It's an entry-level embassy position, but the most exciting way to be on the other side of the planet with you. We'll decorate my embassy office with your band posters. Which ones?" Michael laughed.

"*Embassy* office? It sounds…amazing." Kate didn't feel as elated as he did; she was alone with the joy of her own grad school news now. It was *her* announcement she'd expected to share with *him*. A sadness dropped down on her.

He held her face. "Wait, the best part, the job involves you."

"Me, how?"

"Harrington offered to arrange an audition for a job singing, representing the United States in Bangkok."

"You're serious?"

"Do you know what John Lennon said after he met Yoko at her exhibition?"

"What?" The warmth of his hand on her face made her calm a bit.

"That his old life with the guys was over. He said she became his life. That's how I feel." Michael pulled her tighter and kissed her. "How do you feel? About us? The job? Your opportunity? I know we'd have to move fast. I had to make a decision without you, and I'm so sorry."

"I feel…" She took his face in her hands. Should she even mention the lost piece of mail? The truth was everything to her. Kate shared her acceptance. She had to share the thrilling news, or was it good news, anymore?

"You got into Goodman's program? But wait, I thought—" Michael put his palm to his forehead. "Damn, you're kidding, right? I mean, congratulations."

"The letter was lost in the mailroom. I got in. I always believed we should each follow our personal dreams so we won't end up resenting each other." Kate stroked his face.

"True, but isn't singing your dream? Hasn't it always been?"

He wasn't only her boyfriend and best friend; he was her music partner. Her life without Michael for two years would seem so hollow. She also hated that she would become so dependent on him. Kate shuddered. Her breath went shallow, a pressure started in her chest. Living on campus without Michael was not a pin in her map.

She grasped the window sash with a quivering hand. "If we…when would we leave for Thailand?" Admittedly, her summer internship at an institution before grad school lost its allure compared to life with Michael in Thailand, sharing their music. "All that I've gone through to get into grad school. And what about Jimmy and Brent and Dr. Goodman?"

He hugged her tighter. "I don't know what to say, Kate. I always thought Rolling Hills was your second choice; I mean, I know you were inspired, but wasn't singing always what you dreamed of?" He put his arms on her shoulders. "Kate, I shouldn't have assumed you would… we've talked about being together for so long. Well, not in detail, but we had no details, right? Until this job... and we thought you hadn't gotten accepted into grad school." He kissed her hand.

"Michael, I..."

"I wouldn't have accepted the job if I thought you wouldn't be happy. But what do you think?"

"So I'd have a chance for a paid engagement at a music club in Bangkok? Well, it is my dream come true. *If* I make the audition." Kate was back on the stage at UConn and could hear Mrs. Hawley's words, "I'm sorry, Ms. Ketchum, but you won't be majoring in music..." But she'd had come a long way since then.

"Harrington said the Thai people are crazy for American music. You'd be a star, the way you sing."

Singing in Bangkok. Life in an exotic city—right from her fantasies. If she didn't make the Thai American Club, she could go out on her own, she supposed. Well, it's a start. "Michael, I love you and I want it, but..." It was a huge decision... but life without Michael? The battle inside made her stomach tremble. Truthfully, she couldn't even imagine not waking up beside him each day.

"Kate, I'm confused. Singing was always your passion from when we first met. I know you got excited about Rolling Hills, but you always feared you couldn't make a living singing professionally. This gig will pay well. Honey, say something? Do I need to turn this down?"

Kate looked into his eyes. She wanted their life together in a faraway foreign capital, and the possibility of singing was magnificent.

She knew the silence was killing him. Maybe grad school

was her substitute for not finding a way to sing professionally. She looked into his sincere eyes.

"And Kate, you have plenty of time to build your singing career. You know I have the money to support us until you explode with success. I know you will. We can be together."

He was right; it had always been singing. But what would Kate say to Dr. Goodman and Brent? She would leave to the other side of the planet after she turned down the acceptance. She pictured monks in saffron robes swaying down the Bangkok streets, being in Michael's arms, exploring the alluring city. She fantasized releasing a romantic tune while looking out on the diamonds of the city lights through the windows of the Thai American Club.

"I love you, but...I don't want to be dependent."

"Kate, I've never known you to be dependent. A relationship isn't only about money. The things you give me can't be bought. And we'll be a team; that's what marriage is about, right?"

The bells rang inside her, and the decision took form. It was everything she'd wanted. Kate did have her college degree; hadn't that always been the goal? She had Michael, and her singing career had just been launched, and she would finally push in that first real pin. Maybe Rolling Hills had been a detour, a beautiful detour, but now she was back on the road to her original dreams. "You know what John Lennon also said, Michael?"

"You're killing me here, what did he say?"

"You may say I'm a dreamer. But I'm not the only one." She took his face in her hands. "Yes, yes! And I love you and want to be with you. All three of you, Michael Edward James. And in *Bangkok, singing?*"

"Kate Kelly Ketchum, dear God, let's make each other happy for the rest of our lives. Let's make music together. Will you marry me? How's that for a corny, old-fashioned proposal? Sorry, I know we wanted to do this in a romantic and memorable way...and we're here in my frat room but..." He pictured Hàng, but her face evaporated. Kate was all he could see, Kate in front of him, clear and beautiful.

He lifted Kate to her feet, kissed her, and tucked his face in the crook of her neck. "Have I ever told you how much I love the scent of you?"

Kate laughed. What was his obsession with scents? She saw her mother's face in their kitchen before Kate left for college. "Singing, it's who you are." And her words on their way up the stairs, "You deserve love, Katie-girl."

CHAPTER 31

Michael

NERVOUS IN NANTUCKET

THE SCENT OF salt air told Michael he was home. He adjusted the rear-view mirror as they pulled onto the private road. He would leave the past and move into his future with Kate. Her russet hair swirled around with the breeze from the open window. God, there was something about her that was so good for him. Reaching out, he held the twirling strands away from her face—her perfect face, a place he could always rest his eyes.

"What?" She squinted at him. "What's that look?"

So much like a squinting glance his mother always gave him. "Nothing. Just had to get another peek at how beautiful you are. Make sure I still wanted to do this marriage thing." He caressed her arm, then kissed the ring on her left hand. A simple, beautiful diamond he and Kate had picked out together.

"Funny." She tugged his earlobe twice.

Like ringing a bell for Pavlov's dog, the innocent gesture always had a not-so-innocent effect on him. He noticed Kate was still tapping notes on her thigh. "Nervous?"

"Honestly? Yes. I so want your mother and father to like me."

"My mother will love you, Kate. You two are like peas in a pod."

"Ha. It's the part you always leave out, the other half, that makes me nervous." Kate clasped her right hand over her left. "What about your father?"

"I warned you my father can be arrogant, and the Grand Dame takes the cake when it comes to knowing what everyone else should do. Promise you won't change your mind."

"My parents had a twenty-year jump on me when it came to knowing you. Remember my Dad calling you, *our Michael*, when I first brought you home? I had a heart attack. They already adored you."

Michael laughed. "Well, soon you'll be *our Kate* too. And I'm the one who should be nervous."

Kate laughed. "Anyway, they can't hurt us; we'll be in Bangkok."

Michael knew his mother would love Kate. Mom said all she wanted was for Michael to be happy after his traumas in the war, and Kate was a class act. He wished his father was away on business in Paris. He would be disappointed she wasn't one of his cronies' daughters. She was gorgeous, smart, talented, and fun. Laughing to himself, Michael thought, Kate's Owl & Shamrock shoes would likely get her past his snobbery unscathed. And couldn't Michael count on his father's well-polished social graces for him to behave?

He was grateful his grandmother wouldn't be home. She was on her annual spring shopping extravaganza in Paris. Kate should have her own day without the Grand Dame's opinions or interference. Good timing, Michael thought.

"Grandmother James; she can be scary. Like my father with a wig."

"Michael, not funny. Come on."

The crunch of the gravel ceased, and his car's wheels entered the smooth pavement of his circular driveway. Michael was so excited to have Kate and his mother meet. His mother knew Kate was the love of his life, but had he made a mistake in wanting to surprise her about the actual engagement and the move to Bangkok? But he didn't want his grandmother to delay her trip, which she might have had she known. If Kate and his mother had met at the lake house last summer, this would be much easier, but she'd been in Arizona helping Michael's aunt after cancer surgery.

He watched Kate twist her diamond engagement ring, so the glorious stone was hidden in her hand.

"Sweetheart, it will be OK. I told you, Grandmother is not in town, but when you do meet her in the future, just be you."

Michael's affluence hadn't been something he'd thought much about on the drive until he saw Kate's wide eyes when they pulled up around the circular drive. Parking in front of his family's Georgian home, they sat looking out to sea.

"Oh. My. God. Michael, we're staying at this gorgeous waterside inn?"

Michael laughed; he loved her dry sense of humor. And her teasing lines were said so straight-faced sometimes he had to think twice or search her eyes for her devilish hidden smile.

"Seriously, I knew your family had money—your clothes, your formal manners, and closet-full of Owl & Shamrocks, but, Michael, are you kidding?" She squeezed his forearm.

"You know I love surprising you." Michael tightened his

grip on the leather steering wheel, worrying about his father's potential faux pas. He had to learn to get out of his head more; Kate had always said that. He had to learn to confide in her more, to find the courage to tell her his secrets, his fears. He had to stop being afraid he'd lose her.

"Your surprises, like asking me in your romantic frat room to marry you?" Kate laughed. "That's a story to tell live on-mic at O'Leary's. You just wait."

At some point, he understood Kate deserved to know what she was getting into. He honestly was afraid to prep Kate for the opulence he took for granted. His grandmother's wealth came with a weight attached to it. But now that he had a job, wouldn't his fears diminish? Such freedom. He loved that Kate knew him as just Michael; she hadn't fallen in love with the idea of Michael Edward James, III. Living his life through Kate's eyes brought him a renewed appreciation for what he had. He loved the idea that he could give her the life of her dreams, thrill her. Not just with things—she didn't focus on possessions—but with the chance to let her talent spread out into the world. The chance to enjoy travel and nature beyond the campus.

There was never a time that the splash landing of a duck on the campus pond, an unusual cloudbank, or simply a praying mantis on the handrail at the library, wouldn't stop them both dead, just to watch. He imagined them in exotic places, taking in those peaceful pauses. Sharing their voices in harmony. Those moments when the ins and outs of them perfectly matched. Something he'd never shared with anyone before, except for Hà ng. He cut off his thoughts; it was getting easier.

Michael exited the car and hopped around to open Kate's door. Thank God he didn't have to stay nearby and be suffocated by his family's expectations. Now they would have each other, build their own family. And Kate saw *him*, not his trust fund. *Oh, God, the trust fund. One thing at a time*, he thought. He'd explain how that worked to her later.

Kate wasn't the only one who was nervous, he had to admit. Michael had fantasized about an elopement, but here he was. Kate deserved a wedding, and his mother deserved to meet her future daughter-in-law. He would follow Father Sullivan's rules. Be yourself; have Kate's back.

Opening the passenger door, he offered his hand to help Kate out of the low-slung car.

With her shoulder-length blonde hair coiffed as always, and dressed in a white silk blouse, pearls, a straight skirt, and heels, his mother swept out of the front door and down the stone stairs to greet them.

"You must be Kate; welcome to our home."

CHAPTER 32

PARENTAL APPROVAL

KATE STEPPED FROM the car, leading with one fine leather boot. Looking up at the imposing mansion, she cast another look of disbelief over her shoulder at Michael.

"Call me Christine; so wonderful to meet you. I can't believe we've never met. I'm sorry I have been away so long."

"I'm glad to hear your sister's doing well."

"Thank you, dear." His mother hesitated, then held Kate at an arms-length. "Michael, you didn't say Kate was an Ann-Margret's look-alike." She hugged Kate. "Please, please, come in, dear.

"I'm relieved that you're so pleased. You have no idea, Mrs. James."

"Please, do call me Christine. Mrs. James is, well, it's my mother-in-law's name."

"Christine, can I tell you, I'm just a tad nervous." Smiling, Kate took Christine's arm. "When we pulled up just now, I joked with Michael that I thought your home was a charming waterfront inn?"

His mother glanced over her shoulder at the house. "Yes, it's a bit much for two, isn't it? But then, we do have a dog."

They laughed together.

"We're going to get along just fine, Kate."

Michael stepped in, hugged his mother, and kissed her on the cheek. "Hey, but no ganging up on me, you two." He walked between them up the stairs holding them by the arms.

Kate stopped. "I can't wait to hear you play, Christine; you will play for us, won't you?"

"You're a dear. Of course, Michael and I will play together."

"I want to hear the woman play who taught music to the man I'm going to marry. You must already know music brought us together."

That brought the threesome to a halt again.

"The man you are going to *marry*?" Christine took Kate's hand. "What's this?" Michael's mother turned Kate's hand over to expose the ring and twisted it into its proper place. "That's better. So there's more to the story, Michael?" Christine stared him down. "*Michael*?" She leaned in toward Kate conspiratorially. "Clearly, he doesn't tell me much."

"I can relate." Kate threw Michael one of her Irish darts, a teasing look she knew he understood she wasn't really angry, but a warning none-the-less. "To be fair, it just happened, but he is full of surprises."

His mother's stare and her tilted head was his punishment for keeping things too close to the vest.

"Mom, I wanted to surprise you."

"Mission accomplished. Translation, you didn't have the courtesy to prepare me, and more importantly, Kate. And if I don't know about your lovely young bride-to-be, I can assume neither does your father or grandmother. I thought I was your trusted ally, Michael."

Michael shrugged and implored, "Forgive me?"

His mother turned to Kate. "I apologize for my son's lack of manners. He's usually so gracious."

Michael put his arm around Kate. Was it to give support or get it, she wasn't sure.

"Mom, I'm sorry. I should have told you. It was a dumb idea to surprise you, but I'm so happy with Kate, and I—well, we're moving overseas."

"Overseas? Where? When?"

"I got a great job in Bangkok. With Greg's Dad. I didn't want to say all this over the phone. We leave in three weeks. Sorry if I blew it."

For a long moment, his mother stared at Michael, threw her arms around Kate, then kissed each of her cheeks. The gesture broke the tension. "I've always dreamed of having a daughter."

"Shall I call you Mom after we're married?"

"Oh, I'd be delighted." She hugged Kate again.

Kate felt an immediate bond with Christine. Her sense of humor, her no-nonsense, loving ways. And her love for her son was palpable.

"Mom, honestly, I was afraid to give Grandmother James a heads-up. Wicked Grandma of the West would somehow hurt Kate, or ruin everything."

Kate stared up at him and stepped away. "Michael, you don't give me enough credit. If I can handle my Grandma Kendall, I can handle yours. Christine, shall we start all over." Kate reached out her hand. "I am your future daughter-in-law, Kate. So wonderful to finally meet you."

"I'm honored."

Michael opened the front door for Kate. He dropped his keys on the Louis XIV side table next to the glass dome that housed a gold clock. The majesty of the grand foyer made Kate cover her face with her hands. She shifted her fingers to peek through and was mesmerized by the clock's insides spinning magically. Silently, she mouthed, "Are you kidding me?"

Michael's mother busied herself with her dog, who had come into the foyer to greet her, while Kate looked up at the lofted entrance and the chandelier of a thousand kaleidoscopic crystals that glimmered above.

"Meet the two-story stair rail I kept polished by sliding down it every morning for breakfast." Michael slipped his arm around Kate.

Her eyes scanned upward again, then Kate looked at Michael, shook her head, and whispered, "You missed out, no *Cheerios*? Those horrible Eggs Benedict, I assume, with fresh, hand-squeezed OJ served on silver?"

"Pretty much."

"Michael, look at this spectacular entryway." Kate turned in a circle, arms spread out above her.

"Yes, I've seen it." His laugh echoed in the grand foyer.

Kate leaned over to pet his mother's King Charles puppy that twisted and turned around her legs.

"Off you go, Charlemagne. Michael's father didn't like his son sliding down the banister, and he doesn't like the dog in the living room." His mother pushed open the swinging door to the kitchen, and the dog disappeared on command.

They followed Christine into the living room, and the view through the floor-to-ceiling windows stunned even Michael.

The late afternoon sunlight illuminated the teal blue of the waves below. They lifted and folded into bright white foam that hit the sand and flowed toward them in creamy round swirls. Kate could hear the rhythmic thunder through the glass. Michael stepped closer and put his arm around her. "That's the furnishing I loved best."

"I don't blame you. Wow. Mrs. James, sorry, *Christine*. It's so magnificent."

"It keeps me calm." Her eyes flashed toward the hallway and the sound of a door closing. "That must be Michael's father. I'll be right back."

Kate scanned the expansive room—a page right out of an Art History textbook. Like an exhibit hall at the Boston Museum of Fine Arts, the walls were covered with antique gold-framed, over-sized paintings of Michaels' somber, bearded male relatives in dull oils and sepia tones. Lined up chronologically around the room, they read like a fast-forward history of facial hair, fashion and dressing design.

"I'm picturing the band posters that adorn my dorm walls, Michael. I'm thinking about what you must have felt the first time you secretly slept in my dorm room under the edgy gaze of Janis Joplin." She laughed. "I love you even more now."

The ornate Parisian clock that hung on the wall with a gold-numbered face, splashed with *fleur-de-lis*, could have easily measured time for a *tête à tête* in an eighteenth-century salon in Paris. The ticking sound seemed to countdown their fate, echoing in the high ceiling. Chastising her, perhaps, with its tsk, tsk, tsk.

Kate wiped her sweaty hand on her long cotton skirt. She began her noiseless habit of playing a sequence of chords with the fingers of her left hand on the side of her leg to the beat of the clock.

Sitting next to him on the edge of a gold striped love seat, Kate continued her silent concert on her thigh—thinking in appropriate lyrics effortlessly delivered from her massive manual of memorized tunes. A tune had triggered in her head to comfort her.

Leaning in, he whispered, "What lyrics this time?"

"What? Oh. 'Take it Easy,' that new Eagles' song. You know, don't let your own mind drive you crazy. I feel, well, honestly, so out of place in this formal room. Michael, it's like for the first time, I'm aware of my own prejudice. Something I've never considered."

"What do you mean?"

"My feelings of inadequacy when I'm with privileged people, you know, starting with seeing the affluent customers at the factory."

"So, you feel *inferior?*"

"I always wanted to write them off as superficial and shallow with their values for fancy pens, copy-cat clothes, and cars. I worried they'd look down on me, seeing only a slice of me—my body or my voice, not my person or my brain. But, I realize now, I was prejudiced too."

His mother entered the room with his father. Her tone changed. Solicitous. It made Kate wonder what went on between them?

"Son, good to see you."

His tall, dark-haired father tore off his golf glove, dropped it on the antique telephone table, and turned to Kate.

"Well, who is this lovely, young lady, Michael?"

With Kate's introduction and the double-pat on Michael's back over, his father headed to the bar. "Can I get you something, Christine? Kate? Beer, Michael?"

Kate's eyes flickered from his father to his mother for guidance.

"Chassagne Montrachet, for me, please." His mother moved to stand next to Kate, a gesture of support.

"I'll join you, Christine, please." Kate stepped even closer to his mother, watching the privileged man in plaid golf pants with a Nantucket Bluff logo-collared golf shirt and a matching cobalt blue sweater, its arms hanging jauntily over his shoulders.

His father angled the crystal carafe, filled a double shot glass with the caramel-colored, aged liquid, sprung his head back, and took it in one swallow. "Welcome, Kate." He clunked the carafe down on the granite bar top.

"Dad, you have to know..." Michael began his speech but hesitated.

Christine stepped toward Michael and Kate. "They're in love, John. Isn't she lovely?"

Kate was touched by Christine's support, but she wanted Michael to introduce her and announce their plans properly. And he did.

Pulling Kate close, with his arm around her, he shared the news. "Mom, Dad. Kate and I have a special announcement; I've asked her to marry me, and I'm so lucky she said yes." His words spilled out. "We've been together since I arrived at UConn, as friends, and now. I should have...well, I didn't want to say anything until she answered. And I've taken a new job at the Bangkok embassy. We're working on immediate wedding plans. Oh, and Kate's family is from Glynn." He kissed her on the top of her head.

"Thailand?" His father interrupted. "*Shoe* Glynn?" His father studied Kate, up and down.

Kate saw Michael clench his fists, and she took over. "My parents are with the Owl & Shamrock factory, five generations now."

"Ah, that's your family business? We know it well." His father nodded his approval.

"Yes, for five generations, sir."

"I'd hoped I would have been putting Michael's name on our sign."

Michael could see his mother's eyes filling up.

"Thailand, I'm... so happy for you both."

"Do you work in the business?" His father leaned back in his chair, smiling at Kate.

"No, actually, I'm a senior at UConn about to graduate. I've never worked in the factory." Kate could almost hear Michael's thoughts—no, Dad she's not from a blueblood family, no country club. His posture said he was ready to stand up for Kate. That bothered her. Kate was who she was, and she could fend for herself. He always said he loved that about her. Maybe his father would surprise Michael. Did it really matter? She wouldn't let him make her feel less than. "Mr. and Mrs. James, you actually know my parents."

The small breath Michael took made her smile. She could almost hear him say, Oh God, here it comes.

"Your parents? I don't think so dear; I've never met the owners, only Mr. and Mrs. K., oh and Grandpa K.; such sweet people," Christine said.

"Mom and Dad, meet Kate Ketchum, you know, Mr. and Mrs. K, our cordwainers' daughter."

Kate reached out her hand to Michael's father. "So nice to meet you, Mr. James."

He nearly fell back into the wing back chair behind him. "I...uh, never made the trips to Glynn; that was Christine's purview."

"Kate, you're Cecelia and Kevin's daughter?" Michael's mother moved in behind her husband's chair and squeezed his shoulder. "Isn't she charming, John? Aren't you happy for Michael?"

Where had his meek mother gone? It tightened Michael's throat to see her step forward for him, for Kate, but he worried about the consequences for his mother later.

"Cordwainers..." His father flinched at his wife's grip and glanced down at Kate's feet. "Nice boots. Does anyone need another drink?"

CHAPTER 33

PROTESTING THE PAST

THE EXCITEMENT IN her mother's voice and her father's good cheers were still in Kate's smile the next morning after her call. They were used to her spontaneity, and they were thrilled she'd found love, they'd said. Yes, her mother and sisters would arrange a simple family wedding on short notice. And the thrill of Kate living in Bangkok and singing made her mother cry. "You've done it darling, you've done it, Katie-girl."

Kate's father was happy to have her with a good man. She could almost hear the relief in his voice that she was "normal." Something he'd concerned himself with when she'd slipped and mentioned she had no interest in marriage or kids. In the whirl-wind of their plans, she hadn't spoken to Michael about having children; neither had he. The whole family loved Michael. It was too much to take in—she would be singing in a foreign capital, and she had true love.

The window of Kate's 5th floor room remained open from the night before. A breeze of early fresh May air laced with a pungent wave of weed invaded the space along with a small rise in students' voices outside. The protestors' chants had become the norm throughout her junior and senior years. Shiloh and her SDS members passionately broadcasted speeches through megaphones. Small groups of students shouted out against the war in Vietnam or pro-women's rights or calls for racial equality.

Kate wanted to luxuriate in her personal happiness and push away the campus angst. She slammed the window shut. No politics today, *please*. She was engaged, getting married... *married*. Kate had to laugh. She would take a lot of teasing from her siblings now. Kate, the independent sister who'd sworn off commitment. She welcomed it. It was worth it to feel the joy that showered over her at the thought of the love she'd found with Michael.

Opening the book about Thailand Michael had given her, she took in the exotic scenery—terraced rice fields, golden temples, and coconut palms along the Bay of Siam. Her conversation with Shiloh had been thirty minutes of joyful sharing, crying, and congratulations. Father Sullivan and Kate's pastor would be the co-officiants next Saturday in Glynn. She and Michael had rushed through the Catholic Church's required pre-marriage conference with their confidant, Father Sullivan. Who could have dreamed up this ending? Or beginning, she should say.

Now, she was thinking of her new in-laws. Kate adored Christine. Seeing Michael's father stunned at the news of his only son marrying into a factory worker's family was a moment she would never forget. A moment Michael said he'd secretly enjoyed and smiled about all the way back to campus. He had genuine love, he'd said, not an arranged marriage to one of his grandmother's choices. Kate fantasized helping Michael to release his anger toward them.

There would be no graduation ceremony. Boycott with me, Shiloh had pleaded convincingly. There was bound to be chaos at the event. Best not to be in the insanity with Michael. He'd shared a few stories of the war and his near death by that knife wound with Kate. No wonder he got that faraway look. Lately, she'd been a little worried over changes in him since the campus unrest had escalated. A few times, he seemed like Kate's brother had been after returning from the war, distracted, on edge, a bit moody, but nothing serious and only infrequently. That former haunted look of Michael's had been absent for the past year-and-a-half since they'd started dating and playing music regularly. Kate took partial credit for that, and the rest went to music and Michael's work with Father Sullivan.

Kate downed the final cup of sludgy coffee from the clogged pot in the hallway kitchen. What a relief. So much to think about—a wedding, packing, documents. Confidence was finally creeping in now. Marrying Michael and pursuing her singing career in Bangkok was her true path.

But Kate had to tell Dr. Goodman after the weekend. She'd been out of her office lately on a conference in Washington, DC. Kate couldn't stop thinking of the student out there whose spot she'd taken in the graduate program. Withdrawing at the last minute was mortifying, and imagining Brent's face when he would learn she'd canceled her internship with Rolling Hills was painful. Capriciousness wasn't a trait she wanted to see in herself, and Dr. Goodman had taken a chance on her. Kate searched in the mirror, expecting to see her shame, but found only happiness on her face. She'd done the right thing.

Smoothing her pink chenille bedspread, she looked at her alarm clock. Michael should have gotten out of class and been at her dorm by now to finish working out their plans.

Curiosity got the better of her, and Kate moved to the study hall at the end of her floor to see what was happening in the quadrangle. Stabbing her chopsticks into her Ramen noodles, the scraping sound of the bamboo sticks against the Styrofoam cup echoed in the empty room.

She watched the changing scene below. Like trails of ants, students collided along the perimeter of budding dogwoods and beds of daffodils. They stopped to share some news face to face, grabbed each other or patted backs, then rushed away, bumping into one another, again and again. An ever-growing group of hundreds had gathered at the brick, two-story Administration building as though they had found something to devour. Campus police appeared around the chaos.

Kate could almost feel the emotions of the mob of students compressed around the brick building from five floors up. She debated going down into the insanity of the protests. Thankfully, she wasn't singing today. Shiloh would undoubtedly be there in the thick of it. She'd begged for Kate to perform at their protests after hearing Kate sing. Obliging her loyal friend, Kate had sung at several of the peaceful rallies. How could she harness a crowd into listening like this one, today? Michael had always resisted Shiloh's requests to perform with Kate at events like the massive crowd gathering below. It wasn't like playing for the O'Leary's gang. He said crowds unnerved him.

She wished Michael would trust her enough to talk about

his troubles from his tours in Vietnam. There were times his gaze drifted off to some mysterious place: when the sounds of the protests rose; when speeches blared through a megaphone; when Kate inadvertently ran her hands over the tattoos on his shoulder while making love; or when her kisses brushed the scar that encircled his neck—certain triggers to his dark memories.

While walking together on campus, his step would quicken; he'd pull Kate closer or squeeze her hand tighter or stop to breathe her scent in and kiss her neck. At first, it struck her as so sweet and spontaneous, protective; lately, it felt a bit strange. Was he recalling his troubles from the war again? How would this play into their relationship, their marriage? She had to believe that their life together and her love for him would heal his wounds. But she needed honesty about what had happened in Vietnam for them to start a lifetime together, didn't she? Still, his moods hadn't been troublesome enough to push him to talk—just the occasional distancing.

Although, some secrecy characterized all of the couples in Kate's life when she thought about it. The women always confided in each other, repeating, "Don't tell your father or don't tell your brother I said that, or don't tell Mom." Kate hated secrets in relationships. She wanted communication and a balance of power.

Kate remembered her brother's words, "He'll tell you when the time is right, but just know, that time may never come." That threatened her. Would she ever really know Michael if he didn't confide in her about the memories that made him suffer?

Kate returned to her room to wait for Michael. She glanced up at her family photo with Michael grounded in the center, leaning close to her. Their intimacy was so rich. When Michael went dark and distanced like that, she ached to comfort him, but there was a wall. From her tender, attentive lover, to a momentary inscrutable, brooding stranger. The cloud always lifted quickly when they'd kissed, sang, or were tucked away in nature. Maybe she was worrying too much. She couldn't wait to get him off-campus and on to their life together after graduation. Kate wanted his trust; she wanted to have the open love she'd hoped for with a future husband. She was determined she would.

Kate checked her watch and took the stairs. The spring breeze had an edge, but the sun was winning out. She was sweating in her black leather boots before she reached the crowd. The anti-war, sit-in students filled the expansive grassy area beside the Administration building, thrusting fists in the air, calling, "On strike, shut it down! On strike, shut it down!" The throng was packed in a frenzied circle.

On the edge of the buzzing swaying crowd of jeans and T-shirts, bellbottoms, Fu Manchu mustaches, and mini-skirts, she spotted Michael, standing still, almost frozen, across from her. Kate tensed. Michael seemed immobilized, the only silent note in the chanting chaos.

The protestors cheered at the words squeaking through the megaphone with its occasional high-pitched whines. "These Kent State kids were peaceful protestors, man. Four dead. Could've been you, or you, or you." The President of the SDS pointed at random students, then right at Michael. The group swayed back. Michael's face appeared and disappeared with the shifting swarm.

A spiral of fear burrowed deep into Kate's stomach from

the anger and tension of the crowd as she pushed through the agitated students to reach him. "*Michael.*" She called over and over as she approached.

He turned. What was he thinking about behind those dark, ruminating eyes? His look was unnerving.

Kate hugged him just as a roar of voices and screams rose. The acid-burning smell of a bonfire flared. The flames ignited the snap-snap of firecrackers being thrown into the flames, and the crowd went up on toes to see what was happening.

Michael dropped to the ground, pulling her with him. "Take cover, darling!"

What had he seen that she hadn't? Her panic set in.

His trembling body wrapped around her. Michael's weight was crushing her chest. Her voice was weak. She writhed in fear. "What are you doing...let me up!" Kate's face pressed next to his, the heat of his cheek burning hers. She felt the rumble of his heart and a thundering in her own chest. Tearing at the grass to escape, her nails dug into the soft spring soil.

His body, like a human shield, protected her. From what? An enemy that wasn't there?

Kate yelled in his ear. "Michael, can you hear me? Let me up."

He didn't heed her breathy calls. Panic took over. Tremors spread down Kate's spine. Michael's vice-hold frightened her. His entire body was quaking. "Breathe, darling, breathe. You'll be OK," he kept repeating, huffing air in and out rapidly. "We have to have hope."

"*Oh, God.*" Kate pulled her head down into her shoulders. A second threatening bonfire raged up. The din of the thick crowd of students protesting and the commands of the campus police grew deafening. Scattering students tripped and stepped over Kate and Michael, rolling them both onto their sides.

"Michael, look at me! We need to move." Her tears were pressing to be released. Stay focused, don't panic, she told herself.

"Please, Hàng, please?" His eyes were haunted.

"*Michael*?" He was praying to his guardian angel, Hàng, the word tattooed on his shoulder, Kate thought. "Look at me, Michael."

No answer. He began to rock Kate. A new and frightening thing. She couldn't break away from his powerful arms. One arm under her neck, the other under her waist, Michael clutched her to his chest. She could smell the fear in his sweat. It triggered her own panic. His fiery hot arms and damp shirt soaked through her clothes.

Kate screamed into his face. "We-have-to-get-up! You're hurting me, Michael. Can you hear me? You're hurting me!"

The acrid scent of fumes and the bleak color of smoke surrounded them. Kate managed to curl up in a ball. She sprung open to push him away, then stood and pulled Michael's arm. "Do you smell that, Michael? Something's going to blow. Get up, please get up!"

He finally rose and began to move. His head snapped back and forth as if shaking off a bad dream. They charged down the sidewalk, looking back over their shoulders. The smoke got darker, heavier, and a lick of red flames came up through the edge of the Administration building's first-floor window. Thousands of students moved in a swarm of turmoil, screaming, shuttling in one direction, then the other, to find an escape route through the crowd.

Thirty yards away, in front of the library, they stopped and turned around. Students launched a barrage of fiery bottles through the windows. Billows of black smoke and red-orange flames filled the first floor of the Administration building. Then *boom*—it exploded. Glass shattered. A raging wall of heat blasted them back. Colliding students rocketed into them.

Campus riot police herded the sea of students away from the explosions. "Everybody, move along *now*! Let's go. Back to your dorms or leave. Campus is on lockdown," the commanding voice yelled from a megaphone.

"Darling breathe, you'll be OK." Michael looked at Kate with ghostly eyes and dragged her to the ground again. Stroking her hair, he breathed into the crook of her neck. Over and over, he called out, "Ha`ng, sweetheart. I love you." Then, his one hand was on Kate's breast. His other ran down her thigh and tried to spread her legs. "Push. Breathe."

He kissed Kate hungrily, switching instantly from frenzied fear to passion. Michael's bizarre behavior amidst the riot unraveled Kate's already frayed nerves. "Michael, are you *crazy*? *Stop*! Let me up!" His strength was overpowering.

A new swarm of campus police broke up the crowd. Sirens whined around them in the din of chanting voices. "On Strike. Shut it down. On strike…"

Michael curled his arms around Kate, shielding her from the throng. "Ha`ng, darling, I love you. I'll protect you. We'll be together…" Burrowing his face in Kate's chest, Michael breathed in and out, chanting over and over. "Ha`ng, you're OK, you're OK. Breathe. Push. Push." He smoothed Kate's hair back and kissed her again.

His words finally cut through the chaos in Kate's mind. He'd said, *Ha`ng, darling. I love you.* Michael wasn't even talking to Kate. He wasn't trying to protect her. Ha`ng was not a guardian angel on his shoulder. Ha`ng was his lover, a woman. Kate couldn't breathe; her compassion was at a melting point, tremors of fear quaked throughout her body. What was she feeling? Hollow? Betrayed? Who was Ha`ng? No time to process the whirling, threatening sense of confusion; she held it together. Dragging herself out from under him, Kate urged him, pulling his hand. "Michael. Let's go."

They were far enough away to avoid any damage to their bodies, but a few flakes of fiery debris landed on their shoulders. Kate flicked them off, then patted Michael's head and brushed his back for stray embers, dislodging a paper that was sticking out of his back pocket. It fluttered in the wind and landed near Kate's boot. She picked it up and shoved it in her pocket as more charred flakes of ash and glass rained down, blocking the slanting sun.

Students stood around them, frozen, like small figurines amid black and red flurries in some bizarre life-sized snow globe, then they rushed to escape the fiery embers.

A wave of people changed the tide's direction, sweeping Kate away from Michael.

"Let's go, let's go, Miss," the policeman herded her into a group of panicking students toward the north end of the campus.

"Wait, he needs help…*Michael, go see Father Sullivan*!" Did he hear her amid the screams of the sea of students?

"Campus is on lockdown. Disperse immediately," the announcements blared from the police megaphones. Kate struggled to reach out to Michael, but she was funneled toward her room in the raging river of students taking refuge in the dorms. With her neck stretched around, Kate searched for Michael. In a flashing moment, she saw his dazed face disappear into the chaotic crowd.

CHAPTER 34

Michael

AGONIZING ADMISSIONS

MICHAEL WATCHED KATE disappear into the smoky aftermath of the riot. "*Kaaaate!*" No use. His call was lost in the commotion. His mind was clearing, but the weight on his chest wouldn't lift after Kate's arm was pulled from around him. He wanted to run after her; wanted to explain, find out what she'd seen, how she'd felt? The force of the mob and his heavy legs prevented him. He'd heard her last scream, *Michael, go see Father Sullivan.* He silently repeated her words like a chant as he gave way to the force of the mob.

The flood of students flowed around the lake to the fraternity quadrangle. Michael split off and headed for the church. He needed to see the priest.

Like a foggy mirror clearing with the fresh air, Michael's memories returned in layers. Following the perimeter of the lake, the scenes resurrected—holding Kate down in the riot, making love to Hàng, supporting her during childbirth. Had he called Hàng's name out loud? Called her *his love* in front of Kate? Kissed her? Or was that all in his head? He understood;

the harsh scents and harrowing sounds around Michael had connected him with Hằng and the war. Now, he remembered Kate's voice, pleading him to let her up. He began to see it more clearly—her panicked face as it melted into the flow of students being pushed away by the campus cops.

As he reached the end of the lake across from the church, and the crowd had dwindled, Michael stopped and ran his hand along the back pocket of his jeans. The deckle-edged precious Polaroid was missing from his hip pocket. He'd meant to float it off on the lake with a prayer before seeing Kate at her dorm today. The damn riots had him out of focus. Fuck. He would have kissed the photo, kept it at his lips, breathing deeply, then looked at it for the last time. Kneeling down by the edge of the lake, Michael imagined letting the water take the beloved image from his hands. He breathed and floated the memory off on the ripples of the lake. It hit him hard.

Still, he was hollow and not ready to let the whole story out. How could Kate handle the double blow—Hằng and Hy Vọng, his child. Withholding had been a lie he hadn't even shared with Father Sullivan. What a fucking fake he was. All that counseling using the war traumas as his excuse. Half-truths.

He'd thought the stitches of time would hold the wound closed until it healed. Hadn't he been getting better in the warmth of Kate's kindness and love, her soothing voice? Their music? He didn't want to let it go—that peace he'd come to know.

There was no incense at that time of day at St. Thomas, no choir practice, no sun through the stained glass. It was

Wednesday, May 6th—a date he would never forget. It was not only because of the UConn campus meltdown after the Kent State student killings but because of his own disaster. There was everything to lose now. Why did he ever think he could just bury his past and start fresh without facing it?

Father Sullivan stood in shadow in the choir loft above. With the muffled sounds of the quieting protest off in the distance, Michael lifted each weighted foot and climbed the curved staircase, desperate for the priest's guidance. "Father Sullivan?" His voice sounded haunted even to himself as he slumped into the nearest seat.

"What's happened here? Are you hurt?" Father Sullivan wiped the char from Michael's face with his handkerchief.

"I'm OK. No injuries. None that are visible." Michael fought to keep from falling off the chair from dizziness. "Father…" Michael bent in half, his head dropped into his hands. "I'm fucked up." His words echoed into the arch of the rafters above and came back to him. "And I'm a liar. I'm sorry. That's the only word. I need your help." His voice was an angry growl turned inward on himself.

"I listen; you talk. We'll sort this out." Father Sullivan sat.

His reporting was long—interrupted by choked silences and strings of his shattering story—losing Hà̀ng, leaving Hy Vọng, his loss, his betrayal of Kate. "I fucked the entire thing up. Everything."

"Breathe, Michael."

The choir loft darkened as the daylight slipped away. Father Sullivan flipped on the lights and sat back down to listen.

"I'm sure there's no quote for this, Father." His sweat drip-dripped on the floor like a metronome.

"I wouldn't dare." Father Sullivan put his hand on Michael's shoulder.

Michael continued his confession with his head hung. "I did such a good job of burying it all. Kate had no idea about the extent of it." Michael looked directly into the priest's eyes. "I let her think it was the violence of the war, just like I'd done with you. Wasn't that enough! Wasn't it? You know, when I was with her, my dark side had no chance. I actually thought the torture was over."

"Michael, what is it specifically you want me to help with right now?"

"I don't know." Michael stared up at the altar. "I need confession. I need a plan. I need to heal... I need Kate. And all this time, I could have told her like I just told you."

"Why didn't you?"

"I thought I would spiral down into my darkness and never surface again. Maybe I wanted to keep Hàng's memory to myself. I don't know."

"There's nothing wrong with wanting to preserve your past memories. But you should have trusted Kate would understand that."

"What woman would want to know about a past lover you hadn't let go of?"

"So you feel your memories of Hàng are a betrayal to Kate?

"Yes, not telling Kate that Hàng was still lingering in my head? It was no-win; when I held back, I was less than honest, but when she did learn the truth, it was in the most painful way." Michael turned his head and look into Father Sullivan's eyes. "And I ended up hurting Kate, anyway, breaking her trust in me."

"I think I know Kate well enough that she would want you to trust that she could handle your truth."

A cloud of helplessness settled down around Michael. "Yes, withholding the truth made it seem like I was entangled in thoughts of Hàng when I was honestly with Kate. I don't know what the hell I was thinking? Actually, I didn't know what I was doing today. It was fucking crazy...sorry...I guess I was caught in some strange place between my past and the reality of the protest. Oh, hell, it's not the first time."

Father Sullivan wrapped his arm around Michael's shoulder. "What's happening to you is shell shock. Your mind is still unable to process the pain. I can work with you."

"Shock, all right. For Kate. I think I was saying that I loved Hàng. I don't know what the hell I was doing." Michael could see the look on Kate's face, the confusion, the pain. "How can I ever restore her faith in me, Father?"

"Michael, you have some convincing to do now—to give Kate the peace that your heart and thoughts are with her. To help her to understand what you are going through. I can help. I believe in both of you."

Pushing himself up from the chair, Michael stood on shaky legs.

Father Sullivan took his arm. "If I may, St. Thomas said, 'Faith has to do with things that are not seen, and hope, with things that are not in hand.' Give Kate time. Share your truth and be patient. Have faith, and above all try to have hope. I'm here for you both if you need me."

Michael drew in a deep breath. "Everything is on the line, Father. She's everything."

CHAPTER 35

REALITY REELING

CRUSHED. SHE'D BEEN crushed by Michael's distant, dark look—the look Kate had been compassionate enough not to explore. Exhausted from crying and running the details of Michael's bizarre behavior at the protest over and over in her mind, Kate draped herself over her bed in her robe, staring up at the darkening clouds outside.

What was going on inside him? She should have pushed Michael to tell her the details of what was troubling him. Maybe he wouldn't have broken down or whatever that was he did in the middle of the protest. Where was he now, and was he Ok? He wasn't answering his phone. He wouldn't... no, she couldn't think about him hurting himself. Kate was worried, angry, hurt. Would Michael ever be the same? He needed serious help. Everything had just blown sky-high. That's the only way Kate could describe it—their world had just blown sky-high.

Shiloh knocked and opened the door slowly. "Kate? I just got back."

Shiloh's stare and questioning eyes made Kate look down at her disheveled clothes. "God, I'm a mess."

"You were there! I thought you were safe here, meeting with Michael about your plans."

Stroking the ash from her blouse and pants with quivering hands, Kate handed the photo to Shiloh. "I'm so glad you're here." She hugged Shiloh. Kate's broken words were littered with sobs. "Dammit, how many times did I ask him... was there... someone else? He'd said, 'there used to be.'"

"Sit down, girlfriend. What the hell is going on here?" Propped on the edge of the bed, Shiloh examined the photo. "I don't know what all this means."

"Neither do I. Look. My fiancé with his lover's family, all deliriously happy? And the date on the back. Just before he returned." Kate couldn't swallow. "Shi, I can't bear to think of him alone now, but I don't know how to handle this or comfort him...or me."

"Kate, do you think, maybe—it's over?"

Kate's stomach went sour. She made a small gasping sound as she covered her face with her hands.

"No, honey...sorry, I meant with *her?*" Shiloh put her arm around Kate.

"I'm not stupid. He's carrying her photo around. While he's with *me*. She's someone he left behind, named Hàng." Kate's voice went high, a tone she'd never heard in herself before as she outlined what happened at the protest. "Never mind. I can't take it right now." Kate delivered her words through a thin, winded voice. "I could have handled his healing...his damned mysterious moods, but I can't be his second choice." With fists held tight, her tears carving tracks through her dusty face, Kate felt a gaping hole open in her heart. "I can't have a wall of lies between us. God, Shi, I hate that I was her substitute." Kate felt unsteady, afraid she would collapse.

Kate shivered; she could feel his hands running down her thigh, caressing her breast, and Michael calling out the woman's name in the din of the protestors' voices. *Ha`ng.* Was that Vietnamese? Yes, likely.

Shiloh handed the faded photo back to Kate—Michael's arm around a beautiful, young, cocoa-skinned woman, a smiling family encircling them. Kate could almost hear them saying, *our Michael.* Like a foreign duplicate of the Ketchum family portrait.

"So, what do you want to do?"

"I suppose... I have to talk to him." Kate's pain was physical, as if the weight of his body was still on her, her hands still gripping the grass beneath them. The whole thing was surreal. Was their relationship a deception, his love a façade? "How can I have become engaged to someone I know so little about?" Kate stared out at the hill across the street. Their favorite spot, suffocating in a layer of smoke that hugged the hill's surface and drifted off into the woods.

Michael's loving tone with Ha`ng while his arms were around Kate wouldn't stop torturing her; so tender, so caring, and protective. That softness in his voice used to belong to *her.* The sweetness of his words soured in Kate's mind now.

"Why didn't I follow my instincts, Shi? I promised myself I would stay focused on my education." Why had she let herself get off track? If things didn't work out, there would be no wedding, no travels, no singing together in an exotic country, but mostly, would there be no Michael? No-win. "Thank

God, I didn't cancel my grad school plans." Could Kate pull herself together for her internship in two days? She stared in the mirror. Shiloh was slumped down on the bed behind her. Kate's wild, ruddy hair framed her pale, haunted face in her reflection—a foreign look.

"Shiloh, I can't go forward with this wedding, can I?"

"Oh, Kate. You need to talk to Michael before you make that decision, don't you?"

Kate closed her eyes and spoke with a slow, dull voice. "I gave up grad school to be with him. Rolling Hills, all of it."

"Kate, call him. I know one thing, he loves you. But he does need help."

"And I love him, right?" Kate stared down at the photo. "But who is he?"

Kate jumped at the knock. Maybe it was Shiloh again. She'd gone back to her room to change while Kate took a much needed hot shower. She needed her friend too. Crossing the room, Kate opened the door just before realizing it wasn't Shiloh's signature knock.

"Michael."

"Please, I need to explain. It's not what you think." He looked down at his disheveled condition. "Sorry, I'm...I did what you said; I saw Father Sullivan." Michael stepped into the room and closed the door.

"How did you...there's a lockdown?"

"Fuck the lockdown. Babe, I'm so sorry." He took her in his arms.

"I'm so afraid to hear this right now. I feel...so vulnerable...

it's too raw. What happened to you out there? So, you're OK?" Kate felt chills sizzle down her arms. "It was...so terrorizing."

He extended his arms to her shoulders. "I'm so sorry for what you saw out there in the quadrangle. It must have been horrifying for you. I understand you're hurt and angry and confused."

She turned away and stared out the window. More than you could know, she thought. She couldn't answer. Then her thoughts exploded out. "How many times did I ask you if there was someone else? Still water runs deep, Michael. My brother Karl told me not to pry. He said war stories are best left untold. Your truth was not best left unsaid, Michael, and you know that." Her deep sadness was changing to anger as he turned her around. She pushed away from him and searched his miserable eyes for the truth.

"I just want one chance to be real with you." Michael faced her, took her moist hand, and twisted her engagement ring. Locking his arms around Kate, her body became rigid. He buried his soft words in her hair. "I love you."

Kate pulled away again. It was too much like before when she'd struggled on the ground.

"I want to tell you everything. Please let me." Michael moved beside Kate. She moved next to the bed with her arms wrapped around herself.

He touched her shoulder.

Kate flinched. She wanted to hear the truth; she didn't. Why didn't she have the strength to just walk away from him; he was a liar and a mess from the war. Too much to handle. More so than she'd ever imagined. Why was it so damn easy for him to tell the truth now? Was it because what he was about to say would have destroyed them anyway? The whole thing was so complicated.

Her love fought through the chaos in her mind; it was winning the fight. A deep breath helped calm her enough to push the words out. "Go ahead. I can't *not* hear it now."

He started from the beginning. Kate listened to everything, the whole story of the things that were in his head. He pushed a stray lock of her hair behind her ear.

Kate shook her head. Her long list of troubling questions gushed out without control. "Why didn't you tell me? And where is she? Hah-ng, is that how you say it?" The name had rotated in her head a thousand times since the protest. The tone of his voice when he'd uttered her name—Ha`ng—it held more tenderness and love than Kate thought she would ever find again. It hurt in a way she'd never experienced. Would the searing pain ever leave?

Michael sat next to Kate and took her hand. "I met her in the village where my unit was assigned."

Kate gazed down at her hand in his. His hands. She knew every inch of them, having studied them as he'd played the piano beside her. The memory of them moving down her side on the ground at the protest invaded. She shuddered and waited for the truth. "So... she was a woman from that village?"

"No, she was visiting her parents in the village. She was a professor at a university in the city."

"A professor?" Not just beautiful but a professor. It made his relationship with the woman more real somehow. Kate hated the thought; it cut deep. She was jealous of a woman she'd never met. Kate pulled her hand back. "You were calling out her name," Kate's voice vibrated out the truth. "Michael, you were touching me, kissing me like...you were making love...to her. You have to know how horrible that was for me." Kate took a stuttering breath. "Dammit, you still love her, don't you?" She spit out the words with anger as she imagined Michael on one knee in his frat room, professing his undying love.

Michael's eyes cast away from Kate. She watched him swallow hard and set his jaw. He hesitated, looked at her, then looked down.

"No, it's not like that. Ha`ng's gone now."

"Gone where?"

"She was...I did love her once. She's...a memory."

CHAPTER 36

Michael

TATTERED TRUTHS

HOW TO TELL Kate about his relationship with Hàng? The conversation was doomed with so many similarities between the two women, their warmth, love of family, smart, and compassionate—wanting to save every little soul who needed saving. Hàng's work with the abandoned children in the war held a great irony that had weighed heavy on him. He couldn't think about Hy Vọng, now.

How could he distinguish his love for Kate, so she didn't feel like she was some inferior substitute for Hàng? They were both the type of women he would love. And it was Kate he loved now; it was Kate in his heart. But yes, he loved the memory of Hàng, he admitted to himself. He was haunted by it.

Sharing the truth was impossible while looking into Kate's eyes. How could he say how beautiful Hàng was without hurting or betraying Kate? How could he talk about his intimacy and love for Hàng without Kate comparing herself to his phantom woman from his past? He was going down a path that had no good ending, he thought. Michael struggled to put the puzzle of his time with Ha`ng into words. He weighed each memory—was it a need-to-know, or too burdensome for Kate? For him? But he'd promised not to hold back.

As he began to describe Ha`ng and her family, it felt wrong. Too easy to hear the similarities between the Ketchum and the Le families, both close-knit clans. Or an exposure of something so intimate that belonged to him and Ha`ng.

This was *why* he realized. This was why he hadn't been able to share the details. That kind of sharing would betray both women. And his personal privacy too. But didn't he owe Kate complete openness if they ever had a chance at getting married? Or did some of his story belong only to him?

"I'm waiting, Michael. You're making it harder." Kate's eyes were dark and misty.

He did his best to tell everything, riding that fine line. "I first saw her leaning against a tree, reading a book in English. That's why we spoke. Ha`ng was funny, smart, cared about her family. She taught college—social work; she loved kids; she worked to help kids abandoned in the war."

He couldn't make eye contact with Kate while talking about Ha`ng. Look in her eyes, he told himself; it's part of telling the truth. "We were together for a year, and then I re-upped so we could be together longer. I got called away to another part of the country as the conflict moved." Michael lowered his gaze, then forced himself to look into Kate's eyes again. "We planned to get married when my second tour was over, nine months after my company moved out of her village area."

His hand instinctively went to the tattoo on his arm. He needed to get past the visual that haunted him. The sound of her scream, the shrapnel, her staring, dead eyes—it needed to be told. Just before he got to the part about Ha'ng's violent death, he sat, leaned in closer to Kate. She was trembling. "Are you OK with this?"

"No, truthfully, I'm *not* OK. I'm confused. I'm miserable. You were still in love with this woman when you and I...are you still? Where is she? Are you unable to let go? I'm not sure I want to hear the truth." Kate stood and studied her family photo on the wall, then cast her eyes away from him. "Even if she's far away, is it her you think of when we...?"

"God, no, sweetheart. I know omission is a kind of lie but listen." He faced Kate but kept a few feet between them. Michael squeezed the back of his neck as Kate stared out the window. "I love you, and no, I don't confuse you with her. You're my life now. Sweetheart, she's...she was killed in crossfire." He stood stiff, expecting to splinter apart as he told the story, and watched Kate cover her mouth and lower her head. *Be patient*, he held onto Father Sullivan's advice. He observed every nuance as she stood in front of him—hand to her forehead, eyes closed, her deep breath slowly releasing. Michael tried to read Kate's reactions as she slumped back on the bed in her familiar blue robe.

CHAPTER 37

TENTATIVE TURN

HA`NG WAS DEAD. How could Kate be relieved? That felt so wrong. Her selfish response to the news troubled her. The woman had been violently destroyed right in front of Michael's eyes. Yet with her death, Kate felt a small door had opened again to the possibility of their life together. A worm of guilt spiraled down into her stomach, and a dark cloud outside drew her attention. The blossoming trees on the hill were swaying and bending from the gusting wind. Her brief moment of relief melted as the reality of his horrific loss settled in.

Wouldn't his lover's death have driven Michael's love for her into a permanent place in his heart? Would it ever be possible for him to forget Ha`ng and those violent images? How would Kate know if he was thinking of her while they were together?

Go to him, Kate told herself, but she was immobilized. Standing in place with shock and shame, disturbed by the images he'd put in her head, she suffered an undefinable pain. For Ha`ng. For Michael. For herself. All victims of the despicable war she hated. "If she's…gone, why didn't you tell me? I could have comforted you." Kate's arms went rigid, her fingers spread wide, pleading for understanding. "You should have trusted me."

Michael took her shoulders again. "Kate, I can describe it this way. When I knew I loved you, I imagined ceremoniously folding the memories of Ha`ng like the flag I'd put over her grave. I tucked the corners in tight. Stored it deep inside where I'd hoped those memories would peacefully remain." Michael lightly ran his hand down Kate's arm. "So you and I would have a fresh start. There's no one else, now. Well, no other woman." He took a slow breath. "But there is more to my fucked up story." Michael took her hand.

"*More*, you're kidding?" Kate wilted into her desk chair. Her thoughts were spinning. Every cell in her body was vibrating, on high alert. She studied him but came up with nothing. What else could there be? Another woman? She should make him leave. It was already enough to make her want to end things right there, but *more*?

He rolled up his T-shirt sleeves to expose proof of his past. The scene in her bedroom on that first Thanksgiving replayed in her mind. Kate's fingers tracing the tattoos, her lips against the scar on his neck. You're home safe and sound, Kate remembered saying. When she'd asked about the meaning of his tattoos, he'd answered, they meant *angel in the moon* and *hope.*

Michael knelt in front of her chair with his hands on her thighs.

Shifting in her seat, Kate touched the second mystery, the tattoo that meant *hope.* "If this angel tattoo was your lover, then this word, hope, must be your other secret." Her chest was pounding with anxiety. "Michael, just tell me."

His confession about his newborn slipping from his dying lover's hands into his was the most tragic thing Kate had ever heard. No details, she couldn't hear anymore, torn between comforting Michael and her own pain, as she hesitated and pulled back. Michael had a child? With Hàng? Kate was numb. "Shh. I'm so sorry." She pulled him close, cradled Michael, and kissed the top of his blonde head as he knelt in front of her. They stayed there until his trembles stopped.

He sat back on his knees. "Kate, I was a fool not to confide in you. It wasn't about not trusting you."

Would his mistake leave an irreparable breach between them or end their relationship? In some ways, it was so much worse than merely another woman. That would have been enough. There was at least a chance to soothe that memory away with her own love, maybe. But the loss of a child?

"I can't find the words, Michael. I'm aching for you." Kate's voice went soft again—almost a whisper. "I can't imagine losing your baby."

Michael ran his hand through his damp hair. "I thought I could just bury the memory—that my happiness with you would make me forget. Or it would fade or at least heal, not feel so raw—and, Kate, honestly, it had." He touched her face. "Until the protest." He took a deep breath. "Please tell me what you're thinking. Kate?"

"Honestly? That all our 'firsts' are already taken." Her thoughts spewed out. "The first time you fell in love; the first time you proposed, met your lover's family, the first time you had a child—all not with me. I thought all those firsts belonged to us. And now they don't. It's a loss for me, Michael. Those promised firsts all feel like a lie now. And I might have been able to deal with a ghost, the memory of a perfect woman who had no time to start a fight or burn a meal or disappoint. With time, maybe." She imagined him holding his newborn, another possible first stolen. "But a child, killed in a horrific war in front of you?"

"*No, no*, she wasn't *killed*; Hy Vọng's...well, she's alive."

"What? Alive? She's still in Vietnam?" Kate put her face in her hands. "I always knew there was someone you ached for." They'd never had that talk about having babies of their own. It was not the time, now. Kate hadn't ever really wanted a child. Marriage had not been a priority. At least that was what she'd always thought. She loved children, but she'd craved adventure, to not be tied down. How had this all happened? It wasn't in the plan. She hadn't thought she could ever fall in love so deeply.

A gust of wind fluttered some papers on the end table by the window, and they spun off her desk. Kate watched Michael's eyes follow the sheets to the floor.

"Your eyes, Michael, there's that look, just now. Tell me, please."

"That fluttering sound—it brought back Hy Vọng's first cries. They were swallowed by a squadron of helicopter rotors above us."

Kate's long aching sob released.

"Honey." Michael wrapped his arms around Kate. "I thought I'd actually covered up those brooding moments. Those memories are like a heavy yoke on my shoulders. How could I burden you too?"

She watched a spray of diamonds cast by the afternoon sun on the surface of the courtyard pond below and touched her ring. It had come to mean something else, no longer simply the joy she'd felt to be committed to the man she loved, but she would be condemned to the burden of his past, as well.

"I guess if I'm honest, I was ashamed." He dropped his head. "I was devastated having to leave Hy Vọng behind. My own daughter. Especially when I was with your family and all the kids."

He shared the details of the days caring for Hy Vọng. "I can still feel her soft skin. I had no way to feed her. Then I found a goat wandering in the chaos. It saved her; saved me."

"What did you do?" Kate sat beside him and took his shaking hands.

"There was an old village woman near where I was fighting. I wrapped Hy Vọng in my marine T-shirt with my name in the collar so that her grandparents would know her, and I gave her to the woman. I begged her to bring the baby to her home village. I imagined her safe and happy with Ha`ng's family. Holding all that back from you seems so crazy now to me. I'm sorry you had to see me acting like a madman."

"If hearing about your child is too much for me to bear, it must have been dreadful for you to talk about." Kate breathed deeply. "I'm sure you're sorry...and I'm heartbroken for you—that you lost someone you loved and are separated from your child. But..."

"You've lost trust in me."

"Yes, in our ability to be intimate when it's just us two together. How do I get that back? Can we?" Kate looked at the family photo she'd tacked on the wall above her desk. "I want it back. Selfishly, I admit, I loved feeling you were all mine. That you were wildly and totally in love with only me." Kate took a pencil from the desk and rotated it in her hands.

Kneeling in front of her looking up into her eyes, Michael waited. "Kate, you know I am, right? Wildly and totally."

"Michael, this is my truth, and it feels harsh, maybe cruel to say, but I'm grateful for that protest, your breaking down, or I would have married a troubled stranger."

"Would have married? Kate, no. I'm good when I'm with you. We're good." Michael moved to sit on the chair next to her, his elbows propped on his knees, fingers entwined. He closed his eyes, shook his head, and a strange smile erupted. "I can't believe I'm actually thankful for that violent protest. Oddly, it took something traumatic like that to push it out of me. I'm glad it all spilled out now and not later. But I'm so sorry you had to see that side of me. Honestly, I'm not sure what you saw; I don't quite remember it all clearly, but...we don't have to be strangers anymore. I've told you everything."

Kate watched his familiar gesture, clawing his hair back with his fingers.

"Maybe I needed to look in the mirror and see a hero, a sacrificing hero. That's how I've lived with leaving my daughter behind, by telling myself that she deserved to be with her people." He dropped his voice. "Hằng had a strong perspective about Americans adopting Vietnamese children. She felt the kids belonged in their own culture, if at all possible. She believed the government should find a way to set up sponsorships to place kids with families in their home country."

He looked up at Kate. "And I'd prayed every day that the

face of my infant would fade into a tolerable, gauzy, sweet image—stored away, disconnected from the pain of it all." He touched Kate's cheek. "We've never talked about children, Kate. You did say you didn't think you—"

"I was never sure." Kate changed the subject. It was too confusing, not the time. "Can you live without ever knowing she's actually OK?"

"I don't know...I can't imagine the memories would ever leave me, but I know those memories won't interfere with our love."

"Oh, God, Michael, it's all so confusing. Where *is* she, your baby, or I guess she's a toddler now?"

"A small rural village near the demilitarized zone, I assume. There hasn't been any action in that part of the country since." He took Kate's hand.

"How old is she? If it was before you left Vietnam, what? Almost three?"

"Yes, three...actually, yesterday." Michael's eyes flared. "I hadn't thought...maybe that explains it...the trigger.

"Three years old! In a *war*, Michael." Kate put her hand on his knee.

"If she's...dead, it's too painful to know."

An electrified silence hung between them.

"So, you don't know if that woman even brought her to her family?" Kate stood and walked to the window, imagining him holding his infant. Her twinge of jealousy felt wrong. Kate thought of the kids at Rolling Hills and their pain over being left behind. That pain is more crippling than their disabilities, Brent had said. "She's your *blood*. Isn't there any way to find her?"

"Kate, there's a war going on. How would I get her out even if I could find her?"

"Come here." She put her arms around his neck. "I can't find the right words for this. I'm so sorry for what happened. It's heartbreaking. But, Michael, that doesn't sound like the man I know." She couldn't look in his eyes. "How can we ever get 'us' back? Do I even know who you are now?" Fear of a future dealing with his damage weighted her judgment. She should end things right there? It was too much. How would she ever find the peace, the trust she needed?

Kate pictured life without him. No exotic travels, no music together, no love. The perfect life she had imagined with him. How was this all unraveling so fast? Why did everything seem like a lie now? An illusion. Yet, their loving moments had been so real. "It's like your past has devoured our future. The dreams we had."

"I promise you know me, the *real* me. Can we try to get 'us' back, Kate? It's all out now. Everything about us is right and good."

Was she being too fearful? Disappointment surged through her, but her thoughts rang true, and she couldn't hold them back. "I don't think..." Her practical side said it was the right thing to do. Her words came from her instincts and bypassed her heart. "I think we should postpone getting married. At least for now. I need to process all of this change. Would it help if you saw a...Michael, sitting here you seem so, normal—the, *you*, I knew. It's hard to believe the whole thing at the protest even happened."

"Kate don't give up on us. We haven't lost each other; I am who you thought I was, please? We're so good together.

You know me, dammit." He reached out and pushed her hair behind her ear. "What I withheld, well, yes, it makes me a liar in a way. But everything with you was true...is true. Are you willing to throw that away?"

She could hear his words drifting away. Was she foolish? "I'm so confused now, Michael. It's too much. But I love you. And you need to get help, so you don't suffer anymore. I can't bear to see it again." She had to force her words out. "Maybe you should go ahead to Bangkok and let me focus on my internship for the summer, at least. Give me time to heal, to build my confidence in you, in us. To test my ability to forget the protest. I don't want to have an extra woman in our bed. I can't."

"I know we can find each other again. I am who you thought I was, please?"

Kate hesitated. Her shield of self-protection lowered for a moment. "Maybe, after my summer internship, before grad school, I'll come to Bangkok to spend my few weeks off in August with you."

"Yes, under any terms. At least let me make one of your pins in your map come true."

Kate stared at him while rolling the fantasy around in her mind. The thought of being with him was frightening; being away from him, devastating.

"We can perform, have fun, and just be us." He touched her shoulder.

The offer was tempting—Michael's arms, an exotic vacation, their harmonies, a chance to clear the air, see who they might be together now. See if his past can fade and truly become the past. Maybe by then...in a few months.

Kate pulled at her engagement ring.

He covered her hand. "Wait. We had enough love to want to make a life together. Don't we owe ourselves that much, Kate? Somewhere away from everything that happened?"

The decision formed and felt right. Could Kate get that scene out of her mind? His tender words, his hands running over Kate's body with the chaos around them. *I love you, darling; I love you, Ha`ng. We'll be together.* Those haunting words. She wasn't sure they could ever make love without Kate wondering if he was with her, honestly with her. "God, Michael, I'm miserable about this, but I think postponing the wedding is the right thing. And yes, I'll come to Bangkok, and we'll try."

"Kate, no..."

"It was such a rushed thing for everyone. And my mother and family will understand." The wedding plans were simple anyway, she thought. The break would give her some time to let this all settle-in. "This is too serious a decision to risk making a mistake."

Kate knew her family would be disappointed but not as much if she just said they were postponing because of the rush. And now with her in a summer internship in two days. "I want this to have a happy ending as much as you do, Michael, but I need to know if you are sure you're with me. I need you to heal." The memories of their loving moments flooded her as he stopped her from removing the ring.

CHAPTER 38

Kate

TURNING PRISM

KATE WAS DISORIENTED and lonely. Every landmark held memories of Michael—the library, their dorms, the Student Union, and especially the Administration building that still held the chilling memory of the events that had blown their life together sky-high. Each time she passed by the building, Kate threw a barrage of questions at herself. Did she do the right thing? Maybe she should have canceled her job and grad school and gone with him. No, that felt wrong. Michael hadn't trusted her with the truth once. Would that be a pattern in their life together?

Mostly, Kate wondered if there was room for her in Michael's mind along with his love for Hà̉ng, the horrors of the war, and the ache for his missing child. But could she ever be happy without Michael and their music? Should she even go to Bangkok on her break? Maybe the internship would balance things out a bit and not make everything about Michael and his troubles.

Her mother's words on the phone had been comforting, do

what's right for you, Katie. But there was so much her mother didn't know. It wasn't just the rush that delayed the wedding. What was right? She wished she could talk to Shiloh, but she was traveling.

With the entire campus shut down due to the protests, Kate found herself sitting in the same seat in Dr. Goodman's office, where she'd made her original pitch for grad school. If it weren't for the violence on campus and Michael's meltdown, she would be withdrawing from school to go to Bangkok with him. Thank God, she hadn't taken that step. At least not yet.

Kate had been candid with the professor, she needed a paid internship and a place to live. There would be no living with Michael in the married grad dorm; she couldn't afford a dorm room or apartment. Kate was lucky. Dr. Goodman arranged a temporary job for Kate at Rolling Hills as her required internship, and Kate found herself house-sitting and living in Dr. Goodman's pool house. A win-win, the professor had said since she was leaving for a summer on the Riviera. What must it be like to travel like that?

Falling asleep in Dr. Goodman's gracious accommodations with insects pinging against the screen, Kate thought about her first day at Rolling Hills. She faced her disappointment; there were no paid music internships with the orchestra or teaching, but there was a teacher who had to go on maternity leave. Kate would substitute for her until she returned in the end of July. Only seven students, ages twelve to eighteen. Surely Kate could handle teaching how to tell time to a group the size of her own sibling gang.

How could she ever thank Dr. Goodman and Brent?

Pulling the stack of files onto her lap in bed, Kate finished reviewing the notes the teacher had given her on the students' backgrounds. This was beyond what she'd learned in her classroom training. Brent had so much faith in her, and it meant a real salary for Kate. He was desperate, he'd said; now, so was she.

Kate had to start classroom teaching on her own with no practical training. Everything she'd learned in her special ed. classes was from books, she'd warned Brent. Her "big heart," would be enough, he'd said.

She shuffled the papers and studied the hand-written teacher's notes. All seven children were termed "educable." What did that mean? After reading about the students, Kate had her doubts.

Florence rocks and bangs her head on the wall... Patty's extreme social anxiety interferes with the learning process... Ernie can help if she has a panic attack. Stanley's affect is flat... Ronnie can be aggressive.

Kate was in over her head.

Ernie was intriguing. The teacher had written...*a great sense of humor and the leader of the pack.*

At fifteen, Mary has made minimal progress since her mother dropped her off at twelve years old, the report read. This one caught Kate's attention. Why no improvement after three years?

The teacher's final note read, *Don't get discouraged.*

She set the notes aside on the nightstand. As Kate settled

into her pillow and turned out the light, she imagined Michael and the emptiness he must be feeling, tucked away in a hotel room in Washington without the comfort of their bodies wrapped together. There was a painful hole in her life without him. She was ready to throw herself into the challenge of Rolling Hills to try to fill it.

Would the heaviness in her chest ever subside? She wanted to focus and settle into her new job. To get back on track. Still, the loss was a constant hum in the background that she was determined to ignore. As always, her sympathy evaporated and was replaced by her disappointment, sometimes anger. If only he'd been honest and open early on.

CHAPTER 39

ABLE ADVOCATE

THE SUN ROSE obediently, and so did Kate. On the drive through the beautiful countryside to Rolling Hills, she thought about the small cluster of students she was assigned. Kate parked in the shade of an old tree outside the entrance to the main building. The stream of dampness down her blouse had nothing to do with the humid Monday morning.

She was exempt from the new teachers' tour that Brent had taken her on when she'd made that life-changing candle purchase, nearly two years before. Entering her classroom through the heavy, oak door, her steps were not as light as when she'd first visited the institution. The same blend of acrid cleaner and bayberry and vanilla scent wrapped around a slight lingering hint of urine. She pulled at her miniskirt.

A note was taped to the door of the classroom. Brent had a family emergency, one of the teachers would try to stop in. She was on her own for the morning. Kate took a deep breath and opened the classroom door. Six of Kate's students were already there, but the classroom chairs were empty.

Two students perched like cats on floor pillows in the striped sun. One boy sat huddled in the corner on the floor. A second stood, arms crossed leaning against the chalkboard. A girl faced the wall, banging her head gently. Another was curled up, arms wrapped tight around her lean body, her forehead pressed against the supply door, as though she were playing hide and seek.

Kate blew out a breath and locked her hands in front of her to stop their shaking. She forced a smile. Passing the oversized solid oak desk with a matching chair, Kate knew she wouldn't sit there often; she planned to be with each child, individually.

"Good morning, everyone."

No answer.

A large, plain black and white cardboard clock for teaching time was on the wall within reach. Venetian blinds kept out the New England sun, casting jail bar lines on the hospital-green walls. Springing the blinds open with a pull of the string, dust flew as Kate strained to lift the window to let in some fresh air. It wouldn't budge. Painted shut.

Particles of fairy dust from the bent blinds danced in the shafts of sunlight around the students to the sound of one student's voice repeating, *oh, no; oh no; oh no, she's here.* It was precisely how Kate felt.

When the seventh student still hadn't arrived, and it was ten minutes after nine, Kate became concerned. The teacher she was substituting for wasn't available to show her the ropes, as planned. The woman had delivered her baby girl prematurely, leaving just enough rope for Kate to hang herself. Opening the door to the hallway, Kate looked to see if there was another teacher to ask for guidance, but the hall was empty. Not able to leave the classroom to find the seventh child, Kate decided to begin. Begin, what? God help her.

Some of the children laughed, some smiled, and a few were clearly oblivious to what was going on. Squatting in front of each student, Kate asked their names, seven names she'd memorized: Florence, Patty, Stanley, Sally, Ronnie, Mary. The missing student was Ernie, and by elimination, the young teen girl splayed against the peeling wall, also not answering, was Mary.

Then Kate heard the knock. She crossed the room and opened the door. No one. It wasn't coming from the door. The sound came from behind her in the classroom. No one was moving—another knock. Now Kate began to smile, as well. Something was up. The sound repeated, and Kate zeroed in on her desk, the massive oak teacher's desk with two deep, wide drawers on either side. The tapping came from the right side. She looked under the leg space. Nothing. OK. I'll bite, she thought. Kate slowly pulled open the drawer halfway. The oversized head, nestled down in the deep drawer, spoke.

"Hi." The drawer closed and the mischief-maker disappeared. How in God's name did he fit in there? Kate pulled it out again to the delight of the kids. They squealed and sputtered with laughter.

The head spoke. "Hi, I'm Ernie. What's your name?"

Kate thought she recognized him from the orchestra, the cymbals player. The absurdity of talking to a student in a drawer hit her, and she laughed and answered, "Ms. Ketchum."

"Ketchup? OK, Miss Ketchup, hi." He pulled the drawer

open with his undersized, stubby fingers. "Miss Ketchup, can you give me a hand?"

Kate reached out to him. He had a steel grip, short fingers, and wrinkled hands like an old man. His compact, misshapen body emerged from the drawer, and he hopped up on the desk. The little person with a big head and an even bigger personality gave her a hug.

The teacher's notes were factual, but they didn't convey the teenage person who'd emerged from the big desk drawer—*hydrocephalic, enlarged skull, cleft palate, hair lip that made him lisp, missing vertebrae, club feet, stubby arms, and fingers.*

"OK, everybody, this is Miss Ketchup, and we all have to be nice to her," he announced with confidence.

Kate had an advocate. He leaned over and whispered in a squeaky voice with a slight lisp. "If you want to know anything about these guys, I can tell you. Careful, some of them are retarded, you know."

Unsuccessfully, Kate tried to repress her brief burst of laughter.

Ernie sat on the desk and comforted Kate, touching her arm as he whispered his assessment about each child. He's retarded; she's really retarded. Oh, and that's Mary. I told our teacher about her, but she didn't believe me." Ernie leaned in and lowered his voice even more. "She ain't retarded; I heard her read out loud when she didn't know I was there. True, Miss Ketchup, honest."

"Thanks, Ernie, but you shouldn't be telling me about your classmates, should you? You better take your seat, OK?"

Kate accepted the name Ketchup; after all, what kid doesn't

love it. And she corrected the word, *retarded*, in Ernie's ear. "And now we say, *disabled* or *special*, not *retarded*, OK?"

"OK but they really are retarded, you know."

Mary's vacant expression made Kate want to know the truth about her student. The words on the teacher's note ran through her mind—no improvement since Mary had arrived. Ernie couldn't be right. Kate felt especially drawn to this student's case.

Who could have known what was going on inside the child from the way Mary sat in the corner barely rocking, staring, her arms hugging her scabbed, boney knees, her platinum hair shadowing half of her pretty, narrow face? If not the full-time, exhausted teachers, not Brent, certainly not Kate—who felt every bit of her inexperience as a green and naïve recent graduate who'd majored in music and special education.

All morning Kate tried to teach the class how to tell time. It reminded her of digging a hole in the sand at the beach as a kid, filling it with a bucket of the salty ocean, and expecting the water to stay. Nothing stuck; it all drained out after lunch period. Telling time was the essential skill for these young people, Kate had been told by Brent. It was required for her students to get a job at their residential institution. Everybody's dream—pocket money, and a flicker of freedom and those oh-so-special keys.

It didn't take Kate long to realize, these "unteachables," as she overheard one teacher call them on her first tour, would be a bigger challenge than she thought when she'd read the teacher's report. It made her want to succeed even more. She wanted them to have keys, something to look forward to each day to expand their lives.

Mary kept drawing Kate's attention. When the young teen girl made eye contact, she wiped her hands down her white dress twice as if to brush its little yellow flowers off onto the floor. Her brown leather shoes turned in when she walked with one tattered shoelace dragging.

Responding to Kate's voice at times, Mary glanced up, then down again. She seemed entertained by the streams of splattering afternoon rain slithering down the enormous arched windows. The big moon lamp suspended from the fifteen-foot high ceilings cast a halo over her shiny, corn silk hair.

The light flickered as the classroom darkened from the gathering summer storm. Determined, Kate again rotated the big hands of the black and white cardboard clock. Mary's body moved forward as if she knew the answer, was about to speak, then she flashed her intense blue eyes at Kate, and shrugged. On a rare occasion, an elusive smile was sent Kate's way like the quick flash of the sun on a windy day when the clouds moved fast across the sky.

There was a cacophony of noises in Kate's classroom—vocalizations, grunts, spontaneous, random and uncontrolled, but none from Mary.

When the class lined up for lunch, from short to tall, Mary's reed-thin body stood last in line. Puberty had sent her up several inches in the past year, her teacher had written in her notes. Kate observed Mary and assessed her affect. Engaging her eyes up close, there was a moment, a clear-eyed, vulnerable moment when Kate wondered if Ernie might be right; there might be more to Mary.

CHAPTER 40

Michael

SEEKING HOPE

MICHAEL GLANCED OUT of his third-story embassy office window. The Marine Security Guards were changing posts by the south entrance, sun glinting on rifles, shifting from shoulder to shoulder. Michael was changing, too, feeling much calmer since he'd moved to Bangkok two months before. He'd marked time by that hourly changing of the guard. One more week until he would see Kate. They would be together for a month during her break in August before her grad school started in the fall. In his mind, he hoped it was the beginning of their life together. He would be patient, let her choose the path. Not easy, but he owed her that.

The Buddhist culture, learning the Thai language, immersing himself in arranging arts exchanges between the U.S and Thailand had kept him busy and happy. He'd already snagged the best of the American ballet companies and greats in the music arena. The senior officers and the ambassador were impressed. With full intention, Michael was building a life, a future, for himself, hopefully with Kate.

He examined his hands. Soft, clean—fingers that landed lightly on ivory keys at the Thai American Club each week. Hands that had moved smoothly over Kate's skin, only hers. Those were the images he kept in his mind.

The embassy counselor had connected Michael to an extraordinary Thai Buddhist monk to learn daily meditation. The idea had seemed strange at first. How could he ever empty his mind of the things that had inhabited him for years? Too big a task, he'd explained to the monk. Sitting still and meditating, no way. The one-hour, daily walking meditation the holy man taught Michael—slowly stepping heel-toe through the yard of his new rental home—had worked. Moving through the lush gardens encased in red bougainvillea-covered stucco walls, Michael was aware of his body. Silence, interrupted only by the sounds of a dozen different birds, had begun to replace the clatter in his brain. He'd looked up the Thai names of those musical birds and repeated them in his mind as he identified their tones, and slowly paced in meditation.

When Kate arrived he would shop with her for his permanent house—one she loved. One she might return to someday. He was ready for Kate, ready to restore her faith. He'd be damned if he would disappoint her or let himself down. He wanted to move past the horrors of that protest and his closed-off ways and to open Kate's heart to their new life together. He wanted to earn her trust.

The phone rang. Michael fanned the stack of letters from Kate and his mother and stood up from his office chair, cradling the slippery black handset in the crook of his neck. "Hey, Jeremy. How have you been? Long time no see. Still flying?"

"Yeah, the usual in and out missions. How's the job, buddy? We saw you brought Charlie Parker in for Saturday."

"Yeah, it was a coup. I can get you tickets."

"Maybe just for Cheryl; I may not be back that soon. Listen, Cheryl and I want to invite you to dinner tonight. We keep meaning to... or are you playing at the Thai American Club? Sorry, it's last minute, but I'm headed out again tomorrow."

"No, I'm at the keys on Fridays and Sundays. You're on. Hey, Jeremy, where's the action in Nam lately? Just between you and me." Michael tried to sound casual, just curious.

Supporting himself on the teak desk with one hand, Michael stared at the map on the wall behind him. As Jeremy talked, Michael drove a red push pin into the office map of Vietnam to mark the general area. The Viet Cong had resumed attacks closer to his daughter's grandparents' village. He was shocked. He thought with the de-escalation news lately, he would finally know or could at least *believe* Hy Vọng was OK.

"Seven o'clock work? You there, Michael? These damn phone connections. You there?"

"I'm here. See you at seven," Michael managed to answer.

The heavy humidity resurrected Michael's memories as he left the embassy—the steamy air of Southeast Asia. The same vaporous moisture that had soaked the dull green, military issue T-shirt he'd wrapped around his infant before he'd given her away.

He took the back stairs, followed the sidewalk in front of the embassy, and walked down a side alley to the noodle vendor, Khun Prasaat. As always, the street food cart was parked just off the U.S. Embassy property. Michael had to think—away from his job, away from the putt-putt sounds of two-cycle engines on hundreds of motorbikes, taxis blaring horns, people spilling over the streets swept up in scents of charring skewers of meat, tropical fruits and fragrant flowers—the classic Thai city street scene.

The menagerie of vehicles chattering at each other along Bangkok's main thoroughfare faded as Michael reached his favorite lunch spot. It was his escape when he could avoid obligatory, formal meals or official lunch meetings at the cafeteria.

"*Sawahtdee, Krap, Khun Michael.*" Prasaat, greeted him. Swishing some vegetables, fresh herbs, seafood and noodles in a wide metal pot, red hot from the coal fire beneath it, he served up a generous portion in a wooden bowl.

Michael grabbed a pair of chopsticks from the glass jar, hitched one hip onto the single customer stool, tucked his heel onto the crossbar, and began an endless swooping of the delicious concoction into his mouth.

The air felt just as hot as the heat coming off the flaming pan. Would the Bangkok summer weather ever call a truce with him? It always resurrected unwanted war memories like movies from the X-rated section of a video rental store where he'd forbidden himself to go. The ones he'd labeled *Violent, do not view. Adult materials, X-rated. Play at your own risk. Not for the impressionable.*

How could he do the right thing and at least try to find Hy Vọng to make sure she was safe with her family? He searched for a solution. No way he could find his way into Vietnam with what was going down, he thought. He was a civilian now—an American Embassy official.

It hit him. Jeremy was the rule-breaker Marine pilot. Hadn't

Jeremy himself taken a little orphan, right off the street, sat him on his lap, and piloted the boy back from Saigon to Bangkok in the heat of the war? His friend didn't care about the rules; that was a child's life at stake, bottom line, he'd said.

No, Jeremey didn't give a damn. He wasn't going to abandon that street kid he'd fed chocolate and noodles to over the years since Jeremy had been assigned to the Saigon embassy. The boy had no one. And no Marine had ever betrayed Jeremy and told.

Looking for Hy Vọng in her village just to make sure she was OK was something Jeremy could do. Michael hadn't had contact with Jeremy in so long, but he remembered Jeremy's last comment to him, if there's anything I can ever do for you. There was a small, private airstrip right outside of the village where he'd met Ha`ng. If his buddy learned about Hy Vọng, maybe he would check out the village where Michael had left her? And her grandparents' home village, as well, if he was ever in that area again. To see that his daughter was OK. Worth a try to put Michael's concerns to bed.

The decision was made. After dinner, Michael would come clean with Jeremy in private about Hy Vọng. One long shot, but he had to take it. Kate's words hadn't left him. "That's not the man I know."

He wanted to be that man.

Michael sat at the dinner table that night watching his friends' young adopted boy, An, playing in the living room.

Cheryl told Jeremy's story about arriving home with the scruffy street child to add to their family of five kids. "Like bringing home a puppy that wasn't house-broken," she said, shaking her head.

Jeremy chimed-in. "He'd never slept in a bed, never brushed his teeth—peed right on the floor. Whenever he had to go, there he went. Poor thing. It was a long, tough time for him to adjust. Cried a lot. Caused a lot of chaos in the family with the other kids." Jeremy wrenched his neck around. Sending a warm smile, he nodded in the direction of the child, as if to say, look at him now.

It may not have been much different if he'd brought Hy Vọng home with him, Michael thought. Not that it was ever a real possibility.

After dinner, Jeremy's wife pointed her eyes to their little boy who sat at the table playing checkers and speaking English with one of her other children.

"Sweet as he can be. No regrets." Cheryl's eyes misted. "An!" She called to the boy. He ran to her and snuggled into her arms. "I admit I wanted to...well, I wasn't happy with Jeremy at first.

"Understatement." Jeremy laughed at his own joke.

"Well, you've got an early start tomorrow, Jeremy, why don't I head out."

Jeremy followed Michael to the front hallway. "Glad you could make it."

Michael squeezed the back of his neck and stopped by the door.

"Something on your mind?"

"This is a big ask, Jeremy."

"Spill it, buddy."

The truth came out awkwardly. Every time Michael told it, he could hear the infant's cries.

"Why the hell didn't you tell me this sooner? Damn, Michael, your own kid? Look, give me the details; I'll check it out, see what I can do." Jeremy looked over his shoulder at the sound of Cheryl's voice coming closer. "Look, I don't know when I'll be able to get to that area, could be weeks, months, but as soon as I can, I'll check it out. No promises. I mean finding her...she could be anywhere by now. But, I'll be in touch, buddy. Keep the faith."

"I just want to know she's OK. She belongs with her family." Michael shared the location where he'd left her and the name of Hàng's family village.

"Got it."

"It's best. It's been three years. I'm a stranger; she's with family."

Michael awakened early after a rumbling night of seeing his baby's face in his mind. Imagining her happy, cared for by her grandparents, he prepared himself for no news or weeks without news. He couldn't let himself think of bad news. But the pain of leaving her behind was lifting now that he had taken some action. Imagining Hy Vọng safe with her family wasn't enough anymore. He had to know.

The woman was good for him, Michael thought. No bullshit. Kate would always tell it like it was. This time he would tell her right away. He stood barefoot on the cool, polished teak floor and looked up at the King of Siam traditional portrait and made the call. Kate would be proud of him, Michael thought.

CHAPTER 41

Kate

UNFOLDING MYSTERIES

LINING UP THE class as usual in the big circle Kate had drawn on the floor with chalk, marked with the numbers 1 through 12, she began the exercise. Each student held onto two sequential numbers she'd made with construction paper, representing the hours on the clock.

It had worked great to have Francine call out the hours. "Twelve o'clock," she announced and bumped her head against the wall Kate had cushioned with a foam pad. At times, Francine turned and called the time out without the need for the wall.

Ronnie, a tall willowy boy, had lurched in the corner staring at Kate all summer. Looking down at her bellbottoms, she thought of her blue flower mini skirt suit she'd worn the first day. Ronnie's salacious gaze and his unconscious habit of rubbing or pulling at his crotch had unnerved her, sobered her to the abnormalities of the world within the institution.

Sally held the number twelve high above her head. The boys drummed on the floor with drumsticks, until it was their turn.

Kate sang in rhythm with Francine's words, as Sally stood in the middle of the clock, rotated, and pointed two long, cardboard clock hands while singing to the beat. "Twelve o-clock. Five after twelve, ten after twelve, quarter after twelve..." The class joined in. Kate had seen progress but would the lesson slip into a dark hole in their minds after gym class, as it usually did?

The bell rang. Gripping the door frame, Kate watched her disheveled, lovable cast of characters find their way down the hall to the gym for their exercise program. A solemn blanket of sadness descended. Kate felt like she'd swallowed the basketball that she heard bouncing off in the distance. Teaching, maybe she could handle, but the summer without Michael had been challenging and lonely. Their crackling overseas phone calls had kept them connected, but they didn't fill the painful void. Not singing with him made Kate feel strange, detached from herself. In a week, Kate would be walking out of Rolling Hills to hear the scraping sound of the old, double, green metal doors behind her as she was set free into her future. Her seven young students would hear the same door closing on them day after day, left inside to live out their lives, forever. She shuddered.

Kate was determined to help the handful of students she'd been assigned to teach—an internship she could never have imagined. If she could just teach them to tell time, it would change their lives inside the institution's walls. They would be able to have a job, earn pocket money, or maybe get a job in the community, like Bobby. So far, Kate was making some progress with the students—except with Mary.

Mary was the last to scoot past Kate, her body held in a

curve, arms wrapped around herself, a posture that said, please don't stop me, let me through.

"See you after lunch, Mary."

The girl pulled in tighter. No words. There was so little time left, but Kate was determined to figure out the mystery that was Mary.

"Summer went fast, didn't it?" Brent approached in the hallway, smiled.

Kate held out the intake notes on Mary he'd given her at the beginning of her internship. "Thanks, Brent."

"Here's a letter of recommendation for your file. Have fun on your break in Thailand. Your fall semester's around the corner. And thanks for subbing for Mrs. Norton."

Stepping out of the doorway, Kate summoned her most cheerful voice. "Thanks so much. The students were so good. They're so sweet, those kids." Not a word about her suspicions about Mary to Brent, she'd promised herself. Well, what could she say? Maybe Kate was just imagining there was more to her student.

"Maybe you'll consider applying for a position after grad school. I don't know if we'll have any openings in two years but you'd be perfect. Join us for our concerts any time. By the way, four of your students will finally be getting keys. Good work."

Why did her stomach quiver? "That's wonderful. Oh, Brent, thanks so much. I'm not sure what my plans are yet, but I did love the concerts."

Could she handle teaching there? Full time? Kate imagined how much more difficult it would have been without Ernie to help her unfold the mysteries of her class.

Kate's weekly calls from Michael in Bangkok had added to her confusion. Things seemed so good for him. He'd sent photos of his new home, told her about the famous acts he's secured for performances in Thailand, and always, his sweet loving words left her aching for him despite her underlying fear of trusting they'd be fine.

Sitting on the edge of her classroom desk eating a tomato and lettuce sandwich after reading Mary's file, Kate realized she'd met each morning at Rolling Hills with both excitement and trepidation.

Her last day. How could she explain how repulsed she was by the environment; how much she grew to love the young souls who were in her care? One day there was hopelessness when a child faced repeated failure, and hopefulness another, with even the smallest successes. The yin and yang of the place was perfectly captured by the aromas of the candle and the odors of despair. It left Kate confused.

Any mainstream classroom would have been a breeze no matter how difficult, Kate thought. Those children would leave school and return to a home, a family, siblings, and surely a hug. That one thought lodged in Kate's heart like a festering splinter, and she couldn't pull it out.

The horrors of the institution were partly her projection and partly true. She'd also learned, like life in any world, Rolling Hills delivered the full dimension of human experience in a different context—laughter, sadness, joy, depression, betrayal, loyalty, fight or flight, isolation and belonging, love and hate, and everything in between. It was an awakening, a nuance about context she would never forget. She would have to drag herself away; she wanted to run.

Kate had learned to get down on her students' physical level on the floor or plaster herself to the wall, curl up in a ball, to be real, to relate with them. Most importantly, she thought, she'd learned they weren't scary; they were just different.

There was nothing in Mary's file that would explain why she hadn't progressed in three years since she'd been abandoned by her mother. Not a single parental visit. No contact. Kate noted the address—Connecticut, only an hour away. Strange. From the detailed intake notes, she could imagine Mary's mother sitting in the cracked brown leather chair in Brent's office twisting a limp tissue and fingering the brass studs along the armrest, tearfully sharing her story.

Kate could imagine the desperate words of Mary's mother based on the detailed notes in her file. "Mary's always been like this, poor thing. Can't talk; never could. I can't keep her no more, considering work and all, and not havin' the money for help. And her stepfather promises she won't be trouble."

Why would she say that? There was a clue in that statement. Kate pictured the gaunt worried mother pleading on. "You got to take her, *please*? My Mary can learn though; you don't gotta put her in with the real retards; she can learn, just slow is all. Can't talk, you know."

That stopped Kate. Real retards? More clues. She imagined Mary's mother saying goodbye to her smaller carbon copy. Like a fragile roadmap to her own story, did her mother see herself in blonde-haired Mary's future—underfed, overworked, overwhelmed? She must have kissed her as she left her listless daughter. The escaping breath and the guilty relief that showed in her mother's shoulders as she walked away might have told the tale had Kate been there. But it wasn't in Mary's file; nobody had guessed. Kate could imagine her mother dropping Mary off; she couldn't imagine her never coming back without a good reason. And that held the key, Kate thought.

Mary responded to Kate's voice, glancing up then down when Kate spoke to the class that last afternoon. But when Kate tried to teach the kids their time lesson, rotating the big hands of the black and white clock, Mary's body moved forward, and Kate saw her lips move as if to answer.

What was Mary's story—depression from her mother's absence, a disability, trauma, or a true disconnect that impeded her comprehension? Was her condition treatable?

CHAPTER 42

THE TELLING TRICK

ERNIE WAS THIRTY-TWO inches of genius, and Kate was always fascinated by his insights into the other students. Yet here it was the last day of her internship, and he could barely grasp the concept of telling time or reading. That made Kate confused and so disheartened after two months of trying to teach him.

She loved when Ernie popped-up daily from beneath her desk and treated every child like a friend. Shiloh had dubbed Ernie, Kate's fairy godfather, on their weekly phone call. Each day Ernie would whisper his perspectives on the other students privately with Kate. He'd helped her zero in on a path to each child. When she'd slipped and called him that special name, her fairy godfather, he was thrilled. Kate smiled recollecting his response. "Wait, then I'll need a magic wand, right Miss Ketchup?"

"No you don't, Ernie, just use your smile," she'd told him.

Entering the classroom on her last afternoon, Kate observed the difference in Francine. Ernie's first words about his fellow student had never left Kate's mind. "OK, Miss Ketchup, see that girl, Francine, yeah, she seems retarded, really bad, but that banging she does on the wall, it's kind of like her own music. See? *Ba-ba-ba.* He'd held out one finger and bobbed it up and down to follow the beat like a conductor. As Francine nodded her head in the air to three counts, she would engage the wall, bump-bump-bump—ba-ba-ba, bump-bump-bump.

Kate had succeeded in teaching Francine with Ernie's idea. She'd use the pattern to teach her in between the notes. The excitement of reaching the child through her rhythms was so rewarding. Francine had begun spelling simple words and telling time.

Ernie approached Kate's desk. "Francine is cool now, but what about Mary? You've tried, but Mary's not retarded," he said in his high-pitched nasal cartoon-like voice. "I tried to tell them, but they won't listen cuz I'm retarded." He smiled, held his hands palms-up, and nodded. "Yeah, maybe you need to trick her? She likes you, Miss Ketchup."

It had been useless to remind him to use the appropriate words like special or disabled. No matter what you called it, Ernie was right. Kate needed a strategy—something to make Mary draw back the curtain she'd held between them. Kate had run out of time, only one afternoon left.

Turning around, Ernie faced Kate with a look of realization. "How about you write her a note and see if she looks like she can read it?" He sauntered away, nodding to himself, "Yeah, that's it, Miss Ketchup."

"Ernie, you are just too smart for me." Kate smiled.

"Nope, I'm retarded, remember? I mean, *disabled.*" Ernie grinned, stood up on Kate's desk and got so close she could smell his morning breath, the residue of his toothpaste, his musty orthopedic shoes. He had no self-consciousness. It freed Kate, as well. He approached her as she sat on the edge of her desk, while the others were playing with the individual cardboard clocks she'd made for them. "Miss Ketchup?" Kate accepted that he knew he had her by the heartstrings.

"Yes?" She didn't know what was coming next, but she did know it would be worth hearing. How can you be both repulsed and in love? She was.

"Hey, Miss K?" He smiled and tilted his head at Kate. "Would you come to see me at my concert this afternoon?"

It was a tough decision since it was her last day and she had lots to do, but how could she refuse. "Of course, I will." Kate was still so enthralled with the orchestra, although she'd been disappointed when she'd arrived and the music director hadn't needed more help. He already had two interns in place for the summer. How might that have changed things.

"In the music room, we're practicing lots. Nobody ever comes to see me." Ernie's statement stabbed Kate in the heart. No parents, no one who loved him as their one and only. Kate imagined his young mother gasping at the sight of her newborn's deformities and leaving him behind. Kate understood; she didn't. "Ernie, I wouldn't miss it."

Ernie clapped a dozen times fast and rocked his head from side to side.

Kate saw the pure delight in his eyes, on his face, and in his gyrating hands.

"Whoopsie, daisy." He wiped a tear from the corner of his eye, staring at the droplet on his finger, as though it were a stranger. Then he lowered his head, and his body swayed with embarrassment. "Yeah, Miss Ketchup, you're the first one to come just to see *me*." He skipped down the hallway toward the lunchroom, leaving Kate's chest aching.

Her last afternoon. Kate sat at her desk ruminating about Mary, ready to implement Ernie's idea to draw out the girl's truth. The two old untouched typewriters in the corner on small tables, provided the answer. Slipping across the room, Kate cranked a piece of paper into the roller and struck the stubborn keys to type the words, *I like you, Mary. Do you like me? Miss Ketchup.*

After the lunch break, Kate waited for Ernie's last-ditch effort to work.

As always, Mary returned to the classroom first. Kate took advantage, walked to the typewriter, and read the paper. "Oh, look, a note for Mary." Kate could see Mary was tempted by her announcement.

The young girl's eyes were riveted on the dusty keys from across the room. Slinking closer, Mary sat down at the typewriter.

Hoping she might reveal herself by typing a word or two if unobserved, Kate slipped into the ladies' room to give Mary space. She half-expected the young woman reflected in the mirror to tell her what to do. At nearly twenty-four, Kate felt like a child herself, dealing with the demands of these children.

From behind the closed door, Kate heard him—like an approaching ambulance siren, Ernie's laugh whined and whooped up the hallway and into the classroom. There was no mistaking the joyful sounds of Ernie.

"Hey, where is Miss Ketchup? Maybe she left cuz we're too smart for her?"

Kate could see Ernie through the crack in the bathroom door, shoulders shrugged, hands palms up, bulging his eyes, rocking his head. His usual theatrics. Hearing the giggles of his classmates, whom she'd come to love, Kate imagined the six of them scattered about the room in their favorite routine places.

How could they imagine that the next two hours meant Kate was never coming back if they could hardly tell time? How could they imagine change when there was so little of it in their predictable routine lives? Kate dropped her head against the green, square wall tiles. The thud of her head was clearly followed by a second thud on the wall outside the bathroom. Maybe it was catching.

"Yeah, we're too smart," Francine said. Another squeal of laughter leaked through the door from the group. Then came another soft thud, as someone's head engaged the wall again. Such a thrill to hear Francine volunteering to speak, to express humor. The vocalizing part she played in counting the minutes in the clock exercises had certainly brought her out.

Leaving the cramped bathroom, Kate stood unnoticed in the corner as she observed the students. Can elation and sadness live together at one time in one human heart? The sadness won. Even if Kate started the process, who would see Mary through? Was she opening a Pandora's box for Mary? A pyrrhic victory, perhaps? But no turning back. Dear God, why did they make up something like internships in such fragile situations, with such fragile young people with such tender, young hearts? Theirs *and* hers, Kate thought.

The students were busy playing with the clock.

Mary made her move. She walked around the typewriter twice like a suspicious cat, stretching out her thin hand several times, then withdrawing. Finally, she lifted the drooping page.

Kate kept Mary in her sight and watched her scan the little black shapes lined up on the stark white background. Her back spoke to Kate; the message had clearly hit Mary's heart—the words had broken through. Mary whipped her head around and met Kate's eyes with confusion. They shared an edge of tears, and Mary's shaking hands found her face.

Kate rushed over and touched the young teen's shoulder.

"Miss Ketchuh...I wish..."

Kate froze in place, her breath quickened; she was afraid the spell would break. "What, Mary?"

"I wish..." Her whisper-of-a-voice, silenced for years, was tentative, hoarse and rusty.

"What, Mary, what do you wish?"

"I wish you wuh...my Momma. You wud'na left me."

"Oh, Mary." Kate could only manage a whisper, herself. She wanted to wrap her arms around Mary's frail body, kiss her limp, white-blonde hair. Kate took in the long-awaited moment and tenderly straightened Mary's hair.

CHAPTER 43

Kate

DARING DREAMER

KATE WOULDN'T REMEMBER a thing about what she'd taught her class that afternoon. She'd only felt the anticipation that fizzled through her at the thought of her meeting with Mary after class, and her pressing need to decide what to do about Mary in the few hours remaining in her tenure at Rolling Hills.

Part of Kate wanted to stay and make a difference for her students; part of her was grateful for the natural escape route, the excuse to leave it all behind—the smells, the frustration, the hopelessness. She hadn't shared her thoughts with Michael on their weekly call. She wasn't sure herself how she felt. And admitting her doubts to herself was embarrassing, let alone to Michael.

Kate was no miracle-worker, no saint, no wizard. She'd felt more like an unprepared new grandparent, grateful when the day was over; relieved to return to the quiet of her life after a long delicious day of spoiling her grandchildren—leaving the indulged children behind for their parents to deal with.

Although these children could never be considered indulged. Every precious bit of sweet attention was gathered up like jellybeans in their near-empty Easter baskets.

The flurry of goodbyes sounded at the three o'clock bell. Kate touched Mary's shoulder on the way out. "Can you stay for a minute?"

Mary nodded and checked the empty classroom behind her. She dropped her head. Her words were whisps of air forced from Mary's mouth. "OK, until three o'clock and one minute, right?" She looked at the clock and smiled.

Was it to show Kate that Mary had taken in everything she'd been taught? Mary had spoken. Again.

The cheerful, late July sun angled through the open window and pushed a moist, warm breeze their way. Such a delicate moment. Was it the foreshadowing of a good outcome?

Kate had to take the pressure off of the girl. "Will you help me clean up here?" Watching Mary shuffle the chairs under the desks, Kate thought, this was a no-win situation. She spent a few minutes, straightening up, and trying to figure out what to do. What would happen to Mary if her capacity was exposed? Pulling the wilted piece of paper out of the typewriter. Zzzzzip, Kate read the words Mary had typed; they made Kate queasy. *I love Miss Ketchup.* Sinking deeper into regret, Kate remembered Brent's warning on orientation day, *Don't get too personally involved.*

So, you just cram your feelings down, shut off your heart, give them a vanilla version of yourself? She guessed in hindsight that may have been easier, but the thought of not having connected with Mary felt wrong, as well. Kate knew she was drowning in her own naiveté.

Kate would see if Mary would communicate again, then she'd go directly to Brent's office. The hissing and pinging pipes and a distant dripping sound from around the corner were like music in the background as they spoke. "Mary, you know I'm leaving today, right? To go to school?"

"Yes, buh, you come bah. Nah like Momma."

Mary's trust in her was a burden. Oh, God. Kate couldn't get the words out of her mouth. She just couldn't tell the child that she wouldn't return. Would Kate come back if she could? It was becoming clearer to her that a future at Rolling Hills, or working with special children, was beyond imagining now that she'd seen the realities splayed out in front of her. So many children thrown into the walls of the institution, the dedicated staff overwhelmed, the services underfunded. Maybe Kate was too much of a romantic idealist. Maybe if she'd worked with the orchestra, maybe on her breaks she could volunteer, Kate thought. She wanted to stay; she wanted to run, she missed singing and music. And she still had to get through grad school. "Mary...come with me. Ernie is playing, and I promised to be there. Shall we see Ernie play?"

"Yeah, he plays good."

Kate rushed to the music room with Mary to watch Ernie perform. The orchestra was in good form, but there was no Ernie. Halfway through the piece, in a grand crescendo, Ernie's short, stubby arms appeared amid the back row of musicians, smashing cymbals, one, two three, then he disappeared down into the group again. A burst of laughter rose up inside her; the emotion turned to tears as the song ended.

Ernie approached her, lit up with pride. "How'd I do?"

"Smashing, Ernie, simply smashing."

He held his stomach laughing. "I get it, Miss Ketchup, smashing! Like cymbals, right?"

"Ernie, you's funny." Mary's door had opened. Her face showed her own surprise.

He stared at Mary, then Kate, and started to dance a jig, "Woohoo, Mary!" His arms flailed, his feet thudded against the tile floor. "You're talking."

Brent tapped on the wire-screened window to the music room and signaled to Kate.

"Mary, can you sit here on this bench with Ernie while I talk to Mr. Brent? I'll be right back."

Mary followed Kate's instructions like a resigned prisoner. The jerk of Mary's head in Kate's direction and her brief smile said so much. There was some level of trust and connection. But how much? In Mary's world, was Kate just another mother figure who would abandon her? "I'll be back, Mary." Hadn't the girl heard that painful phrase before?

Glancing back at Mary, Kate talked to Brent at the door. How different her childhood was growing up in Glynn surrounded by dozens of siblings, cousins, aunts, and uncles, compared to Mary's sad beginnings. Kate used to hate that feeling of always being within earshot of some relative. Now she realized what a circle of safety she'd had surrounding her.

"So what's this about? Your departure?"

"Brent, Mary isn't disabled. Well, not in a way that she can't *undo*. At least, I think so."

"What? Kate, I appreciate your enthusiasm, but I think Ernie's had an influence on you. He's been saying this to Mrs. Norton for over a year now. You taught the girl. Do you really believe Ernie?"

"No, I believe what I saw today." Kate stepped closer. "She spoke to me, wrote a note on the typewriter. Honestly."

"Really? You're serious."

Kate handed over the paper with the two notes on it.

"I'll be damned. How did you ever..."

"Isn't there any way to get Mary out of here? Anywhere she can go? What's the law?"

"She can only be released if her mother signs her out. Except for an outing."

"So can we find a different place for her? A foster family, somewhere? She doesn't belong here, Brent. I can't bear to leave, knowing she could have had a better life. I mean, I know Rolling Hills does its best, but—"

"No need to hedge; this place is a nightmare...but, yes, we do our best." Brent sighed. "So to answer your question, her mother would have to sign her out and give up parental rights." And frankly, I couldn't in all conscience let her go back home with a mother who'd never returned. In my mind, the stepfather's suspect. Mary's chances for safety are probably better here."

"Why do you say that?"

"Just based on her mother rubbing her arm while she spoke to me and the way she pleaded for me to take Mary...saying the stepfather promised Mary wouldn't be any trouble. You read the notes, Kate. And Mary folds in on herself at the slightest touch. If you read between the lines, there could be abuse involved. That's my hunch."

"Hunch? But doesn't anyone follow up, or do some kind of home visit when kids are dropped off like this?"

Brent stepped back and crossed his arms. "I'd just arrived

here when this all happened three years ago, Kate. They live an hour away. I'm not sure what was done. Maybe it fell through the proverbial cracks like a lot of things in our world. There are sixteen hundred residents here...look, I shouldn't have to defend myself to you, Kate. I know you're passionate but..." His tone turned cool.

"Sorry. No, of course you shouldn't." Kate retreated. "Just so I understand, if her mother released her rights to Mary, the State would let her live with some nice family somewhere? A foster home?"

"Technically," Brent rubbed his stubbled chin, and sighed, again. "I'm an optimist, but I don't hold out much hope in finding a family who wants an older child who doesn't communicate and might have a background of abuse. As heart-breaking as it is. And who knows where the mother is after three years? She never answered any of our communications. And with a possibly abusive husband?"

Kate thought of the address from Mary's intake file she'd jotted down just in case. What would she do with it? She was tempted. What if Kate could find Mary's mother? "Maybe Mary has relatives? Has anyone ever checked that out? I mean—?"

"None were listed. Kate, look, you're new at this work. And I appreciate your dedication to these kids this summer, but the woman was bruised and not very bright. She refused to list her one sister as next of kin. Said they were estranged. The woman has never been back to see her Mary, and she's proba-bly...look, I'll check into it, and if Mary talks and is functional, I'll make sure she's moved into job training and relocated to a safe, campus residence. You have to feel good about that."

"Thanks, Brent." Kate didn't feel good, not good at all, but it was clear from his tone she had more than overstepped.

"You may have a natural talent with these kids. But, Kate, don't get involved, please. This is bigger than both of us. I'll pass this proof on to the social worker to investigate, OK?" Brent folded the typed paper and put it in his jacket pocket.

Kate looked over her shoulder at Mary who sat listening to Ernie.

"I know you, Kate; I didn't hear your promise. And what it took for Mary's mother to leave her child here, we don't even want to know. I don't want you to take offense. But you are just beginning to understand this world. You're only an intern."

They both turned to look at Mary, who sat, slumped over and sad on the bench.

"I love that you're a dreamer; it's admirable, but you might be dreaming up a nightmare for Mary." Brent folded his arms and dropped his gaze. "Disappointment in the known might be better than what she'll find in the unknown."

Kate returned to Mary's side, burning with anger. Even if there were sixteen hundred residents, didn't every kid count?

CHAPTER 44

Kate

REVERSING FORTUNE

KATE SIMPLY WASN'T cut out for it, she realized. The direction she thought would light her life up, had been a detour to a dead end. Pacing, regretting, and crying were her constant trio of self-tortures during the weekend packing out of the pool house.

Ernie's casual response to her departure, surprised and admittedly hurt Kate until she realized the kids who were lifetime residents, like Ernie, had no experience with someone staying, no expectation of loyalty, no sense that anything was permanent except the walls of Rolling Hills.

There was no resentment toward Kate from the rest of the class. They probably knew nothing else—just a long line of teachers who had come and gone. Ernie had simply waved and run up the hall. "Bye, bye, Miss Ketchup. Remember, I'm your fairy godfather." Her leaving was the norm, it seemed.

Mary was a different story. There was nothing Kate could do to console her. She'd pushed Kate's hand away when she'd tried to touch Mary's face. Slumping into the corner of the hallway, the girl had sobbed between words. "You neva eva comin' back. Just like Momma."

It had been profoundly discouraging for Kate to have released Mary from her self-imposed wall of disabilities. Without Mary's cooperation in coming out of her shell, there was little chance she would be released to a life outside the institution. Mary still hadn't spoken with anyone else but Ernie. What trauma could have had such an impact on the girl?

After announcing Kate's decision not to continue her studies with Dr. Goodman's graduate school program, Kate was miserable. Her mentor's look of disapproval and disappointment had melted Kate into a puddle of shame—after everything the director had done for Kate.

Dragging herself through the motions, gathering her things from the pool house, Kate's guilt was red hot, burning her from the inside. Her newly chosen career of uplifting children and making their lives better wasn't what she thought it would be. When the summer term was over, leaving Mary and Ernie was beyond the most painful thing she'd ever had to do, but working at a place like Rolling Hills where there was so little hope was impossible for Kate.

When Cousin Patrick swam his awkward lap in the pool, his parents' joy had been palpable to Kate. She knew she'd made a difference teaching the petrified boy to swim, a big difference. It had changed his interaction with the world. Why had Kate been so naïve to think she could change such a deeply entrenched place like Rolling Hills? No, the scent of bayberry could only cover up the desperation that would always be there.

The weight of being a *quitter* rode on Kate's shoulders. Her siblings were right when they'd teased her; she did want to save the world, at least Mary's world. Being entangled in the lives of disabled children in the future, no matter where she taught, wasn't a fit, she realized. She couldn't keep a professional distance; she couldn't save every child.

The absence of hearing her voice go out to an audience had left her empty inside. Kate needed to see her mother—to take time to think. Nothing else in her world made sense right now.

The trip home to Glynn felt the same; it felt different. The same route, the same familiar streets, but Kate carried something new with her—the one thing she feared the most—the heaviness and shame of failure. and a car full of her belongings with nowhere to belong.

She shrunk down into the driver's seat as she crept up Washington Street. Not wanting to see anyone, not wanting to explain quitting grad school, not sure about Bangkok, she just wanted to sneak in the kitchen door and seek comfort in her mother's arms like a child.

Kate pulled into the narrow driveway and noticed the abandoned hand mower by the side of the house. Only the grass pushing up between the concrete runners on the left side of the driveway had been cut—a sure sign that her dad's back was out of whack again. Her whole life felt out of whack.

Everything had been so wonderful when she'd first left home. Every return trip for the holidays over the past two years had moved her life forward, until now. She was the prodigal daughter who'd returned to the place she'd always dreamed of leaving.

Watching her mother's shadow against the kitchen window blind, Kate wondered where to start—the protest, Michael's past, his lover, his child, Mary's situation, her quitting grad school? She had piled up a hill of decisions and problems to sort through with her mother on her day off. Kate was relieved; everyone else would be at the factory.

Closing the car door quietly, Kate took the stairs to the back door. The family had been disappointed but understanding about the delay of her marriage in May. Still, she'd never really explained the real reason for the change.

The story Kate told was a joyful one of Michael getting the most exciting job in Bangkok and her acceptance into grad school with a full fellowship. All true but not the whole truth. They would find a new date for the wedding on her winter break, she'd said. Would they? Why damage the family's image of the charming guy who had become like a fourth son? If things turned out right with Michael, she didn't want those details about the protest and his past to haunt their future with her family.

As she reached for the tarnished doorknob, Kate thought of the label she'd given their relationship—a global-commuter-marriage until grad school was over, she'd explained to the family. A strange concept for the Ketchums, but they'd always known her life would never be like theirs. As long as she was with Michael, her over-protective father and brothers were OK. His dedication to the Marine slogan, Semper Fi, always faithful, was good enough for them. To her newly-formed-feminist-self, gleaned from Shiloh's Women's Consciousness-Raising Group, that thinking seemed very sexist. She could undoubtedly survive without a man beside her. She would never let them know about his troubles and their near miss. The story hadn't ended yet so why tell the tale?

"Mom." She opened the door. Enfolded in her mother's hug, and within seconds, Kate lost her usual control.

"What is it?" Her mother peeled her away and examined Kate's watery eyes. "Sit, I'll make the tea."

How does she keep so calm in the eye of the storm? Kate waited for the tea kettle to whistle. Even that annoying whine made her feel relaxed, there in the kitchen where Kate was safe, where she could finally tell the truth and not be judged.

"Mom, I truly don't know where to start."

"Start with how Michael is? How has he settled into Bangkok and his new job?"

"We talk on the phone every week." Kate assessed Michael's progress, telling her mother how happy he seemed. Sharing descriptions of Michael's new house from the many photos he'd sent, his exotic life in the Buddhist country, and the offer from his boss for Kate to audition to sing at the Thai American club. Just describing his life there, made Kate happy she'd agreed to go.

"Mom, I need your advice."

"And advice, you know I have plenty of that." Her mother let out a short laugh and placed a cup of hot Lipton in front of Kate.

Kate slid her tea away and hid her face in her hands, elbows on the table.

"Something tea won't solve, I assume." Kate's mother rubbed her hand in circles on Kate's back. "So, love, romance, wedding, school? Let's hear it. Wait, you're not..."

"God, no."

Her mother huffed down into her oak chair. "Thank God for that."

"Michael and I...well, we didn't spend time together before he left for Bangkok for that to happen. There's no chance of that." Kate shared every gruesome detail of the protest, and their agreement to postpone the wedding. She described her pain over distancing from Michael, and the whole complicated story.

Her mother sat back and sipped her tea. "He made a terrible mistake, not trusting you. But it seems it's about more than that. His shame? Worried he would hurt you? No woman wants to know they've been kept in the dark. I'm sorry, honey." Kate's mother sipped her tea. "When trust is broken, it goes deep inside. But his whole breakdown so long afterward worries me. Will he get help?"

"He was seeing a priest on campus, Father Sullivan, my choir director. He was a Marine chaplain; he counsels Vietnam vets. I thought, and Michael thought, he was healing. So, it seemed. When we we're singing and together, the torture quiets, he says. I didn't notice much, just a far off look sometimes." Kate sipped her tea. "Mom, I thought it was what happened in the war, not his mourning for his lover and their child."

"We would never have guessed he wasn't at peace. How sad to have to leave his child." Her mother covered Kate's hand.

"Heartbreaking." Kate shared Hy Vọng's story and Kate's suggestion that Michael should attempt to find her to ensure she was OK. "I think knowing she's safe might be just what he needs to soothe his conscience. What do you think? Should I go to Bangkok and try to build our trust back? He seems so good on the phone. Mom, you know I love him, but I don't want to follow him and be shattered again. Maybe it's not about Michael so much now; maybe it's about me." Kate put her head in her hands. "The way he called out to me, the way he touched me thinking I was her." The automatic response returned, chills down Kate's arms and that sick feeling in her stomach. "Will I ever feel he's loving me and not her? If he'd confided in me when we were friends or first dating, it might have been so different. Maybe not."

"Men can be so damn senseless sometimes, their own worst enemies."

"Mom! I can't believe you just said that." Kate had to laugh. The moment of intimacy and openness between the two women felt refreshing.

"If we're going to be close, I have to be real. You're not a little girl anymore." Her mother joined in the comic relief and laughed. "So your thought is to visit Michael, then come back for graduate school?"

"Mom, that's another thing. I'm not...I withdrew from the program yesterday. God, I sound like a maniac." The entire story of Rolling Hills and Mary took two more cups of tea to tell. Kate tried to explain how profoundly discouraging it had been to leave Mary behind with her isolating barriers down. She would be so vulnerable to a flood of raw emotions. "It seemed so hopeless at that place. I know it's just me. I'm not cut out for it. Like you said, I'm a dreamer. I never really knew what that meant until I worked there."

Kate understood; she wasn't someone who could stay objective. There was no way she could remain emotionally detached. The children's lives had become inexorably a part of hers. "How the hell are you supposed to stay detached and still do your job? I made such a big mistake. And Dr. Goodman went to the mat for me. I'm just so mortified, Mom."

"Kate, remember what I told you when you were so upset in school when you made mistakes on your tests as a child?"

"I remember, you said, mistakes are your friends." Kate let out a small puff of laughter.

"Let's do this. Let's make this one, your friend. This was a powerful lesson to learn. What's done is done and with good intention. You have a chance to get back on track, to sing again. I imagine you've missed that part of you?"

"Like I'm missing an arm, seriously." Kate sighed.

"Kate, singing, it's who you are, like I always said. It seems you have nothing to lose visiting Bangkok. That's another dream of yours, right?"

Kate nodded and smiled.

"You can have your audition and see where your relationship can go. See if he's willing to get past this with counseling. Forgive him. He's suffered, Kate, and there is one thing I know for sure—Michael loves you, and you deserve that love." Her mother flashed her eyes toward the door to the parlor. "Don't stay here where you'll have to explain every little thing to everyone until you figure it out yourself. Protect Michael; no one needs to know all this. Trust yourself and go now. Find out if you belong with our Michael."

CHAPTER 45

Kate

FAR-FLUNG

HER MOTHER WAS right; Kate would leave tomorrow. When had she last had fun? His letters were so loving. Michael had said he was aching for her and wanted to explore moving forward with their relationship. Kate's passport and ticket had been in hand weeks before; he'd made sure of that. A quick departure the next day was easy once she'd changed her reservation at the airport.

The original plan was for Kate to visit her family for a week right after her summer at Rolling Hills. Traveling to Bangkok for the remaining four weeks until the fall semester started had no strings attached. They would just see how things went, he'd said. With no graduate school now, Kate had the option of staying with him longer than a few weeks.

She needed to talk to Michael. When Kate tried to call him, she'd only heard the familiar crackle on the line. So frustrating. She hadn't thought to surprise him with her early arrival in Bangkok, but as always, international communication was unreliable.

When she couldn't reach him, and it was too late for a telegram, she'd decided to go ahead.

Kate smiled, anticipating the look on his face and the way he would locomotive toward her and sweep her up. Who wouldn't want a greeting like that? She wouldn't let his demons take control. The thought of singing together at the Thai American Club sent chills over her body like fluttering confetti. Talking to her mother had always helped Kate to clarify her thinking.

It was good to see the family for dinner. Her mother played the perfect role in celebrating Kate's upcoming audition and being with Michael again. Her father was glad she wasn't going to grad school. Why do that when you're only going to have children, anyway, he'd said. Kate didn't respond. Funny, traditional Dad didn't take issue with her living with Michael out of wedlock. He wanted his little girl happy with Michael. For the first time, Kate agreed with him for different reasons.

Before bed, Kate slipped downstairs, stretched the phone cord into the kitchen pantry, and called Shiloh to share all of the news.

"Oh, Mary, and Ernie, all of it breaks my heart. But you did the right thing, Kate. Leave it to the professionals." There was a silence on the line. "And as for Michael, God, Kate, I have no answers for you, but it's worth trying. I hate that f-ing war."

"I'll miss you; I have missed you. I'll write often." Kate felt an ache for her old friend and their nights sitting cross-legged in the dorm on Kate's bed, figuring out their futures.

"Don't think I'm not coming to Thailand. Winter break, I'm on your doorstep."

"But truly, Shi, I'm not sure I'm staying; we're just—"

"You know, once you see his eyes, you'll be staying."

Kate knew that was a likely possibility. "Thank you. If I'm there, I'll count on your visit. How's Harvard Law?"

"I'm working flat-out and feeling purposeful. And picture me, I wore my serious suit today."

"I'm sure you look the part, but don't change too much."

"Don't worry, my hippie garb awaits me at home, and I wore my best bandana."

Shiloh's signature, echoing laugh made Kate pull the phone from her ear and smile.

"You're doing the right thing. Like your mom said, you'll be singing again. Don't you just love that woman?"

"She's the best. And so are you." Shiloh's support was always touching. She'd been there through it all. "Thanks, Shi."

"Kate, your mother's right—forgive him; see if he'll get help; you two are so good together. We all have our demons."

"I'll try, and you're right; we are good. As long as all the secrets are out, maybe we have a chance."

CHAPTER 46

EARLY ARRIVAL

SONGS WERE THE structure of Kate's day. Was there ever a time when lyrics weren't rolling around in her head or escaping her lips? Sometimes she didn't notice the music; she was so used to her brain's duality—her thoughts and that background hum of lyrics. Walking down the Pan Am hallway at the Boston airport, she smiled and felt happy for the first time in days. Kate remembered Michael's funny comment. If far in the future they ever did an autopsy on her, they'd find two brains in Kate's skull—like a cow has two stomachs—one normal and one a jukebox.

Sometimes the lyrics were related to what was happening to her at the time. Was it her subconscious that chose just the right selection for the moment? Lifting one of a thousand recorded vinyl messages, and lowering the needle of her sharp memory, it would play them in the background of her mind.

She walked faster down the Pan Am hallway to Gate A2. The opening line to the Box Tops' song rotated around in her mind again. Michael had given her *a ticket for an aeroplane.*

Her first flight ever, and she would be traveling around the globe, passing over three continents. One big dream fulfilled, foreign travel. And living overseas in exotic Thailand, that was a fantasy she never thought she'd really have. Maybe now, she would. Michael had said he had a renewed appreciation for everything, watching the Thai people live their kind and peaceful Buddhist lives. He was more peaceful.

Would she sing, *lonely days are gone*, being with a man like Michael—honorable, musical, dedicated, and romantic? How can you ever thank a mother who puts your best interest first? If it weren't for her mother urging Kate to let the past go, and to leave Mary's future to the professionals, the departing look on the silent girl's face would have been enough to make Kate unpack and cancel her flight. Would Mary's words ever cease to haunt Kate? "You wud'na left me."

Turning the corner at the end of the long hallway, she heard the flight announcement. "First Class passengers for Pan Am flight 101..." Kate took out her first-class ticket. First-class, first flight ever, so many firsts. Would they make up for the ones she'd lost with Michael?

The stewardess fussed over her, offering her a drink. Sitting in the leather seat, lounging and drinking a Tom Collins, Kate continued to open up the package with a bow on it that a life with Michael could offer. She was beginning to be more hopeful their match would work. He would be so surprised that she wasn't going to grad school.

Kate leaned her head against the cool plane window and cozied into the book on Bangkok, reading about the Buddhist culture. Turning the pages, she took in the beautiful countryside and the golden temples. There was truly nothing familiar about the exotic city. It wasn't remotely like New England—the blazing sun, the ever-green vegetation, the weight of the moist air, or the tropical rain she'd read about on the flight. There was nothing Kate could relate to from her years in New England as she looked down on the marshmallow clouds.

By the time her flight landed, she was already in love with the idea of the crazy adventure she was on. There was no regret that she had snipped the tether to grad school and Rolling Hills.

With the luggage porter in tow, she exited through customs amid the chattering of the foreign language. She couldn't read the signs of Sanskrit squiggles. The thrill had an underlying layer of apprehension. But the thought of pushing in that first pin on her map was too thrilling. She wouldn't let herself succumb to fear of the unknown.

Standing in the throng of people, Kate dialed Michael's office on the airport phone. It rang and disconnected. On the second try, Michael's assistant answered.

"Hello. Khun Nin, it's Kate Ketchum."

"You are calling from the States, Madame?"

"No, I'm here, um, at the airport." Kate could hear her own heart pounding.

"Oh, you are a week early, then."

"Yes. Please don't say anything to Mr. James. I couldn't get through on the phone, and I want to surprise him."

"Yes, sorry, our lines were down, again."

Kate tapped her fingers nervously on her thigh. "Can you keep him there for a while? And can you help me get to his house, please? A cab, I assume? I have the address. And Michael's household help, Nong, I've spoken to her before on the phone. Would she be home, do you know?" Kate felt giddy and admittedly petrified.

"Oh. Nong is away on her day off, and I'm sorry, but Mr. James has taken the day to review the upcoming show's venue. He should be home by dinner time, Madame Ketchum. Welcome to *Krung Thep.*

"*Krung Thep?*"

"You know this is what we locals call Bangkok. Well, you would be challenged by the full name; *Krung Thep* is just a short nickname. Our city is so wonderful they wanted to sing all of its praises: *Krung Thep Mahanakhon Amon Rattana-kosin Mahinthara Ayuthaya Mahadilok Phop Noppharat Ratchathani Burirom Udomratchaniwet Mahasathan Amon Piman Awatan Sathit Sakkathattiya Witsanukam Prasit.* We Thais like to take our time, you know."

The foreign words made Kate's head buzz. Maybe coming without having reached Michael was a bad idea, she thought.

Nin's soft laugh made Kate relax a bit.

"I'll need to practice that, Khun Nin."

"But I am keeping you waiting. So sorry. No taxi necessary for you, Madame; I will send an embassy car and driver and the emergency house key to the airport for you."

"Thank you so much, Khun Nin." Kate was relieved. The complicated clatter of people speaking the tonal language Michael had described now sounded like a song she could never learn to sing.

CHAPTER 47

FIRST PIN

AGITATED CLOUDS RUMBLED above, and the air was heavy with the weight of an impending storm. Kate tucked into the back seat of the black embassy limo. Was her nausea from jetlag or excitement over this new overseas world she'd fantasized about since childhood?

Kate's 'taxi' turned onto Michael's street. Where was it? Not a single house was visible along the dead end road. Each property had a high concrete wall around it with glass shards along the top ledge. What was it that was so threatening that those precautions were necessary? Chills ran down Kate's arms. Rainy season with its deluge had brought snakes into the flooded streets and the powerlines down, the embassy driver said in his lilting English.

Women with warm smiles held colorful sarongs high to traverse the ankle-deep muddy waters. Watching the Buddhist people adapt to life's ups and downs had taught Michael so much about acceptance of what was, he'd told her. She needed those lessons now. Her planned romantic reunion with

Michael was going well despite the flood; he'd be home that evening. Still, Kate had some lingering doubts about coming. Did Ha`ng still live in his head? Could she let her fears go that he was with Ha`ng and not Kate in their intimate moments? Stop, Kate. She'd promised herself she wouldn't repeat images of Michael's past. She wouldn't let that be contagious.

The driver looked back at her and spoke in broken English. They would have to walk the rest of the block to the house. *"Mai pen lai, krap."*

Kate repeated one of the few phrases Michael had tried to teach her, remembering to add the feminine ending, kah. *"Mai pen lai, kah."* The phrase meant, it's nothing, never mind, not to worry. That wonderful, comforting Thai phrase she'd practiced that Michael had said would get you through anything. Nothing like a simple flood should throw you off or disturb your inner peace, the Thais would say.

She thought of the tones and laughed to herself. Did she pronounce it right, or had she said something completely different like, I want to ride an elephant. The musicality of the language was fun for her and Michael when they practiced Thai on the phone. Now it held a danger in the tonal errors you could make that invariably meant something unintended in the monosyllabic language.

The driver opened the back door of the embassy limo for her, and the steamy air whooshed in. Signaling for Kate to wait, he handed her two keys and a small towel to dry herself. Lifting her two pieces of leather luggage, he held them over his head with his wiry, muscled arms.

As she stepped out of the back seat, Kate felt a snake slither around her legs. She jumped and let out a quick, "Oh!" Her first encounter with Bangkok rainy season. Would she ever make peace with those snakes? Kate held her long, gauzy cotton skirt up as the driver guided her through the knee-high water, politely keeping his gaze to the side. She was glad she hadn't worn heels, but her taupe leather flats wouldn't take well to the swell of muddy water either.

Standing in the deep brown rushing liquid, Kate used the oversized, old-fashioned key Khun Nin had given her to unlock the gate to Michael's home. Little red bougainvillea flowers from the garden swirled around Kate's knees like a welcoming red carpet. A thick line of the lovely blossoms floated in the rushing water and clung to the huge iron gate frame, refusing to be washed away into the street.

She looked up at the two-story gracious stucco home with a porch that wrapped around two sides. Home had such a different meaning now that Kate didn't have one.

Could such a foreign and exotic culture ever feel right, she thought while trudging toward the front door against the insisting flood water? Kate had begun to fall in love with all of the richness of life she'd seen in the colorful book. There were no photos of snakes and floods in the pages of the gorgeous book he'd given her. She laughed.

Exploring a city with a twenty-one-word name was an invitation to the biggest adventure she could imagine. She felt nervous but somehow in her right skin. Why wasn't she petrified of a place so dramatically different from anywhere she'd ever been?

Kate thought of her mother's diagnosis of Kate's childhood attraction to all things foreign—wanderlust. Bangkok was Kate's first real taste.

The embassy driver deposited her luggage on the covered porch outside the front door and returned to take her arm. It was just a flood that would soon recede; nothing the raging sun couldn't handle tomorrow, she repeated to herself. This no-worry Thai philosophy was just what she needed. Let it go—Rolling Hills, Mary, graduate school, the protest. It was over, *mai pen lai, kah.* She let out the deep breath she was holding.

She thanked the driver, opened the door, and called out for Nong, just in case she hadn't gone home to her family on the other side of the Chao Phraya River. Everything was gleaming. Kate admired the teak floors and left her shoes just inside the door, a Thai tradition. The massive carved dining set, cushioned rattan chairs, and lounges in a stunning batik design were so inviting. A fresh scent of coconut and lemon laced the air.

Exploring the house, Kate smiled when she saw the coffee mug from O'Leary's she'd given Michael, upside down on a batik runner that decorated a hand-carved chest in the dining room. Framed photos of them together—playing at the Student Union, Kate smiling in his kayak on the lake, and Michael's first Thanksgiving with her family—surrounded an arrangement of white orchids on a shelf behind a baby grand piano.

It was too tempting. Kate sat and opened the keyboard cover. Perhaps, it wasn't just the environment at Rolling Hills that had made her blue. Maybe she was mourning the loss of her true self—her singing.

She gazed around at the sweeping room with floor to ceiling glass that opened to beautifully manicured gardens and trees laden with unfamiliar fruits. The flower-covered stucco walls provided total privacy. Her finger hit middle C, and the note echoed in the welcoming space. Please let things work out. Their phone conversations and his letters had made her more confident that the changes in his life—the job in music, his meditation, and getting away from the campus unrest—had settled Michael's mind.

The graceful carved stairway that led to the second floor made Kate cover her face with her hands and laugh. When she took her hands away, would it still be there? Too spectacular. Make yourself at home, Nin had said. Home, what a gorgeous home he'd made for them. He was right; she loved it.

Kate wanted to call her mother to describe the place and to share her joy. If she called Shiloh, they would scream and laugh together, as always. Kate would do that when the twelve-hour time change allowed, not at 5:00 AM US time.

Upstairs she found the master bedroom. Stripping away her soaked clothes, she hung them over the tub and put on her robe. The jet lag was setting in from her long trip and a twelve-hour time change—Boston, London, Bangkok. A hot bath was in order.

In the master bedroom sitting room, Kate stopped. The space had been outfitted with rattan furniture with sage-colored palm designs on a fresh cream-colored background on the cushions. Paintings of the Thai countryside hung on the wall. Staring at the large bed, draped with a beautiful blue batik coverlet and pillows, she made a promise to herself. She would push away the images of the protests, Michael's voice calling out for Ha`ng. She promised herself she would be with the Michael she knew, here and now.

A new addition to the room made her tear. A cozy Mama-san chair now sat next to his deep, round, overstuffed rattan Papasan chair in the spacious niche where Michael said he loved to sit and read overlooking the garden. The house photos he'd sent a week before had no such chair. The matching Mamasan chair was obviously a thoughtful welcome he'd planned for her arrival to say she belonged. Positioning it at a comfortable angle facing his over-sized chair seemed to promise the intimacy and honesty they would share in their future.

CHAPTER 48

Michael

RETURNING RHYTHMS

EVERY LIGHT IN the house was on. Not like Nong to leave them on when she'd left for her day off, Michael thought. He scanned the windows. In the master bedroom, stood the shadowy outline of a woman. She turned at the sound of the clanging gate closing. A second of confusion, then clarity, then a tightening in his chest. *Kate*?

He burst through the door, nearly broke the key in the lock, and took the stairs two at a time, calling out. "*Kate*? What the hell; you're really here?"

She stood in the master bedroom, wrapped in a white bath towel holding a shirt to her chest.

"Oh. Uh, do you want me to...do you need to get dressed first?" The realization of their situation brought him back to reality. He'd promised to take it slow, on her terms. He didn't want to blow it. He'd fantasized about their reunion so often, he'd gotten ahead of himself.

"No, I..."

Michael took three long strides and swept her up in his

arms. "I can't resist. We can argue about it later." He couldn't let her go.

"God, I've missed you, Michael Edward James." She kissed him.

"Let's just stay this way, so we don't have to face the challenges."

They laughed together.

"Michael, you've done such a beautiful job with your home."

"Not for long. This one's a short-term rental. I have a realtor who will help show us around; I wanted you to help me choose my permanent place. I mean, just in case we…in case you want to visit again. What do you think?"

"With those blue eyes of yours pleading like a child, how could I resist? That would be fun. Really fun."

He leaned in for another kiss. "Thank you for coming. I promise it's going to all work out. You will love it here for these weeks. And then, well, we'll see."

"Michael." She tucked the towel in tighter around her chest and signaled for him to sit in the overstuffed nest of a chair. "I'm not going to graduate school." Her embarrassed laugh echoed in the high ceiling. "I sound like you now."

"What happened, I thought…"

Michael listened as Kate explained her departure from Rolling Hills—the disappointment about Mary's fate, the bleakness, the mismatch, and missing singing…and missing him.

Michael sprung out of his chair to embrace her. "You did the right thing. Tomorrow, let's go find our new home. You won't regret your decision to leave grad school, Kate."

Rushing into things hadn't been Michael's plan. He would leave the pace of their reunion and intimacy up to Kate. He offered her the master bedroom that first night so they could take things one step at a time. He went to wash up and returned to say good night. She wasn't there.

After a momentary panic, Michael found her tucked into his guest bedroom, where he'd planned to sleep. She had the covers over her head, like a kid ready to say, *boo*. Her hand waved out from under the covers. He loved seeing her back to her playful self.

Kissing her extended hand, he took her back to the beautiful master suite. Without words, their rhythms just fell into place where they'd left off, with passion, like the first time they'd made love. He made sure to whisper Kate's name when he touched her, giving her the comfort that he knew she deserved. There was only Kate. They were a couple again. Curved-in behind her as they drifted off to sleep, he sensed no tension, no fear on Kate's part that he wasn't there with only her, alone.

CHAPTER 49

HELLO FOREIGNER

KATE LAY NEXT to Michael, studying his profile as the dawn made its way through the slice in the curtains, lighting one side of his face. Two words always came to mind, chiseled and refined—a contradiction that argued its way to creating a face she could look at all day long.

Were they really together? She propped herself up on her elbow and ran her eyes over the tattoos on Michael's shoulders. Remembering the morning she'd first seen them in her childhood bedroom on Thanksgiving, Kate's throat tightened. Those enigmatic Vietnamese characters on his shoulder that told his tragic story. But now he was calm and happy. He'd even seemed light-hearted.

Michael stirred a bit.

Their first night in Bangkok had been so blissful. They were truly lost in it. Untouched by his past. Troubles had faded into the background. She was relieved she'd dropped out of grad school. A career without music, compared to singing and being with Michael? And to not starve doing what you loved? Such a gift—if her audition worked out, she could contribute to their life together and send money to her family. Having a partner who shared her passion for music in an exotic place like Bangkok was all new and thrilling. A charmed life.

Kate fingered the traditional *phuang malai,* the garlands of strung jasmine that hung from her bedpost. The sweet fragrance of the petite, white flowers had put her to sleep and calmed her that first night amidst the cool blue walls of his master bedroom. Her life that had been fraught with uncertainty now seemed calm. "Are you awake?"

Michael faked the snore of a grouchy hibernating bear.

"You're so predictable. How did I know you were going to do that silly snoring bear routine?"

"Because I only have five jokes, remember, I used number five last night; now I'm back to number one again." He opened his eye on the shaded side of his face and kept the other tight against the glaring laser of light. Like a comedy-tragedy theatre mask, she thought. Light and dark. So kind and easy to be with in the present. Kate would set her mind to forgetting the darkness of his past.

Flipping onto her side, Kate stared up at Michael, and tugged at his ear lobe. "Playing and singing with you again— will be pure ecstasy. There's something so... I don't know..."

"Soulful? Sexy?" Michael ran his hand down her side and laughed.

The intoxicating scent of Jasmine necklaces, swinging from the rearview mirror, captivated Kate as the cab inched its way through the city. Their appointment with the real estate agent was a thrilling first day for Kate. Was it the aroma of those fragile white flowers that made her breathe in deeply, close her eyes, and smile? Or maybe it was the darling faces of the Thai children that swarmed around the open taxi windows at every stoplight or traffic delay to sell her the floral strands. Kate knew she would buy their flowers a thousand times while living in that hectic haven. The faces of Mary and Ernie flashed in Kate's mind. The distance between these children and the Rolling Hills students was more than half-a-world away. She had to let her regrets go somehow.

What was it that allowed her to drop her guard and settle-in, instantly? Maybe it was the children scattering freely on the streets at such a tender age. Their freedom spoke to Kate of the teeming city's safety and friendliness. Perhaps it was taking those hand-made garlands from the little girls' cocoa-colored fingers that was her first and purest connection? Or was it her fascination with their melodious voices that charmed her, *Sawatdee, Farang. Khun chap chai mali, chan*? "Hello, Foreigner! Choose mine. Oh, please buy my jasmine." Surely, her comfort with all the newness began with the Thai children.

Michael and Kate stepped from the cab in front of the Imperial Hotel and got into the awaiting Mercedes. The agent was not a typical soft-spoken, Thai woman, who tucked her smile into her respectful bow, her wai. She reminded Kate of whom? It came to her—a Thai version of Shiloh.

Kate laughed.

She was an attractive Chinese Thai with gorgeous thick black hair that she flipped over her shoulder when it fell on her listings page. Her tight skirt and an overabundance of gold jewelry, among other attractive attributes, and the sound of the bangles clinking, made Kate sentimental. She missed her friend.

After viewing a dozen houses, they made their choice. A unanimous choice. They left in a cab with the keys to do some exploring and waved goodbye to the woman, who zipped away in her Mercedes.

At the stoplight, the taxi driver shooed away the street urchins like pesky gnats as they pressed in and left their little handprints on the window glass. He apologized to Kate and Michael, worried the children were annoying the elegant American couple, no doubt.

Kate politely insisted that the taxi wait. Michael translated for her, *Karuna, khun phak thi ni, dai mai kah?* Sir, please wait here a moment, can you please? Kate had to buy one Jasmine chain from each child just to see the warmth of a smile spread across their sweet faces. How could you choose among the choir of angels who's unabashed eyes fixed on Kate. Big, round, deep brown chocolate eyes.

The first Thai cultural norm she'd embraced—lovely, innocent eye contact. "Why don't we do that in our culture?"

"Who said we don't?" Michael engaged her eyes until Kate laughed. Why was an enduring look only for lovers, inappropriate in her own culture, suspect even, she thought. Kate was eager to learn that gaze-lingering ability for the benefit of the journeys it would take her on during her possible life in the exotic Buddhist country. The friends she might make. Who might Kate have been had she been born into that world, instead of her close-to-the-vest Irish clan? She was a child again, innocent again—learning at every turn.

The driver's head turned around at Michael's words. "You speak Thai very well. You are a professor, an embassy official?" he said in his native language.

Kate didn't realize that Michael had been taught the most formal high dialect of the King. And the few phrases she'd learned from Michael, little by little over the phone before her arrival, made her sound like a polished educated person too. His more formal spoken Thai told everyone that Michael was of high rank by the phrases and words he used. They'd been treated like royalty. The depth of the Thais' bow, their traditional *wai*, hands pressed together, indicated they thought she and Michael were of high status. She laughed with the images of the crumbling factory in Glynn in her mind.

CHAPTER 50

MONOSYLLABIC MANIA

AS THEIR THINGS were moved into the new house the next Saturday morning, Kate walked with Michael near the embassy along the main street, *Soi Sukumvit*. The thoroughfare was filled with sounds that were becoming more familiar.

She was beginning to fall in love. Yes, those are the right words, *fall in love*—with the culture, the people, the food, the openness, the gentle Buddhism—a cocoon of comfort, like home, an exotic home. Maybe it was the jasmine or the traditional gold Buddha pendants dangling around every Buddhist's neck? Or maybe it was the whole of it that was much more than the sum of the parts. Beyond any explanation, Kate immediately connected at the heart, and Thailand became her home.

Was it when the Thais gazed into her strange stranger's eyes, assuming friendship, seeking a common humanity that made her feel she belonged? Was that what freed Kate to take down her walls—those unnecessary barriers to another human being?

The unidentifiable scents of strange food being sold by street vendors intrigued her. "Michael, what is that scent?"

"Fried cow brains, chicken saté grilled over coal, and lots of luscious curries."

"Cow brains, you're teasing me." She punched Michael's arm. He wasn't.

Kate had been excited to try out her Thai language. It came naturally to her over the first week. The musicality of the tones made the words easy to learn and hard to forget—like a song—although the idioms, colloquialisms, and the fast pace of the local's words still left her spinning a bit.

They took a taxi to the new house, and as Kate disembarked, she practiced that simple greeting with the driver, "I hope you are well." *Khun sabai dee reu kah?* Her words were understood. He responded in kind.

Yes, she was well and so happy.

The double wrought iron gates opened to their future home on Soi Ekamai, 63rd street. Perfect—a large stucco home, teak trimmed, with full-wall glass windows and doors, tiled patio on three sides, four bedrooms, a separate quarters for the traditional Thai household staff, and a garage and outdoor kitchen to the side—a must in a tropical home, Kate had already learned.

"Welcome home, Katie-girl." Michael lifted her and walked through the door, kissing her.

"Oh, excuse us." Kate slipped down out of his arms.

Inside the house was Nong, the household help, a petite woman with soft brown eyes and an embarrassed smile. She was dwarfed by the large open main room with high-ceilings and shimmering, classic teak floors. Nong bent her head and bowed with her prayerful hands held high in front of her face as a sign of deep respect—greeting Michael first, and then Kate, with a bow. A reverse of America's "ladies first" world.

Kate copied the wai, and Nong blushed.

"She is a little uncomfortable with the honor you just showed by the high placement of your hands and your deep bow, you're humbling yourself to her. You'll catch on," Michael explained.

"Oh." Kate and Michael removed their shoes.

"*Sawatdee kah, Madame. Dichan chye, Nong. Yin dee tee dai ruchakcan. Sabai dee reu kah?*"

"Nong says she's happy to meet you; she says her name is Nong and asks if you are well."

"I'm so happy to meet you, Nong—are you well?" It was Kate's first real try at a longer exchange in Thai.

Nong pulled back in surprise; she seemed thrilled that Kate could speak Thai. And clearly, Kate's correct tones had conveyed her meaning.

"She knows American wives rarely arrived with language skills," Michael explained.

"*Wives?*"

"It's assumed, honey...oh, not by me." He laughed with an edge of nervousness.

Nong's eyes sparkled, and she giggled behind her hand. "*Khun phut pasah Thai, geng maak.*"

Kate had reached her language limits and turned to Michael.

"You speak Thai, so well," Michael translated for Kate.

For Kate, there was no describing the thrill that passed through every cell. She was living on the other side of the planet. Was it knowing her mother sat in her overstuffed wingback chair rotating her rosary for Kate every day with a direct line to the big guy upstairs that provided some kind of protection? She didn't know. Was her irresistible passion for the unknown a genetic gift, or an inexorable curse from some Irish immigrant ancestor who fled the famine determined to survive? Was it that invincible feeling that allowed her to boldly come to Bangkok? Her face muscles ached from smiling. Kate was farther and farther away from the pain of leaving Mary behind.

She would bury that guilt in the din of the forty-four consonants written in inscrutable *Sanscrit* and the five tones of the clattering *Siamese* language. She loved that monosyllabic mania—and being here with Michael.

"Kate, I can't read your expression." Michael led her around their new house, room by room. "It's perfect isn't it?"

"It's joy, Michael, pure joy. And I don't mind at all that there's no kitchen." She poked her head around into the dining room, laughing. "Well, at least *inside* the house." She opened the door to the outdoor kitchen.

The traditional gold Buddha on a long chain swaying from the rearview mirror hypnotized her. Whipping back and forth, as their taxi driver's deft detours around divots, street dogs, and water buffalo, delayed them on their adventure. "I wanted to show you the countryside, what do you think?" Sitting in the back seat together, Michael put his hand on her thigh as she gaped out the window.

"I couldn't have imagined this."

"I want to spend some time with you at the Saturday Market too."

"I'm in." Kate shook her head in wonder as they passed lines of women in sarongs bent over, working in flooded rice paddies, with straw hats tilted in the breeze. Passing the roadside carts, Kate scanned the usual vendors selling coconut water and noodles with raging hot Thai curry sauces. A man wielding a glinting cleaver cut cubes of pineapples with precision, slipped them onto bamboo sticks, and passed them through the taxi window. Delicious.

As the black clouds broke, the downfall swallowed the sounds of the street dogs barking their greetings, the chickens squawking, and the groans of the buffaloes. Kate liked this tabula rasa way of living—starting fresh in an alien world that was hers to explore.

"This is going to work, isn't it? Us, I mean." Michael's pleading eyes touched her.

"Yes, it is." She squeezed Michael's hand. As the deluge splashed down the windshield, splat, splat, splat, welcoming Kate to her first tropical Thai rainy season, she felt her past wash away. Every mundane thing that had defined her, every mistake Kate had ever made, and the fears around Michael's loyalty, seemed to evaporate in the newness.

After they arrived back at their new home, Kate affixed her childhood world map to the master sitting room wall and pushed the first pin in, marking Bangkok. Like a shaking up of her childhood Etch-a-Sketch. A do-over, she thought. Finally, this felt like being the real Kate.

CHAPTER 51

Michael

AUDITIONING AGAIN

HE STARED AT her, sleeping beside him, watching the dawn wash across her face. The first Monday morning with Kate. They would go to the embassy together for her audition. It would be a breeze; he knew that. Nin had thought to give Mr. Harrington some recordings of Kate, and he was already anxious to hear her sing. Michael could picture Harrington in the frat house, offering him the job. So ironic that going halfway around the globe had finally brought Michael and Kate together.

Her eyes fluttered open.

"Breakfast in bed, Ms. Ketchum? Energy for your audition?" He pushed back the curtains and let the day in. "Nervous?"

"Only in a good way. I'm feeling my Irish luck this morning."

Michael put the tray on Kate's lap and slid his own onto the silk sheets. A green creature scooted across the ceiling and stopped just across the room from them.

"Oh my God, what's that, a lizard?"

"A gecko. They're harmless; they eat mosquitos. And they're

good luck; if they make their tsk-tsk-sound seven times, you're in for something good."

Kate sipped her coffee. "If I were home, I'd have screamed and gone to get the broom. But I read that in a Buddhist country, all life is sacred. I believe I'm in for something good." Kate tugged on Michael's earlobe.

"Yes, you are." Michael kissed her bare shoulder. Especially in our life...together again."

"He is kind of cute, but what if his little suction cup feet give way?"

The gecko's call started, and Kate counted. "One, two, three...a perfect seven. "OK, he can stay."

"There you go, the Thais would say your successful audition is guaranteed."

Passing the Marine guards at the door to the embassy, Michael saluted. The sprawling white concrete buildings, nestled in a garden of trees and plantings, stood out in the middle of busy Bangkok.

"Michael, it's huge."

"We don't like to understate, we Americans." He laughed. They stopped for his mail at his office. Michael sat Kate in his swivel chair. She smiled at the cluster of framed photos of her on his desk. Turning, she looked at the map of Vietnam behind her. "You and me with the maps. What are the pins?"

He had been tracking the Vietcong and U.S. attacks to ensure they weren't near Hy Vọng's village, but he didn't want to bring that up. "Just places where the fighting's taking place."

"Oh."

"Kate, they're not places where I'd been with... with anybody."

She stood and put her hand on his arm. "It's fine, just funny, you and me with the maps. That's all I meant."

"OK. Let's head over to the Thai American Club; Riverrun will be there. You're going to love these guys."

The all-glass sky-scraper venue was perched on the penthouse level with a stunning view of the Chao Phraya River and its network of busy canals that twisted in between the buildings and temples.

Michael enjoyed seeing Kate's reaction as she gazed down at the magnificent King's Palace, its rooftops splashed with gold leaf.

Michael imagined Kate singing to a packed house of expatriates and local executives. Framed by the gold velvet curtains, he pictured the city lights smiling back at her at night like a second audience.

He introduced the band members—a Pilipino lead guitarist, a Japanese drummer, Thai rhythm guitarist, and an American expatriate on keyboards for times when Michael was engaged with visiting performers.

Nin arrived. "They're excited; they've heard your recordings. Mr. Harrington is on his way. So good to see you, Madame Ketchum."

"Would you feel comfortable calling me Kate?"

"I could do, Khun Kate, less formal but more polite. OK?"

"OK, Khun Nin."

"No, *Khun* is unnecessary. I'm just Nin to you."

Michael smiled. "Just roll with it; you'll catch on," he whispered.

Harrington greeted them and sat in the back of the room for the audition. The band was set to perform the songs they'd played with Michael for months. Familiar and perfect for Kate.

With the steam rising visibly from the city's expanse outside the glass walls, Michael pictured Kate singing in O'Leary's, rocking the crowd. He knew she was thinking of her failed audition at UConn and the punch to Kate's gut that came with her rejection from the head of the music department. She'd talked about it all the way to the audition.

Kate grabbed the mic and delivered her best blues, country rock, pop and soul.

Michael watched Kate's eyes flickering between Michael at the piano and the smiling faces of Nin and Deputy Harrington.

Harrington's offer was ensured by Kate's crystal sounds. His words were a shot of pure elation. "Fantastic, they'll love you. Nin will talk money and draw up a contract and set up the schedule with you."

And that was that. Kate thanked the band and left with Michael down the elevator.

"I can't believe it. Michael, is this really happening?"

"Thanks to that Gecko, right." Michael was so happy for her and for himself. Things were going so well. "You deserve it. Now let's go celebrate.

CHAPTER 52

ON WINGS

WALKING THROUGH THE Bangkok weekend market with Michael the following Saturday, Kate saw so many exotic, unfamiliar things—prickly fruits she had no idea how to eat, unfamiliar fish and fowl, vegetables, sweet treats, and cages of birds. They stopped at every stall. Kate fantasized with Michael about a purchase, asking what's this and what's that. "Shall we have a pet bird?"

He smiled, explaining that these Thai birds aren't kept as pets to coo at and say, "pretty bird."

Kate put her finger into the cage to touch the soft feathers of the little gray and black birds with red beaks. "Then what do they use them for...wait, they don't eat them, do they?"

"No, no, just the opposite. Tradition says we should release them to the sky, like Buddhist believers do, to gain merit. The belief is that merit is a force that comes from doing good deeds; it attracts good circumstances into a person's life, they say."

"Think of it as grace, credit on the big guy's books, I guess."

Michael laughed and lifted a cage that held several hopeful, chirping, feathered friends.

"Oh, so many charming Thai customs."

"Tomorrow is your twenty-fourth birthday. Shall we follow Thai tradition?"

In all the excitement, she'd forgotten. Twenty-four, and she had everything she could ever have wanted. And more.

Michael paid the Baht and bought a cage filled with the sweet creatures.

In the middle of the sunlit, grassy field, in the shadow of the King's golden palace, Kate pondered her future with Michael as the birds cocked their heads and eyed her. Could the fluttering flock sense their impending liberty? Their imminent release to the azure atmosphere made Kate shiver with an awareness of the fulfillment of her desire for freedom. She never thought she could be committed to a man and feel free. She was wrong.

Michael unlatched the gate on the birds' metal prison. "You ready?"

Was he speaking to Kate or the birds who trembled in anticipation of their release? Kate shared their disbelief and their momentary hesitation to escape the open door. Could she also fly away from home, everything she'd known, without regret? Was their relationship and maybe marriage, the cage, or the sky?

"You open the door, Kate. It's a metaphor." Michael held the cage out and she opened it.

Kate touched her engagement ring. Her throat tightened at the fluttering and flapping sounds that encircled them. The birds' happy tweeting activated her excitement to see them emancipated to their natural lives to soar above.

Dropping the empty cage, Michael lifted his arms into the air watching the birds scatter to the sky. The thrill of their freedom took hold inside Kate, and at that moment, she felt her new-found courage to free herself to fully follow her passions, to love Michael openly. No fear of flying with this man she loved.

Michael put his arm around her, still tracking the escapees above them. Kate would stay with Michael; they belonged together. She would thankfully perch feather to feather, on a sturdy branch with a bright bird of a different breed beside her. In that instant, she understood the profound power of that charming Thai tradition of release that inspired her—a moving metaphor for freedom and taking flight.

After weeks of singing together and the ongoing questions about the woman living with Mr. James in the traditional culture, it had all made sense. Things had been so peaceful and loving. They were ready.

"I think my family took our marriage announcement well on our phone call, don't you?" Kate stopped on their walk down the embassy hallway.

"Cecelia set the stage and everyone followed. I love that about her. Your father showed more emotion than anyone." Michael laughed.

"She puts me first, and he's sentimental at heart. And Christine was so sweet. I mean she really cried…"

"She always cries. But in a good way." Michael took Kate's face in his hands. "We're doing this, wow."

Was it possible that he was free to love someone again?

And not just someone, but *her*, his best friend, his musical match. "Are we crazy?" Kate's gaze lingered. That face she could look into forever.

"Probably the sanest thing I've ever done." He kissed her.

"We will do this again when we have home leave, right? For our families?"

"As often as you want." Michael winked and opened the door.

She'd never expected to be married, let alone say her vows in an office at the Bangkok Embassy under the portrait of the King of Siam and an American flag. Still, they hadn't wanted to wait a minute longer.

Kate swept her hands down the lavender silk suit created for her by a local seamstress. Michael looked so handsome in his blue suit. He handed her a purple orchid from their garden.

Slowly spinning it in her hands, Kate had never felt so certain. I do. Two words that would lead them to a life together in the most wonderful city she'd come to know from Nin with its twenty-one-word Thai name—the City of Gods, the Great City, the Residence of the Emerald Buddha, the Impregnable City of God Indra, the Grand Capital of the World Endowed with Nine Precious Gems, the Happy City.

CHAPTER 53

LUCKY KEYS

AFTER A MONTH performing four nights a week at the Thai American Club, Kate and Riverrun had attracted a room full of regulars. Kate peeked through the curtains at the crowd seated at the twenty-five white, linen-covered tables with an expansive view of stars and city lights through the floor-to-ceiling windows. "Michael, remind me tonight when I come down off the cloud to call Shiloh; it's her birthday."

"Impossible. It's October already? I lose track of time here somehow. No changing seasons like at home to remind me, I guess. OK. Here we go."

The manager approached the stage.

Michael had a strange expression on his face; Kate couldn't read it.

On her breaks, she loved watching the waiters move about serving drinks to the Thai and American business executives and embassy officials and their spouses. The servers wore traditional Thai costumes—white Nehru-style jackets with five buttons, knee-length silk pants with a wide sash at the waist, and high socks and dress shoes. Fingering one of the timber pillars carved with lotus flowers that flanked the inside wall of the stage, she took a slow breath to relax.

"Ladies and gentlemen, it is my pleasure to introduce Kate and Michael Ketchum-James, or as I like to call them, the K-Js, and their fabulous band, Riverrun."

The Thai American Club manager had given them their new name for nights when Michael had sat in. Kate liked it. She'd earned her reputation for drawing a crowd over the weeks performing with Riverrun. But, for Kate, the nights when Michael was free from work to join them were the best.

Stepping through the purple velvet curtain onto the stage, the anticipation on the diners' faces and the round of enthusiastic applause sent a familiar spray of chills down Kate's arms. With Michael on the piano and keyboards, Riverrun was in tune and ready. Settling onto the polished bench, Michael stretched his fingers.

They performed a variety of American songs in every genre, giving Kate the chance to sing her favorites. "Let me do this forever," she whispered.

Private thoughts and images of romantic nights together with Michael made the lyrics sizzle and the sensuous tones of a love song come alive.

Kate was known for that. She hadn't lost her ability to move an audience, especially on an international stage with a crowd that craved American tunes.

Mid-song, Kate saw her through the smokey room in the back of the club by the bar in the dim light. With the spotlight focused on Kate, she couldn't be positive. But when the woman turned, and the lights of the bar hit her, there was no mistaking the glitter and glow of those bangles and spangles; it was Shiloh.

Nearly losing the lyrics, Kate skipped a beat but caught up and tried to focus and finish the song. One glance at Michael's grin, and Kate knew he'd arranged it. She tried to catch Shiloh's eye, but her best friend was standing at the bar, deep in conversation with a tall, lean, good-looking guy in a leather vest. Something about him was familiar. Nin joined them, and the trio continued an intent conversation. Nin was more animated than Kate had ever seen her. What was going on?

When the song was over, Kate literally ran from the stage, moved through the tables, and threw her arms around Shiloh.

"Surprised? Happy birthday to *me* from your one and only husband. *Husband*!" Shiloh threw her head back and released her signature, wicked laugh.

"What? That devil, Michael. I knew something was up. His face tells all now."

"You, the I'm-never-getting-married girl. It's a good thing, Kate; you were terrible at playing the field. No offense."

"And Shiloh, you were a world-class whore. No offense."

"I'm flattered."

They laughed some more.

"God, it's good to be together. Our first, great, foreign adventure."

Michael joined them, and Shiloh jingled him a big hug. "So glad you made it. How was your trip?"

"Michael, the tickets arrived early, the plane was on time, driver waiting, couldn't have been better. But listen, I want to introduce you to someone. Come on."

As Kate drew nearer, she recognized him. Was it Adam

Anderson, the lead singer for the Keys, three-time Grammy winners? It had to be him—lanky, long dark hair, in a black T-shirt with two gold keys on it. He leaned against the bar, sipping a Singha beer, and stared at Kate through the crowd as she approached.

Kate turned to Michael and whispered, "Is that really Adam Anderson? Why is he talking to Nin? Don't tell me you brought the Keys to Bangkok, Michael?

"No, I wish."

"No, this is all about you, Kate! You won't believe what he wants." Shiloh stopped them just before they broke through the crowd to the bar area.

Adam continued to talk to Nin while nodding and watching Kate.

By the time Kate stood in front of him, she was giddy. Star-struck.

Shiloh introduced Kate and Michael to Adam.

"I was just talking to your assistant, Nin, is it? Shiloh was kind enough to connect us."

Her eyes were so wide, Nin looked like she was going to explode. "Mr. Anderson is interested in some assistance."

"How can we help?" Michael seemed so cool. This was his business, Kate thought. He was already used to moving among the stars and talking with famous people in his embassy role.

She'd lost track of Adam's words as soon as he'd ask for Riverrun to be the substitute warm-up band for the Keys in Singapore the following weekend. Something about his current warm-up group getting sick. It wasn't the answer Kate had expected. She gathered herself. "Nin would have to talk to the manager here; we would miss a three-night commitment." Oh my god, did she just say that to Adam Anderson? So embarrassing. Kate shouldn't have hesitated for a second.

Nin nodded, wide-eyed, with a clear signal. "I will take care of it, Mrs. K-J."

Michael jumped in, clearly disappointed. "Well, I'm actually committed those nights; I've booked the New York City Ballet next weekend. I'll be tied up here."

"No problem as long as we get you, Kate, and Riverrun, of course." Adam signaled to a tall, thin man who stood nearby. "David will take care of the flights and accommodations. And contracts go through you, Nin, correct?"

Kate didn't dare breathe a word about how much she'd be paid.

As if she'd read Kate's mind, Shiloh drew a dollar sign in the air and silently clapped behind Adam.

It was clear Adam was used to getting what he wanted, and he didn't handle the minutia. Nin was too lost in her fan-fascination to handle things in her usual detailed way. It was better than singing for tips. Who cares? Kate was opening for the Keys!

"Gotta go. My luck hearing you sing tonight. Mind-blowing." He smiled at Kate. "And thanks, Shiloh, great idea, I hope you'll be my guest at next weekend's shows in Singapore." His look lingered. Adam handed her a card and kissed Shiloh's flushed cheek. Shaking Michael's hand, he glanced at Kate. "Lucky guy."

Every head in the club turned as he disappeared through the gossiping crowd.

"That did just happen, right?" Kate still had her eyes on the closing elevator door. "Shiloh, you're amazing."

"Do you need an entertainment lawyer, perchance?" Shiloh laughed. "I'm only two years shy of the boards."

Michael kissed Kate's cheek, ordered a round of drinks, and toasted, "to Kate and the Keys."

"I wish it were to *us* and the Keys. It's so sad you're tied up." Kate touched Michael's arm. "Aren't you the least bit disappointed? And I'll miss seeing the New York City Ballet with you. I'm so damn nervous."

"Honey, this was always about *you*. I'm just a guy on the piano accompanying a woman with magnificent talent." He hugged her.

Kate put her arm around Shiloh. "In Thailand, on your birthday, you give gifts to others. You coming is the greatest gift, Shi. Thank you. You always show up at the best times. I'm indebted."

"You got me through the loss of my brother, and you rocked those protests for me, Kate; debt paid, and who's keeping score. I do have a week to kill; how about I join you in Singapore; I'll change my ticket and go home from there."

"Really? Fantastic."

Kate wanted to share the news with the band members, who were on stage breaking down the set. They'll be ecstatic. "You guys have a drink and catch up; I want to tell the band."

Kate passed Jeremy and his wife's table. She knew they had been good friends to Michael when he'd first arrived. And she knew about Jeremy's offer to help locate Hy Vọng.

"Kate, it was wonderful; so glad we could make it."

"Good to see you both. We're remiss in not having you over for dinner." Kate hesitated, trying to remember Jeremey's wife's name.

"Well, getting married, singing nights; you've been busy settling in. But we'd love to anytime."

Jeremy leaned over to convey his words, privately, through the chattering crowd. "By the way, tell Michael I'm sorry I haven't been able to make any progress on our little mission. But I haven't given up."

"I'll tell him." It had been months since Michael had asked Jeremy to check on his daughter. And months since they had talked about his child. Wouldn't finding her give Michael the peace he deserved? The whole thing had settled into the past—Ha`ng, Hy Vọng, the protest. There was no sting around it anymore. No fear. The past had been overlayed with the peaceful life Kate and Michael had built in Bangkok over the nearly three months since she'd arrived. And now the most thrilling thing that had ever happened to her—the Keys.

The band members threw their arms in the air, did some secret, brotherhood-handshake that involved elbow-bumping and back-thumping, then hugged Kate.

"It's my friend, Shiloh, you should thank." Kate nodded toward the bar at her fashionable friend. "I'll see you guys at rehearsal tomorrow. Lots of work to do."

As Michael, Shiloh, and Kate worked their way through the crowd to leave, the room was a blur of excited voices, as Kate floated out with the surreal news. The Keys.

CHAPTER 54

Michael

SILENT CRYING

"A FUCKING MIRACLE," Michael muttered Jeremy's words like a mantra with each swipe of the windshield wipers during the two-hour drive through the monsoon. And while Kate was in Singapore, no less. He'd tried to reach her numerous times, after Jeremy had choked-out the news to Michael on the phone. Was the child his pilot-buddy had found really that same infant he'd handed over to the old woman? His child?

It had been too much to expect to find her—one little girl in a war-torn country. After months with no news about Hy Vọng from Jeremy, Michael's mind often returned to his list of justifications that had helped soothe his guilt. She was safe with her family. His unit had to pull out; how could he have taken care of her? She'd had no papers, on and on. Mostly, he'd repeated Hằng's passion that orphaned children should be placed with Vietnamese families first. How could he justify taking Hy Vọng from her family, having already taken their daughter from them. Hằng wouldn't be dead if she hadn't followed Michael.

The moisture inside the car had wilted the map in Michael's hand. The back of his blue golf shirt was soaked—partly the heat, partly his anticipation, partly his panic over not reaching Kate. She would be in transit to their home on a flight tomorrow morning from Singapore. If Jeremy was on time, Michael estimated a four-hour drive round trip. He would be home in time for dinner tonight and to get things settled before Kate's arrival in the morning.

Was he fearful that Jeremy hadn't found Michael's child, or fearful that he had?

Steam rose from the narrow, poorly-paved road that led to the designated meeting place in Chon Buri Province on the east coast of the Bay of Thailand. Liquid wavy lines were sucked skyward by the mid-morning sun—a kind of reverse-rain—vibrating like his stomach since Jeremy's phone call. Michael had to fit the pieces of the puzzle together. Jeremy's clipped call had left him with only fragments of the story—enough to know his pilot buddy had found a child carrying Michael's marine T-shirt near a bombed-out orphanage.

"Damn lucky. I've got her with me; I should bring her back, right?" It was clear, Jeremy had assumed Michael's answer would be yes. "I know you're weren't planning...but I'm sure you're up for the challenge for this little sweetheart, right? Can't leave her here, man. There's nothing left."

Silence.

"I mean, I could turn her in to the authorities with the others. She'd be safe—but Michael..."

Damn phone lines. "Sorry, Jeremy, what did you say?" Michael's answer came from somewhere beyond logic and thinking. There was no question; she belonged with him.

He'd said yes when Jeremy asked if Michael wanted him to bring her back; he'd said yes.

Listening to Jeremy's instructions with no time to think, Michael agreed to meet him at an old landing strip in Sriracha used for covert missions.

That's not the man I know. Kate's words, spoken after he'd confessed he left his child behind, had haunted Michael. What kind of man wouldn't welcome his child? A child with no one to care for her, wandering around with a half-dozen orphans in tattered clothing with no surviving caregivers? Maybe the irony of Hope's name was about to change.

What Michael and Jeremy were doing was illegal, using government property to fly a secret mission for a civilian embassy official. Taking a Vietnamese child from her country without authority. He'd possibly lose his job. Michael didn't care; she was his flesh and blood.

Don't assume the worst; that's what Kate would always say when things were tough. Their life was so good now. How would this impact them? Maybe it would be a joy. Couldn't it all work out over time like it had for Jeremy and his wife? Couldn't they make it work?

He rubbed the stream of sweat from the back of his neck. The pink stuffed bunny he had bought at the PX sat next to him on the seat. He didn't even know what else he needed. Except to know his child would not meet the same fate as her mother. The relief he'd felt that Jeremy had found her, only a few villages away from her grandparents' home, had begun to untie the permanent knots in deep places inside him.

Now he had different concerns as Michael headed up the road toward Sriracha. Was she healthy? Who had taken care of her? Now that it was a reality, the idealized romantic reunion had Michael perspiring. Would she be afraid of him? Did she look like him? Like Hàng? Would she forever trigger in him the memory of his lover's violent loss? Or could he stay in his daughter's smiles. And could she smile after what she might have seen? What had she suffered? Had she been in any action? So much news Jeremy's rushed phone call couldn't convey.

After Jeremy's early morning call, Michael had grabbed a crib, adult and child-size rocking chairs, three different sizes of clothes from the PX—and had them delivered while he tied up things at the office. Did she even sleep in a crib? He couldn't imagine leaving her in a bed at night. What if she rolled off and got hurt?

Michael took the turn at the end of Sriracha village and entered the designated path through the endless crop of small red peppers. They clung in clusters to the bright green plants like tiny, wrinkled, red Christmas ornaments.

A flock of children flowed in around his slowing vehicle, waving and helping to move a stubborn water buffalo from his narrow route. At the end of the bumpy trail, villagers lined the path, waving to welcome Michael and his blue foreign car like the only attraction in a small-town parade. It was as though they knew his mission. He was always amazed at how news traveled in the countryside. Had Jeremy called some village leader? Some contact he had from previous secret drop-offs? Or was it just the excitement of having a *farang*, a foreigner, arrive in their village, which they knew always had brought the plane?

Then Michael eyed the long break in the crops far across the field. Like an earth-colored marine buzz cut through the acres of green and red. A dirt path long enough to land a small plane. Long enough to bring his daughter home to him.

"*Sawatdee. Sawatdee, farang.*" Hello, foreigner. Returning their greetings, Michael felt the heavy heat drop over him as he got out of the car. The big brown eyes of the children studied him.

He walked out on the dirt airstrip to look for the plane. It was late. God, please let her be safe. Daddy's here, Hy Vọng. Yes, he had to remember to call her Hy Vọng, not Hope, although that was all he wanted to feel.

Daddy. Was he ready to be an instant father? He imagined Jeremy finding Michael's little girl wandering through the rubble with her tattered tribe. The image sent a tightness through his body. Reminding himself to breathe, Michael rechecked his watch.

He stood at the end of the rustic runway surrounded by the fields of tiny red peppers. A dozen children clustered around him with such sweet smiles he had to squeeze his eyes tight to prevent his tears.

He gripped the front of his damp shirt.

All heads turned as the quiet of the early morning was split by a buzz that became louder and louder as the small plane approached. A humming sound that seemed to drill into Michael. He ran his fingers through his hair and wiped the sweat from his forehead.

The squeals and cheers of the children. The whine of the landing gear. The thud of the wheels touching down. Every sound made his hands tremble.

The small plane skidded. He caught his breath. It came to a stop twenty yards away. Twenty yards from his child. The daughter he'd fantasized about tucking into his arms for a bedtime story. A fairytale with a happy ending; please, no more nightmares.

A young Thai man in tan pants and an oversized American military shirt appeared from the shed and dragged a set of portable steps up to the side of the plane.

The small door opened, and Jeremy appeared, holding a petite child draped over his shoulder, dressed in a soiled, white dress. Was she...? The child moved; yes, she was alive. Michael's relief was audible. She was no longer an abandoned orphan, but was she Michael's child? Here in front of him? Only steps away? He could hear the quiver in his own breath. A dry and silent crying.

Hy Vọng clung to Jeremy's neck, her face buried in his fatigues as he stood on the platform at the top of the steps shading his eyes to find Michael in the crowd.

Michael waved. Was this the tiny baby he'd held for just one long day and one intimate night before abandoning her? The petite toddler who was his blood, yet now a stranger.

"Hey, buddy, she's OK, she's OK." Jeremy's choked voice called out.

The children's voices silenced around him. Michael bolted toward her, stopping at the bottom of the steps.

"Take it slow, OK? She's skittish, finally calmed down."

Michael's eyes scanned the child who kept her face hidden in Jeremy's chest as they descended the last step. He saw it in his friend's dark look. Jeremy had more to say.

"What? What is it?"

"Her family village. Good thing your plan to get her back to her family failed. Entire village gone. Devastation everywhere.

Sorry, buddy. But it saved this little one. She wouldn't be here if she'd made it home to her grandparents." Jeremy shifted her onto his hip.

Ha`ng's family gone? Michael studied her limp hand on Jeremy's shoulder. Her fingers, those tiny fingers. Bigger now, but still so vulnerable. The half-moon fragile fingernails. He couldn't breathe. Ha`ng's family gone. The news took time to sink in. Hy Vọng was their only legacy. Still, he waited, aching to touch her, afraid to frighten her. Michael's legs felt weighted. He stepped in closer. "Hy Vọng, it's Daddy. Hy Vọng?"

Hy Vọng turned her head and engaged Michael's eyes.

Dear God. Ha`ng's face, Ha`ng's complexion, his own honey highlights in her brown hair, his startling blue eyes, his child. He pulled her warm hand closer, ran his thumb over the back of her soft skin, and kissed it. "Hi, baby girl," he whispered in Vietnamese. Every part of him tensed as he tried not to fall apart and disintegrate into a pile of emotion.

Did he see the corners of her mouth turn up slightly? Michael inhaled deeply. What the hell was he feeling? Guilt? Relief? Fear?

No. Pure love, like an explosion in his chest.

CHAPTER 55

Michael

SHATTERING HEART

THE CHEERS OF the village children at the airstrip frightened Hy Vọng; she shimmied up Michael's chest, and perched on his shoulders, holding his head with her sweaty hands.

Michael patted Jeremy on his back with his free arm. "God, thanks, buddy." Weren't they cut from the same cloth, Michael thought, looking into his comrade-in-arms' watery eyes? Not that Michael was a hero, but he'd always put his fellow marines first, to do what was right, even breaking the rules, like he'd done rescuing Greg Harrington and Jeremy too. What was it, passion? "Semper fi, my friend."

Jeremy opened the car door for Michael. "Listen, you need to back channel this buddy. Take the covert route and move fast. You don't want her to go into temporary foster care until they get around to checking out your story. Seriously, not to scare you, but it could all unravel fast, going through the system." Jeremy handed Michael two polaroid photos of Hy Vọng and a folded piece of paper. "You'll need these and see this guy for the paperwork. The rules aren't always right, you know."

"Right. No way I'll let them take her now. Over my dead body. Thanks."

Hy Vọng wrapped her arms around Michael's neck. "You're OK, Hy Vọng." He spoke his rusty Vietnamese and settled her into the front seat. "Wish me luck. And I owe you. I owe you bigtime, Jeremy."

She still hadn't spoken, but he was grateful Hy Vọng hadn't screamed and cried when he'd put her in the car. What would he have done if she'd pushed him away? He was grateful that the movement of the car and the swipe of the windshield wipers during the first fifteen minutes of the two-hour drive back to Bangkok had lulled her. Now she was asleep on the seat beside him, grasping the stuffed animal he'd brought to comfort her. What would he do when she awakened? Thank God, he still remembered much of the Vietnamese he'd learned.

He reached down and brushed a swath of her two-toned hair from her face and rested his hand on her chest, feeling her heartbeat through her thin cotton dress. The regular rhythm reassured him. He just wanted to get her into the safety of their home.

As he approached the city, he nervously tapped the steering wheel. Reality settled in, and a new set of concerns inhabited Michael's mind. Could he learn how to be a good father to this three-and-a-half-year-old? He'd certainly had no role model. Would the little girl shatter their world? Would Kate be ready to face motherhood? Her comment in their early days together flashed through his mind; she'd never thought she was cut out for kids. They'd only been married a few weeks. Having a child would require so much care. Not to mention the roll-of-the-dice on his career and the legal challenges. He'd barely had time to prepare himself for the child's arrival and hadn't considered the consequences. Pondering Jeremy's advice, Michael made the decision to follow it. He wouldn't trust the system.

First, Kate had to accept his troubles from the war, his lover, and now his child from his lover. Not just an idea or memory, but a permanent part of their lives. And Kate's budding career, singing? He could never deny her that. He wouldn't have to, right? He had Nong to help. Two things he knew for sure about Kate—she was compassionate about children in need and passionate about family. Still...

The changes for Hy Vọng continued to sink in as he drove on the main highway into Bangkok. Would she want to sleep on the floor like Jeremy's little boy? Cry constantly from the unfamiliarity of it all? And the language, how would Kate communicate with her, and Hy Vọng would be exposed to two new languages, English and Thai, and the food, adjusting to Thai culture and city life, living indoors? He huffed out a long breath. Michael's torturous thoughts wouldn't stop. Emotions pulled at him, fear and joy in a battle for his heart. He rubbed the stream of sweat from the side of his face. What if legal issues took her away from them, a warning Jeremy had given Michael? *God help us.*

Hy Vọng's big blue eyes had opened and studied him just before they'd drooped, and she'd drifted off again. What would his father and grandmother say about having a Vietnamese girl as their heir? Michael didn't care. His mother would be surprised but thrilled, and he had no worries about the Ketchums. Telling Hy Vọng's story over and over to family would be so hard. Her past was so inexorably linked to such tragedy, her family's, her mother's. He tightened his jaw.

Michael checked his watch; they'd be home in five minutes. He'd left home a man thrilled to have married the woman he loved; he'd return home a father. Surreal.

He felt so inadequate for the job. They were strangers; they weren't. What would he feed Hy Vọng? It was Nong's day off. He wished he'd planned better. Well, there hadn't been time to prepare. His daughter needed a bath. She needed everything. He knew nothing.

He moved through the flooded street. The thick fog had dragged the night in early. Michael didn't want to get stuck now and traumatize the child further with the knee-high swirling waters and the darkening sky. He could tell from the brown water's depth, there was no way to get through the street to the house by car; he'd have to carry her. Hopefully, she wouldn't wake up.

He parked, lifted Hy Vọng and her rabbit from the car and walked the final block to their house. She remained still, so light and limp over his shoulder like a rag doll. The dank smell of her dirty clothes brought him back to the war. He shivered, and held her tighter, imagining what he and his frail daughter had in common. The tat-tat-tat, the boom of the explosions. How close had she been to the violence that had haunted him? His mind was slipping down into those thoughts, forbidden thoughts of Ha`ng. Hy Vọng uttered a soft sigh, and Michael thought his heart would shatter at the tender sound.

She lifted her head and twisted one fist in her eye.

His tremors subsided. Michael needed to get her indoors,

fed and clean in the soft pajamas he'd bought with the pink butterflies. Please don't breakdown now, he told himself, not with his precious baby in his arms.

CHAPTER 56

BEGGING EYES

THE DOORBELL RANG. Kate tossed her silk robe over the rocking chair and threw on a pair of jeans and a T-shirt. At the bottom of the stairs, she stopped. The outside porch light cast a glow around drenched Michael. What was he carrying? No, *who* was he carrying? "Oh my God, Michael." She crossed the cool wood floor and pulled open the door.

"Kate, I'm so sorry; the phones were—"

The din of splattering rain swallowed his words. "Shh. Explain later." Kate took his arm, drew him inside, and closed the door. Swiping a stream of rain from Michael's forehead, she kissed his cheek.

"I'm sorry. It all happened so fast. I—"

Kate put her hand to the child's face and looked up at Michael. "Hy Vọng?"

He nodded.

The moment was fragile. Kate held her breath. Moving a strand of damp hair from the child's face, Kate whispered, not wanting to startle her. "Hello, Hy Vọng."

The petite girl with drooping, sleepy eyes pulled away and tucked her head in Michael's neck.

Michael stumbled, his legs went weak, and Kate guided him to the rattan sofa.

Hy Vọng slipped down into his lap, the damp stuffed bunny in her grip.

No longer just Michaels' child now, Kate thought—Hy Vọng was now their child, *her* child. Kate put her hands to her chest and tried to clear her tension with another deep breath. Too many emotions to process. A rumble of questions rotated in her mind. Focus on the child, she thought.

"It's OK, sweetheart." Kate wanted to take the child in her arms, but she waited, letting Hy Vọng take the lead. "She's so delicate and beautiful. Is she OK?"

Michael nodded, and raked his hand through his hair. "I think so. Jeremy found her near a bombed-out orphanage. There were other kids; he got them to safety."

Hy Vọng turned her head toward Kate.

"Oh Michael, she has your blue eyes. I didn't expect that."

"Yeah, pretty unusual. It's been a long day. But she seems OK, physically anyway. Not sure what's she's been through."

Kate saw the fear in Hy Vọng's eyes. What had this child suffered?

Michael's voice caught in his throat. "She came so close."

Kate's eyes filled, and she leaned her head against Michael's shoulder. "I can't believe this is real."

"You're a blessing, sweetheart—you showing up at home at this moment. What does that say to you?"

"It says, I moved my flight up because I missed you; I love you, and we have an instant child." Kate put her head back against the sofa and let out a short laugh laced with irony. "She's alive."

"And we're together." Michael leaned back and slumped against Kate. "Oh, damn, what about your concerts? Shiloh's visit? Sorry honey. How was it?"

The power of his child's rescue and the relief of her presence put everything into perspective for Kate. "We'll talk later, so much to tell you about. Not important now." Kate stroked Hy Vọng's cheek, then pulled out a corner of her T-shirt, and wiped the child's damp legs and dirty bare feet. "Sweet one, you're safe now."

Squirting off the sofa with her bunny, Hy Vọng scurried across the room and curled up in a ball in the shadows under the dining room table.

"Hy Vọng, it's OK, honey." Kate headed for the kitchen. "What's the word for rice?"

"Rice? It's, *com*."

"Can you go upstairs and get her some pajamas, Michael? I'll heat some rice."

Michael stood. "Good idea. I'm not thinking."

"And bring the little pink blanket, OK?" She knew Michael needed a job to pull himself together; she did too. It wasn't the first time she would deal with confusing or unusual behavior in a child, she told herself. Kate peeked under the table, keeping her distance.

Hy Vọng looked up, her eyes wide with fear as she rocked her bunny.

"*Com*, Hy Vọng, *com*?" The child stopped rocking and put out her hands, cupping them like a beggar, her eyes pleading.

Kate shuddered, imagining Hy Vọng on the streets, her tiny

hands extended, waiting for something for her empty stomach. "You're breaking my heart, Hy Vọng." The thought of her having no family, no one to comfort her was too much to bear.

"Glancing back from the outdoor kitchen through the wall of glass, Kate kept Hy Vọng in her sight. With trembling hands, Kate served a portion of warm rice she'd found in a white rice cooker into three bowls. In slow-motion, she placed the bowls and three sets of chopsticks on the floor and sat cross-legged at a distance, across from Hy Vọng under the table. "*Com*, Hy Vọng? Rice?"

Hy Vọng's hands dove into the small bowl and shoveled the rice into her mouth.

The gesture shot through Kate, and she closed her eyes and took a deep breath. *Please, God, help us to do the right thing.*

Michael came into the dining room. She could see his dry jeans and bare feet from under the table. He shuffled a turn. "*Kate?*"

The rise in his voice showed his worry. Such an emotional day he must have had, Kate thought. "Down here, Michael. I think we need to just meet her where she is, OK?"

He joined them, and Kate wrapped the blanket around Hy Vọng. They sat quietly, their clicking chopsticks lifting rice into their quivering mouths. Plucking a chopstick full of rice, Kate held it to the bunny's mouth and watched Hy Vọng's response. "One step at a time," Kate whispered. "Let her come to us, Michael. We have all the time in the world."

"We do?"

Escaping their hideout under the table, Kate brought them small glasses of fresh pineapple juice she'd found in the refrigerator. She set a quarter-full one in front of Hy Vọng.

"*Không, không!*" Hy Vọng kicked at the juice as Kate leaned in. The liquid puddled on the teak floor and soaked Kate's jeans. Hy Vọng's face twisted and scrunched, and she cried.

"She's saying, no. *Không* is *no*."

What could Kate do? Memories of Mary guided Kate. Patience. She wanted to hold Hy Vọng but didn't dare encroach on the child's space. Kate did the only thing she knew to do—she distracted Hy Vọng by singing as she wiped up the spill with a kitchen towel. After the first few notes, Hy Vọng stopped crying and riveted her eyes on Kate.

"Those arresting blue eyes. Like looking into yours."

"Look how your voice soothes her, just like it does me." Michael reached over and touched Kate's arm. "I think you found a bridge."

They sat listening to the rhythm of the rainy season pinging on the windows. "What if you play, Michael; I'll sing. Maybe that will bring her out from under here. We have to get her cleaned up and into bed. Look at the dark circles under her eyes."

From the piano, they could see Hy Vọng across the room. Michael began to play, and Kate sat next to him. "OK, what do you think? 'Bridge over Troubled Waters' or 'Raindrops Keep Fallin' On My Head'?" Kate nodded her head to the storm raging outside.

Michael smiled and leaned into Kate. "How about Carpenter's 'Close to You'?"

"Ha, that's perfect; if only she understood the lyrics." In the middle of the first verse, from the corner of her eye, Kate saw a movement. She continued the tune substituting lyrics directed at Michael. "Don't look now; someone's coming."

Hy Vọng slid along the sleek hardwood floor and squatted a few feet away, listening, swaying with the bunny crushed to her side.

"Just keep playing." Kate hooked her arm around his waist.

Hy Vọng moved closer.

"I didn't know I was about to become a mother?" Kate sang. "At least it was painless." Kate squeezed Michael's arm.

"You're kidding? *What* was painless?"

"Childbirth. My becoming a mother. No labor pains." Kate flicked Michael's arm. "One of these days, you won't get away with your secrecy." She looked at Hy Vọng, who sat fixing the ragged T-shirt around her bunny only a few feet away. "At least *you* did all the labor for my delivery." Kate slapped her arm and scratched, pinching an insect between her fingers. "Oh no, she has fleas, Michael."

"Fleas. Damn. So, you're an instant mother? That means we're more than just *us* again." Michael touched Kate's face. "Sorry."

"Some things just put life into perspective. And I know from our past few months, and from this mission you arranged, that you are the man I know and love."

Michael nodded his head toward his daughter, who squatted nearby, a yellow pool of urine spreading under her. "You sure? I think the hard part's about to begin."

"Is she really right across the room from us?" Kate kept her voice low, snuggled into Michael's back, and massaged his earlobe between her fingers.

"You know when you do that I'm back in your bedroom in

Glynn—that first Thanksgiving when I first knew I loved you." He rolled over and propped himself up on one arm. "I know you won't sleep until you know everything."

"So true."

Michael shared his call from Jeremy, his manic shopping spree at the PX, the rescue, his child arriving on the plane amidst the red pepper fields in the remote village. He gave her the details she wanted. He'd learned to do that for her, to thrust his words up over his wall, Kate thought. That's how she would describe Michael learning to share his life with her.

"You were amazing with her, Kate. The way you calmed her, bathed her, sang to her in the rocker."

"And tomorrow, we'll need to decontaminate the entire house from these fleas." She snapped at another one that landed on her arm and laughed.

"Sorry, babe, Nong can help. I never thought Hy Vọng would quiet down. It was your melodies that finally did it."

Kate kissed his chest. "Well, and the warm bath and pure exhaustion."

"Like you were her mother."

Kate heard the word "mother" barely escape his throat.

"You're thinking of Ha`ng. It's OK. I am too. Naturally, you would."

"But I feel like I should push away thoughts of her, you know? I'm not thinking of her... that way... " Michael ran his hands across Kate's face like a blind man, never wanting to forget her. "I love you."

"I know; it's complicated. The horrific memories Hy Vọng being here must bring. Don't be alone with it. Let me in, OK?"

"It might not be easy to undo any trauma she'd experienced.

To get Hy Vọng to feel comfortable with us and know she's safe." He held Kate tighter. "I think of my own pain. How long it's taken to get it under control."

"We'll do it together. And we don't know what she's experienced. She might do better than you think, in time. Hà̛ng might be peaceful now that her baby is safe."

Saying his lost lover's name out loud had made it more real, a woman whom Michael had loved. Hearing her name also made it less painful. Kate felt the veil of Michael's secrecy pull back, letting in the light of his truth.

The ache in Kate's chest subsided a bit. It would get easier, she thought. And they had each other, and Kate had a child. The one thing she'd never felt the natural desire for in her life had appeared. No decision had been necessary. Kate laughed, pulled back, and searched Michael's eyes, his face lit by the band of moonlight coming through the window. She ran her hand over his shoulder with the Hy Vọng tattoo. "You seem so... good."

"That's the music and you."

"And having Hy Vọng back. Powerfully healing, I imagine. You must be exhausted, and I'm so jet-lagged too. We better get some sleep; she might not sleep through the night. But speaking of music. Now, *I* have a surprise for you—my all-of-a-sudden husband and father-of-a-child."

"Shoot." He put his hands behind his head to listen.

A gecko's call, *tsk, tsk, tsk,* came from the high ceiling above them. Kate counted. "Seven, that's good luck, again. I might get to play again with the Keys."

"Babe, that's great."

"Adam hinted at it after the last show. Well, more than hinted."

"Oh hell, we didn't have a chance to talk about your shows in Singapore. Honey, I'm sorry."

A little voice called out across the room in the crib—a short cry, then quiet.

Kate released her breath. "She's just dreaming."

"Aren't we all."

CHAPTER 57

Michael

INSTANT FATHER

HY VỌNG'S CRY at dawn lifted them both out of bed in tandem. "Honey, you sleep; I'll get her. You're off-kilter from traveling and performing."

"Are you sure you...well, you have to start fatherhood somewhere." Kate threw Michael a kiss and slumped back onto her pillow.

Day one of the rest of their lives. Michael stood, staring at Kate curled up exhausted, with her wild swirls of red hair across her pillow. He'd wanted this life with her, but he hadn't expected the little extra bonus. Hy Vọng cried out again; he'd better get his semper fi going.

He had no idea *what* his daughter was used to eating. Certainly, she hadn't been breast-fed as other children would have been, even well past her age. Did she ever have a bottle? She was too old for one now. Would it have soothed her?

He hoisted the soaking wet child, grabbed an outfit that looked like it would fit, and headed for the bathroom.

"You're one little stinker." She stiff-armed his chest and

screamed as he struggled to wipe her with a warm washcloth and wriggle her into her shirt, diaper and shorts. The clothes were much too large for the petite toddler. It would have to do; he wanted to get her fed. Michael grabbed one of his silk ties and slipped it around his neck.

"Sh, sh, are you hungry, little one? I'm going to feed you now."

Her arms softened, and she sniffled on his shoulder as Michael padded downstairs to the kitchen. "That's it; don't worry. Daddy will take care of you." He cut up some pineapple pieces, and her sounds of pleasure, as she sucked on the luscious ripe fruit, made him smile. "Some things you just can't fight, right, honey?"

He sat Hy Vọng in the oversized dining chair boosted by a pillow and strapped her in with his favorite Italian silk tie. She ate the leftover rice porridge Nong had made for him the morning before she left. "Everything will be fine, Hy Vọng."

Reaching her arms out, she pumped her little fingers, begging for more fruit.

"Not too much, or your tummy will hurt." He gave her one more piece of mango and a cube of pineapple then washed her sticky hands and face. She resisted, but he made a game of peek-a-boo with the washcloth to distract her. It brought back his mother's smile. "Your Grandma Christine will be over the moon with you."

Slipping down from the chair, Hy Vọng ran into the living room and climbed up on the piano bench. Her little fingers couldn't open the heavy cover to the keys. "Uh, uh!" She slapped her hands on the lid as if she were playing.

Michael laughed. "So you *are* your father's daughter. Shh,

Mommy's sleeping, sweetheart." *Mommy*, the word sounded strange but beautiful to him. They'd skipped the honeymoon and had plunged right into the demands of their new family life.

The raucous Hy Vọng was making was worse than her playing the piano could possibly be, so he opened the lid. "OK, let's play quietly. He took her one finger and played the notes, "You are my sunshine, my only…" Hy Vọng pulled on Michael's thumb and placed his hand on the keys.

"Go ahead, play; I can't sleep anyway."

Michael turned to see Kate sitting on the landing, holding her knees in the turquoise Thai silk robe he'd left at the foot of the bed for her. "Uh oh, Hy Vọng, look who we woke. Good morning. She ate like a tiger—porridge, mango, and pineapple. So far, so good."

"Seems like you're a natural father. And courageous, oh, and loyal. Have I told you how much I admire that about you?"

"I have no idea what I'm doing. Do you realize I've never even held a child—not since Hy Vọng was a newborn?"

Hy Vọng banged on the piano, and Michael called over the noise.

"Kate, I've been thinking. We need to go home right away. Introduce Hy Vọng to our families. Maybe have that family wedding we deserve. That is, if the lady says yes."

"I could never in a million years have imagined such a romantic proposal. It almost beats the frat room." Kate laughed, which made Hy Vọng throw her head back in imitation. "But seriously, shouldn't we settle in for a while with her? So much change, Michael."

"Except I have to get back here in two weeks to host the

Alvin Ailey American Dance Troupe. Then we'll put our life back together here with Nong's help."

Silence.

"What you don't like modern dance?" He laughed. "Seriously, Kate, does that sound good? By the way, I totally forgot, Nong doesn't come back until Friday. I gave her some time off so we could settle in. Had I only known. How about we leave day after tomorrow. Give us time to pack. Can you call your family; I'll call my mother today from the office?"

"Sure. Can you imagine; they'll be so happy." Kate put her hand out with a small marble Buddha in it that she'd bought at the airport for Michael. Hy Vọng took it and put it next to her bunny.

"I need to get her paperwork in order and book flights at the Embassy today. It might take some time. I'm concerned about that. Can you take over today for a few hours?" Michael hesitated. Was it right to worry Kate about the fragile situation around the paperwork and legal issues? Not until Michael checked it out with Jeremy's contact at the embassy and he knew the details. Maybe it would all go smoothly. "I'll bring dinner home, so we don't have cooking to worry about, OK?"

Michael saw a look pass over Kate's face he couldn't identify. He hoped she wouldn't ask about Hy Vọng's documents in detail; he'd already stepped over the line, taking his daughter illegally, and now forged papers. He didn't want Kate implicated. There was no other viable way, really. How could he prove Hy Vọng was his daughter? It was all circumstantial— the T-shirt, finding her near the same village where he'd left her, the old woman's admission to Jeremy that she'd left Hy Vọng at the orphanage, the child's penetrating blue eyes? That didn't seem to be enough to translate into a good case. And there was no family left to verify his claims of fatherhood.

Even the slightest risk of Hy Vọng being taken away made him shudder. Forged papers avoided the channels fraught with risk and hoops to jump through. The back door was how Jeremy had handled his little boy's adoption. And that child wasn't even his. It was logical to Michael's mind. And he wanted to get Hy Vọng home to the U.S. where he could use the family lawyer to pull some strings and get her properly documented.

The release of Michael's guilt that had gouged at his gut for three years had been replaced by a fearless protectiveness and a kind of euphoria when it came to his rescued child. Michael could count on Jeremy's friend in the Visa office who had handled An's paperwork for Jeremy and his wife—a former Marine who wouldn't let him down. Michael would talk about the backdoor route he was taking for Hy Vọng with Kate tonight once he had all the facts.

Hy Vọng tugged on Michael's shirt. Spontaneously, he hugged his daughter. She didn't pull away. Did she sense he was her father, just like he knew without a doubt she was his child? Things were going better than expected, he thought. Their new life together would be busy with activity now that they had an instant child. Michael would learn all the usual things every parent of a toddler faced and the unusual challenges of a traumatized refugee. He had no idea one little girl could create such chaos and such joy.

Wrapping his arms around his daughter, he kissed the top of her head and hoisted her onto his hip. "OK, guys, I've got to salvage our car from the street and get to work."

As he kissed Kate, Hy Vọng squirmed down from his arms and scooted to the piano. He put his hand to his chest. He couldn't resist. Sitting down, he played and began to sing, "You are my sunshine, my only sunshine." Why was it so damn touching that his daughter wanted him to play the piano? Looking down at Hy Vọng, Michael understood; it was the connection to his mother teaching him to play as a boy. He was passing that down, something he'd never dreamed would ever happen.

As he squatted down with her to say goodbye and tried to disentangle her, Hy Vọng clung to him and screamed. Peeling her arms from around his neck, he thought his chest would explode again. "It's OK. Daddy will be back soon." He kissed Kate and clicked the glass door shut.

It was overwhelming to have his baby back. All worth it now, all his suffering, his injuries, his mental torture, all to have his and Ha`ng's child, now Kate's child, in his arms, he thought. He could almost feel Ha`ng's gratitude and her arm around his shoulder in thanks. Michael turned back and crouched down to Hy Vọng's level. He kissed the glass then made a funny face. Her crying stopped for a moment. He waved goodbye; she pouted.

The healing from his shame over leaving Hy Vọng in Nam behind had begun; he felt lighter, excited, as he left the front door. Sludging through the few inches of floodwaters that remained, Michael rescued his car around the corner. "Our daughter is safe," he said out loud to Ha`ng.

CHAPTER 58

MANAGING MOTHERHOOD

HY VỌNG STOOD at the door sniffling. Her hands cleared away the condensation that appeared on the glass as the air conditioning met the steamy hot day.

"Sweetheart, come to Kate." Hy Vọng had seemed so ready to connect after the affection she'd shown to Michael. Kate was hopeful. The child ran back to the piano, struck her hands on the keys, and called out in Vietnamese. The language barrier was such a challenge. It took away Kate's greatest weapon when it came to reaching the child. Words. Patience was needed, Kate knew that, but she so wanted to close the distance between them. Had she expected the child to run into her arms and love her instantly like in a romantic movie?

The challenge of Mary came to mind again. Kate couldn't let herself think of that now. But this time, when Kate had the breakthrough with her new daughter—and she would, she told herself—Kate and Michael would be there to give Hy Vọng the life she deserved.

Picking up Michael's old dictionary from the dining table,

she tried to make sense of the complicated, tonal language. Just like with the Thai language, mistakes were easy to make; a simple tone change would change the meaning of each word.

"Hy Vọng, hungry?" Kate pronounced the strange words. Dancing the pink bunny on her knee, Kate tried to lure Hy Vọng closer. Was Kate's awkward Vietnamese communicating what she'd intended?

Hy Vọng shook her head, no, and Kate slumped back onto the carved, high-back dining chair and sighed. With Michael gone, Kate could finally let down the façade. There was no way she would let her elated, new husband know she had a second of hesitation about bringing Hy Vọng into their new life. Husband? Fiancé to husband had all happened so fast. Kate knew they could never have been just friends if she'd caught sight of him for one minute. She laughed. It felt right—a quiet wedding reception at home, maybe with Father Sullivan offici-ating a blessing. Her family would be so happy; they loved Michael, and they would embrace Hy Vọng.

She pictured him kissing his daughter, comforting her on his way out the door, and Hy Vọng reaching for Michael. But Kate's motherhood was still only a concept. Obviously not an emotion Hy Vọng nor she fully felt yet. Last night, Kate had felt in control; this morning, she felt at a loss.

The unrelenting early sun angled onto the hardwood floor spotlighting Hy Vọng and her pink bunny. Slipping into the kitchen, Kate spotted a can of maple syrup. A touch of home, she'd brought Michael. No dairy, Jeremy had told Michael. Children who'd never had dairy didn't have the enzymes to digest it, he'd explained. Keeping an eye on Hy Vọng through the kitchen window, Kate made French toast with sweet syrup and no milk, no butter—ah, coconut milk. She pulled it from the fridge—the perfect temptation to get a neglected, street child to scramble up onto a chair and join Kate while she ate breakfast.

Luring her with the luscious sweet plate of food, Kate helped Hy Vọng up onto the chair, and her little hands ripped at the treat—no utensils necessary. The first thing she'd eaten that wasn't rice or fruit.

Their first day alone had started well, Kate thought, shuffling the breakfast dishes into a stack. How could she have been so selfish to be jealous of a fragile child who'd suffered so terribly?

Kate couldn't help but think of how leaving Mary behind, so exposed and vulnerable, had knocked Kate off her game, as her grandfather would say. She'd been powerless. It wasn't her job, Brent had said. True enough, but this child, this beautiful child, Hy Vọng, was her chance to do things right. Kate hadn't really expected they would find Hy Vọng amidst all the destruction. Now that she was here, Kate would never have to leave her behind.

Still, something was off, but Kate couldn't pinpoint it. What was it that was clawing at her insides? She re-ran the scenes since Hy Vọng had arrived yesterday. The picture cleared—it was Michael's shift in attention. Kate would have to adjust to that. For the brief time they'd been together as newlyweds, Michael had made her feel like she was his whole world. He'd kissed Kate goodbye this morning, but that special, lingering *I can't wait to see you again* look was given to Hy Vọng on his way out the door, not her. Well, wouldn't that be natural after all the trauma, all the years he'd tortured himself? Kate would have to adjust to sharing Michael's heart. But seeing him with his baby girl and the changes in him, Kate knew she had more of her loving man than she ever would have if his child hadn't come back into his life. He would always have been unresolved, incomplete. In the end, Hy Vọng was a gift to both of them.

Kate faced her disappointment over canceling the Thai American Club again, so they could go on leave to take Hy Vọng home. That music connection was like another way of making love for them. Well, it was only postponed, wasn't it? She could schedule new performances when they returned from their home leave. She hoped she wouldn't be replaced after cancelling so often.

Life was moving fast. Calling her family would be a thrill. Everyone would be supportive, and her sisters would laugh that she, too, had a child unexpectedly—the Ketchum girls' legacy. One way or another, Kate thought. You just had to laugh at the irony.

The fragile voice of Hy Vọng talking to herself and her stuffed animal and doll while playing under the dining room table added a counterpoint to Kate's nervousness.

After breakfast, Kate would call to postpone her shows. She was excited that they had the bond of a child to love and raise together. But the timing, just when Kate had a chance to resurrect her singing career, was unexpected and threatening, she had to admit. There had been little serious discussion about having children; they'd been too busy dealing with whether or not they could work as a couple. Kate took in a deep breath and consoled herself. It would be OK. They just needed time. Focus on Hy Vọng. Her needs. Be the grown-up, Kate told herself.

Kate spent the morning under the dining table with Hy Vọng making the bunny sing. Using every kids' song she could remember, Kate sang out loud, rocking her body side to side— M-I-C-K-E-Y M-O-U-S-E.

Repeating some version of her own lyrics through a spurt of giggles, Hy Vọng sang, "em, cee, ee, em, ee."

Kate put her hand to her chest. Small things, it was always the little things that touched you with kids. Then another surprise. The child climbed the stairs with her toys in her fists, repeating some chant Kate couldn't comprehend, as if Hy Vọng were singing to herself. Kate followed.

Upstairs, Hy Vọng ran to the rocking chair, banged on it, saying the same phrase over and over. That was more than a hint of hope for Kate. Moving slowly, she lifted Hy Vọng and her dangling toys, and sat on the rocker, and sang, "would you like to swing on a star, carry moonbeams home in a jar?" The flutter of Hy Vọng's closing eyes was so touching. The ragdoll child, slumping in her arms, melted Kate's fears.

Lunchtime had worked too. Once Kate figured out what Hy Vọng was saying. "You're hungry, honey, com?" It wasn't even eleven o'clock. Hy Vọng chewed bits of chicken off the sate sticks and pushed fistfuls of mango and sticky rice into her heart-shaped mouth. Her eating with such desperation, made Kate lose all worries about herself, about Michael, about her singing. There would be time for that; right now, this young girl, their daughter, needed her.

Picking up the phone, Kate called the embassy to cancel her next two weeks at the Thai American Club.

She liked that all of her singing engagements were booked through the embassy's American-Thai arts exchange with Nin. No language struggles. Miraculously, the phone worked. "Hi, Khun Nin. How are you? Something has come up, and I'm sure Michael told you we're taking home leave. I'm so sorry, but Michael and I—."

"*Mai pen lai, kah,* never mind. Great news, Mrs. James."

Nin's English broke into a staccato of syllables that blended into one long accented sentence over the fuzzy connection. "They loved your warm-up act—they want you—Southeast Asia Tour. You'll tour in Krungthep, Hong Kong, Manila, Jakarta, Singapore, ending in Krungthep. Twelve shows, fourteen days.

Damn these phones. "Wait. Can you repeat it? The *Who?* Sorry, you got cut off."

The phone line cleared. "Not *The Who.*" Nin laughed. "The *Keys.*"

"Me, playing with the *Keys, again?* When?"

"Tour starts Saturday! Riverrun is so excited. I've already told them."

"So exciting, but I'm afraid it's impossible; Michael and I have to take home leave. We've had..." Had Michael shared his news? She wanted to be discreet. "Nin, something's come up."

"Don't worry, you go to the States later."

Michael must have changed the plans. The news was dizzying. Hy Vọng started to cry. Squatting down, Kate put her arm around the toddler and kissed the top of her two-toned hair. Hy Vọng didn't pull away. "Dah-Dee."

"Did you say something, Kate?"

"Yes, I'm very excited." Was Kate supposed to tell anyone about Hy Vọng's rescue?

"So good. Don't worry, Mrs. James. I'll take care of the Thai American Club—two weeks off. You start when you come back, OK?"

Hy Vọng squiggled off the piano bench, ran to the front door, and stood with her hands and nose pressed to the glass, calling out the Vietnamese word for "Daddy." The one word repeated by Michael that had stuck in Kate's mind. Then she turned and ran to Kate, "Dah-dee."

"Who's that?"

"Oh, Khun Nin, it's no one. The radio." Kate stroked Hy Vọng's hair to calm her.

"So, you and your band are tight now. Ready to tour with you—they know all your songs. Please hold, I have a call from the Keys."

Images blurred through Kate's mind: performing at O'Leary's, harmonizing with her mother at church, singing with Father Sullivan's choir, learning to read music with Michael, singing overlooking exotic Bangkok, and now the thrill of being the warm-up act *on tour* for the chart-burning Keys. Being on stage again and the applause. Kate could see her mother's glowing face; it's all Kate had ever wanted. Michael had arranged it for her.

Kate could hear Nin's distant voice on her other phone. "Yes, Mrs. Kate James accepts your opportunity. Please send the contract. The offer is perfect. Thank you."

Wait. Mrs. Kate James? So she would tour as Kate James? Where did her Ketchum go? Kate sighed, and Nin came back on the line.

"What time you can come today? Riverrun wants to meet with you."

They would have to decide on their sets in a matter of days. Kate was ready; but with the Grammy-winning Keys for an entire tour? Amazing.

"Keys' agent says everything's all set."

"Khun Nin, I can't..."

"Can't hear me? Bad connection? Don't worry, good money offer too. Much more than Thai American Club."

"Oh my God. Don't tell me, I want to be surprised. But, I have something I need to do today; I can come tomorrow." They would have to ask Nong to come back to fill in for her at home with Hy Vọng. Kate kept her eye on her fragile girl. Michael must have had trouble getting the papers and had to delay the trip home, she thought. The timing was all working out.

Nin laughed. "Mr. James loves you to sing. We all see his face. What do Americans say, *chance of a lifetime*, Mrs. James?"

Kate's stomach tightened. How could she accept it? Not after all Michael had been through to find his child. He had a packed program coming up at work. And now she would leave for two weeks? Not after Hy Vọng was finally here. She glanced at her new daughter. They had a long future ahead with Hy Vọng, and they'd worked so hard to make this music dream happen for Kate. There would be other tours, right? Kate knew that rang false. Not the Keys. If Michael had arranged it, she wanted it.

She was thrilled, then hesitant. The whiplash of emotions took turns building the conflict inside her—postponing seeing

the family's faces when they brought Hy Vọng home to celebrate their marriage, or tasting the music dreams that she'd
nurtured for years.

"Are you there? Phone line is always trouble. Ok, see you
soon. You're smiling big, right, Mrs. James?"

"Thank you, Khun Nin. Yes, I'm smiling big."

Kate hung up. Her laugh exploded. "Oh, my God, touring
with the Keys." She clapped her hands and danced around the
room.

Hy Vọng left the front door and moved toward Kate. She
clapped and copied Kate's laugh and spun around too; the first
playful interaction they'd had.

"Oh, Hy Vọng, sweetie. Dear God, I'm singing with the Keys
again."

CHAPTER 59

Michael

PERILOUS PAPERS

MICHAEL OPENED THE gate and swept his car into the driveway and came to an abrupt stop. He held the precious paperwork in his moist grip—a forged birth certificate for his daughter, Hy Vọng Ketchum-James. He was glad they'd hyphenated their names; he could give Kate her due and Hy Vọng a bond to Kate.

How many times had he said that phrase to his friend in the Visa section behind closed doors? "My daughter's papers, my daughter, *my* daughter." He'd actually hugged the guy.

Jeremy was right; the blood tests didn't always confirm paternity accurately. Too risky. The quick Polaroids Jeremy had taken at the airstrip had worked. Her documents were fake but functional. Michael would feel a lot better when they'd landed in Boston and passed through customs. Once he was home in the States, he would even use his father's influence to do whatever needed to be done to make his little girl a legal citizen.

Climbing the stairs, he saw Kate twirling around the living

room and Hy Vọng clapping and laughing. Damn, Kate was fantastic. Give her a few hours, and she could change the world.

"Hey, my beautiful girls, what's happening?" He pushed the door open, and Hy Vọng ran to him and handed him her bunny. His legs weakened, and he lifted his featherweight daughter into his arms. Would he ever be able to stop the fluttering in his chest when he held her? He switched into Vietnamese. "Were you dancing with your Mommy?"

Michael moved closer to Kate, who looked...what was that look? Ecstatic? Exhausted? "Made me want to cry to see you two through the door. Jet lag got you, honey?" He pulled Kate close. "Did you ever think we would be standing here the three of us, a family?" He kissed her. "You're speechless? My Kate with no words?" He laughed. "By the way, everything's set. Hy Vọng's birth certificate, the tickets. Unreal. But we need to talk."

"Yes, we do. Michael, thank you. Oh my God, it's so wonderful. I spoke to Nin. You devil."

"What about Nin?"

The afternoon monsoon began its own show as dark clouds swallowed the sun like a light switch had been turned off. A crack of thunder made Hy Vọng bury her face in Michael's neck.

"Aw, it's just thunder, sweetie." He pulled Kate in closer with one arm. "Nature's drumroll seems to be right on cue, right? So, what's up with Nin?"

"I called her to cancel the club dates—"

"Then we're all set. Sorry honey, we'll get—"

Kate separated from Michael's arms, stepped back, and ran

her hand back through her hair. "Nin gave me your news. Don't be funny, Michael. I'm going on tour with the Keys? I can't believe you did that for me."

"You're serious? The *Keys*, again? That's fantastic. How did that happen? When?"

"Wait, but you know this. The Keys replaced their warm-up act with Riverrun and me to finish their *Southeast Asian Tour*. A fourteen-day tour. We're the new opening act."

"That Nin, she's the best." Michael hugged Kate and rapid-fired three kisses. "Baby, you deserve it. Wow!"

Hy Vọng reached out toward the piano, "Uh, uh, Dah-Dee." Michael let her down, and she ran to the lacquered bench. Another crash of thunder jolted the house. Hy Vọng started crying and dove under the bench.

Michael followed. "It's OK, honey. The sky is celebrating." He sat her on his lap and clapped. "Let's clap for Mommy. She's going to be a star." Michael used the English word, *Mommy*.

"Mah-mee." Hy Vọng sniffled, then turned to Kate and clapped. Michael loved that; it was the first he's seen Hy Vọng respond to Kate as Mommy.

"When's the tour, Miss Superstar? And why that look?"
Silence.

"I'm confused; I thought you arranged it, Michael? It starts Saturday."

"Saturday. You don't mean this coming Saturday."

Kate's face reflected the dark storm outside.

"You do mean this Saturday. Shit." Michael tried to absorb the impact of the curveball that had just hit him in the chest. When would he realize that trying to protect Kate was a kind of lying. It always backfired. "We already have the airline tickets. Damn, I need to get Hy Vọng safe, back in the states...I was hoping, as a family.

"I was so conflicted. I was going to say no. I thought you'd talked to Nin. I thought maybe you couldn't get the papers until later. Wait, what did you mean, bring her back safe?"

Michael slumped down onto the piano bench. "Confession time."

"Michael, not again."

"Yes, it's me again. I didn't want to worry you last night. And honestly, I didn't want to face it myself." He stroked Hy Vọng's hair. "The birth certificate, it's forged. I've got some work to do to prove she's mine. She could be taken...it's happened, Jeremy said. At least she could be held temporarily, maybe permanently. I don't want to even say it out loud. What I did was shady, well...illegal, Babe."

Kate covered her face with her hands. "Dammit Michael, why didn't you tell me last night? I hadn't even thought of that. I would have refused Nin, stood my ground...Nin assumed I'd say yes, so I thought you'd arranged it. The way she'd worded it. Nin was so excited, and she'd already engaged Riverrun. Honestly, so was I. Michael, you understand right, The Keys?"

"But I did say we needed to leave right away with her."

"I thought it was just your excitement and your work commitments, not fear of losing her!"

This was not the way he'd imagined their trip home to the States. He needed Kate's support. Despite his shaking hands, just the thought of their little family of three together meeting everyone had made him smile all the way home from the embassy. Coming through customs as a couple with a child was the most convincing way to smuggle the child in, he'd thought. It had been a fast-forward blur from a childless couple to becoming a family, and sure, there were plenty of years ahead of them, but the news of the concert tour took the wind out of him.

"When will I get out of living in my head?" He closed his eyes, gathering his mental balance, and breathed in the humid air laced with the sweet jasmine that he'd snipped from the stucco wall outside. Ground yourself. The scent helped his heart to slow a bit. He sighed, focused on the miserable look on Kate's face, and imagined her happy, singing on stage, hitting those insane notes of hers. He sighed. Could he put the trip off? But wouldn't that jeopardize Hy Vọng, even his job, if people saw him with the child? There would be questions. Hell, he'd already jeopardized his job. Could he stand not being there when Kate hit the heights? What a fucking choice to have to make?

Kate put her arms around his neck from behind. She said nothing for a suspended time. "I wish you'd told me about her documents. I want this chance at my career so badly, but how can I jeopardize things with Hy Vọng. I'd never forgive myself."

The deluge slapped against the patio tiles outside, rhythmic, like an excited audience. Plus, would it change their lives? Once she got out there, she might never be able to give it up, never be able to resist that high again, Michael thought. "I won't lose you again, will I?" He tightened his arms around Hy Vọng. She rubbed Bunny's face against his.

"Darling, that's never going to happen. We're too tight. We have a family now. You know how I feel about family...and you, and us." Kate put her arm around his shoulder.

"I've seen your face at O'Leary's; this will be the difference between a candle and fireworks when you hear the applause of thousands of people. We know you're meant to do this." Michael closed his eyes and hugged Hy Vọng to his chest.

The emotional catch in Kate's throat was audible. "When have I ever deserted you? Dammit, Michael—not through your lies, your troubles, the challenges of my fitting into your family; I've been here for you."

Michael gazed out into the garden and watched a small monkey swing over the wall into the papaya tree. It swiftly stole the ripe papaya he'd been meaning to pick for days. Michael paused and huffed out a breath. *Fulfilling a dream that's been driving her since childhood? I have to find a way,* he thought.

Kate stood with her arms wrapped around herself.

"I can't take this from you." He sat at the piano with Hy Vọng in his lap.

Moving next to him by the piano, Kate hugged him from behind.

He didn't want to separate from the man he'd become. He inhaled a deep breath to connect with his child's scent—the slight fragrance of mango and maple syrup on her shirt, that innocent aroma of her skin.

"Dah-Dee." Hy Vọng banged her hands on the keys, playing a dissonant, thunderous pattern with the low notes.

Kate squeezed him tighter. "Our family is more important."

"Wait. What if I take Hy Vọng to my mother's lake house? Nobody's there. I'll get Hy Vọng into the States and have some time alone with her to adjust." Michael stroked his daughter's hair. "Kayaking, being in nature. That always soothes me, and she'll love it, won't she? The peace and quiet? Being with her daddy. Can we keep this secret from our families for two weeks until you get there to enjoy the looks on their faces?" He kissed Hy Vọng's head. "It will give her a chance to settle in before meeting everyone."

"Darling, you are the supreme secret-keeper." Kate walk to the side of the piano and squinted her eyes at Michael. "It could work. Right after the tour, I'll catch up with you, and we'll go meet the families. Oh, and there is the minor detail of a small wedding reception. I'll talk to my mom." Kate ruffled Hy Vọng's hair; her eyes showed their child was becoming frightened from the tone of their conversation. Kate added a cheerful aspect to her voice. "Couldn't that work, Dah-Dee? Then I'll just go back to the Thai American Club and enjoy what I love, and we'll be a family again in Bangkok after our home leave."

"I think that could work." Michael rocked Hy Vọng in his arms. The splatter of the storm got louder. With the foggy, dripping windows all around and the high ceiling, it seemed they were inside some grand aquarium. Michael imagined Kate sitting on the hillside at UConn trying to follow his instructions with sheet music in her hands. He could hear her voice threatening to bring down the arches of St. Thomas Aquinas, and Kate holding him in the riots when he though his soul would spill out on the sidewalk, and her love stitching him back together. What kind of a bastard would take this chance from her? He had to trust. "Listen, Hy Vọng, you hear it?" Michael took her small hands in his and clapped again. "The rain sounds like applause for Mommy."

CHAPTER 60

HIGH NOTES

BACK STAGE AT King Chulalongkorn Concert Hall, Kate watched the stagehands rebounding from side to side like pinballs testing the sound and setting up for the show. Sitting on a Fender speaker with a mic in her hand, she couldn't help laughing out loud.

This had actually happened. They had gotten married by the embassy chaplain. They had a child. That Saturday, she'd left for two weeks on the road, and now she was back in Bangkok for the final show. Kate Ketchum-James. Too strange to sing under any name but Kate Ketchum. But being connected to Michael and being married in the eyes of the Thai public was a good thing.

The usual emotions battled inside her—the tingles encircling her entire body from the mind-blowing musical experience she was having, and the pain of loneliness at having no one to share it with except the band members. They were great guys, but she didn't really know them well, and their harmonies were no replacement for the intimacy of Michael. But each night when the music started and the first note came from her mouth, the shaking and that ache subsided; it was pure bliss.

"Testing, testing." The sound guy, Rodney, went about his job, and Kate sang a few bars of one of the songs she and her band had written. "It's all about the music..."

"That's good, Kate. We're good. I put some water and a hand towel over on that stand for you on stage left; it's gonna be a hot one tonight. The AC is never enough to win out over 100 degrees and 90% humidity." He took a towel from his shoulder and wiped his face.

"Thanks, Rodney." She was just a bit hungover from the two-week, city-to–city-tour. Could it have been more than a few drinks she'd had in post-concert celebrations every night? Was she drunk from the experience of singing to a crowd of not dozens, not hundreds, but thousands in fascinating foreign places?

We've got *capacity*, they'd said every night in every city, Manila, Jakarta, Kuala Lumpur, Hong Kong, Singapore, and now back to Bangkok. Or was her high from seeing the banner with the Keys and her name suspended over the main streets of major foreign capitals? Or the sizzling high she got from the press surrounding her after each show, flashing photoshoots for the *Bangkok Post*, *The Times Herald*, *Rolling Stone*, while they waited for the Keys to come out of the stage exit. She hadn't imagined the fame by association she and Riverrun would receive.

"Ms. Ketchum-James, how did you get your start in the U.S.?"

"Oh, in the church choir with my mother and a tiny club named O'Leary's."

The cameras flashed. That always made Kate laugh.

"Mrs. James, how do you feel playing with the Keys?"

"There are no words. We're so honored." She called the band over. "Meet Riverrun."

"*Kate? Kate?*" The questions went on.

Overwhelming and glorious. Kate wanted to transport her mother there to share in the joy of the dream she'd had for her daughter. She wanted Michael there too. That was the sad note in her musical nights. She'd missed him, and she wanted him to hear this knockout applause at her final performance and to share all her tales at the after-party.

She'd tested her own vocal cords in the ladies' room. The sound against the white tiles made her confident she could produce the same tones that had worked for her the night before. And the night before that. Riverrun had been at their best, although the first song was a little rough for a few bars last night, she thought. But their rehearsal today had gone better. She clasped her hands together to stop the shaking. The familiarity of the routine, singing night after night, had done nothing to take down the shivers and butterflies before going on stage.

The Keys band members were so supportive, and she was sure they weren't just being nice; they seemed impressed, chattering about wishing she could warm-up for them every night. It was an offhand comment by lead singer Adam Anderson, wasn't it? Did he really say, "That's no warm-up, Kate." He'd paused.

Kate had choked.

Without missing a beat, he'd added, "No, that was no warmup; the audience was sizzling hot when we came on stage."

She took her position at the mic, her band tweaking and tuning the strings one last time, as the heavy red curtain swept back for the final night. The black pantsuit with red flowers and lime green vines hand-embroidered down the legs she'd worn to perform had gotten a bit tighter. Could it be from their overindulgence of room service food and booze during two weeks on the road? It was getting a little out of control.

The spotlight hit her, stabbing her eyes, blackening out the audience, and the raucous applause was deafening. This was no O'Leary's crowd; this was no factory floor. The walls were solid teak to the vaulted ceiling. Massive portraits of the King of Siam flanked the stage with the red, white, and blue flags of Thailand moving from all the excitement in the hall. How could she describe her feelings as she hit the bridge of the song, and applause built from a few hands clapping, to the crowd calling out, "Kate, Kate, Kate, Kate, Kate?" The volume rose to a sound she'd never heard—thousands of simultaneous hands together, voices in synch, blending her chanted name and their applause raising into a roar like a full-on locomotive. No, like the deafening machines of the shoe factory at full-tilt. The sound pushed her back on the stage. It filled her up. This was a noise she could hear forever. How had she come to this place half-way around the planet from Glynn?

The screams, frenetic bodies, and fists punching the air, surrounded her. Kate could hardly breathe. Her face hurt from her perpetual smile. Her joy wasn't just about the audience's adulation; Kate loved knowing she touched them with her voice and the lyrics. As she ended the set, Kate shifted to the side of the stage, feeling humble.

Nin stood behind the curtain smiling and clapping.

Kate's knees gave out, and she hung onto the mic stand and planted one hand on the pebbled surface of the Fender speaker. It was bigger than any emotion she'd ever felt; how could she ever contain it?

CHAPTER 61

Michael

EQUIVOCAL ENTRY

THE LONG HOURS of delay in transit from Bangkok to Boston agitated Michael. Thankfully, Hy Vọng had slept for the first leg of the trip from Bangkok to London. Sunken into the plush Singapore Airlines first-class seat, Michael felt himself nod off. In the gauzy distance, he heard the voice of the stewardess stopping by with beverages.

"Thirsty, sweetheart?" The stewardess handed a small glass of milk to Hy Vọng, and she drank it before Michael had a chance to revive enough to stop her. He'd learned the hard way at home in Bangkok that his daughter couldn't digest dairy, never having had it from birth, when Michael had forgotten Jeremy's warning.

A short time later, Michael felt the warm stream run down his leg and smelled the stench. He had to change his slacks and Hy Vọng's diaper and clothes. She squirmed and cried as he cleaned up her mess.

"I'm so sorry about the milk." The stewardess was clearly frustrated but helpful.

"How could you have known?" Michael searched in his carry-on. Fortunately, Kate had packed a few outfits in case of delays. The nearby passengers were suffering from the odor but mostly had compassionate words for this helpless father. Not a good start for his unhappy girl. Michael prayed for the flight to be over.

Waiting in the long line at Logan Airport among the bustle of families, tourists, business travelers, and soldiers returning home, Michael held his breath. He was exhausted and desperate to get his child into his own country, even if it was illegally.

So many stares at the blonde man with the Asian child. Was he imagining their curious thoughts? *Is she adopted? Did he have an Asian wife? Where's the mother?* Maybe they just saw she was cute. He hadn't thought about Hy Vọng's acceptance by others. In Bangkok, it wasn't uncommon to see American parents and Thai children. But then wouldn't his father and grandmother see his love child, Hy Vọng, as another liability? Sweat beaded on Michael's forehead, and he wiped it quickly, not wanting to show any of the tension that was ripping at his insides.

Breathe, he thought. Just be Hy Vọng's father. That's what Kate had told him. Engage with the child, not the agent; it would seem more natural. He stepped up to the counter and handed over his passport and her birth certificate. Michael kept his eyes on Hy Vọng, straightening her little blue cotton dress, pulling up her lace-edged socks, and adjusting her patent leather Mary Janes. "You look so nice for Grandma."

The customs agent looked at Hy Vọng. His question hung in his lingering look. "So, Michael James, you work for the embassy in Bangkok?"

"Yes, my first year there."

He turned over the black diplomatic passport. "Traveling alone?"

"Meeting my wife...for our little girl's birthday with the family."

"Tough traveling with a child, huh?"

"After two tours in Nam, she's a breeze. Aren't you, honey." He shifted Hy Vọng from one hip to the other and played the military sympathy card. "Just a few weeks of home leave to see family."

"Birthday? Says here, her birthday was May 6th."

"Oh, well, we were overseas, so now..." *Keep the story simple, so you don't trip up*, Michael thought.

The customs agent's intense gaze flickered from Michael's eyes to Hy Vọng to Michael. *Keep your face relaxed, seem natural, kiss your little girl, call yourself Daddy, make him believe she's yours.*

Dear God, don't let her speak Vietnamese. Wouldn't she speak English if she'd been with him all along? He hadn't thought of that. She's an American child. He realized he was squeezing Hy Vọng's leg, and he relaxed.

The customs agent touched Hy Vọng's hand. "What's your name, sweetie?"

Hy Vọng mumbled some Vietnamese words and hid in Michael's chest.

Oh God. Michael shifted her to his other hip. "Amazing, she's learning Thai already."

The agent flagged a colleague from across the room.

With shaking hands, Michael held on tighter to Hy Vọng. "You hungry, honey?" *Pay attention to your child. Ignore the other two agents and their whispers, and the agent nodding in your direction. Dear God, please help me. Not after all she's been through.*

The second agent took over. "Just sit her here on the counter."

Michael looked back at the original agent who had gone down the hall and entered a door marked, "Security." He took a deep breath. "Are you tired, angel? We'll be home soon. Here, hold onto Bunny."

"Seriously, you can sit her on the counter. Must be tired holding her all this time."

Michael didn't put her down; he would fight for her. He would never let Hy Vọng go, not to anyone.

The second agent's stern face shifted and was lit by a smile as he made that one sound, that one critical sound Michael had waited for—*ka-chunk.* "Sorry for the delay, sir, we were due a shift change."

Was Michael's sigh audible to the agent as the imprint landed on a page in his passport? It was a sound of freedom that would always repeat in Michael's mind.

"Enjoy your home leave. My colleague tells me, you did two tours in Nam. Me too. Thank you for your service."

"Thank you, sir." He turned so the agent wouldn't see Michael's eyes floating in liquid that threatened to overflow.

Hy Vọng's hand dragged through the warm, pristine lake water leaving a miniature wake behind. She'd come to love the kayak slicing through the gray-blue water, riding tucked between Michael's legs with Bunny in her lap. He could see it in the way she relaxed and the giggles that followed each time he settled her into the boat. His daughter's furry comrade was beginning to show some wear from their days playing at Michael's family house in the Berkshires. Taking walks in the woods and cooking meals had left their marks—matted fur, stains here and there. Michael had tried to put her beloved Bunny in the washing machine, but Hy Vọng would have none of that.

After nearly two weeks, Michael was beginning to show some wear as well, he thought. Hadn't he lost weight? His shorts had begun to slip down off his waist a bit, and he'd noticed dark circles under his eyes in the mirror this morning. There were many causes for his restlessness, and he'd found it hard to sleep without Kate beside him.

Michael had no crib for Hy Vọng to keep her safe. Should he put a mattress on the floor? That didn't work; Hy Vọng was used to the ground. She'd curled up next to his bed on the floor like a puppy on their first night at the cabin. Being on a blanket pile on the floor seemed to comfort Hy Vọng, but Michael would soon have to break that habit. He was afraid he'd step on her when he got out of bed in the morning or at night when sleep escaped him.

Why did that break his heart seeing her coiled up alone on the floor?

It had been a few days since he'd heard from Kate. He imagined her surrounded by her new fans and at after-concert parties with the Keys. Her usual excitement was palpable even over the inferior international phone lines.

The high he felt for her had quickly transformed into dark loneliness as the line disconnected. He missed the hell out of Kate, and keeping up the secrecy with his mother was tough. His two calls home had made it worse. Telling lies, always telling lies, pretending he was in Bangkok. He'd almost slipped more than once. The anticipation of sharing the news with his mother made him pace at night as Hy Vọng curled up sound asleep on her blankets. But he resisted sharing such delicate information on the phone. It had to be in person, and she needed to see her grandchild's face.

"What a clear connection for a change," his mother had said on his last call to her. That made him want to tell her everything. Spill it all and get on to celebrating with her and her new granddaughter. It wouldn't be long now. Kate would be back in a few days. If he could just hold out. The joy of the good news came with the story of Ha`ng's fate. That story, he didn't want to share with his mother. The consequences of telling all to Kate after holding back so long was fresh in his memory.

CHAPTER 62

Michael

HIDING HY VỌNG

MICHAEL TIED UP the kayak on the old splintering pier. October was so beautiful on the lake, and Hy Vọng pointed at every quacking duck and honking goose that flew overhead. She leaned back into his chest. Her petite body swayed left and right with the rhythm of the oar as she held on. Her hands, even the sight of her hands, made him choke up. He loved when she wrapped her fingers around his thumb and spoke his favorite word, her favorite English utterance, Dah-Dee.

There was something hypnotic about that gurgling sound of the paddle moving through the water. How far he'd come since first arriving at this place after Nam. He had a wife now, whom he loved deeply, and a child he'd rescued. Kate's singing career was taking off, and he was happy with his job in Bang-kok. He would never have guessed any of this good fortune would be his while lying in the bloody grass with his lover's body and his baby in his arms just a few years ago.

Studying the familiar pines that lined the shoreline, tall and straight, Michael stopped rowing and drew in a breath.

He loved their scent blended with the fragrant clematis that crawled up the summer cottages dotting the edge of the lake. There were days he had to carry Hy Vọng when she refused to leave the lake and cried all the way from the pier to the house. Holding her under her arms out away from his body, with her legs kicking wildly, Michael worked to avoid the impact of her hard-soled shoes against his thighs. His daughter regretted the end of the day in the kayak just as much as he did. Today was one of those days. He never wanted the sun to set.

Once Hy Vọng saw they were getting in the car, she settled down. Did she associate riding in the car with the day he'd brought her home? They pulled up to the Daly's Grocery Store. Michael been the recipient of the Daly couple's kindness since he was a child at the quaint, green and white shop with the rockers on the porch. Their Tootsie Roll stash was endless. Hy Vọng knew what was to come.

"Hey, Michael. Hi, sweetheart."

Hy Vọng ran to Mrs. Daly to collect her prize.

"Wait, let me open one for you, dear."

Coming out from behind the counter, Mr. Daly squatted down eye to eye with Hy Vọng. "Is that good, honey?" He looked up at Michael. "By the way, your mother just called an hour or so ago."

Michael froze in place and went into his well-trained emotional lock-down.

"I didn't realize Christine thought you were still in Bangkok."

Shit. His mother hadn't come to the Berkshire house in years. Well, she would now, Michael thought.

"A little awkward. She was checking on the house. Seems you might get a visitor. I couldn't lie."

The quiver ran up and down Michael's arms and found its way into the pit of his stomach. He picked up some Spic and Span, Cheerios, Wonder Bread, eggs, and a can of Spam and tossed it on the counter. "Oh, how wonderful. Thanks. I was going to call her tonight to surprise her, anyway."

"Yes, you said something about a surprise the first day you arrived, so I didn't mention the child."

"Thanks, Mr. Daly. Michael released a breath of tension. Not a surprise I wanted to share over the phone. I thought Hy Vọng needed a little time to adjust first. You know, jet lag, new place."

"Well, she's doing just fine, aren't you, honey?" The silver-haired proprietor stood and ruffled Hy Vọng's hair. "So now your darling doll will meet the families?"

"Uh, yes, of course. Waiting for Kate, first."

"You're a lucky man, Michael; Kate's a good woman. Liked her right from the start when you came for your little visit last summer. You're visiting your father and grandmother next, I guess?"

Mrs. Daly stepped closer to her husband.

Michael watched the eye exchange between the couple. Mrs. Daly shot her husband a look of warning to stop him from whatever he was about to say. She filled in the seconds of silence. "Well, I'm sure your father and his mother will be thrilled."

It was no secret to Michael that in the early years when she'd visited the lake house, his condescending Grandmother James, the Grand Dame of the James family, had caused a rift between the kindly shopkeepers and herself. He knew the Daly's were referring to his grandmother's racism and elitism.

"Tell your mother to stop in if she has time. We miss her; it's been years."

Michael thought of his mother pleading with his father to spend more time relaxing at her family's simple lake cottage, but he'd often used work as an excuse not to go. More important things to do. Still, the cottage held warm childhood memories for Michael—alone with just his mother.

CHAPTER 63

Michael

STING OF SECRECY

ALL THE WAY back to the house from the Daly's Country Store, Michael rehearsed his conversation with his mother, as Hy Vọng unwrapped and finished her little log candies. He wouldn't let himself think about his father and grandmother's reactions, but he was glad he'd practiced telling the Daly's his story about Ha`ng and his past when he'd arrived with Hy Vọng.

The caretakers of so many of the vacation houses on the lake, they were news central. They'd known him since he was a baby; they knew his stories from when he'd returned from the war and he'd called them to tell them he'd survived those tough years. They didn't seem to have a prejudiced bone in their bodies when he'd brought Hy Vọng to see them.

Michael kept his mind on seeing his mother after his months of absence. No doubt his mother was on her way, speeding through the winding roads, leaving a rooster tail of fumes behind her. She would have thrown a few things in her leather luggage after her phone call with Mr. Daly and would be here in several hours to see her only son, her hands aching from clutching the steering wheel.

Back at the house, Michael made a grilled cheese sandwich for himself, just as Kate had taught him in college. Buttered bread and cheese in tinfoil, pressed with a hot iron. "No muss, no fuss," she'd say. No dairy for Hy Vọng—he pressed a spam sandwich she'd come to love and cut it into tiny squares perfect for tiny fingers. He never had trouble with Hy Vọng when it came to eating. It should have made him happy, and yes it did, but he knew her enthusiasm came from the days when she must have been starving. He bit his lip at the thought.

Hy Vọng finished and licked her fingers, and Michael wiped her hands and face. "*You*, little girl, need some rest."

"*Không, không.*"

"Never mind, saying *no*, young lady, you need your nap. Someone special's coming to see you." He put her on the floor with a pillow, a blanket and Bunny next to the striped porch glider. Bridging another pillow over her like a little lean-to to keep out the bright sunlight that still washed the porch, he sang to her. It would soon be shady.

Hy Vọng was out in minutes, those long lashes slowly fanning, then closing.

Michael listened for his mother's tires on the dirt driveway through the screened-in porch while Hy Vọng napped. The squeaking sound of the old porch glider sliding back and forth seemed to soothe her. It took him back to his own childhood. Sitting with his head against his mother's shoulder, they would watch the sun angle down through the trees, lighting up the lake at sunset, and listen to the loons say goodnight as they settled in across the lake at dusk.

He was relieved Hy Vọng hadn't picked up on his tension; she'd be in a much better mood, having had a nap.

What could he tell his mother that would take away the sting of his secrecy? Like Kate, his mother didn't appreciate being on the outside looking in when it came to him. But how could he have told her over the phone? Wouldn't that have been worse? He would rather have the option to look into her eyes, hug her, let her see her new grandchild. Wouldn't his mother's disappointment from being marginalized from the truth just evaporate when she saw Hy Vọng's bright azure eyes? Her little rose-shaped lips, her honey highlights on her dark brown hair. It looked so much better than the wild condition it was in when Hy Vọng had arrived at the airstrip. Kate had performed a miracle on her hair, trimming it to chin-length, so the ends tucked in.

Michael reached down and stroked Hy Vọng's face. She was beginning to adjust to people now. Hadn't she let the Daly's hold her at the country store? Yes, it took a Tootsie Roll or two, and yes, it had taken nearly two weeks, but then his mother had a certain openness, a warmth few could resist. She and Kate had been arm in arm within minutes of their meeting. Yes, any hurt his mother felt would melt at the sight of her granddaughter, he thought.

Michael heard her black Mercedes come to a skidding halt behind the house. Who else would screech into his driveway? The car door slammed, and her crunching steps moved around the side of the house on the gravel path, past the blueberry bushes to the lake-front porch. *"Michael? Michael!"*

He could see she was running by the time she rounded the corner of the porch. It would be best to have their discussion before Hy Vọng woke up, he thought. Let his mother focus on her granddaughter later. Michael stood and rushed to open the screen door.

She wasn't her put-together self. Her blonde hair with dark roots showing, no makeup, wearing his Harvard sweatshirt with her grass-stained gardening jeans. Michael had never seen his mother looking so unkempt.

"Darling, I can't believe it..." Her trembling arms ensconced him and wouldn't let go. "Why didn't you tell me you were back?" The up and down of her shoulders and her soft cry began, and she spoke between sniffles. "If I hadn't called the Daly's about the house...if I wasn't so happy, I would...I never dreamed you'd go overseas again after four years in that god-awful war, then the Bangkok surprise, and now you're here at our cottage without telling me." She wiped her eyes, sniffed, and stood straight. "Sorry, you must have a reason; I didn't mean for my mom-guilt routine to slip out."

It crushed him to have hurt her. He hadn't thought their reunion would bring back memories of his return from Vietnam. All those years apart. He hadn't thought of that. "Mom, I'm sorry. I'm crazy. I didn't mean to hurt you. To leave you out." He spoke in a whisper.

She stepped back and straightened her clothes and her hair. "Well, you certainly did that. Again! But why?"

"I have so much to tell you, and one thing to show you." He kissed his mother's cheek, pulled away, and swept his arm toward the pillow and his sleeping child. "Shhh! Your granddaughter is asleep."

"My *what*? Where?"

"Over there, asleep beside the glider."

"My *granddaughter*? Kate had a *baby*? You didn't tell me you had a *child*, my *grandchild*? Wait, she couldn't have... Heavens above, Michael, what's happening between us?" She put her face in her hands.

"Mom, it's OK."

Hy Vọng sat up, clutched Bunny, and rubbed her eyes.

"Hi, Honey, did you have a nice sleep?"

Hy Vọng buried her face in Bunny.

"I'll explain, Mom. We just got her two weeks ago. It's OK, sweetheart." He switched to Vietnamese, "Yes, this woman you can trust. She's your grandmother."

"What did you say to her?"

"Just introductions. Mom, this is my daughter, Hy Vọng; it means *hope*."

His mother bent over, put her hands on her knees, and looked down at Hy Vọng. "Oh, honey, don't be afraid. Let me see your sweet face. Tell her, Michael."

"Hy Vọng, honey, look at Grandma." Michael could see his daughter's eyes scan his mother's face, flutter closed, then open again. They flashed at Michael and back to his mother, as if to ask, is this someone I can trust; will she hurt me, Daddy? That vulnerable, fearful look always burrowed inside him and caused a tightening in his chest. Hy Vọng stood and scampered to her father. "Dah-dee."

He sat on the glider and held her so his mother could see her face. His daughter cast her spell on his mother as he knew she would. The familiar way Hy Vọng furled in fear when she met someone, then spread open like the petals of a morning glory with the stranger's smile or kindness was irresistible. His mother dropped to one knee. "Oh Michael, she's so adorable... so fragile. How old is she?"

"Four, in May."

His mother drew her hands to her chest, taking in a quick breath. He imagined her heart bursting open just like his had the day he'd met Hy Vọng at the airport. Could that have only been a few weeks ago?

Hy Vọng kept her gaze down at Bunny.

"My God, Michael... I'm confused. When did you decide to adopt? She's Thai?"

"Mom, I have so much to tell you."

"Clearly. And I, you. But, later, dear."

"Wait, why were you checking on your lake house? Are you OK?" *Was his father up to his old tricks with another woman?* Michael's fists tightened.

"I'm fine; later, dear. Just wanted to do a little renovating. Right now, I'm looking at the sweetest child on earth." His mother's look changed as she studied Hy Vọng's face lit by her electric blue eyes. "Oh my God, Michael, her eyes." His mother looked up at him. "They're *your* eyes?"

"And *yours*, Mom."

"She's *your* child? And now, *my granddaughter*?" She bolted upright; with her mouth open, she searched his eyes.

Michael was wordless.

Wouldn't it be cruel to describe his love's destruction as it really happened? Images that might linger in his mother's mind forever like they do in his.

Wouldn't she be ashamed of him that he had waited to go back and find his child? He would deliver the violent part of the story with softened words, words that could be left to linger in her mind with only sadness, not the vivid realities that he'd had to bear.

"Mom, she's mine. I had a…" He hated to call Ha`ng a lover. "A woman I loved, we planned to move here after the war, get married. She…she died in the war."

"Oh, Honey, how devastating. I'm so sorry. But wait, that was over three years ago."

Michael shrugged and nodded.

"Michael, you held that in for all those years? God love you." She shifted her hands from Michael's face to Hy Vọng's cheeks. "Your Daddy needs to learn to let people in who love him, doesn't he?" His mother kissed Hy Vọng's tiny fingers and smiled. "She is simply mesmerizing with those blue eyes. "Hello, Honey. I won't hurt you."

Hy Vọng stepped closer and showed his mother her stuffed bunny.

Michael's mother stroked the matted fur of the favored toy. "Where was she all that time? Who took care of her?"

"I had to leave the baby in a village woman's care. I asked her to bring Hy Vọng to her grandparents' village. I only found her a few weeks ago through a buddy pilot in Nam. She was in an orphanage that got bombed. The village where I left her was destroyed."

"I can't image this angel in a war. Wait, where's Kate? Does she know? You'd told her long ago, I assume." She looked up at Michael. "*Michael?*"

"Mom. I only told Kate recently that I'd found her. But she's known…for a while. It all happened so fast."

"So this is why you called off the original wedding?"

"I know, I know, I'm an idiot. I nearly lost Kate. Who wants to hear about a former love and a love child? Honestly, I couldn't talk about it without falling apart again. And I never thought I'd ever be able to find one child in a closed-off, war-torn country." He could feel his throat closing.

"Oh, Michael, where is Kate? Why isn't she here with you?"

"Kate's singing on tour with the Keys. That's another crazy thing that happened just before I left for the States. We decided she should go."

"The *Keys*; she must be thrilled. But she must want to be here with her husband, doesn't she? Oh, Michael, is everything OK between you two?"

"Yes, Mom; we're good now. Kate was the one who insisted I keep looking for Hy Vọng."

"Oh, too much to take in, Michael." His mother kept talking in a cooing, sweet voice to keep Hy Vọng calm as she asked Michael questions. How did Kate get her concert tour, when would Kate be home?

Christine put her arms out, Hy Vọng came closer, and she lifted her granddaughter. "That's right, sweetheart, don't worry, Grandma Christine won't hurt you."

Not quite awake yet, Hy Vọng put her head on his mother's shoulder. Michael could hear his mother's deep sigh. It wouldn't be long he thought that his little girl would walk around displaying that irresistible smile openly with no hesitation. Once she spent time in his own mother's tender arms, once she was spent time with the Ketchum clan, once Kate was home.

"So, Mom. Please. What's going on with you? Are you OK. Why the lake house all of a sudden?"

His mother looked into Michael's eyes, then looked away, and continued to stroke Hy Vọng's hair. "Just needed a respite from…well, from everything."

"You mean, Dad."

"I want to fix my house up. Just in case I want to spend more time here. A place that's mine. That's all. I've been away so long taking care of your aunt."

His mother kissed Hy Vọng again. "Frankly, I worry about your trust fund."

The thought of no financial resources spun around in his head. He could handle it. Once he figured out Hy Vọng's legal issues, he'd be all set. He could support his own family.

"Let's not talk about this now. I have an idea for you regarding the trust; I've had a lot of time to think about my exit strategy—whenever I have the courage. I haven't been a total fool all these years; I have a nest egg. But let's enjoy this child for now."

They were silent. Michael drew them both near. What a feeling to have his arms around his mother and his child. The first moments with his mother gave him a tender taste of having his own family. "Mom, I'm glad you came. The bastard doesn't deserve…well, I'm just glad you came."

She kissed Hy Vọng's cheek and looked into her striking eyes. "And I assume there is more for you to tell *me*, as well? I know my enigmatic son. But then who cares about all our dramas when your new granddaughter is right in front of you? Let's focus on this cherub and stop all this chatter. Everything will work out OK, won't it, Hy Vọng?"

"O-K." The lilt in her small voice and the separated syllables surprised Michael. "Aw, that's a first. I guess she's copying me.

I'm always asking her, OK? OK, Hy Vọng?" Michael looked at his mother. "Are we *OK*, Mom? I'm sorry for all the intrigue. If it helps, I'm so happy in my life with Kate, and now, Hy Vọng."

"After hearing what happened to you in that god-awful war, it means the world." His mother put her hand on his shoulder. "And you have the international job you always wanted."

Michael held back the news from the telegram he'd received that morning from the Embassy. "I know what we all need. Let's take the north path with Hy Vọng? So much wildlife and birds for her to see." Michael hoisted Hy Vọng up onto his shoulders. "Birdies Hy Vọng? And Mother Nature and Mother James? My favorite combination since I was a boy. Let's show Hy Vọng what family feels like."

CHAPTER 64

CLOUDY CEILING

AFTER TWO WEEKS, Kate's voice pulsing out over the throngs of thousands and the backwash of applause hadn't lost its thrill. As she left through the stage door into the sticky gauze of the humid night in Bangkok, a cluster of fans almost made her want to cry. Bodies jumping like delighted children; their excitement was contagious, flashing shivers through her despite the heat.

Some faces were familiar—regulars from the Thai American Club. *Kate, can you sign my shirt, my program, my chest, my bald head*—they called out in broken English, British English, Aussie English, and languages she'd never heard.

Being American had some magical allure in the chaos of 1970. If she were in the US, wouldn't she be thrust back into perspective, into the dining room at O'Leary's, certainly not upfront on the finest stages in the country? Wouldn't she be a dime-a-dozen back in the US—her reputed good voice and good looks, aside?

She held no illusions, but she had no resistance to the allure of the fans and letting her voice go out into the rafters of famous, foreign venues.

The message was clear, no matter the language, no translation necessary. *We love you, Kate. We want to take a reminder of you with us.* Kate scribbled her name over and over, hugged, and smiled, and tried to forget. To forget that this wouldn't last forever, this surreal tour, this euphoria, this perfect place where her voice was heard in so many ways. To forget who she used to be, a small-town girl in Glynn. Would she still fit in? To forget that Michael was alone in the mountains with their new-found child.

When the last autograph was signed, she went back inside and stood at the edge of the stage, looking out across the empty seats. Stagehands wrapped wires from wrists to elbow and packed mics away behind her. Kate wanted one last look. Could the room still be vibrating? Pure joy didn't dissipate quickly.

"Need something, Kate?" Her drummer asked.

"What? Oh, no, just one last look."

"It was great, wasn't it? The band's in the car, outside the double doors. Time to celebrate."

Driving with her band members in the limo to the hotel, the din of the concert faded in her mind. What would it feel like to go back to the Thai American Club? To be in her life with Michael and Hy Vọng again? Her thoughts fought for attention in the band's animated conversation that surrounded her.

Kate twisted her wedding ring and took in the city lights as they road under a street banner suspended overhead with her name on the line just below the *Keys—Kate Ketchum-James and Riverrun*. Could a human have two hearts, she wondered; it seemed Kate did. She wanted to be with her family and Michael and their new daughter; she wanted to be on stage with her fans and that glorious thundering applause that told her she'd touched them.

Being an absentee mother was not the kind of parenting she understood. How would they work it out? She had no idea. In Kate's world, mothers stayed at home with children or worked near home while grandmothers watched their children. Mothers made soup or French toast when you were sick. Mothers sat in the kitchen drinking tea and listening when you needed advice. Mothers were there for you. But this was a different world. And she'd never had that ache to be a mother. Would motherhood swallow her future after all?

Kate stepped out of the limo and was surrounded by fans again. Over the past three weeks, fame and public recognition had swept into her life like a brush fire through dry fields, and their champagne tour had been a pure luxury. She loved every minute of it, knowing her singing had caused so much joy.

Entering the magnificent hotel, Kate laughed as she rode the elevator with her delirious band members. The guys were bumping fists, exchanging some secret handshake, and talking in broken English all at once. This was no typical warm-up gig, her band members had assured her.

"Without you, Kate, we would be in a fleabag hotel."

"Yeah, all sleeping in one room."

"Along a muddy klong somewhere in the other end of Bangkok."

"Party in Adam's suite!"

Kate stared up at her hotel ceiling, her hands behind her head. There were no circles of yellow stains from leaky pipes overhead; instead, floating above her in the Italian Suite was a painted ceiling reminiscent of the Sistine Chapel. Whipped cream clouds against a sky blue background with beams of light beckoning. How her life had changed.

Sighing, she moved to the lounge chair overlooking the twinkling cityscape and finished her Singha beer. Where did the tour time go? Wisped from her life in seconds. Her room service tray beside her soon held a half-dozen wooden chicken saté skewers gnawed bare and stacked purposely like a pile of pick-up-sticks over a smear of peanut sauce. Beside the kindling were three empty amber beer bottles. The delicious snack had awaited her after the post-concert party fanfare. Her face ached from smiling at the glorious fun of it all; her body felt lit up, aroused from the admirers rushing her for autographs, the excess of everything—stimulants and stardom.

CHAPTER 65

REPEAT PERFORMANCE

THE DOORBELL RANG. Kate wobbled her way to the hotel door. She shouldn't have had that third beer on top of a night of toasting with Dubonnet Rouge, but she'd been so dehydrated. Who's visiting at midnight? "Who is it?" she called out.

"Special delivery. Champagne?"

The door swung open, and there stood Adam holding a bottle of champagne high above his head.

"Ha! I think I've reached my limit. But, come on in." She'd been nervous around Adam at first. He was a Rock superstar, but after a few nights of after-parties and seeing how playful he was with everyone, she felt comfortable with him. He'd taken her under his wing, and she could feel her career taking off—her feet almost levitating off the ground.

"Well, what have we here, champagne and a superstar?" She could hear a slur in her own voice.

"Congratulations, you were fucking amazing. Check these out from last night—the Keys are below the fold, and you and your Riverrun guys are above it!" Adam dropped newspapers and the ice bucket on the table and wriggled the cork out from the magnum. "You owe me." Adam laughed as the foam fizzled onto the rug. "And you, Kate, tonight was the best for you, the fucking best." He kissed her cheek.

"Come on, Adam; I'm just the lead singer for the little local warm-up band, riding on your coattails."

"Not anymore, Kate."

She offered him the box of chocolates some anonymous fan had sent to her room. He took one of the accordion white paper cups, popped the candy in his mouth, spun around, and shot the crinkled paper into the nearby trash can.

"Two points. I'm impressed." Kate laughed. He was fun; the parties were a blast. Yes, Adam was flirtatious, but wasn't he that way with everyone? It didn't seem aggressive; she overlooked it as harmless; he'd never crossed the line.

"True, you're a warm-up band singer, and damn, you can heat up a crowd." Adam stepped in a little closer and downed his champagne. "Kate, you're going places; you realize that, right?"

Was it true, she wondered, or was the crowd electrified with anticipation of Adam and his headliner band?

"Hell, that ravishing red hair of yours, glow-in-the-dark green eyes, your knock-out voice. Get ready to launch, kiddo."

Launch. There was that word again. She had to admit she was flattered by his compliments. "Your mouth to God's ears."

Adam casually pushed one side of her hair behind her ear and smiled.

An ache ran through her. Michael's special gesture. Chills sizzled over her arms as she thought of the first time Michael had tucked her hair behind her ear at the fraternity house and the charge of electricity that had run down her spine. She imagined their celebration had Michael been there in her hotel room in Bangkok.

"I'm not blowing smoke, Kate, you were a smash hit. I want to help you really break out." He hugged her.

Smashed was right; she stumbled back a step. Adam caught her, and *she* caught sight of her glowing face in the dresser mirror. She didn't recognize the woman in the arms of the tall, lean man in the back leather vest. Who was that red-faced woman with those woozy eyes? Michael's wife? Hy Vọng's mother? Cecelia and Kevin's daughter? Christine's daughter-in-law? The scent of little white fragrant chains of jasmine that hung from the bedpost reached her. A gift Michael had sent Kate—the same aroma she and Michael had made love to, the fragrance that had filled her bedroom in Bangkok. She could see Michael's face hovering over her.

She was high enough to have clouded judgment, but just sober enough to know better. She stared at the person reflected back at her. She was suspended between two worlds.

Glancing at the empty beer bottles and her reflection in the mirror, like a slap, awakened Kate from her fantasy. A memory emerged that stopped her cold—Michael and Hy Vọng cuddling with a pink bunny on their rattan sofa in their home in Bangkok. She stepped back.

"Careful, Kate." Adam steadied her and led her to the chair. He perched on the edge of the bed across from her. "Sit. Listen, I have an offer for you."

"An offer?"

"I know you have the 'honey, I'm home' husband thing going on, but that's for a whole lifetime, right?"

"And there's—" Kate cut off her words; she'd almost forgotten that Hy Vọng was still a secret that hadn't been shared.

"And...how about three more weeks warming up for us in Europe? Seven countries, three days each. Then head home." He leaned over and held his hand out. "What do you say? Then you can play the wife."

She prickled at his words, *the wife*. "Europe? Oh, my God." She was hypnotized. Resisting Adam's flirtations she could do, she told herself, but missing out on the chemistry of the crowd? "I'll have to make a call."

"Yes, call Michael, but we leave tomorrow night for France. First concert is in fourteen days. The band's going to take a two-week respite on the Riviera, first. On me. Join us if you want. We'd all love that." Adam took off his bandana from around his neck and touched her shoulder. "Getting hot in here."

The phone rang. Kate jumped. Who else would be calling? "Excuse me, Adam, this is probably Michael."

Adam didn't pick up the hint to leave.

Kate picked up the receiver.

"Hey, Babe, how was your final night?"

"Glorious! Seriously, mind-blowing. Impossible to explain. Well, maybe it wasn't the *last* concert night. We need to talk." Sounds like crumbling paper filled the line, then cleared.

"Honey, I've missed you. A lot's happening here too."

Michael's voice sent a chill through her. Kate waved at Adam and silently signaled she would call him later.

He gave her a thumbs up. "See you in the morning, gorgeous." Adam winked on his exit and closed the door.

"Who's that?"

"Adam Anderson."

"And he calls you gorgeous? Kind of funny."

"Oh, he's just a smartass; I said I knew it was you when the phone rang." *Did she slur again?*

"I see. Sounds like you've been partying. Glad you're having fun. So, you're at the Imperial Hotel? Wow, pretty swank for a warm-up band. I guess I figured you'd stay at our house? I called Nin, she gave me your number."

Was Michael's voice heavy with questions and suspicion, or was it Kate's imagination? "Last minute surprise. Never mind, I'm not partying now, just a few beers alone in my room. The guys were so excited. Adam put us all up here at the Imperial Hotel, *on him*." Kate's stomach quivered as she dropped into the jade silk chair. "Adam just stopped by with news clippings and to congratulate me. I miss you. So much. We had a packed house again tonight. I got lucky with my voice; it really opened up."

"You got lucky when you were born with that voice, Kate."

It was so good to connect with Michael even through the poor phone line. "How is Hy Vọng doing? I keep thinking how strange it was to have met her and left the next day." The beers had made Kate vulnerable; her throat squeezed with emotion. "I hate the timing, Michael. There's so much I'm missing. But I confess, this was the time of my life." Kate fidgeted with the white phone cord, coiled it around her finger, and delayed the news about extending her tour. I got your telegram about your mother's unexpected visit. How did it go with her? Was she thrilled?"

"She came to check on the house, and here we were. The Daly's got a call from her, so I had a head's up. Still…"

"Oh, my God. What a shock for her. Was she angry you didn't tell her?"

"She got over it when she saw her own eyes in her grand-daughter's. But yeah, she doesn't like secrets."

Secrets, Kate thought. It was time to talk about the European tour.

"What about Hy Vọng? Is she adjusting? I should have been there." Kate was aware of her own continuous chatter. Her delay of the truth about Adam's offer. Noticing an envelope next to the news clippings with her name on it, Kate slid her fingernail under the edge, and ripped it open. The amount on the check was stunning. More money than she'd made from two jobs in a year in Glynn. For singing a few nights and a few rehearsals? She gasped, then laughed out loud.

"Babe, you OK?"

"Sorry, I'm here. But I just saw an envelope Adam left me. My pay for the tour for five thousand dollars!" Kate threw herself back on the sofa, delirious. She'd known the base pay, but the percentage of the door proceeds Adam had added in, blew her away.

"Wow, Kate, very cool. You deserve it. The big time. Honey, it's getting tough here without you. Can't believe it's been almost two weeks; feels more like a year. Hy Vọng just squirmed up onto my lap. Hold on. Don't pull the cord darling, say hi to Mommy."

Silence.

Thunder cracked in the background.

"Dah-dee." Hy Vọng whined at the second boom.

"You're OK, Hy Vọng. Kate, I have so much to tell you, and life through this telephone line is really getting old. Hold on;

I need to calm her down. When will you be—? Hy Vọng just pulled on the cord again, sorry."

"Here, honey," Kate could hear his mother's voice, "come with Grandma. I'll take her; you talk to Kate. Hello Kate, sending my love and congratulations on your concert tour."

"Hello, Christine! Michael, tell her I send love too. Is Hy Vọng, OK? Does this happen often? It's the sudden sounds, right? Like you. Oh, Honey, it's tragic what she must have gone through." Kate dropped the check on the table.

"She's doing better. Mom's so happy about Hy Vọng. We're having a good time. I'm looking forward to bringing Hy Vọng to meet the Ketchums."

"It feels wrong for my mother and father not to know. Especially now that Christine's there. I'm going to call them." Kate held her breath. "What about your father and grandmother? Do they know?"

"Mom told them. That's another story. Kate, I miss you at night when it's quiet. Well, I miss you when it's not."

"Aw. Honey, me too." She took a breath, held it, and exhaled. "I need to talk to you about...another opportunity." Kate grabbed another beer, opened it and drank. "I'm just going to put it out there. See what you think?" She talked about her European tour extension. Could he hear the quiver in her voice? "There would also be a two-week vacation break, a chance to rest between tours." Why mention the rest stop was in the Riviera; it seemed cruel considering Michael's situation, but she wanted to tell the truth. Wasn't she always asking Michael to be more open and honest? "On the French Riviera. It's all so strange, the timing, Hy Vọng, and my big break. Michael, I love you and miss you. I'm so torn. You know how much I've wanted this. I know it has to end. But two week's rest and the chance to see the French Riviera?" Kate felt woozie. "Another three weeks touring through Europe, and I'd be back. Then, we'll celebrate Hy Vọng, and go home to Bangkok." Her mind cleared, did Michael even have the option to extend his home leave? "If you can work that out with your boss."

"Dah-dee."

Hearing Hy Vọng's little sobbing voice was sobering. Kate put her hand to her chest and felt her high from the concert and the alcohol evaporate as she reconnected with her alter egos again—Michael's wife, Hy Vọng's mother. "Honey, never mind; I shouldn't have brought it up."

The battle between two weeks basking on a beach on the French Riviera with Adam and his band and rushing home to Michael to see her family again to introduce Hy Vọng surged. So much travel, but Kate imagined the warmth of holding Hy Vọng in her arms and having Michael's arms around her. She'd worked so hard to escape Glynn and now she was conflicted— Paris or Glynn? A laugh rose up. It was a choice she'd never imagined having to make.

CHAPTER 66

Michael

PEAS IN A POD

HE'D ALMOST TOLD Kate; nearly spilled out the truth about the job. How could he? She deserved to finish the tour carefree. Hadn't he been the one to encourage her to pursue her singing? He would damn well not be the one to tell her, no, you can't go, or give her any bad news. That wasn't the husband he wanted to be. And what resentment that could bring. Surprise, Kate, you have an unemployed husband, a new family, and our home in Bangkok just across town from your hotel is about to be packed-up.

He needed time to pull things together; he had an idea for himself, and meanwhile, he'd let Kate have her joy. It was only three weeks, well, five weeks. True, more than a month would be tough. "Babe, go for it; we'll be fine. I can get the time off; do some work arranging gigs from here."

"Oh Michael, I can't, truly. It feels wrong."

He closed his eyes and pulled Hy Vọng closer. He was grateful Kate couldn't hear his sigh. "I don't want us to be the reason you miss out on this big chance—all of it." How often would this situation arise in their lives, he thought. "Remember your mother's deep regret? Most importantly, we have each other, right? A long life ahead of us."

"You're right, Michael, we do, but the idea of going on tour doesn't feel right to me."

"I love you. It won't be long we'll be back together with Hy Vọng."

"And we'll have the Thai American Club shows, Michael."

He was silent.

"What's happening, Michael?

"Hy Vọng just squirmed down from my lap, and she's turning the light switch off and on."

Kate hesitated. "Michael, you know that high from performing when you know you've reached the audience. Remember, in the Student Union? You know how much I love that feeling, and I admit it's addictive. Thank you for understanding. You know that you and Hy Vọng are everything to me."

"Dah-dee."

"I admit I needed you to confirm that, to fill the crack in my confidence. I trust you, but I confess I'm afraid something will change."

Why was he insecure? Some guy calling her gorgeous? Or was he afraid of the allure of her break-out touring career?

Michael changed the subject. "It's been slow going, but she's saying a few words in English. She loves to kayak on the lake. Anything to keep moving; that makes her happy."

"Just like her new mother."

"Yes, you're peas in a pod, darling—unpredictable, adorable, and irresistible." Michael laughed. "So we'll see you when?"

Kate's moment of silence hid behind the echoing twang on

the line. "Michael, I'm going to skip the vacation break with the band. I need to see you. I'll be home the day after tomorrow. I'll have ten days at home, counting travel days. I have to book flights to Paris on October 21st. The tour starts on the 23rd in Paris and runs three-weeks. Last stop Dublin, Ireland, on November 13th. Plenty of time to get home for the holiday."

"Thanksgiving. Our holiday." Did Kate hear him let out a long breath? "That's great, sweetheart. Really great! And Ireland, that's exciting, back to your roots."

"I can't wait to tell my Mom about it. Wish she could have seen this tour."

After Michael hung up, the conversation whirred in his head. Joining his mother on the porch, he sat on the glider beside her with Hy Vọng between them. Silent lightning flashed on the other side of the lake.

His mother squeezed his hand. "You didn't tell her about losing the job, did you?"

He took a deep breath. "Nope."

"Or the trust fund?"

"Nope."

"Or being homeless?"

"How did you guess?" Michael pulled Hy Vọng closer and stroked her hair. "Didn't want to worry her; we'll talk in person."

Christine's eyes searched outside through the screen.

Was she judging him? Michael took her hand. "Mom?"

"You're a good man." His mother hesitated.

He knew she had something more to say. "But?"

"An infuriating man at times, but good."

Time passed quickly while his mother visited and they waited for Kate to arrive back in the States. With Hy Vọng napping, Michael could be alone for the first time in weeks. His daughter had become such a part of him. Strange to have both his arms and legs free to move about as he hiked the north path up along the lake shoreline. No dragging Hy Vọng along like a little Koala bear clutching his leg, no hoisting her like a prattling parrot perched onto his shoulders or trying to cook holding Hy Vọng and her scruffy Bunny in his arms. He laughed.

He enjoyed the thud of his walking stick on the dirt path navigating the familiar tree roots and rocks. His teen memory of stripping and whittling the sturdy tree branch into the gnarled hiking aid made him smile. He could identify every call and chitter of the birds overhead in the pines, lindens, and silver maples. His mother had taught him the name of each tree and bird sighting from an old dog-eared Audubon book and a volume of *Native New England Trees*. He decided to find those weathered volumes and teach the words to Hy Vọng. A kind of legacy.

How the hell had he become this father overnight; how had this all happened so fast? He needed time to think through what he wanted to do now. Father Sullivan's first words returned, "What do you love?"

Michael stood in the dappled sun at the highest point over-looking the lake, where the entire sparkling view stretched out in front of him. The air smelled so sweet and so clean it tickled his lungs as he inhaled deeply. There were two things allowed in the trust that he could get away with if he moved quickly, his mother had said. His grandmother couldn't reverse buying a house and giving a percentage of his trust to charity.

He had the perfect charity in mind.

His thoughts were interrupted by a car whooshing its way around the lower lake road below. He had no doubt it was Kate. Sharing the urgency of the speeding car, Michael broke into a run toward the cabin.

CHAPTER 67

Kate

CHANGING WINDS

WHIZZING DOWN THE twisted road past the familiar lush scenery in her rental car brought Kate back to their first summer week in the Berkshires. It was surreal to go from the lights of the stage to the sun slicing its way through the green canopy of trees. The screaming, applauding crowd was replaced by the sigh of the wind and the pine scent of the lake shore. Nothing else was in sight but an audience of squirrels that stopped and popped up on hind legs to watch her swish by and the occasional cast of hawks swooping down from the azure sky like a welcoming committee.

Passing an enormous split-trunk tree, Kate wrapped around it with a sharp left turn. She couldn't miss the symbolism—the dichotomy between the new life she was moving toward on the lush country road and her fantasy life singing on foreign stages.

The shift from the crowded, hectic city to the countryside was pleasant though. The lovely weather and cool mountain air that had replaced the wet blanket of humidity in Southeast

Asia should have made breathing easier. But Kate was driving to a cabin on a lake in the woods to become a first-time mother, to be in Michael's arms, to see her mother-in-law and her family's reactions to Hy Vọng, and to celebrate Kate and Michael's marriage. Crazy. So many thrills, and then she'd be gone again in ten days for Europe. Kate could barely breath.

Why was it nearly every international phone call either Michael or Kate had made to each other delivered news of some fork in their road, a calamity, a dramatic reveal? Kate longed for their peaceful days at home in Bangkok.

During the twenty-four hours in transit to Boston from Bangkok after Kate's tour had ended, she'd run a continuous loop of their relationship in her mind. Her life in Glynn, before Michael, had been so routine and predictable, but hadn't she prayed every night since her childhood for unbridled adventure? They say be careful what you wish for. Could Michael be any more adventuresome? Could he be any more complicated, frustrating, wounded? Could he be any more loving and loyal, tender and goddamn gorgeous?

God, she missed him. Kate never thought she would find a man who shared her passion for music, let alone supported it. Or one who would make her want to get married. Michael caused such a fork in *her* road.

Now, *she'd* been the one to cause the fork in their road together. But as she approached Michael's lake home, she knew she'd made the right decision to spend her tour break at home. How could she have thought otherwise? Wanderlust, that disease of desire, can affect the eyes, she thought, blinding you to what you need. The dark swamp of sadness for not being there for Michael and Hy Vọng, that had lurked beneath her joy, had dissipated with her decision to go back to the US before the next tour. Michael and Hy Vọng needed her; she needed them. It would be an exhausting turnaround, but these few days at home was better than nothing.

Kate sped around the curve on the lower lake road in her rental car. The reality surrounding Hy Vọng was beginning to sink in as she replayed the child's scream. What if she wasn't adjusting? What if it was a nightmare getting her to acclimate to their lives?

Kate had seen it all at Rolling Hills—damaged or fragile children, their struggles, their strangeness—a world of challenges. But hadn't she been able to break into Mary's world? Hadn't Kate seen a small crack in Hy Vọng's wall in Bangkok when she'd rocked her with her doll and Bunny in the white chair?

Pushing the fear away, Kate imagined Hy Vọng snuggling up to her, calling her Mah-mee—the daughter of her own that was never supposed to be.

❖·❖·❖

Kate came to a halt in the driveway. Parking her Toyota rental next to the stately black Mercedes, she got out and straightened her jade Thai silk blouse, pulling the fine fabric from her moist back.

As the emotion she'd been holding back rushed to her eyes, she started to run along the side of the house to the lakefront entrance. "Michael!"

His voice echoed from above her. "Babe! Up here."

Kate looked over her shoulder, scanned the hillside, and followed the rustling sound in the bushes. She caught a glimpse of Michael lunging through the underbrush toward her, sliding down the hillside, dodging trees as if he were glade skiing.

"Be careful; you're crazy!" She rushed toward the edge of the slope laughing and waited for him to emerge.

Michael lost his footing and took the last ten yards on his tail. He landed in front of Kate, sprung up, wrapped his arms around her, and lifted her off the ground. "I *am* crazy. Crazy without you."

And then there was his kiss and the signature gesture tucking her hair behind her ear.

"He makes a classic hero's entry, and she's swept off her feet," Kate announced, pulling away to look in his eyes. "Is it you?" How did she ever feel right without him? Could a heart thunder this loud without exploding? And why did love feel like an ache, like pain? Her tears broke through as she clung to Michael again.

He kissed that tender spot in the crook of her neck. "We need somewhere private."

"Oh, Honey, have you already forgotten everything? I'm a woman; you know we need to talk first."

"Do you not get it? That graceful entry was foreplay."

His laugh was the reward she wanted, and to wrap herself in the rhythm of their corny banter she'd missed. "Where's Hy Vọng? Your mother?"

"Inside, napping. I went for a hike to pass the time. Needed to think."

"Don't go ruining everything by thinking. Just stand here, hold me, and breathe with me."

They didn't move for minutes until the sun ducked behind the hill, leaving them in shadow as if a spotlight had gone out.

"We have a little time before Hy Vọng wakes up. Let's sit out on the dock and get that talk in."

The stories flowed. His and hers. Hy Vọng—the challenges, the joys, her flashbacks, and her progress; Kate—the foreign capitals, the concert tour, the thrill at her first taste of fame.

"I'm so excited for you. I'm picturing us on the hillside at UConn, you practicing to sight read. Wow. Babe, you've got liftoff!"

She touched Michael's face. "So now tell me what you haven't told me. You know what I mean, the truth I've always had to excavate out of you when we've been apart." She shifted on the bench and looked into his eyes. "Whatever caused the hesitation in your voice on our last few phone calls. I know you, Michael James."

"This is big, Kate." He took her hand and squeezed.

"Oh, God, Michael. Just tell me. Whatever it is, we'll handle it." Her stomach had come to associate Michael's confessions and revelations with nausea and a tightening. But couldn't it be something good? Everything lately had been marvelous—finding Hy Vọng, Kate's concerts.

"I got a telegram from the embassy, and…" Michael took the wrinkled paper from his jeans pocket and unfolded it.

"A telegram?" In her current world of wild, impossible dreams coming true, she couldn't let herself believe the news could be anything but wonderful.

"Well, and a phone call from Harrington."

A promotion, maybe. He'd done so well. Kate prepared herself for another adventure.

"It's been burning in my pocket since yesterday."

"Honey, you're making me nervous. Are you being

promoted? Wait, we're not being *transferred* are we?" She couldn't leave Bangkok so soon. But she knew assignments were at the whim of the State Department.

He flattened the paper out on his leg and swept it with his hand several times as if the news could be wiped away. "No, I... lost my job."

The sound of their world starting to crumble was almost audible to Kate. "*Lost?* Why?"

"Well, fired, really. Babe, I misappropriated government property and forged documents and well, basically kidnapped my own kid. If it wasn't for Harrington, I could have ended up in jail. I really let him down...but what choice did I have? Thank God, he's got my back."

OK, OK, let's be calm, she told herself. Kate made a mental list. The promise of the Thai American Club, gone; the charm of Bangkok, the friends they would never know, their first home, and their future life together there, gone. The birds were back in the cage. Life had been a ticker-tape parade since she'd arrived in Bangkok. Now she'd be sweeping up the confetti on the morning after.

"So..." Kate let the loss sink in. She asked herself the questions she'd designed to survive the tough times, the past times whenever things had gone wrong. *What could be good about this? What good can I make of this?*

Sometimes, like now, it was hard, really hard to see the good in the bad. Find the good; there must be something, Kate told herself. Nothing came, until it did. "So I assume this was punishment for using embassy resources to rescue Hy Vọng?"

"Yes. I'm sorry—the forged paperwork and Jeremy and the

plane. It was the only way. Harrington saved Jeremy and the Visa officer's skins too."

"Then, a small price to pay, right? A replaceable job for your child's *life*?

Michael tilted his head and squinted his eyes at Kate. "I love how you do that." He kissed her hand. "Just when I think you'll be upset or furious, you get that quiet thing going, and then you're so damn logical."

Kate's fears around money flooded back. She stopped them. "Wait, we have no worries about money. We're fortunate for that. You have your savings, your trust. Remember, I'm being paid for these tours. We'll figure it out." That was a first, she was the breadwinner.

He held her, and they watched a pair of ducks drag their legs across the surface of the lake and take off. "Just like old times, back at UConn."

There was silence until the ducks were out of sight. "Wait till you see Hy Vọng again, Kate. She's ours now."

Michael's mother put her finger to her lips to prevent them from waking Hy Vọng. The cottage family room filled with hugs and whispers as the two women reunited.

"I don't know how I can wait." Kate crossed her hands on her chest.

"It's time for her to get up anyway."

"Michael, no, don't wake her; let her come to me, like before."

"She's much better now, you'll see." Michael cracked the door and peeked into the bedroom.

Kate longed for that feeling when her new sleepy daughter would curl into her lap. She wanted to repeat that tender, heart-clutching emotion she'd felt when Hy Vọng had snuggled close to Kate that first night together—singing to her in the rocking chair in their bedroom in Bangkok with the pink Bunny tucked under Hy Vọng's chin.

She could almost taste the irony. Kate had spent her entire time in Glynn trying to avoid becoming a mother. How often had she denied herself, prayed for it not to happen? Now she ached for this little girl to come close. It was so unanticipated to have her alive and with them. Imagining the village collapsing around the child, Kate wanted to put her arms around Hy Vọng and never let go.

From the glider across the room, Kate could see into the bedroom where their daughter was asleep on her pink quilt on the floor.

"Hy Vọng, sweetie?" Michael crooned. She didn't stir.

"Honey, it's OK, leave her be. I'm so excited, but she might wake up cranky."

Don't expect some romance at first sight, Kate told herself. Mother was a word her child would grow into at her own pace. Kate couldn't wait for her bright blue eyes to open.

Hy Vọng's body twitched. She stretched and rubbed her eyes. That beguiling twin reflection of Michael and his mother came out of the bedroom.

"Sweetheart?" Kate used her softest voice and held out her arms. She'd expected some reticence, but Kate hadn't thought the child would push her away. It was nothing like that first day together.

"Oh, honey, it's OK; it's Mommy." The word came clumsily

from Kate's mouth. The room went dark as the afternoon sunlight was swallowed by a cloud.

"*Không, không*!" Hy Vọng held her head and shook it.

"What is she saying, Michael?"

"She's saying...no, no. Just waking from a dream."

"Dah-dee, Dah-dee," she wailed. Hy Vọng ran across the room and climbed up Michael's leg.

Kate watched Michael soothe Hy Vọng. Wrapping his arms around his child, he held her tight, rocked her, and started a kind of humming chant. Hy Vọng whimpered until she was caught up in the rhythm of Michael's sounds, and the hum began to soothe her. Her sobs subsided into little wounded chirps and sniffles.

Covering her face with her hands, Kate could picture Michael during the UConn campus protest. That first experience with his torture had been terrifying. A chill spasmed down Kate's arms.

What trauma had her new daughter endured? How would it manifest? Be patient, she told herself. Isn't that what she'd learned in Rolling Hills. Why was it so different when it was your own child?

She could feel her mother-in-law's eyes riveted on her with sympathy. Christine moved to sit on the striped glider next to her, put her arm around Kate, and pulled her close. "Honey, I'm so sorry. She'll be OK. It happened when I got here too."

"She let me rock her that first night, I just thought..." Kate fidgeted with her ring, then let down her guard and leaned into her mother-in-law for comfort.

Michael sat in a chair next to Kate, holding Hy Vọng. "Sometimes this happens when she's startled or with someone new. And she just woke up. She'll come around." Reaching out, he covered Kate's hand. "Sorry."

Kate had so wanted to put her arms around her new daughter, to feel the soft skin of her sweet face.

Hy Vọng turned and pointed at Kate and muttered something in Vietnamese.

Michael answered, "That's Mommy."

Her husband and his child shared the bond from the wounds of the same torturous past and their own language, Kate thought. And now the arms that had comforted Kate were engaged.

CHAPTER 68

BLESSED BEGINNINGS

MICHAEL PULLED UP to the curb and turned to look at Hy Vọng in the back seat with Kate. "Come on, honey, we're going to meet your grandparents and cousins and aunts and uncles."

Kate was glad she'd sat with Hy Vọng. It had given her a chance to connect. She regretted that there had been so little physical contact between them since she'd arrived yesterday. The child was still shy about her new mother. Still, there had been no screaming and anxiety attacks like the ones that had marked her child's past either.

"You're such a lucky girl, Hy Vọng Ketchum-James." Michael hoisted her from the back seat of the car.

"Bunny." Hy Vọng pointed back to the car.

"I'll get it for you." Kate rescued the raggedy rabbit, kissed it, and handed it to Hy Vọng. She clutched her toy, flashed a quick smile, and tucked her head into Michael's chest. Hy Vọng had even smiled when Kate had given her the tattered toy before bed as well.

"I know it's hard for you, Kate, but we'll get there; she just needs time."

"Except, I don't have much of that right now."

Michael put his arm around Kate. "You're so patient. She'll come around. Who can resist you?"

"I guess, we'll have lots of time when we get home…I mean, wherever. Michael, at some point we need to talk."

"Kate, I know you're a decider, a doer; me, I'm more of a contemplator, a procrastinator. We'll talk, I promise, and we'll decide together after your tour. Right now, welcome home, Katie-girl. Here comes the bride and her instant child." He laughed.

"Say a prayer she'll be OK meeting our big, crazy family."

They climbed the familiar steps to the Ketchum's row house, as Michael's mother pulled up behind their car and caught up to them at the steps.

"Perfect timing. Christine, come meet your in-laws and out-laws." Kate laughed and put her arm around her mother-in-law.

"So everyone was fine with your secret wedding in Bangkok, right?"

"Yes, along with all my other confessions. Wedding by telegram, Hy Vọng, and our arrival all shared by phone last night."

"Oh boy, you two. I'm looking forward to seeing your parents again. It's been so long."

The same red door, the gray painted porch, those wide-eyed windows that revealed all, welcomed them.

Michael paused at the door. "Look at us." The sun reflecting in the glass panes mirrored—a family. "Kate, how did we get here?"

Kate put her hand to his face. "Didn't it start with me saying something about you not being the man I thought you were?"

"How about now, Mrs. Katherine Ketchum-James?" Michael shifted Hy Vọng to his other hip and kissed her head.

"Now? Honey, you are that man."

"OK, you two love birds, let's meet the family." Christine stroked Hy Vọng's hair.

"Hy Vọng, get ready, here comes some big, loud, love." Michael turned the doorknob.

A gush of emotion rushed through Kate; she was home; ironic the place she fought so hard to escape would always be *home*, and Kate wanted Hy Vọng to feel the safety of their buzzing hive.

The roar of greetings made everyone tearful, and the wave of love nearly knocked them over when they entered the parlor.

"Congratulations! Welcome to your wedding and baby shower." Kendra and Karen hugged Kate.

"Did we miss anything else? It's not your birthday is it?" Kate's sister Kelly's sarcasm was light. The kind of teasing that made Kate laugh. "Damn, now I have to give your Town car back."

"Kate, we missed you. It's not the same here..."

"It seems like forever." Her twin cousins hugged her.

"Everyone meet my wonderful mother-in-law, Christine, and Hy Vọng, our new daughter." Kate called out to the room full of family.

Kevin, Karl, and Keith, and her father did their guy thing, patting Michael on his back. "Man, how the hell did you get her out of Nam?" "We need to hear it." "Good job, brother." Like a receiving line, the family waited for their turns to hug

Kate, pat Michael on the back, greet Christine, coo over the baby, and ask the million unanswered questions.

So much Kate had missed—her mother's face, her dad's bear hugs, her sisters' warmth, her best-friend cousins' closeness, her brothers' antics.

Kate wished Shiloh hadn't been traveling; it was disappointing that she hadn't been able to come. Their connection was infrequent now as their lives had become more complex, but when they spoke on their weekly phone calls, it was as though they'd never parted. They'd seen each other through so much.

Children were gathered in the dining room, as always, playing chutes and ladders. Her mom and aunts' cooking sent alluring aromas of roasted chicken and potatoes and blueberry pie into the parlor. A Carvel ice cream cake sat on the table with handwritten words, *Welcome Home, Mr. and Mrs. K-J and Baby Girl.* Kate smiled, imagining the decision to write *Baby Girl,* not sure of the spelling of Hy Vọng. Time had such strange effects, she thought; even Grandma Kendall was smiling. Did she really say *Oh bless her, she's so adorable and those blue eyes?* Kate's Aunt Maggie placed a plate of carrot and celery sticks with a small plastic bowl of ranch dressing onto the coffee table.

"*Katie-girl.*" Cecelia came out of the kitchen, wiping her hands on her apron. She wrapped her arms around Kate and sighed. "This is what I've been waiting for. How are you, darling girl?" They broke into a song, "I'll take you home again, Kathleen." In perfect harmony. Then her mom broke into tears.

"Oh, Mom, I've missed you." Kate pecked her mother's

cheek a dozen times and broke out laughing. "I'm so happy, Mom. Come meet Hy Vọng."

"Please let her stay calm," Kate whispered to Michael as they introduced Hy Vọng to Cecelia.

Any three-year-old would be startled by the din of conversation and the boisterous crowd, but the dozens of colorful balloons above her were keeping their child engaged. So far, so good, Kate thought.

"Mom, she can be a little wary of new people."

Hy Vọng tucked her head into Michael's chest, then looked up again, stretching her arm toward the dangling ribbons.

"You want some balloons, pretty girl? Michael, her eyes; they're absolutely startling, and those highlights in her hair, she's you. I just want to squeeze her; she's so sweet." Kate's mother gathered a few balloons and tied them to Hy Vọng's wrist. "Look up, honey, see how pretty?"

Cecelia jiggled the ribbons, making the balloons twist and wriggle above them. That brought a squeal of delight and a smile.

Michael spoke to Hy Vọng, trying to elicit a thank you from her. Hy Vọng's foreign words were lost in the conversations around them.

"We have a surprise guest." Kate's mother opened the kitchen door and invited Shiloh into the parlor.

"Oh my God, Shi, I thought you were traveling and couldn't make it." Kate hugged her friend and fought back her tears.

"I cancelled my plans and decided to surprise you. And your baby is so adorable. Look at your husband holding that cutie pie." Shiloh leaned in close to whisper. "Look at you, snagging a man who's handsome *and* a *feminist* to boot. I can't believe it. My best comrade, Kate, with a child, and without gaining a pound."

"And no contractions either." Kate laughed. The sound of Shiloh's jingle-jangle from her silver hoops and bangles made Kate sentimental. "This was the one time I couldn't hear you coming. We have so much to talk about, Shi."

"Yes, and long overdue." Shiloh nodded toward Michael and Hy Vọng and smiled. "I told you it was more than singing. *Way* more. I can't leave you alone for a minute, Kate; you broke all your commitments. Weren't you the *I'm never getting married or having children* friend?" Shiloh hooked her arm through Kate's and squeezed, as Michael approached with Hy Vọng. "And Michael, look at you, Daddy of the Year." Shiloh kissed his cheek.

Hy Vọng pointed at Shiloh's silver, musical bracelets. "You want these honey?" She slid two of them onto Hy Vọng's arm. "Look who else is here." Shiloh turned Kate and Michael around. "You're already married, but it wouldn't hurt to get a blessing from the one who introduced you."

Father Sullivan shook Michael's and Kate's hands. "Who would have guessed the trouble I started." He shook Hy Vọng's hand; the balloons danced above her.

Everyone took a seat on the sofa, a folding chair, or on the floor. Kate's father led Michael to his Barcalounger, that sacred throne her dad inhabited most hours when he was home.

"Kate, we want to hear all about your tour but first, son, tell us how you came to get this little darling back?"

Hy Vọng squirmed down off Michael's lap and silently hid between his legs at the base of the chair.

Michael recounted the dramatic landing at the airstrip, the

threatening airport entry, and Hy Vọng's adjustment at the lake house, her love of the soothing kayak rides.

The food, a brief ceremony, a party, and the stories went on into the late afternoon.

As the celebration was ending, Michael appeared nervous. He hesitated and cleared his throat. Hoisting Hy Vọng into his arms, he took Kate by the hand, and moved next to his mother. "Can I just say something everyone?"

Kate looked at Michael with no clue as to what was to come.

"This...all of you... *this* is the family I've always wanted."

A visible wave of emotion passed over the gathering. Even Big Kevin and Grandpa had to brush away a tear.

"Son, that's not fair to do to a never-let-them-see-you-weep Irish family, you know." Kate's father started a round of contagious laughter that ended with Hy Vọng's giggles.

CHAPTER 69

UNWELCOME NEWS

WHEN THE FESTIVITIES were over, and everyone had left, Michael and Kate took their sleepy child to Kate's bedroom to put her to bed. Kate tucked Hy Vọng into one of her brother's sleeping bags next to her on the floor. "You sure she'll be OK here for a while?"

"She's fine, just exhausted." Michael turned out the light. "My mother went to the factory with your parents. A little private shoe shopping. It's still early, let's go visit with Shiloh downstairs; she's come so far."

Shiloh shared her stories of law school and her latest activism.

The wall phone rang. Kate, answered. "Brent?" Stretching the cord, she tucked away into the pantry for privacy and listened to his nervous voice.

"Kate? I can't believe you're in the States. I was calling your mother, hoping to get a message to you. I didn't expect... I thought you were in Thailand."

"I'm home to celebrate...it's a long story." Kate quickly

explained her marriage to Michael and told Brent the news about Hy Vọng's rescue.

"Wow. Lots going on in your life. Congratulations. Listen. I really hesitated to call you, Kate, even more so now that I hear why you're home."

"It's no bother, Brent, but what's going on?"

"Given your special relationship with Mary. You're the only one she's talked to so far. Well, you and Ernie."

"Mary and Ernie? I'm confused, what is it?" The last time she'd seen Brent had been so hard for Kate, at the end of her internship, the disappointment over Mary, explaining to Dr. Goodman why she was leaving for Bangkok and quitting grad school. Hearing his voice opened a wound.

"Look, I know things didn't work out and you were only an intern for eight weeks, but you had such success with Mary. I wonder if you…"

The pause made Kate impatient.

"I'm headed to see Ernie in Windham Hospital."

"*Hospital*, what happened?"

"It's Mary…and Ernie." Brent shared the story of Mary's near-rape by Ronnie, and Ernie's heroism that had put him in the hospital. "Mary rocks herself all day. Ernie has been asking for you. I don't think he can imagine how far away Bangkok is."

"Oh, Brent. Will Ernie be OK?"

"He'll be OK but he has some healing to do. Took quite a tumble down the stairs."

"When was this, Brent?"

"It happened two days ago."

"How can I help? Maybe Mary will talk to me."

"Well, yes, and Ernie's been asking for you at the hospital—pleading actually. I thought. I don't know what I thought. I knew you couldn't just up and come back, but maybe just talk to Ernie on the phone. Since you're here on home leave, would you consider paying a little visit? If you have time?"

"No, no, you were right to tell me. I know you didn't expect me to come half-way around the world. But I'm just a drive away. I...just need to talk to Michael first. You're sure they're both OK?" Kate twisted the cord around her finger.

"Well, there's damage, for sure. But they'll heal. Well, Ernie will."

Kate sighed and closed her eyes. Michael will understand.

"Let me call you back. Five minutes, OK?" Kate held the receiver to her chest and took a deep breath.

Michael opened the pantry door. "Kate, what's going on?"

Kate hung up the phone. A numbness descended on her. She found herself in Michael's arms, then pulled herself together and prepared to share the news that had set fire to her stomach. "Michael...Shi," She took a deep breath.

"Honey, what?" He had that furrowed-brow she'd seen on his face when anything went wrong concerning her. So loving and protective.

"That was Brent." Kate looked in his eyes.

"Oh, I know this look." Michael guided Kate into the chair. "What's going on?"

"I need to go to Rolling Hills tomorrow."

"Oh my God, what happened?" Shiloh pulled out the chair next to her. "Kate sit down and tell us."

Michael sat and took his *I'm listening* pose—legs crossed, leaning slightly forward, hands folded in his lap.

Kate relayed the story from Brent. "Mary's gone silent, hasn't talked since, rocks herself all day. Michael, I may be the only one she'll talk to. And Ernie. I just can't bear to think of that sweet guy...he's been asking for me. I'm so surprised by that. When I left, he was so non-chalant." Kate told them about Ronnie, the uneasiness she felt around him. "I should've known; Ronnie always made me uncomfortable the way he looked at Mary...and me. I didn't know what I was doing. They were all so...different. So little control over themselves. I wasn't sure what was out of bounds there—what I should have reported?"

"Damn." Michael put his palm to his head. "But you can't hold yourself responsible."

Kate wasn't sure if Michael's response was sympathy for the kids or disappointment over her leaving or both.

"I'm so sorry, Kate. For all of it. But aren't you taking on a little bit too much. I mean..." Michael went silent and gazed at her, then looked out through the open kitchen door. "I have a physical tomorrow morning for Hy Vọng your mother arranged with your family doctor. I really want her checked out. But I should go with you to see them, for support."

"Michael, why don't I go with Kate. We need some girl time anyway. It's only an hour away; we'll be back by lunch."

"Thanks, Shiloh. OK, well, you drive down tomorrow, make the visit with Shiloh, and I'll get Hy Vọng's check-up and let her settle in here a bit."

"That works. We still have days together. Let me call Brent back."

CHAPTER 70

LOST INNOCENCE

KATE NEARLY BUMPED into Brent as she entered the main building. "How are they? Sorry, Brent, you know my friend, Shiloh."

"Good to see you, Brent. And I'm so sorry about Mary and Ernie."

"Brent, Shiloh's going to do some candle shopping and take a tour around Rolling Hills while we're at the hospital."

"That's fine. I'd give you a ride, Kate, but I need to run some quick errands afterward."

"No problem. I'll meet you at the hospital, then afterward I'll come back to see Mary."

Brent held the door for Kate. "My wife's art is on display in the cafeteria, Shiloh, if you're interested."

"Sounds good."

"Shi, I'll meet you back here in what, in one, two hours?"

"That works." Shiloh headed down the hallway.

"Oh, sweet Ernie..." Kate thought about Ronnie, the uneasiness she'd felt around him. Her student always made her uncomfortable, the way he looked at Mary...and Kate. She hated his habit of rubbing his crotch. Kate realized long ago that she hadn't known what she was doing in that internship. Should she have reported him for his nervous, compulsive habit? It had never gone beyond that. Kate's stomach twisted at the thought of the incident.

Brent went silent and gazed at her, then looked out through the open door. "See you there." He revved up his VW bus and hastily exited the parking lot.

Windham Hospital wasn't far, but it felt like an eternity getting there. Kate turned into the parking lot, and a dusting of snow fell onto the car. Late fall was early for flurries, but New England was funny that way, unpredictable.

With the car in park, Kate thought about that constant line she found she'd had to navigate lately. She didn't want to be so grown-up just yet, making these kinds of choices. What do we owe ourselves, and what do we owe others? She was giving up her precious time with Michael, Hy Vọng, and her family. After all, Kate had only been a summer intern, and she'd left because she just wasn't cut out for all of the heaviness and complications.

Why was she getting involved again?

A slight feeling of resentment leaked into her compassion. Kate was beginning to understand what being an adult meant. Love meant you got tangled in people's lives for better or for worse. This felt like the 'worse' part. But wasn't Mary dealing with understanding the adult world in an even more profound way?

Exhausted and nervous, Kate's defenses were down. She wanted to talk to Brent before she visited Ernie. Caustic antiseptic scents coupled with the floral aromas escaped from the hospital gift shop. A bait and switch. Scents. Michael had made her so aware of them. Who wouldn't fall deeply in love with mornings lingering in bed with caramel-thick roasted coffee, the aroma of fragrant jasmine hanging from the bedposts, and Michael's muscled arm marked with an angel tattoo, draped around your naked shoulder? Every part of her wanted to turn around, go home to Michael, and return to Bangkok. But there was no longer a home in Bangkok.

While waiting in the busy lobby as agreed, Kate weighed her decision. Should she mention Ronnie's behavior, or was it just too late for that information to be helpful?

Brent approached. "Thanks for coming. Ernie keeps asking about you. I didn't tell him you were here."

Kate thought of Brent's kindness in caring for the kids, his brilliance at starting the candle factory, and the orchestra. So dedicated. And yet, he'd fallen short when it came to Mary, Kate thought. Today, he looked so haggard.

"Ernie will be so happy you came. Mary will be too..."

The tangles had begun. She wanted to turn and run, but Ernie's whispered advice in Kate's ear that first day of teaching made her soften. It was the least she could do.

"I'm glad you told me. Like you said, I'm the only one Mary's ever talked to. And she's, well, complicated. And God, I'm happy to be able to see Ernie."

"Let's have a cup of coffee first. I'd like to chat about Ernie."

"Sure. Should I be concerned?"

"No, no, just want you to be prepared." Brent opened the

door to the hospital coffee shop. They sat by the window with the steam rising from their cups and ghostly, white fog swirling outside.

Kate gazed through the frosted glass, then turned her attention to Brent. "First, how's Ernie? You said he's better?"

"Better yes, but you need to prepare yourself. Bruised all over, purple eye, teeth shattered, sprained muscles in his leg. Most of that from Ronnie flinging him down the stone steps after Ernie jumped on Ronnie's back like a miniature Sumo wrestler."

"God, what an image. It hasn't left my mind. What courage."

"Everything's healing. Except."

"Except what?" Kate leaned forward.

"How can I put this? It knocked the innocence out of him. You know how he was. Ernie knew people could be cruel about his stature and disabilities, but he was always our joy factory. This was his first-time experiencing personal violence." Brent took a breath. "Ernie threw himself right in the fray when he saw Ronnie on top of Mary with his pants down. He stopped Ronnie from smacking the poor girl when she tried to fight him off."

"Oh, my God." Kate put her hands over her eyes as though she could somehow prevent herself from imagining the scene. Her entire experience at Rolling Hills felt like a book she'd read with a bad ending she wished she could re-write.

Kate remembered the first time she'd seen Ernie's short arms reach up out of the orchestra to play his cymbals part, the triple-smash that had charmed her. She wanted to bring him back to those sweet early days when he'd appeared in the desk drawer on her first day of her internship; the months when he was her upbeat advocate guiding her through each day, giving her his special insights into the new and challenging world of Rolling Hills. She smiled at the memory of her informant—telling her the inside stories of her troubled students—who was disabled, who wasn't. And Ernie was the only one who'd seen the truth about Mary. A kind of raw, instinctual wisdom no one else around Mary had, not the teachers, no one. And now he lay in the hospital—bruised and battered, crushed in every way.

"OK." Kate took in a deep breath and let it out. "So," Kate's eyes were focused on her empty cup, "Look, I admit I was pretty naïve about Rolling Hills, well, everything when I worked for you." She looked up.

Brent was still; he locked onto her eyes. Straightening his back, the sound of his chair scraped back drawing the attention of the woman at the next table.

Kate lowered her voice. "What is it, Brent?"

Brent leaned in closer and cleared his throat. "I understand how you felt when you left. A place like Rolling Hills is tough. Not enough facilities, not enough staff. So many dark things happen, even when we do our best. You did so much for our kids in your short time with us. Your efforts with Mary. And you were only one young intern. I put you in a tough situation with no training, so let's blame me. And I'm sorry the experience made you change your mind about your career."

His viewpoint took her by surprise. "I thought I...thank you for that, Brent. I learned a lot. I guess I was always meant to sing. I'm performing now in Bangkok."

"Fantastic. Let's see what we can do now. Let's go visit a certain young man and bring back his faith in people."

"How?"

"There's a young woman who came around the planet to be with him when he needed her. That's pretty convincing that there's still good in the world. Right?"

CHAPTER 71

FAIRY GODFATHER

THEY SIGNED-IN and walked the long hallway to Ernie's room. The wide door was propped open. The sight made Kate's every muscle tense. She cleared her throat. "Ernie?"

Ernie turned his head toward her. His face lit up with eyes wide and an open-mouthed smile. "Miss Ketchup? Miss Ketchup! How did you get here?" Ernie's leg was wrapped in bandages, his eye puffed and purple, bruises on his swollen head, his two front teeth chipped in an angle.

An ache gripped Kate's chest. She dropped her pocketbook, put her arms out, and pretended to fly like an airplane in circles toward him. "I flew thirty-six hours, half-way around the entire Earth, to see my hero." She reached the side of his bed, afraid to hug his damaged body. It was a white lie worth telling.

He exploded with tears and released a low-pitched howl like a wounded animal. The sound suspended in the drab room for an unbearable length of time.

Brent stopped the nurse at the door, signaling Ernie was OK.

Ernie wiped his face on his gown and let out another muffled wail into the white cotton sheet. Kate slid a chair close to the bed.

His howl resumed, then he sniffed-in his final tears. "You love me, Miss Ketchup, huh?"

Kate was stunned by his pure innocence, his new seriousness. "Of course, I... do." The feeling was there but the words, I love you, that were rarely uttered in her family failed her. "Ernie, you're my fairy godfather, remember?"

"I'm not your fairy godfather anymore. I tried. I couldn't." Ernie dropped his head. "Mr. Brent, Miss Ketchup didn't come around the whole world. She only came halfway," he said into his chest between sobs. "You showed me the globe, remember?"

Kate smiled to see a spark of the old Ernie. She held his hand to her cheek, the only part of him that seemed to be left undamaged.

"I tried to stop him. Miss K. He was—"

"I know. It's over now. You did stop him, buddy; you did." She kissed his hand.

Kate arrived at Rolling hills, and went to find Shiloh. They met by the door and followed the fluorescent-lit hallway. It was empty, in-between classes. The sound of their voices echoed in down the long hallway, as Kate relayed the story to Shiloh. The warmth of her friend's arm on her shoulder as they walked brought Kate back to the Music Department and her failed audition. It was a tender memory when her new college friend had met Kate at the top of the stairs to comfort her. "Thanks for coming, Shi."

"Of course."

Shiloh's hug was much needed, as the familiar scent of sanitizer, layered with the aromas of the candle shop, made her realize Kate was really there in that dreary place again. Kate tapped her thigh, and tried to find the right song. None came.

"What can I do to help Mary?"

"You'll find a way to break through again. I know you will."

Kate wasn't a psychiatrist and knew nothing of counseling damaged girls. She'd stumbled onto her success the first time, and it had never been repeated, she thought. The institution's committee had refused to believe that Mary was functional. If Brent hadn't seen the proof, the typed pages, he wouldn't have believed her either.

"Even if I get Mary to talk, then what?"

"Talking might be the only path to healing from her past. If she would ever talk to a professional." Shiloh touched Kate's shoulder. "This is beyond me. And you. I'll wait in the gift shop for you, OK? You need to be alone with Mary."

"Thanks, Shi. I'll walk with you; I want to say hi to Jimmy. I'm meeting Mary in the music room in five minutes." Shivers vibrated down Kate's arms as she entered the candle shop with Shiloh where it all had started. "Isn't life crazy, Shi—from a candle to a failed career and back to singing?

"Crazy good, Kate."

Jimmy stood behind the cashier's desk just as he had been on that fall day two years before. He caught sight of Kate, dropped his head, and rocked left and right, laughing. "Miss Ketchup!" Jimmy said into his chest, repeating his pogo-stick jump.

His movements brought it all back—Jimmy, the orchestra,

Dr. Goodman, Kate's internship, a storm of memories ending with the unimaginable—withdrawal from grad school and her whirlwind marriage to Michael. Now she was a mother and a rising music star. Surreal.

Taking a deep breath, Kate tried to purge the sadness. She couldn't break through it, as she had before. She couldn't focus on any shred of good they had in their lives—a safe place to live, food, fun playing sports, the orchestra, playing in piles of colorful, fall leaves. It was nowhere near enough for a child. Her context had changed, now that she had everything, now that her life had moved forward at hyper-speed and expanded. Now that she was a mother, she could only see hopelessness in the place.

Hy Vọng's face after her rescue from the destroyed orphanage was fresh in Kate's mind too. She knew Rolling Hills was not the same situation, but she ached for these kids who had no family.

Jimmy turned his head toward the wall and stuck his hand out toward Kate. "I didn't know you were real—two bayberry towers, six vanilla votives. Tell Mr. Brent I shook your hand, OK?"

"This is my friend, Shiloh, remember her?" Kate so wanted to hug Jimmy, but she knew that would distress him.

Jimmy rolled his head around and brought his chin to his chest. "OK, OK, I'm looking up now." His head angled up. He engaged her eyes for a brief moment. "Hi."

"I'm so proud of you." Kate opened the bag of gifts she had brought from Bangkok and took out a white T-shirt with her K-J Riverrun band logo on it. "For you, Jimmy." She held it up to her chest.

"That's you, Miss Ketchup with a microphone. Your mouth is open. Was a song coming out when they made this picture?"

"Yes, Jimmy I'm a singer now. I sing for lots of people."

"You like it. I see in your face. I like playing my saxophone."

"I'll never forget that Jimmy, believe me."

"Remember, you sang that night after the concert when I played, and I was so good."

"I was so proud of you. Where is Mr. Brent?"

"He'll be back in three minutes and five seconds."

"Jimmy, I'm going to see Mary in the music room. Take care of my friend, and tell Mr. Brent, OK?"

"OK. In two minutes forty-seven seconds. But if Mr. Brent is late that time might not be exactly right, OK?"

"Don't worry; whenever he walks through the door is fine."

CHAPTER 72

PROMISE AND PASSION

WHEN KATE ENTERED the Rolling Hills music room, the memories surrounded her. The piano Michael had played to accompany the impromptu jam session after the concert was in the center of the room. Ernie's tarnished cymbals lay on the piano bench. She closed her eyes, trying to forget his battered condition. Kate had arranged to meet Mary here so that they could be alone. There would be no practice today, on a Sunday.

Kate sat on the bottom bleacher and waited, wishing she were back in Bangkok. She and Michael would be practicing right now for a weekly performance at the Thai American Club. They would be harmonizing, that intimate time that made them feel so connected.

Music was their oasis, she thought, the place that suspended them from all their cares and their pasts. But that was over. She'd been free of Rolling Hills. Why had she come back? This was not the quick, happy visit she'd expected to have with her two former students.

Mary walked in with her head down, escorted by a counselor. The teen's body seemed to have matured in the brief time Kate had been in Bangkok. She had the figure of a young woman, yet she still wore one of the three homemade dresses she'd rotated each day when Kate had taught her. Now the dress stretched across her chest with the buttons nearly ready to pop. Kate remembered how her brothers had teased her the summer she'd blossomed, seemingly overnight.

"Mary?" She reached out to touch Mary's shoulder, but she curled it away from Kate. The gap opened between them—that same distance that had taken Kate months to close. Mary crossed her arms. Silence. Kate crossed the room, turned on the sound system and mic, and started to sing. "You are my lucky star."

Picking at the white flowers on her powder blue cotton dress, Mary didn't budge.

"I brought you something." The T-shirt brought no reaction. "Mary?" Her eyes were dull; the only light was a flash of sun flickering through the blinds. She squatted and curled up in front of the bench. Folding her hands together like a fragile bird, Mary tucked them tight into her lap—a protective position that conveyed her vulnerability. Kate could hear Mary's words spoken when they'd last been together, *You wudna left me.*

"Remember, when Ernie hid in the desk drawer, Mary?"

Nothing.

Brent tapped on the window.

Still silent, Mary followed Kate's instructions and sat on the piano bench like a resigned prisoner.

"How did it go with Mary?"

Standing in the doorway with Mary in her sight, Kate smoothed her blue linen slacks, buying time, trying to get a fix on how to answer Brent.

"Not so well. This time feels different. She has twice the reason to stay behind her walls now. Brent, isn't there any possible way to get her out of here? Anywhere she can go? Being here must be terrifying for her now."

"I'm frustrated too, but by law, she can only be released if her mother signs her out."

Kate had the information she needed, Mary Anne Johnson. Mother's name Martha Lee Johnson, 23 Avery Street, Kutoma, Connecticut. If that really was her address. She'd researched it on the last day of her internship—an old historic colonial town somewhere near the Thames River. If she could get her signature to give up her parental rights, maybe Brent could figure something out for Mary? But what documents did Kate need? Maybe, Michael's lawyer could help. There wasn't time for that.

Brent's long stare unnerved her. Was it a supportive look or a threat? Was he reading her mind? She couldn't tell. Kate had to do something, but she couldn't involve him.

Couldn't she just go and see if the mother was willing?

"Don't do anything crazy, Kate."

"I won't do anything crazy, I promise." But she had to try. That wasn't crazy was it? She couldn't imagine Mary living at the institution...especially not with Ronnie still here. Kate looked over her shoulder at Mary, and a spray of chills sizzled down her spine. Shiloh should be finished buying her candles, and she wouldn't mind traveling an hour with Kate to give this hair-brained scheme a try, Kate thought.

"So if her mother signed documents to release Mary out of here, then what?"

Brent crossed his arms.

"I mean, theoretically." The idea took root inside Kate.

Brent looked down the hallway as though expecting someone to overhear his words. "I'd have to refer her to social services. Maybe they can help. But, honestly, Mary's so troubled, finding a permanent home won't be easy."

"They have to. Someone just has to." Kate looked back at Mary. Would anyone want to take the silent teen? If they could only get to know her. Although Kate didn't really know her, she had a warm feeling about Mary. Her expression and watery eyes when she'd read Kate's note from the typewriter and the first time she'd spoken and looked into Kate's eyes.

"Meanwhile, I've made sure she's in a safe residence." The board already thinks I'm some hippie flake from the last time I presented Mary's case and she refused to talk."

Kate couldn't read his far off look.

"Look, I know better than to think I can stop a romantic idealist in her tracks, but you don't work here anymore; it's not your concern. I'm not your boss either."

"I understand." Kate shifted and glanced back at Mary. I'm not your boss, he'd said. Was that tacit permission she'd heard embedded in his warning?

"I think I know you, Kate; I didn't hear a promise."

"Brent, everyone needs you here. Please, remember it was my idea, not yours. I know I was a naïve intern, but there's a female ancestor in my lineage I'm named after and, well, my mother says there's no denying that her passion got passed down to me." Kate let a small laugh escape. We'll blame it on her.

"Even if I forbid it, you'll do it anyway, right?"

"It's wrong not to."

"Then, please call Michael; it's wrong not to."

"I'll call him, I promise." The afront to her independence annoyed her.

Brent put his hands on his hips. He looked like he wanted to say something. The slight nod of his head made Kate think he was giving her permission. Kate turned her head in Mary's direction.

"Kate."

"Yes?"

"Oh, hell. I don't give a shit what the board thinks." Brent pulled a document from a file he held in his hand. "You'll need this. And thank you. Maybe you reminded me that I've lost something working in the system."

"Lost what?"

"My passion."

CHAPTER 73

Michael

TRIBAL TRIBUNAL

CHEERIOS FLEW ACROSS the kitchen table. Kate's five-year-old nephew laughed, flicking them back to Hy Vọng. She made Bunny pretend to gobble them up. Their giggles were therapeutic for everyone.

The story Kate had shared on the phone with Michael was the topic of the breakfast conversation. Plates of French Toast and scrambled eggs were passed around amid opinions.

"So, Shiloh's joining Kate, that's good. She has to get the mother to sign, and then what?" Cecelia poured more coffee for Christine at the stove.

"Then, hopefully, Brent is going to have social services work on finding her a foster home placement," Michael reported the plan.

"You have an extraordinary daughter, Cecelia. I can't imagine how that young girl will feel to have a chance at a new life after four years in that horrible place."

"Thank you, Christine. Kate gets something in her head, there's no stopping her."

Michael grabbed a cloth to wipe up the dribbles of orange juice Hy Vọng had spilled on the table. "If they can find a place. Not easy to take in a troubled young teen, Brent says. We'll hear more when Kate gets home tonight. I wish I could have gone with her." Michael snatched Hy Vọng up from the table. "OK, little one, let's get you cleaned up and dressed. Be right back, Mom."

Hy Vọng reached down and grabbed one more fistful of the crunchy circles and stuffed them into her mouth.

"Michael, can we talk?" Cecelia followed him upstairs to Kate's childhood bedroom. "I'm thinking, although I haven't spoken with Big Kevin, and I'm stabbing in the dark here..."

Michael kept glancing at Kate's mother as he shuffled through the luggage for an outfit for Hy Vọng and ran a brush through her silky hair.

"I can't imagine letting that young girl stay in that horrible place. Not with that boy still there. Next time...well, I don't want to think about it. Maybe it's bold and a little crazy. I don't know the laws, but we could use a little crazy around this place." Cecelia released a short laugh.

"Are you suggesting? What are you suggesting?"

"I'm not sure. Truthfully, Mary's story touches me deeply. You've met my younger sister, Maggie, who lives two doors down. She's so patient. She's one we all sent our kids to when they went through their terrible teens." Cecelia ran Bunny up Hy Vọng's belly to kiss her. She giggled.

"Now *that* giggle was a delicious reward. Anyway, Maggie has a way with them, you know. She's a seamstress, and the girls loved making clothes with her. She lost her only baby in childbirth, a little girl with Down's Syndrome, the year her husband was killed in a car accident. She would love to have Mary. Anyway, Michael, I think I'll talk to my sister about Mary."

"That's a big undertaking, Cecelia."

"You're probably right, but this has been a painful thing for Kate ever since she learned about Mary. And it might bring a purpose to my sister's life too. "This is what family does."

"I'm beginning to understand that." Michael nodded and smiled.

"Can you imagine years of pretending in silence? They still don't understand exactly why Mary won't talk. It's a mystery. Had to be some trauma?"

Michael hoisted Hy Vọng into his arms. "Maybe her mother couldn't afford to take care of her daughter?"

"Then why did her mother never visit? My guess is the household wasn't safe. Who knows? I do know, I'm happy Kate took another route and left Rolling Hills. Singing is who she is, Michael."

Michael gave Hy Vọng her toys. "And who doesn't love who she is?"

Cecelia hugged them both. "Well, it's a long shot, but I'll talk to Kate when she gets home, and she can broach it with Mr. Bradley."

"A long shot, but why don't *I* explore it? I'll chat with Brent and my family's law firm."

"By the way, your mother is so lovely. Thank you for bringing her; she's family now; it was such a pleasure. Who would have guessed you and Kate would ever have connected? And your mother and me already old acquaintances. Well, I need to get on with the day. See you at dinner."

Later, through the kitchen window, Michael spotted a man

bending over, hammering a sign into the little-patch-of a-front lawn next door. For Sale. The arguing neighbors Kate had always complained about were leaving. If that house ever goes up for sale someday, I'm going find a way to buy it, she'd said.

Michael took Hy Vọng and stood outside on the steps to the kitchen. "What do you think, Hy Vọng? You like Glynn?" The wind sent a flurry of leaves down on them. Hy Vọng reached up and tried to catch them. Just weeks until Thanksgiving. He kissed his daughter. He had a lot to be thankful for.

A quiet had settled over the kitchen with Kate's parents at their shift by the time Michael returned. Entering the house, Hy Vọng scooted out of Michael arms and made a beeline to the kitchen table, where Christine sat sipping more coffee and staring at two documents. Hy Vọng took advantage of the crack in the pantry door, pulled it open, and searched out the treat. "Dah-dee, Dah-dee." She went up on her toes to reach it. "Cee-ree-o."

"She said, 'cereal', or was it 'Cheerios?'" Michael sat down at the kitchen table next to his mother. "Mom, did you hear that?"

Christine quickly folded the two pieces of paper she was reading and slipped them into her pocket. "Oh, honey, she's going to do just fine, isn't she? Aren't you, sweetheart?"

Christine got up and reached the Cheerios for Hy Vọng, then sat again and folded her hands in front of her. "Michael, you must be spinning from all this. But I am so grateful—a daughter-in-law I love already, and now this little one." His mother turned to him and put one hand on his forearm. "My life is so different now."

Michael covered her hand, looking into her moist eyes.

Her voice thinned with emotion. "I wake up every morning, and...and the realization comes...I have a family of my own."

Her words brought matching emotions in Michael. "Mom? I get it. This is our family now."

"I'm not going to be some sideline, some decoration for your father, or a disappointment for your grandmother to gossip about anymore."

Hy Vọng climbed onto Michael's lap as if she knew he needed her near. He kissed her soft hair. "Mom, this is how family should be, isn't it? But, what's really going on? You're hiding something." He pointed to her pocket. "Something I should know?"

"Probably so. Call me a coward." She slipped the folded papers out and set them in front of her.

"Never. You're just picking up my bad habits, Mom. What's the secret?" He sprinkled some Cheerios on the blue placemat, then put his hand on his mother's quivering shoulder.

"Sorry, son, I'm so happy being with you and this big loving family. Makes me realize..." Christine lined up the tan circles in the shape of a heart for Hy Vọng. "I need to finally make a move. Build my own life with people I care about and enjoy. I know that 'family' isn't biology, or formalities, legality, or possessions; let's just put it that way." She spread the documents out. "It's from your grandmother's lawyer. So personal of her to send her news through a lawyer, don't you think?"

Her twinge of sarcasm surprised Michael.

"I'm sorry to burden you now. That's why I was going to the cabin to think. What is the right thing for me? I'm so weary of holding up the front for your father. I haven't truly been happy in years. And there you were. Talk about a sign. And there's more." She shifted to the second paper. "A letter from your father."

CHAPTER 74

MARTHA'S GHOST

BRENT'S WORDS OF warning cycled in her head as Kate drove the twists and turns on the slick Connecticut back roads with Shiloh. The chards of frosted, spiked grasses along the roadside felt like a threatening message. Walking on thin ice.

"I didn't expect to elope with you after your marriage celebration. Why is it feast or famine with us?" Shiloh laughed.

"I'm sorry I dragged you into this."

"Yes, how could you dare drag me into a cause?" Shiloh huffed a laugh. "And by the way, my friend, I thought you said you weren't an activist. Well, we needed an adventure."

"Let's hope not too big an adventure. I hope we can make this happen, Shi."

Kate was glad she wasn't doing this alone. But was she imagining things? Maybe it will be a simple explanation and a signature.

No longer connected to Rolling Hills, Kate felt she could ensure Brent some immunity, if things went wrong. She didn't want him to suffer any consequences for her actions.

"I've got to find the right words to convince Mary's mother. That's the key."

"If she's still there." Shiloh straightened her blue bandana, and a familiar shimmering of bangles made Kate smile.

The dull look in Mary's eyes had made it impossible to turn away, get on a plane, and return to Kate's singing life touring Europe. It was one day out of Kate's ten days at home; how could she not? "It won't be easy for a mother to just sign away her rights in her daughter's best interest, will it?"

"I guess it depends; if she's protecting her, it might be. I don't envy you having to do this, Kate, but I admire it." Shiloh turned the radio knob to a Motown station.

Then, Kate could...what? There was no sure next step, only hope that a stranger would open their hearts to the struggling girl. Kate's thoughts layered as she drove. Would she save Mary from Rolling Hills and damn her to an even sadder situation? Still, there was no option to walk away now. One step at a time, one critical step.

If not, then what? The *ifs* were too many to ponder. Not the least of them was how Mary's stepfather figured into this.

Kate knew nothing about domestic abuse. If Brent was right about the bruises on Mary's mother's arm she'd rubbed when she'd sat in his office, what would Kate find behind the door of Mary's former home? The questions rumbled inside her. Was it abuse? Was it just Mary's mother who was abused? Maybe it was some other kind of trauma when it came to Mary. There was nothing physically wrong with the girl that would prevent her speech, recent tests after the near-rape had shown.

"I'm so glad you're with me."

Shiloh squeezed Kate's hand. "You have that you-need-music-look on your face." She turned up the radio.

They listened to the upbeat tunes as the morning became grayer, fitting the mood of the old town's outskirts with its dreary, century-old homes in ill-repair. Small farms were dotted with crumbling barns, wobbly like a house-of-cards with scraped red paint barely tinging the wide decaying planks. Kate imagined the barn siding clawed at by feral cats until the streaks of graying wood had shown through. Spotted Holsteins lingered under old oaks, sheltering from the dense fog that rose like upside-down clouds from the valleys.

With the creased map in Shiloh's lap, she navigated for Kate. "Turn here on Route 5. You should see the center of town soon."

Around a bend, a rustic wooden sign welcomed them, *Kutoma, Connecticut.* Following the one-mile frontage along Kutoma Cove, they passed mid-century colonials and early Victorians that clung to the coastline—some with facelifts, some sagging from old age. Like seeing double, the homes reflected in the gray lake water, a quivering upside-down skyline.

Kate turned off the main road and followed Shiloh's directions to find the Johnson's address. Small white cottages perched on berms dotted the narrow two-lane road. Like Legos, they'd sprung up alongside the stately, large colonials and Victorians with turrets painted purple and classic colonial blue.

"Just a few blocks farther."

Following the numbers, Kate pulled over. There was no 23 Avery Street; the short street ended at 12. She could see the last house from her misted car windows. The homes were nothing exceptional, notably well-cared-for small white mid-century colonials. "Now what?" Kate released a long-held breath, sipped the dredges of her coffee, and crushed the cup. A dead end. "Maybe this is going to be harder than we thought."

A postman with a leather satchel in a blue uniform appeared out of the foggy blanket. He was pushing retirement age from the look of his silver hair and his sloping shoulders.

"Mailmen know everything in a town like this." Shiloh rolled down the window.

"Let *me* go, OK?" Kate got out of the car and intercepted him. "Excuse me, sir?"

"Morning, young lady. Tourists? Here for the ghosts?"

"Excuse me?"

"We're famous for them. That's why you're here, right? Ghost chasin'? The houses on tour are hair-raisin'." He shaded his eyes and laughed.

A haunted New England town. Great. As if she needed her hair more raised than it already was, Kate thought.

He smiled, clearly proud of his town's heritage.

"No, sir, I think I wrote it down wrong. I'm looking for... I came to visit my dear aunt, Martha, Martha Lee Johnson."

"Next street over, number 8."

"Actually, she told me to meet her at her job, and I left the address at home. Dumb. My first time, here."

"Niece? You must be Martha's sister Ethel's girl, the runaway."

Oh, God, she hadn't meant to get into a conversation. "That's me." Kate tapped a tune on her pant leg. She hadn't meant to have tea with the guy either. She'd just wanted the address.

He shifted his heavy brown leather mailbag to his other shoulder. "What's your name again?"

Kate stuffed her hands in her slacks pockets as though she could hide her lies. "Kelly."

"Hmmm. That don't sound right. My memory must be failin'."

"I use 'Kelly' now." If that's all he knew that freed Kate up for a story. "I'm back. Straightened out. I teach school in a small town in Massachusetts." Kate's lies rolled out easily, like being in one of her high school plays. But she didn't want to go too far.

"Good for you, Missy."

Kate flashed a pleading smile at Shiloh.

"Hey, Kelly, let's go." Shiloh added to the subterfuge.

"I'm coming." That's my, uh, step-sister."

"Hello, Miss." The postman waved at Shiloh and continued. "So, you want the Old Sea Captain's Inn. Now that one's the best ghost palace we have. I get chills just walkin' up the step to deliver the mail." He shook and held himself. "There is one pretty girl ghost in the garden that appears sometimes. He winked. She works in the kitchen."

Kate tilted her head in confusion. "A ghost working in the kitchen?"

He laughed. "Your aunt, Martha, I mean, not the ghost. Works in the kitchen, nice lady. Husband works at the inn too. Groundskeeper."

The postman's face flashed a different look, and the friendliness in his voice changed at bit at the mention of Martha's husband. Kate couldn't quite read it.

"Just make a U-ee and take a left, the old inn's up on your

right; built in 1754. White picket fence. Enormous tulip tree in front. Can't miss it. Inn's been painted blue. Have a nice visit."

Kate thanked him, got back in the car. "Shi, did you notice his change when he mentioned the husband? Or was it just me?"

"Yes, I don't want to know what that was about."

Contemplating what possible words she could say to get Mary's mother to sign the release, Kate drove the few blocks and pulled up in front of the Old Sea Captain's stately colonial inn.

A man was kneeling, bent over the garden on the left side of the property under an enormous tree. Its large leaves shone gold against the blue front of the inn. He turned when their car arrived, stood up, and walked toward them. He was handsome, mid-forties maybe, with one knee on his overalls soaking wet from kneeling in the garden's moisture. "Good day, lovely ladies. Henry Johnson, groundskeeper. Can I help you?"

Johnson? Kate flashed her eyes from the man to Shiloh. Could Brent's guess be correct? Was he an abuser? He seemed so kind and polite. Kate stared at his weathered hands, his nails filled with dirt. Was she looking at the man who had possibly destroyed young Mary? She couldn't let her mind go to where those hands might have been. The terrors they may have caused. "We're...we're checking to see if there is a room for the night?" Kate clenched her hands around the steering wheel and tried to keep the suspicion from showing in her eyes.

Shiloh tapped Kate's arm in warning and whispered. "Stay calm."

"Luggage? Happy to take it in for you." The man moved closer. Again, the charming smile.

"What?" Oh, God, she hadn't expected to stay. It was only an hour's drive back to Rolling Hills. For someone who didn't want to raise suspicion, Kate hadn't planned very well. It was too easy. She hadn't really expected to find Mary's mother so effortlessly.

"No luggage. Just decided last minute to check out the ghosts. For my students, I'm a teacher and—"

"Side door entrance. Anna'll help ya. Enjoy your stay." He returned to his weeding. But the last glare of his ice-blue eyes chilled Kate as they scanned her body. Had Mary's poor mother been accosted by those filthy hands and terrorized by those azure eyes? They fit right in with a town full of ghosts. And so smooth, you would never see him as a predator. Was he?

"Pretty charming, huh?" Shiloh's bangles sent a shiver of clinking sounds through the car as she hugged herself.

"Maybe we're imagining it." A shower of fear ran over Kate's shoulders and down her arms. Any New Englander worth her salt believed in hauntings. What had Kate expected Mr. Johnson to look like—wild hair exploding through his cap and sinister gray eyes? But still, something about his mannerly surface left more of an impression than any ghost tale could. Kate couldn't let her mind go to Mary and her stepfather and those soiled hands. As Kate parked the car, she started to hum a soft song to block the images.

It struck Kate, if this were pre-Michael or pre-concert-tours, she'd be digging through her purse and under the car seat, nervous about finding enough cash to pay for tea, let alone an overnight in a fine New England inn. Kate pulled out her credit card from the supple Italian leather wallet she'd bought in Singapore. It was thick with dollars and a few thousand Baht. "I've got this, Shiloh." It was better to have a room, just in case.

The inn was quiet. Anna, the owner, settled Kate and Shiloh into comfy chairs in the library for a hot cup of tea. The light scent of musty books mingled with the earthy tea aroma was so New England to them both. Shiloh's magenta skirt and hippie print blouse screamed out against the gold velvet chairs. Kate's Thai silk blouse and linen slacks must seem just as foreign, she thought. The unconventional duo drew the attention of a conservatively dressed elderly couple sipping tea in the corner. Kate smiled and waved.

"My son will give the two of you a proper ghost tour in forty-five minutes after his errands, and Martha will bring you Earl Gray tea," the Proprietor said.

Martha Johnson, herself, was being served right up to Kate, along with their tea. "Shi, say a prayer this works."

"Maybe we'll find ourselves on the highway to home sooner than we thought." Shiloh took off her shawl and dropped it over the back of the chair.

"Earl Gray?" The pretty woman set the cup and saucer on the side table. It struck Kate, the soft-spoken woman wore a floral dress, the same fabric as a handmade one Mary had worn. The waitress also had an older, withered version of her daughter's body; her clothes hung loose on her lean frame.

"Thank you." Kate wanted to find a reason to chat. The room was empty. It wasn't dinner time, yet. "Do you live here? I wonder if I can ask you a question. Is it Martha? I'm Ka—, uh Kelly, and this is my step-sister, Sharon." Kate knew she needed to keep her story straight in a small town.

"Pleasure. What can I do to help?"

"I met a girl who...who looks exactly like you." There was no time to take a softer approach.

Kate and Shiloh followed Martha's glance out the window to the man digging up the wilted annuals surrounding the tulip tree. The woman rubbed her arms as if to quell a line of chills, as did Kate, followed by Shiloh.

"Mrs. Johnson. Please sit for just a second. No one's near. I want to talk to you about Mary." Kate handed the woman a Polaroid she'd taken in the classroom on her last day.

Martha leaned back onto the green-striped satin wallpaper to support herself. She shuddered, stared at the image, and held it to her chest. "My Mary! She's grown so since she was stole."

"Please, Mrs. Johnson..."

"Maybe you should be calling me, Martha."

"Martha, I'm not here to cause trouble for you. I know what happened. I know you meant well by putting her in the safety of Rolling Hills." Kate snapped her head and looked outside to ensure Mary's stepfather was still in the garden. "I just want to help Mary. I was her teacher. We don't have much time." Mary's stepfather would likely be coming inside soon with the black clouds gathering from the pending storm.

Martha looked up at Kate and whispered. "Is my baby girl, Mary, alright?"

"Yes, well, no." Kate helped Martha to sit and settled herself into the adjacent chair. Shiloh stood in support behind Kate.

The woman folded her bony hands in front of her. A

yellowish-green stripe of discoloration marred each hand. She pulled them down under the table. "No mind, dresser drawer caught my hands."

A cool breeze swept by them. Kate looked around for an open door or window, expecting Mary's stepfather to appear.

"That cold—it's the girl in the lavender dress. You know, a ghost."

Kate had heard of hauntings in old New England homes, but she hadn't ever actually experienced one. She shivered. Shiloh hooked her hand into Kate's arm and squeezed a message of support.

"Honestly, Mary needs you, Martha. Needs help badly. An older boy at the school tried to...accost her." Chills raced down Kate's spine. "Another boy stopped him, and he got seriously hurt."

"Oh, God. So, everything's OK, right, he didn't get into her?"

Martha's expression, "get into her" caught Kate's breath. "Everything's not OK, because Mary is in danger in that school, especially now that she's maturing, you understand? And Martha, we both know there is nothing wrong with Mary, is there?"

"Mary's retarded, can't talk." Martha pumped her folded hands nervously and dropped her head. "Truth is, I told her nevah, eva talk to them or tell anyone, or else her stepdaddy..."

The familiar speech pattern brought it all back to Kate. "She talked to me."

"She did?" Martha put her head in her hands.

Kate slowly pulled Martha's hands away and looked in her eyes. "But now we need to get her out of there. And we need your permission, so she can have a good life."

"She can't come home here. I lied to my husband, the whole town, they went huntin' for her. He'll do bad things to me and her." Martha shook, twitched like an injured animal, as though shaking off thoughts of her husband. "He nevah wanted kids; he just wants me. And me having Mary, and her getting to be a teen and all."

"No, don't worry. I'm not talking about bringing Mary back to *this* town with her stepfather here. Martha, I know you love your daughter, or you wouldn't have put her at Rolling Hills. But that's not the right place for her now that she's a young woman. We want to keep you safe too." Kate took the paper out of her pocketbook. "If you sign these papers, it gives permission for her to live with a nice family, a normal life." The story formed only seconds before it left Kate's lips. "If we can just get the papers signed, I can get her out."

"Where would she live?" Martha engaged Kate's eyes in a way that she couldn't carry out the fantasy any longer. Lying didn't come naturally. Could she really promise to fulfill that fantasy for Mary?

Shiloh pulled Kate's arm back, and jumped in. "Your Mary will have the kind of family who wants to raise a nice girl. And she'll need money."

Kate was stunned at how smooth Shiloh was. Why hadn't Kate planned her story better. She tried focus on the conversation, but she couldn't stop thinking about Mary and what happened on that staircase. What in God's name was Kate doing here interfering in places where she had no right, no power?

"Money? I don't have much." The woman looked at her empty hands.

"No, no. Let me explain. I'm an attorney; there's money to help children like Mary, yes money from the state for her education." Shiloh nodded her head for Kate to take over.

Brilliant. Kate wasn't hopeless anymore; she had means to solve this problem. Michael had taught her about the power of money; Kate used the lesson. "There are funds to compensate *you* for setting up Mary in a good place too."

Shiloh's eyes got big, she bit her lip and nodded encouragement for Kate to go on.

"You understand? You won't have to worry or pay it back. You can go somewhere nice. Away from here, from him." Kate flashed her eyes outside. "Anywhere you wish."

Shiloh chimed in again. "You'll have a nice nest egg. Every woman should have a nest egg."

"For a rainy day...yes. I ain't neva had one. My momma did." Mary's mother stared across the room. "That's how she left Daddy."

Framed in the old windows of the library, Martha's husband was gathering up his tools in a wheelbarrow.

Martha began to shake. "Can't tell him about Mary. For sure, he'll kill me."

The idea became fully-formed somewhere in Kate's mind. Thank goodness Shiloh had thought of money. "You'll have your own. You understand?" Kate stepped in front of Martha to block her view of her husband. "A new start. Maybe with your sister, Esther, in New Jersey? Or you can stay here. Do whatever you want with it."

Martha wiped her hand down the front of her faded dress, that familiar gesture of Mary's. "Money for Mary too?"

It started to come together. Kate had hope. She was creating a scenario even she had begun to believe. It wasn't a fantasy. Kate could make it come true. At least the money part.

The look on the woman's face encouraged Kate.

CHAPTER 75

TRUTH TELLING

THE LIBRARY DOOR opened. Anna, the innkeeper, walked in. "Martha? We have customers in the dining room, and Henry's coming in from the garden. He won't want you to be talking to these nice guests."

"I'm her niece from New Jersey." Kate was getting in deeper; a cold dampness wrapped around her.

Martha took off her white ruffled apron, folded it carefully, and looked up. "Anna, truth is, this young woman's a teacher, found my Mary. We can trust her." She held up the photo.

"Mother of God. You *found* her?"

Martha shuffled side to side, and glanced out the window. "She wasn't really lost, Anna. I...I brought her to a residential school called Rolling Hills. I needed to hide her from Henry. I told Miss Kelly the truth about what my Mr. Johnson...well, what he did to me and Mary. Now I need to tell you the truth, Anna."

Kate stepped in. "Anna, I can have Mary moved from the institution to a nice home if her mother signs this release.

Since Mr. Johnson isn't her legal father or guardian, he will never have to know."

Martha turned from Anna to Kate. "It's the ghosts, you know, he can't help it. The ghost's got inside him." Martha lifted her dress to reveal the newest of her blue and purple bruises on her thighs. "I made him mad. It's not his fault. Please. He finds this out, he'll kill me. But I gotta help my Mary. I can't take worrying about her no more."

"I knew he was a bully, but honey, we never thought it went that far...you never said a word." Anna put her arm around Martha. "Oh honey, you can't be putting up with that, you've got to tell the police."

Please don't frighten her, Kate thought. "She will be getting a grant from the state for Mary, and her daughter will be adoptable if Martha signs the documents."

"And I'll get some walkin' money too. I can't call the police, please, Anna. I can leave and go live with my sister. She has a nice life. But don't get Henry mad. He can't come after me; he doesn't know I have a second sister, Edna."

Anna glanced out the window, and hesitated. "Go, Martha, dear; go sign for your baby girl. Jack will distract Henry. We'll deal with this later."

"Miss Kelly, I'll show you a route to get out of town so you can stay out of sight; it's best." Anna gave Kate directions.

Kate went to the ladies' room with Martha and counted out the ten one hundred dollar bills she'd gotten at the bank for travel.

"Martha, the support money is a thousand dollars." The unsigned papers were shaking in Kate's hand; the lies were hanging in the air around her.

"One thousand?" Martha walked back and forth on the white tile with her hands over her face. "One thousand?"

"I wish it could be more." Kate was relieved Martha said she would leave Henry. The money would save both mother and daughter. It justified Kate's dishonesty, didn't it?

"More? No, that'll work just fine for my nest egg. I neva thought I'd have…" She wrapped her arms tight around her middle.

"And Mary will be taken care of?" With the woman's shocked face in the mirror, Kate spread the papers out and handed Martha a pen.

Martha took the pen and hesitated. "Does this mean I can't neva see my Mary again?"

"No. It means Mr. Johnson won't ever know where she is. It means she'll have a chance for a better life. You just get in touch with Mr. Brent Bradley at Rolling Hills if you need to once you get settled at your sister's place. I'm just going to take a picture of you signing. It's what you need for her official release." Kate felt like some gangster, making a payoff, some drug deal.

"Thank you." The tearful woman signed the paper, took the money, looked over her shoulder and stuffed it down her dress. "This might be my walkin' money, someday soon."

Sooner rather than later, Kate thought. "I need to go, Martha. I'll tell Mary you were the one who arranged to help her." Kate folded the document and put it in her oversized pocketbook.

"Thank you, Miss; thank you for helping my Mary. And for this, God bless you." Martha patted her chest where her new-found fortune hid.

Slouching down in the car, Kate and Shiloh waited until Henry had left the yard. Like a soldier in a fox hole, Shiloh peeked over the dashboard, and scanned the scenery outside the car windows for the enemy before sitting up. "Shi, I'll drop you at your car; I'm delivering these papers right away."

Shiloh grasped Kate's hand. "You should have been a lawyer...or a liar."

"Couldn't have done it without you." Kate let out a breath and a nervous laugh, and the tension released a bit.

The car pushed exhaust into the chilly afternoon air as they left the haunted town. As the sun dropped over the cove, it cast shadows of the turrets and church steeples onto the shimmering water like a foreign skyline.

Mary was in her new single room in a large, dilapidated group home on campus that housed a dozen other young adults. Kate tapped on the door, and Mary opened it. At the sight of Kate, she broke down. Mary's whimper drove into Kate's heart, and she grabbed the edge of the bed for support. The trip had been exhausting. "I'm sorry, Mary. I had to go somewhere. Everyone wanted you to be safe; do you like your new place and a room all to yourself?"

Mary's mouth moved, but no sound escaped. Her lips quivered and pulsed, a kind of practice, Kate thought. Like priming the pump, calling deep inside herself for her words. Nothing. Then Mary began to utter words, not sentences, but strings of utterances that said enough. "Mama neva eva, but you...

came back Miss Ketchup. Wahhhhh." Her wail was so much like Ernie's cries.

Kate put her hand to her chest. "I'm going to get you out of here, OK? But I need a little time. You'll live with a nice family. Trust me; I will come back."

The promise was sincere, but the plan was hollow. Nothing had ever erupted such emotions inside Kate. Nothing had ever made her realize how blessed she was. The exchange between them made her explode with love for Michael, Hy Vọng, and Kate's big, crazy, dye-stained family—Kate's loving mother and father, her scruffy brothers, her wild and nurturing sisters, her singing, her own perfect life.

Kate took the hallway to Brent's office. Her feet were weighted as she departed; she was sinking into a quicksand of responsibilities.

Her promise to Mary had just come out of her mouth. No filters; just hope. It weighed heavily on Kate. Was this just another nail in her singing career's coffin? Before she could tap on his door, he opened it.

"I'm wearing the linoleum out in here from pacing. Goddam, what happened? I had such regret when you left. That I actually hadn't stopped you. Was I nuts? If I hadn't had a board meeting, I would have chased after you. I should have; they've had it with me anyway."

"You didn't let me go; I disobeyed your orders, remember?" Kate pulled the signed paper from her pocketbook. "She signed it. Legit, not forged. I promise. Here, look, I took a polaroid photo of her signing it."

"Shit! Sorry. Here, sit down and tell me."

Kate shared the whole brutal story. "You were right. He

was an abuser. And I can't even describe how... I'm so sad for that woman. But I can't let my mind go there. She's leaving him, thank God. Please, help me keep my promise to get Mary out of here."

Brent reached for the phone. "It's in the works. I got a call from your lawyer. We are damn-well going to make this work. But it might take time to find the right way. I mean since she's a single woman."

"My lawyer? What single woman?"

CHAPTER 76

Michael

ILLUSION OF PERFECT

MICHAEL PULLED OUT the kitchen chair and sat next to his mother. "Dad *wrote*? Why didn't he call you? Is he angry?"

"No, but..."

"Mom, I've been...well, I've been deliberately not retuning his calls. You understand, right? I don't even want him to meet Hy Vọng." Michael covered Hy Vọng's ears. Anger erupted in his low voice. "I'm not going to subject this angel to that selfish son-of-a-bitch. I don't want him to have any influence or claim on her." He hugged Hy Vọng tighter. His tone made his child stretch her neck to look up at him with wide eyes. He took a deep breath.

"Dah-dee."

"If Dad does accept her, it will only be to display her for attention like he does everything else—my war medals, my trophies. Like saying, 'Look at me; I'm not prejudiced. I have a Vietnamese grandbaby from the war.'" The venom spilled over his words. "I won't watch him try to turn her into his perfect grandchild on display."

"He was upset that you never called him back. He says, it hurt him." Christine explained that his father had been removed as CEO by the Chairman of the Board, fired by his own mother. He would never starve, clearly, but he was mortified and lost.

Michael listened as Christine tried to convey what his father had been like when she'd met him—loving and fun.

"He was such a sweet and attentive father when you were a baby, Michael. He stood up for me, at first, his eighteen-year-old pregnant girlfriend."

Her insights confused Michael. Was his view of his father that of a child?

"Grandmother's pressure and your father wanting to be someone...for you, for me; ironically, it drove him to be the less-than-honorable man he is."

"Mom, I'm so sorry. I didn't realize Dad was in jeopardy. Damn, that company has been his life."

"It's so sad. No matter how he tried, he was never enough for his mother. I'm not trying to justify what a pompous man he's become over time. He can be despicable. Maybe you become like the people you spend time with." Christine reached across the table and touched Michael's arm. "Just so you have an understanding, he wasn't and isn't really all bad inside. He took a lot of pressure for getting his girlfriend pregnant." Christine rubbed the back of Hy Vọng's hand. "But he's broken now. After his cow-towing to his mother, and her mortifying him with the company board time after time, she's destroyed him."

"That's tragic, Mom, but let's see how or *if* this changes him for the better."

"If only his father were alive—you would have loved your

grandfather—but once he died and Grandmother took over, all hell broke loose." Christine stroked Hy Vọng's hair. "It's an evil legacy, and Michael, I'm so proud of you for breaking the choke chain."

"The medals and the awards on display, the perfectly posed professional photos of Dad and me, they seemed... just for show, Mom."

"He was proud of you."

"It appeared so artificial, elitist, such bullshit. Just like the pictures and portraits of you and him he put all over the house, so loving, and then he cheated his ass off. Sorry, Mom."

"I understand. I do. Sometime, I'll show you the photos I took of you two early on. He does love you in his way."

Everything took on a slightly different meaning for Michael; maybe the love in those photos was sincere beneath the illusion of perfect. But it wasn't enough.

"In his letter, he wanted to warn you. Well, your trust fund... has been dissolved." Christine stared at the letter. "Grandmother's handiwork. Your father wanted to know if you needed help."

The news swirled in Michael's head and settled quickly. Why did Michael feel relief? He'd just lost millions of dollars, but the freedom made him feel light; his shoulders dropped, a smile crossed his face, he burst out laughing. "I don't know why I'm laughing. I know; I'm no longer the privileged son of a multi-millionaire who is owned by his mother." He took his mother's hand. "And all it took was four years in a hell hole, tragic loss, and my mental health. Seriously, it's no surprise. I knew once I turned down being the official '& Son' on Dad's building it would be all over. I'm glad it is."

"Well, and you missing all those holidays you spent with Kate's family or abroad, and not playing Grandmother's puppet, to be honest, Michael. At least when you were away in the war, it gave them a legitimate way to explain to their friends why you weren't there, and he could bask in their sympathy."

"We've both been controlled by the James' family tradition of...I don't even know how to describe the control and selfishness. I'm relieved. But, Mom, I never thought about the culture of the family holding Dad hostage too."

"Grandmother had her losses too."

"What do you mean?"

"I try to see things from her perspective; it was the only way I could survive her all these years. A widow at forty, a pregnant, unmarried, unexpected daughter-in-law, a grandson who refused to carry on her family's legacy, and a son who couldn't live up to her standards." Christine paused. "Not that I have much sympathy for her, but if I try to see it from her jaundiced eyes...her loss of control, you know." Christine refilled her coffee, added two teaspoons of sugar and stirred slowly. "Still, there's no air to breathe being married to your father the way he is. Understanding him and having some loving memories doesn't mean I can be with him. I'm so weary of living up to someone else's expectations, all the rules for show. Your father's extracurricular activities and the whole country club society knowing. Not being allowed to teach piano—too bourgeoisie."

"I'm glad you'll be OK financially, Mom."

"I'm fine. The handwriting was on the wall pretty early on, honey. I've been putting some money away. My investments have done surprisingly well. Actually, I'll be better than fine, and I think I'll just start up my piano studio again." Christine cast her eyes down. "I've always worried about what Grandmother James would do to you and your trust."

"Is that why you *stayed*?" Michael stood and the chair crashed to the floor behind him.

"*Không, không.*" Hy Vọng wriggled out of his arms, ran into the other room, and flipped on the TV.

"Don't worry. She just said, no. It's her standard when she doesn't like what's going on."

"I agree with Hy Vọng, *không.*"

"What?" Michael laughed.

"Sorry, just needed a little humor to release the tension." His mother sighed.

"I get it, but seriously, Mom, that's not a life I cared about. And I hate that you had to tolerate it for my future." Michael ran his hands over the tabletop. "I have savings; Kate and I have our whole lives ahead of us. And she's the breadwinner anyway." He laughed. "Is that great, or what?"

"Yes, of course. But, you realize you still have options, Michael."

"What do you mean?" Michael kept his eye on Hy Vọng who sat in Big Kevin's brown leather lounge chair enthralled by a cartoon show.

"I called the lawyer this morning at your father's suggestion. According to the terms of the trust, at age twenty-five—"

"At Dad's suggestion? He knows the fine print?"

"Yes. The lawyer says, you have the right to buy a residence if you don't have one and donate up to a million dollars to a charity, within thirty days of the closing of the trust."

Michael leaned forward. "A *million*? Are you kidding? That's odd. I don't understand."

"I guess your grandmother didn't want to have a homeless grandson to embarrass the Grande Dame. People talk you know. And look at the attention you'll get for the family name as a major donor when it hits the covers of a dozen magazines." Her words dripped with sarcasm.

"Well, that solves everything, Mom."

"Everything? Except for an income for my jobless son when you've just started a family."

"Mom, don't worry; I've got this idea." Michael explained his plan to start a foundation to assist families to adopt orphaned children in war-torn countries. He'd already hired an attorney to research the plan. The business plan was ready and the charity was nearly established. "I had lots of time at the lake house to think too. Timelier than I'd ever thought. I don't need to fundraise, now; I can underwrite it myself."

"Then you just need employment. Flexible employment." Christine glanced out the kitchen door and nodded toward Hy Vọng. "For your sweet one."

The idea came easily. "I hadn't thought to run the charity, but come to think of it—I'll need a CEO. I've just interviewed and hired myself." Michael had another thought about his future with Kate and Hy Vọng too.

"Just be sure to get a passionate adoption attorney. You, of all people, know how overseas adoptions can be."

"You're reading my mind." Michael knew his mother was right. He needed a trusted ally on his staff. He smiled. "I just happened to know an up-and-coming lawyer I can trust, who wants to work with kids."

"Who's that?"

"A hint. You can always hear her coming." By the time Michael would have the non-profit up-and-running, she'd be sitting for the bar. And wouldn't Shiloh be perfect with that tough-minded passion of hers?

"I think I can guess. Perfect. Imagine all the little Hy Vọngs out there." The idea elicited a hug from his mother. "Brilliant."

Michael contemplated another idea that had been percolating ever since Kate had returned. He just might have figured things out for his new family, and he had a feeling Kate would approve.

"As for me, I'd better get my renovations at the lake house done."

"So, you're leaving Dad, now?"

"I just want to put things in place and have options, Michael. It's complicated. I don't know how I feel about the timing. He'll need me to get him through this."

"Are you *serious*?" Michael righted the chair and sat.

"I know that sounds ridiculous for me to be concerned about him after all this, but…let's see how the trauma changes him."

"It's your call, Mom."

"Maybe you'll change your mind about Hy Vọng at least meeting her grandfather, someday. Forgiveness is powerful, son. I'm not suggesting you include your grandmother. That's *your* call."

Hy Vọng returned, reached up, and put a Cheerio to Christine's lips. "Hung-ree?"

"Did you hear that?" Christine munched on the crunchy

golden circle. "The thrill of watching that child adjust is so touching, Michael. You see how it's the little things that make your life?"

"I do get that. She teaches me every day."

CHAPTER 77

Kate

THE PLAN

STOPPING TO BUY a new stuffed animal to replace the matted and mildewed pink rabbit was a necessity. There had to be a substitute while the original Bunny was laundered. Kate joked with Michael that she was afraid of a plague outbreak from the grungy toy. She'd gone to three stores to find a match and was glad she had. It had been an innocent distraction to balance out her disturbing day and a way to connect with Hy Vọng. It wasn't until she walked through her parents' door that the full impact of the day hit her. Kate slid into her father's chair with the new stuffed animal.

"Hy Vọng, I'm your new bunny." Kate squeaked out a cartoon voice. Lured by the talking bunny, Hy Vọng giggled and climbed up onto Kate's lap. Holding her new daughter was just the therapy Kate needed. It seemed Hy Vọng instinctively knew it. Kate kissed the top of her head, hugged her, and sighed out the terrors of the day.

"Kiss, kiss." Hy Vọng's words surprised Kate. With her head resting back against Kate's pounding chest, Hy Vọng introduced the stuffed animals to each other in English. "Bunny, see Bunny."

Hy Vọng was no longer only Michael's daughter, Kate was beginning to fall in love with the vulnerable child. How would she ever leave for the tour with everything that had gone on with Hy Vọng, with Mary and Ernie? Her priorities had shifted with the sounds of Martha's trembling voice, Mary's wail, and Hy Vọng's word, *Bunny*.

Michael came into the living room and stood behind Kate's chair with his hands on her shoulders. "You're home. I just heard from my lawyer. He got a call from Brent. So, you did it?"

"Oh God, Michael, it was crazy. Thank God I had Shiloh with me. And thank God you didn't come; you would have lost it and killed the guy." Kate tried to delay; retelling the story would be chilling.

Hy Vọng pushed the rabbit into Kate's face for a kiss. "Oh, good girl. Michael, Hy Vọng said a new word, *bunny*. She made them talk to each other."

"Today, she said 'Cheerios,' or maybe it was cereal. So exciting. But I'm dying here. Tell me what happened?"

Kate worked to capture the horror of the day in words. "I shouldn't have made such a promise to Mary. I'm praying Brent works fast."

"He did." Michael knelt in front of her chair.

"What? He called? I know that look, Michael; what have you done without me knowing?"

"So cynical and suspicious, Kate Ketchum-James. It was your mother this time; don't blame *me*. She's cooking up a plan."

The doorbell rang. Michael headed for the door. "I'll get it. You two look too cozy to disturb."

Cecelia and Maggie came through the door bringing in the November chill.

"Aunt Maggie, so good to see you. You look great."

The lean brunette in a smart red outfit approached slowly and gave a little wave to Hy Vọng. "Oh, your sweet daughter's doing so well, Kate. I knew in time she would. Your mother told me about Mary at, what's it called, Rambling Hills?"

"Rolling Hills. I know, it was so dreadful, Aunt Maggie, but the director is working on finding her a home."

"I think he found a home for her." Kate's mother and her sister wrapped their arms around each other, standing like two guilty children who'd had their hands in the cookie jar.

"How do you know about Brent's search? Wait, what's going on here, Mom?" Kate dragged out the word, Mom with a warm tone of accusation and a squint.

"Kate, I have always wanted a child of my own, after my losses; you know that… and when your mother told me about Mary…"

"Wait, Aunt Maggie, you're the *single woman* Brent mentioned?"

"Well, dear God, who could leave that girl in that place, Kate. Michael's lawyer is helping me to petition to be her foster parent, and who knows, hopefully later, adopted mother."

"And your Mr. Bradley is helping." Kate's mother winked. "But we can't get ahead of ourselves."

"Yes, we don't know if they will approve a single woman. My mother called her lawyer; he said he'll work on finding a way. Your father and I might have to…well, we'll figure it out."

"I don't want to know what that means." Kate shot a look at Michael.

Kate's mother put her hand on Kate's shoulder. "Katie-girl, I know you. Would you ever sleep in peace if we left Mary in that place?"

"We are going to get Mary tomorrow for a trial visit...on a temporary basis until the legal issues are all worked out." Michael stood and put his hand on Kate's other shoulder.

Kate held onto Hy Vọng, closed her eyes, and silently cried. Hy Vọng didn't pull away; she touched the tear on Kate's cheek, then snuggled into her chest.

Clearing her tension with a deep breath, Kate delivered her thanks through a tight throat. "You two are the best. I can't believe it. Thank you, Aunt Maggie. Mary is sweet. God, I hope it works out." The good news was a threat to her concert tour, but Kate knew her priorities. She had to be there to support Aunt Maggie and to be the bridge, didn't she?

Hy Vọng put Bunny to Kate's lips. "Kiss, kiss."

"Can I talk to Kate alone, everyone? Can you take Hy Vọng? I think she'll go with you two." Michael lifted her and the bunnies and her doll and passed them on to his mother and Cecelia. The transition worked. A first. They took her to the kitchen, her favorite room.

Kate sat like a rag doll in the overstuffed chair. "I'm over-whelmed, exhausted. Michael, this is all above my pay grade. It's all too much. But I'm so grateful."

"You need to rest up for the tour...you leave in eight days. But you need to see that Mary gets out of that place before you go—even if it's a temporary thing until things get straightened out."

"Is it too selfish, Michael? Everything is so complicated now just as my career is taking off. I can't desert you with all this."

"Eh! Don't argue, Ms. Singing Star. You're just tired, and you'll eat those words. You have to go." Michael leaned over and hugged Kate close. "You have fans to think of, commitments, and your own dreams. All these family things will settle down. We need you happy."

"But Michael..."

"I'm not pulling any more pins off your map, darling." He lifted Kate from the chair and put his arms around her. "And I don't want you to look back and regret. Like your mother did. I've seen that look on her face when she tells that story. Not because of me, Hy Vọng, Mary, no one."

"Things are rolling around like marbles in our lives right now. I'm dizzy."

"Don't get too dizzy, Kate. We need to talk about Ernie."

"Oh God, I can't even think about what will happen to him."

"After all you did, we can't stop here. We're going to have a nice dinner, get some sleep tonight, and take a ride to Rolling Hills in a caravan."

"A what?"

"Here's the plan. Your Mom and Dad will drive with Aunt Maggie to sign papers and pick up Mary for a temporary visit. There are a lot of steps like interviews and home inspections for any permanent situation for Mary. It could take time. Pray it works. Once we get them off, you and I are going to get Ernie. He'll be up and out of the hospital tomorrow, and you're taking him on a rehab vacation to the fabulous town of Glynn."

"Michael, really? I felt so miserable leaving him behind and taking only Mary. Will they let us?"

"If you don't try, then you're not the woman I know."

Kate launched out of the chair to hug him. "Very funny

turning that line around on me. You've been a busy boy, Michael. I won't ask how you did it."

"I'm thinking a little duet at O'Leary's this weekend will cheer everyone up. Including the love of my life. Warm-up for your tour. What do you think?"

"Sounds wonderful. Just what the doctor ordered."

CHAPTER 78

SHOE ELF

"DAD, WHERE'S ERNIE?" Kate came into the living room of her parents' row house.

"Try the factory showroom with Grandpa K," her father said, dropping the corner of his Boston Globe—a luxury read for his day off.

"The factory, again?" She wasn't sure hanging out there was a good idea for Ernie. So recently traumatized, and there were so many strangers. But why was she so protective? He was a young man who knew how to make the best of everything. A lesson for her, as well.

Kate headed up the street to talk to Ernie about his return to Rolling Hills. She was loath to face discussing her departure for her European tour with Ernie and Mary. A mist fell on the street as Kate passed an abandoned house, it's porch window shattered—another sign of the changes in Glynn with the closing of another factory. Of course it would be a gloomy fall day, she thought, as her foot slid on a pile of slick maple leaves brought down on the crooked sidewalk by last night's rain. A dog let out a lonely howl from behind the house. Kate pulled the hood up on her UConn rain slicker. No matter how much Michael and her mother had encouraged her to pursue her singing dreams, leaving everyone felt like abandonment.

The weekend respite for Ernie had turned into a week, thanks to Brent. It seemed like a good idea at the time for Kate to advocate for more time for Ernie to stay with her family. He was having such fun, and he was recovering well from his wounds. Now, she wasn't sure. Maybe he'd settled in a little too well, and his re-entry into his institutional home might be harder on him. Kate would drive him home before she left. *Home*, the word didn't fit that dank institution for Ernie.

Maybe she'd stop to see Father Sullivan on her way to her hotel overnight-stay at the airport. She could use some of his inspiring quotes right now. True confession—Kate was thrilled that in two days she would head to Paris, despite that ever-present conflict that came with leaving. She knew when she hit the stage, she would feel like herself, again.

The factory's main door was locked with no second shift today; she went around back to the customer service measuring room. The gray metal door stood ajar; inside, Kate saw Ernie. Standing on a wooden shipping crate, he was lit up and glowing like an angel from the big metal lamp that hung overhead. On the factory fitting table, Ernie measured one of the customer's children for her wooden shoe last, to make her first custom shoes. Her parents looked on with pride.

Grandpa K stood back against the wall, smiling with his arms folded, watching Ernie.

"I'm the Shoe Elf, and I'm going to make you the prettiest shoes in the land."

The word *elf* had felt so wrong; it sank in Kate's stomach like a rock. Did *he* make that up, or did the little girl, or her parents? Kate stepped forward, then stopped herself, and held her breath.

At the same time, Grandpa K held up one hand to delay her interruption. He flashed a thumbs-up, and nodded—indicating he'd seen Kate's instincts to let it play out had already kicked in.

She couldn't protect Ernie from everything. In seconds, that sick fear Kate had that Ernie would be made fun of, or be rejected, evaporated with the little girl's giggle and hug.

"He's my shoe elf, Mommy." Dressed in pink like a ballerina, the child threw her arms around Ernie's neck. And then, the reassuring reward was delivered—the fawning parents' smiles.

Who could resist Ernie? Kate couldn't. And when he'd called *himself* the shoe elf, it was different than if anyone else had, wasn't it? How could anyone be so vulnerable and turn it into courage?

After the child's parents had paid for their order of patent leather shoes and brown leather oxfords and left, Ernie did a dance around the room.

"Did you see that Miss Ketchup, Grandpa K? I sold some shoes."

Kate choked a laugh up. Any fear she had over exposing Ernie to the outside world melted away—her misgivings about him being capable of life beyond the walls of the institution began to dissolve with Ernie's happiness and pride in his success. He'd loved the factory from that first day, he said—a place she'd spent her entire young life trying to escape.

A pyrrhic victory. She'd given Ernie what he deserved. Now she had to return him like some unsatisfactory purchase after he'd discovered a belonging he'd never known—a family.

Kate signaled to her grandfather that she needed to talk to Ernie alone. The weight of having to take him away from his first taste of independence made her pace nervously.

Grandpa K patted Ernie's back. "Great job, a true professional. A man worthy of working in leather."

Ernie's face said it all as he saluted and stood at attention. "Ready for our next customer, sir."

A worthy man. She'd almost forgotten he was a young man. Nothing in his stature or his childlike affect was there to remind her. Then couldn't he handle the reality of his return to Rolling Hills? It wouldn't be his first disappointment; he'd found a place in the institution, making everyone laugh, helping every child to find joy.

When had he ever had such a look of satisfaction on his face? Oh yes, she'd seen that look when he'd popped up out of the orchestra and slammed those two big brass cymbals together the first time she'd seen him play. Smashing, Ernie, simply smashing.

What was it about Ernie that he could burrow so deep into her heart? He'd become such a part of her life—like a child in his unfiltered love, like an old sage in his observations. A contradiction of brilliance and innocence. Taking him from the factory and the family would be tough; dropping him at Rolling Hills would be even tougher. The thought of leaving him in that place after what happened with Ronnie made Kate shiver.

CHAPTER 79

NO RETURNS

"THAT'S OK, MISS Ketchup; I knew I was going back." Ernie didn't show much emotion when she'd shared their departure time in the factory yesterday, nor as everyone waved goodbye. Not his usual exuberance, but he'd smiled and waved back.

Turning in the seat, he watched Kate's family disappear behind him through the rear window. Ernie settled back into the seat next to Kate, gazing far off into the fields.

Had Kate even taken a breath since they'd pulled away from Glynn? Ten minutes into the trip, her words came out. "Ernie, I wish—"

"Don't worry, everyone has to leave me. I know that. I was too ugly, even for my parents." His high-pitched voice delivered the words that stopped Kate's breath.

He didn't say it looking for sympathy; his tone was filled with compassion for Kate's position. That made it worse, somehow.

"I had a cool time in Glynn."

She searched for the right words; were there any?

His voice was barely a whisper, but the words reached Kate. "I'm ugly, but I could've made my parents laugh."

Kate pulled off the road and stopped at the gate that opened to a long dirt road to a farm. "Ernie, you think that's why I'm taking you back? Because you're... *ugly*?" Her heart pounded so hard she could hear it. "That is *not* why I'm taking you back to Rolling Hills. I—"

"It's OK. But I figured you're family's keeping Mary, and she's pretty, like you, Miss Ketchup."

Kate's hands were shaking. She squeezed the steering wheel. "Dammit. There is no way in *hell*."

"Mr. Brent said, you're not supposed to say hell or damn or shit."

"Hell, damn, I don't give a shit!"

Ernie gasped and covered his mouth with his wrinkled hands, and laughed.

Kate had that *I-have-to-do-this* feeling. She worried about putting too much burden on her family, creating chaos, and then leaving. But fearing for Ernie's safety after what had happened with Ronnie? No. She had to find a way to keep him out of that place.

There was no plan, nothing beyond that instinct. Her mother would say, do the right thing. What was the right thing? Was that her Nana Katherine's spirit inside her, again? OK. Nana Katherine, I asked for adventure, but...this was one adventure Kate couldn't walk away from. She was going to damn-well turn her car around and take Ernie back to Glynn until she figured things out. She would call Brent and ask to have Ernie's stay extended again, then investigate the options, talk to Michael and her family. Of course, her mother would agree. The same look was on her mother's face as Kate and Ernie walked out of the kitchen after saying goodbye.

Maybe he could live with Grandpa and Grandma Kendall? Seeing Ernie with her grandfather in the factory made that seem possible. Her paternal grandmother was judgmental about Kate, but she was kind to kids. Well, maybe Grandma Kendall was a tad full of herself and a bit of a grump, but not to Ernie. Unless they were too old? A million thoughts were processing, but they all led to Ernie becoming a Ketchum like Mary. He had the right soul for it, the right sense of humor for it, the right to belong.

"You are not going back, Ernie. Are you OK with that? If... I can find a way, at least for a while?" Kate didn't want to promise too much, but there was no *if*; she *would* find a way.

"Pull over, pull over." Ernie reached for the door handle.

Kate thought he was going to be sick. "Hold on, I have to find a place." Fifty yards ahead, was a country store. She skidded onto the crunching gravel.

He leaped out of the car and did that hysterical dance of his—hands on crooked hips, elbows bent, bowed legs, a kind of clog—a wild Irish jig.

The next day, as Kate discussed the situation with Michael, Ernie came through the front door, panting as though he were being chased. The door slammed, and he launched into the foyer. Moving toward the parlor, balancing an Owl & Shamrock shoebox on his undersized hand, Ernie took off his jacket and tossed it on the low brass hook in the hallway Kate's father had installed for him.

With his short body in silhouette, backlit by the sun through the beveled glass insets in the front door, Ernie bent in half and let out his muffled guffaw. He threw his free hand over his mouth. His signature snuffles put Kate back to first meeting Ernie in her classroom—his endearing sound that always heralded Ernie was up to something—some secret, some surprise.

Kate didn't have to see him in the light to know Ernie's classic grin had just spread over his moon face.

"*Miss Ketchup*!" He caught sight of Kate in the corner, ran toward her, and stopped short of knocking her over. Ernie bent over, peeked at Hy Vọng upside down through his legs, waved at her, and smiled.

Hy Vọng came crawling out from behind Michael's legs calling, "Ernie."

Kate held her breath. Ernie always had a way with kids. She remembered what Brent had said—with all of Ernie's misplaced organs and deformities, his heart is always in the right place.

"I forgot to tell you. I missed you so much after you left school, Miss Ketchup, that I walked in circles for days. Yeah." He put one foot out and shuffled around in circles as if his foot were nailed to the floor. "I pretended I didn't care so you wouldn't feel bad about leaving. Yeah. And I didn't want to ever leave Mary, you know. So, look." Ernie displayed a watch Grandpa K had bought him. "I really could tell time, Miss Ketchup; you taught me. But, I had to stay in our class to help the other kids who couldn't. You know? But now they got their keys." He saluted Kate. "And now, Mary's with Aunt Maggie, so…"

Her throat squeezed shut with emotion at his admission.

"I saw your picture in the paper. Yeah. You're famous." Ernie pantomimed singing with a hand mic, mouth wide open, writhing like a rock star.

"You clown." She leaned down and kissed his head.

"Aw, you kissed my head, Miss Ketchup. Everybody does that in this family." Deflecting the tender moment, Ernie pointed at Hy Vọng. "Grandpa K and I were cooking up something at the factory for Hy Vọng, Yeah. I'm late. Sorry."

Hy Vọng toddled over toward Ernie and held out Bunny to him. He took it, held it in the air, and spun around. "Hey, Bunny Boy." He kissed it and gave it back.

"Look. You like your new shoes, Hy Vọng?"

Sitting next to Hy Vọng on the window bench, Ernie opened the box and rustled the tissue. "Look what I got for you, Hy Vọng."

She reached out.

"Say, 'red,' Hy Vọng. Your favorite color, *dow*, red." He pronounced it in Vietnamese and pointed to the shoes.

"Ernie, now you're speaking *Vietnamese*?" Kate smiled.

"Mr. Michael told me how to say it."

"Come on, Hy Vọng; I'll let you see what's inside the tissue, say 'red.'"

Hy Vọng searched in the paper and pulled out a red shoe.

"Yes, it's red," he repeated as he strapped it on her foot.

"Wed." Hy Vọng touched the soft leather.

Ernie whipped his head around toward Kate for approval, as Hy Vọng added another English word to her ever-growing vocabulary.

"Now say, *Shoe. Shh-oooo.*" Ernie adjusted the second

red leather shoe on her other foot. "Pretty. Red. Shoes." He encouraged Hy Vọng to say the words, over and over, tapping on each shoe.

"Pitty...wed soo."

It was all Ernie needed to hear. He hugged her and laughed. "Yes, Hy Vọng, pretty red shoes."

Pointing to Ernie's thick-soled orthopedic shoes, she said it again, "Pitty wed soos."

Ernie fell back laughing, holding his stomach.

The burst of joy caused contagious giggles from Hy Vọng.

"We're getting there, yeah."

Kate put her hand over her mouth and went silent. A pressure built behind her eyes, and she leaned against Michael's shoulder.

The door opened, and Mary arrived. Maggie's sewing talents had transformed her from a gawky, gangly fifteen-year-old into a stylish young lady.

"Maggie made me a new dress. Ernie, I'm neah you now, staying wid Maggie."

"Miss Ketchup told me. That's cool. Mary, you're talking. Woohoo!" Ernie spun around.

"I know." She cast her eyes down and laughed.

"Hey, Mary, Kate said I'm not going back to Rolling Hills yet either. She said, hell and damn too. So, I believe it now."

"Miss Ketchup, I'm going to stay here too, ain't I? And you ain't neva eva gonna leave right?"

The way Mary communicated was the awakening that Kate had hoped would materialize for the lithe, young girl who'd huddled silently in the corner at Rolling Hills. But was Brent right? Did Kate set Mary up for the most tragic disappointment yet? She could only hope Michael's family lawyer could make it happen, even if Maggie was a single woman. Maybe her parents could sign for her. Kate knew nothing about these kinds of things. Adoption was never an issue in a family that popped out babies at the tip of a hat.

Cecelia put her arms around Kate and Mary at the dinner table before she took her seat.

Mary tilted her head toward Maggie. "I'm staying, Ernie, cuz I think Maggie's gonna be my new mom."

The adults shot a glance of concern, shifting their eyes from Mary to each other, then shared hopeful glances and smiles.

Cecelia broke the silence. "Everybody hungry?"

On the good side, Mary was talking, and her strange verbal patterns were already fading. There was hope as her occasional sunny smiles broke through the gray fog that had hung over her eyes. Kate wouldn't feel comfortable until the legal requirements were met for Mary to stay.

CHAPTER 80

Michael

"YOU MUST BE exhausted. Did you enjoy singing again at O'Leary's? It's been a while." Michael snuggled closer to Kate in bed.

"Yes, something about knowing everyone in the room. I love that, Michael."

"The applause was maniacal."

"And my own cousins wanted an autograph; I had to laugh. The smaller crowd, it felt like...I don't know—"

"Like home."

"Your parents were so sweet to keep Hy Vọng in their room on our last night together." Michael kissed Kate on the shoulder.

"Honey, are you sure I'm doing the right thing? Because I confess, I really do want this tour."

"I understand what's enticing you. I can't have you miss out on this. I only wish *I* didn't have to miss it."

"But Hy Vọng? She should come first. And there's Mary and Ernie. Are you confident the lawyer can pull this off? God, it makes me sick to leave. I'm not sure you *do* understand, but thanks for not making me feel bad about going." She whispered in his ear and nibbled at his earlobe.

"Now you're being predictable." He laughed. "It's only a few weeks. We'll survive. We've been through this before, and I know if you give up this big chance, you'll always regret it." He stroked her arm to calm her.

Kate threw her leg across him. "I'll miss you."

"Kills me, I can't go with you, Babe." The thought of not being there to share it with Kate, produced an ache for him.

"I keep wondering, after the tour, then what?"

"Honey, have faith we will figure out everything when you get back." The plans were forming in his mind.

Michael's arms came around her.

"Oh, did you make the call to Brent? About Ernie? God, there's too much going on."

"Oh, damn. Yes, he called me back amid the chaos when you were bathing Hy Vọng." Michael squeezed Kate's shoulder and whispered, "Thing is, Ernie's always been adoptable since his parents dropped him off as a newborn eighteen years ago."

"Really?"

"Brent said, no one's ever given him a second look over the years. I mean...he's, well, an odd character, but you were right, he's great. Look at him with Hy Vọng."

"Oh, Michael, we can't *not* keep Ernie here." Kate laughed. "And me, the woman who didn't want commitments."

"Kate, sometimes, I feel bad about all the accommodations you'll have to make because of Hy Vọng, Mary, and Ernie—an adopted daughter and two other children who depend on you being here. But it was the right thing in all cases, babe."

"And now I've passed all that responsibility onto my family."

"Cancelling the tour was never an option, Kate."

"And what about going forward? Stopping the momentum of my singing career would be like deciding to stop breathing. Nana Katherine's complicating the hell out of my life." Kate glanced heavenward. "Maybe someone else would do the right thing and stay home from the tour, but Michael, you're right; I just can't."

The alarm went off, and Hy Vọng ran into the room. "Dah-dee. Mah-mee."

"Good morning, Hy Vọng." Kate stretched out her arms to her child.

Crawling up onto the bed, Hy Vọng cuddled into Michael's side.

Kate kissed her. "I have to eat and throw some last-minute things into my carry-on. And I smell breakfast, complete with bacon. You hungry?" Kate tussled Hy Vọng's hair, planted a line of kisses along Michael's square jaw, and flew out of bed with the sound of his sigh behind her.

CHAPTER 81

Kate

HEATING UP

THE FLIGHT FROM Boston to Paris seemed interminable. Kate wanted to land on the stage singing; she'd missed that high so much. The magnificent view from Kate's first-class window kept Kate from worrying about all the people she'd left behind—the bright-white cloud formations pierced by shards of sun and the landmasses below etched by silver rivers. She had to believe things would work out; it was meant to be. It didn't hurt to have the money and a clever lawyer to handle legal details. Brent said he would do everything he could to make it happen for those two young people. Tapping her plastic cup of orange juice on the tan tray, Kate smiled, and leaned her head against the cool of the window.

She'd experienced a kind of disassociation, when it came to singing on stage—a distancing from all of Kate's responsibilities and concerns. Sometimes, that distancing worried her. What was wrong with her that she could lose those yearnings for home and her loved ones the minute she'd hit the road? Kate never thought she'd be like a homing pigeon. Despite her desire for an exotic life overseas, despite the pact she'd made with herself to escape her life in Glynn, would she ever be able to stay away from home for long now? Why did love sometimes feel like a burden? She'd fallen in love with two lives.

Kate's mother's idea was a good one. Michael and Hy Vọng would stay with her family for a while until they bought a house. Michael could figure out his refugee children's foundation, and Kate's family was just the support he needed.

But where would their little trio land? Kate and Michael had talked about it in bed each night but hadn't come up with a decision. Round and round they discussed the pros and cons of every place that came to mind. She just couldn't see clear to living in Glynn, although Michael seemed attracted to that idea. And she couldn't imagine giving up singing just when it was ramping up, maybe ever.

But would singing give up on her? The tour with the Keys would end in three weeks. She had some inquiries about a tour of her own with Riverrun, but nothing solid. Kate felt more like a city girl now, but wasn't the countryside a better place to raise their daughter? How would she handle any possible tours in the future, as a mom?

Maybe she had a dark and light side, just like Michael. A kind of selfishness—leaving right in the middle of such serious life-things. Now that she had a life beyond what she could ever have conceived of, she didn't want her newfound fame to contaminate her perfect life with Michael. She wanted to stay; she didn't; she couldn't. Singing was who she was, her mother had said over and over. She had to stop this continuous loop of conflict. She handed her empty glass to the stewardess and prepared for landing.

Stop, just focus on Paris, she thought. Could this career ever give Kate anything but a see-saw of conflict? She had to admit; she resented that.

As she sat in the Paris airport lounge, Kate ran a list of songs through her head, and her mind rushed into the details of her tour. She'd transformed, become someone new. Kate's fans adored her, the press scrambled to interview her; she was the American sweetheart. They had no idea she was a girl from Glynn. Anyway, that was the past, and now she was the female lead singer with her own band, Riverrun. Even as a warm-up band, they'd topped the charts in their new world. She could never have imagined the banners over foreign capitals with her name on them.

"Had a nice flight, Kate?" Adam appeared out of the crowd at the Paris airport.

"Honestly, leaving Michael and my new daughter was a bit emotional. I enjoyed the scenery. Fantastic. I can't believe I'm in France."

"New *daughter*? You never even looked pregnant." Adam laughed at his joke until he saw Kate's face. "Hey, sit down, what's up?"

Kate shared her stories. If she was going to make this her lifestyle for now, she wanted to be real, get closer to her band members. Maybe she wouldn't feel so lonely.

During the two weeks on the *Southeast Asian Tour*, she had learned very little about the band members of the Keys or her own Riverrun musicians with their tight schedule, except for their favorite drinks and the key they liked to play in; she would change that.

"Adam, did you ever have to make a choice between…"

"What, family and living the dream?"

"Well, yes."

"Every time I break up with a woman I love." Adam laughed. "But I'm not the commitment type. I've accepted that. Two of the band members are married. They seem to pull it off OK. Well, one's been divorced twice. Too complicated for me."

"I know this is my last concert. Thank you so much for the incredible opportunity. It was unreal."

"Was? You don't think I'm letting you go now? You're just getting started."

"I just...thought it was a two-tour fantasy." Kate sat up straight in her seat.

"We'll see how you feel after this tour of Europe. You're going to fall in love, trust me. It will blow you away."

The European tour was every bit as exciting as the first one—packed houses, but on the first night, Kate noticed something different when her voice went out over the crowd. She was on key, yes. Her tone was good. But it was her lone voice, and she missed that inexplicable duet feeling. Like when her mother's voice and hers blended in the church choir and became more than two parts. Or when Michael's voice bonded with hers in the student union and blew everyone's mind, including hers. The band's background harmonies fell short for her. Something was missing.

For twenty-one nights, she was applauded, followed, adored. She wrote her name, so many times she was spinning. The Eiffel tower lit outside her hotel window, guards changing at Buckingham Palace, the finest hotels—it was a fairytale.

She looked forward to her phone calls from Michael to find out what was happening with Hy Vọng, her family, Mary, Ernie. Her mother was right—thirty-seven aunts, uncles, and grandparents could certainly take care of two more teens in the family. No drama.

Adam's over-the-top generosity, the long rehearsals, and the loneliness when Kate returned to her room late each night, caused her to rethink her next move. Kate began to plan her own tour—what continent this time? Her map was filling up with a scattering of pins. But with no Michael, no Hy Vọng, and no emotional intimacy, no way. Get up, travel, perform, greet the fans, party, go to sleep. Get up, travel, perform, greet the fans, party, pass out, on and on. Not that she wasn't grateful. It was an over-the-top amazing life, but was it hers? No, she didn't want to be a warm-up band; she needed to have her own tour, choose where and when to go, and try to walk the tightrope of her desires.

She felt responsible to Riverrun. They were having the times of their lives. Single guys, trying to make it. If she ended it here, what would that do to *their* dreams?

In her nightly, fuzzy calls with Michael, she had the same things to say. Amazing sights, capacity crowds; I miss you all. Trapped in a cycle of luxury and success. Kate had to laugh—it was like the thermostat was turned up too high. Like having a Thanksgiving feast every night of the week—at some point, you just wanted a burger and fries.

CHAPTER 82

Michael

TOURIST SPOT

BEING WITH THE Ketchums was just what Michael needed. Hy Vọng had begun to speak a few English sentences from so many family members engaging with her. When her buddy Ernie came home at night for dinner from his part-time job at the factory, he taught her English vocabulary. Hy Vọng was a regular in Cecelia's kitchen at mealtime, scribbling in her stack of coloring books to the tune of the clinking pots.

Michael had to decide what came next, besides all the paperwork and resolving legal issues for both Mary and Ernie. But what about their own trio?

Kate seemed different on the phone lately. He imagined it was hard to be alone on the road. Alone, with thousands of strangers every night. The highest high, the lonely low of the hotel room while decompressing from the intensity of it all. She'd gone to Europe, but not carefree, he thought.

The details were worked out with Michael's family lawyer, and the documents he had for Hy Vọng now showed her as legally adopted by Michael and Kate. Michael could travel with her wherever they decided to live. Was it the right thing to do, to keep uprooting the child? And yet, Hy Vọng seemed to be adapting, as she was exposed to new things, he thought. She'd been through much more than he would ever know.

"Cecelia? Can we talk?" Michael pulled out one of the kitchen chairs and sat.

"Of course. Do you mind if I finish this spaghetti sauce? You've noticed, I'm a great juggler." She laughed. "How's our Katie-girl?"

"That's what I wanted to talk about." He spun the white ceramic saltshaker around on the oak table. "I'm OK; I'll soon have a job I can do anywhere. A meeting in Boston now and then, some overseas trips. Well, honestly, we're better than OK." He knew his context was dramatically different from the Ketchum's idea of OK. "But I'm not sure what's right here."

Hy Vọng ran into the room. "Dah-dee. Er-nee." She pointed at Ernie, who was doing a headstand in the dining room.

"Yes, that's Ernie, honey; he's funny, isn't he?"

She ran back to play, giggling. Michael's eyes followed his petite daughter until she was out of sight. It was a kind of love he'd never experienced.

"Isn't it wonderful?" Cecelia nodded toward Hy Vọng and put a cup of tea down in front of Michael. "I'll tell you what I once told Kate, here in this kitchen. Michael, you two belong together. Hy Vọng will be fine if you two are fine." Cecelia stopped stirring her creation in the dented Revere Ware pot. She sat on the edge of the chair next to his, a wooden spoon dripping with her famous red sauce. "Taste?"

Michael tested it. "Delicious. Perfect."

"Salt?"

"Hmm? Nope."

"Michael, you and Kate are young, and you've taken on such responsibilities. Look at what happened with Ernie. He's become a part of the family. And we'll get Mary straightened out in time too. There is no way we can send her back now."

"Yes, my lawyer said, he's making progress."

"Like I said to Kate, I think thirty-seven Ketchums, Callahans, and Kellys can handle one teenage girl and a shoe fairy. We have a family formula."

Michael laughed. "What's that?"

"A good dose of love and a pinch of humor. Well, sometimes more than a pinch is required."

Michael shook his head and laughed.

"As long as Hy Vọng is with the two of you, she'll adapt. Wherever you three are together is home. Remember that, Michael."

"The only question is, where?"

"You'll check with Kate first, won't you?" Cecelia's stern look melted into a smile.

Michael was getting used to the Ketchum's dry humor. "I guess you two have been talking. Yes, I've learned not to mess with a gorgeous, red-headed Irish woman. I mean, no offense."

"I'll take that as a compliment."

Michael drank his tea, gazing at Cecelia over the rim. "I know it would disappoint you and Kevin Sr. and everyone to not have Kate and Hy Vọng nearby if we move far away. I bet you never thought that the curly-haired boy who came to buy baby shoes decades ago would steal your daughter away some day, did you?"

"I knew years ago that Kate would never be happy in Glynn. And I understood from day one she had that wanderlust that can't be denied. She's her great-grandmother Katherine's carbon copy. Truthfully," Cecelia looked into Michael's eyes and hesitated. "I was stricken by the wanderlust, too, although I never had the chance to follow my dream." Cecelia looked over her shoulder, although there wasn't anyone within earshot. "Don't get me wrong, Kevin and the kids were more than enough for me. But the singing did call to me. I can only imagine being on stage like Kate with thousands in the audience. What a thrill."

"Yes. It excites me even from an ocean away." Michael treasured the rare moment of intimacy with Cecelia. "So, no regrets, Cecelia? I mean on your missed opportunity?"

She hesitated. "None now. But never mind me. It'll disappoint us more to see Kate unhappy. Her soul lights up when she's singing."

Michael watched Cecelia stare out into the distance.

"And the way she was when she arrived here with you and Hy Vọng and her career on fire, that's gift enough for a mother."

"Cecelia, I'm not sure what the future will bring or where we'll end up, but this will always be home too. And isn't it time I call you, Mom, or... is that OK?"

Cecelia put her hand over his. "I'd be honored, Michael."

The sound of something breaking and the neighbors' nightly fight drifted through the open kitchen window. Cecelia stood up and shut it.

"I know how to shut them up for good." Michael grinned.

"If only."

"Seriously, I have an idea, actually. What if I bought the house next door? We'll shut them up for you, and when Kate and I visit, we can stay next door. A kind of vacation home."

"Ha. I never thought of Glynn as a tourist spot."

The word, ha, and the sound of Cecelia's laugh reminded Michael of Kate.

"It's not fair to crowd you in all the time." Michael watched the news sink in, and Cecelia's face glow.

"Brilliant, Michael. I'm thrilled."

"We need to stick together. We're family." Michael knew his decision was the right one.

CHAPTER 83

FEMINIST FINALE

KATE SAT IN the green room, looking in the mirror.

"Two minutes, last performance. Your folks' home country, Kate," the stage manager called from outside Kate's windowless room offstage.

"Thanks, Rodney." A surge of energy went through her. There was still a high every time she went on stage to the rolling applause. How could she come down from this dazzling thrill, singing every night, and then settle into being a mother and wife? There would always be a life half-full on tour. There would always be a half-fulfilled dream at home without her music high.

So hard to be apart from Michael. She'd finally found the love she'd sought—this exasperating, loving man who somehow fit just right, and an unexpected, adorable daughter, Hy Vọng, who hadn't had time to fit in.

How long before Hy Vọng would cuddle into Kate's lap, letting her new mother rock her, teach her—passing on the legacy of love her mother had shown Kate. She wanted to make that happen. She would make that happen. Somehow. Kate ran her fingers through her hair and stopped the constant what-ifs from taking over the joy of what she was about to do.

It wasn't quite jealousy Kate was experiencing; still, if she were regularly on tour, would Hy Vọng ever feel like this woman named Kate, who came in and out of her life, was her mother? She had to shake off her guilt, her conflicts. Kate was singing to another sell-out crowd.

"Thanks, I'm ready," she responded to the curtain call. Ireland, who would have believed when her aunt told tales of her trip to their family homeland, Kate would be singing there. This one was for Kate's mother. In the span of two tour circuits, Kate had seen so much of the world. She imagined pushing two clusters of pins into her old world map, five countries in Southeast Asia and now seven more in Europe. The adulation of thousands of followers, the love of one man. And soon, she promised herself, a child who loved her.

Adam's words lingered. "Let's talk tomorrow before you go. I have another offer, I think you'll love. Break a leg. No, better yet, break a heart."

She knew this feeling. Things were getting too complicated. The last night of the tour, and another offer from Adam. Was there any going back? She finished her make-up and smiled. *There she is in the mirror, Kate, the singing star you've always wanted to be.*

That alluring sound began—the calling, stomping, and clapping, demanding that she show up. How could she quit? Her mother had never even had the chance, and now Kate did. But touring alone was different. A privileged homelessness.

She waited for her cue. The band was already set on

Dublin's St. Xavier Hall stage with their instruments ready. With the energy of a thousand fans, standing up, shoulder to shoulder, the renowned venue was throbbing.

The announcer's introduction echoed in the concert hall, and everyone sat. Kate stood offstage stroking the velvet curtain and listening to the man at the mic sing her praises. He told the audience the story about Adam discovering Kate. Adam owned her success in many ways. She'd read interviews that gave the Keys credit for Kate's skyrocket launch in Asia and now Europe. Was it selfish to go off on her own with Riverrun? She was grateful; Adam had made her into a budding star. She knew that's how it often worked in the industry, if you were lucky, really lucky.

Kate shook off the tension, rocking her shoulders. For her, it was all about reaching the audience. The connection. Knowing she'd made their night magical. And who could resist the hypnotic sound of an adoring crowd?

The musical cue sounded. Kate smiled and bounded into the spotlight; it followed her out onto center stage. The clamor of applause and screams from the crowd welcomed her. When her eyes adjusted to the brightness, it was like looking out on a glowing moon. A black-out surrounded the massive multitude. Only the blurred faces on the fringe were visible to her from the blind spot that those hot lights created.

Engulfed in the glaring light, she began to sing. That always freed her of any nervousness. The band was dead-on tonight, she thought. Everything was perfect, no, perfectly imperfect.

Lost in the steamy splendor of her performance, Kate knew she'd delivered—songs that rocked, sad songs, and upbeat ballads. The spotlights dimmed for the last love song. The house lights went on. She wanted to see the audience for this song, to try to connect her ache to theirs.

"Too precious to leave behind." She sang the slow soulful lyrics of her first hit song, acapella, before the band joined in— the first song she'd ever written herself. Her voice was loose and sensuous. She added a rusty edge to her delivery. The irony and the lyrics created a desire that rose up from inside her and coated her voice with emotion, drawing rolls of cheers from the audience, and then silence.

Her words touched something tender in the crowd too. Kate sang it for anyone who'd left home to pursue a dream, and those who held the hope of someday launching. The words touched something true in herself too. Clicking the mic back onto the stand, she folded in half in a bow and dropped like a marionette.

Lone voices called out from the concert hall. One here, one there. "Kate, you're the best." "We love you, Kate." Whistles, and then a "Katie-girl!" from somewhere near the front. She signaled the band and sang an encore verse, squeezing every bit of passion from the lyrics.

When the lights went up, amidst the resounding applause, Kate put her hands in a prayer position at her chest, and bowed again, stage left, stage right. Then she shaded her eyes with her hand, walked to the edge of center stage, and squinted at the front row.

Did she really hear her mother's nickname for her? His baritone voice?

"Katie-girl. We love you." The familiar voice called out again.

As Kate approached the front of the stage, the clamoring

crowd crushed forward with T-shirts, programs, pens, and paraphernalia, hoping for an autograph. Kate gasped and held her breath when Michael emerged from the front row and nudged through the throng.

"Katie-girl!" His smile, his voice, the flutter of his hands applauding, arms raised above his head, and the feigned touch of an Irish accent he added to his calls sent a jolt of emotion through Kate. She erupted into tears, then laughter. Covering her face with her hands, she peeked out at Michael to see if he were real.

Kate signaled him to come up. He hitched his hip on the polished edge of the stage and hopped up next to Kate and kissed her—a long and lingering kiss. What a breathless moment.

"Excuse me a minute; we need to have a little chat." Kate took Michael aside. The audience cracked open with laughter and applause.

A repetitious rhythm of anticipation came from the band behind her. Leaning in close, Kate turned off the mic and dropped it to her side. "Oh my God, you're crazy. But, where's—?"

"Don't worry; she's at home, asleep."

"Home, *where*?"

"At home, babe. Right now, it's a mile from here in a hotel with Nong.

"You brought Nong to Ireland?"

"She was thrilled for the adventure. And Nong knows Hy Vọng. From now on, home is wherever we're together and you're singing."

Kate's mind was spinning with the possibilities. "You would...

do that for me?" One look at the smiles on her band members' faces, and she knew Michael had planned it all. "Why Mr. James, I do believe you are a true feminist." She kissed his cheek and felt her throat close with emotion.

The crowd clearly loved the couple's intimacy. "Aw." They clapped in rhythm, encouraging the encore.

Michael laughed. "If being a feminist means getting everything I want, then gladly." He reached down, took the mic from Kate's hand, flipped it back on and spoke into it. "Can I play for you?"

Kate swept her arm toward the empty piano bench inviting Michael to sit, and he relinquished the mic to her.

The band made small tuning sounds on their instruments. They were ready, and the hall went silent. Raising the mic she announced, "I guess we're having another encore." Kate shrugged. "Are you all up for that?" The laughter and applause brought her a wave of happiness.

Michael's fingers fluttered over the keys and played the lead-in. Leaning over his shoulder, she settled into the warmth of his back, and put the microphone to her lips.

It was a first. She had it all. Kate's throat was too tight to let out the notes as her joy took over.

A rustle of anticipation fluttered through the crowd—then quieted. The drummer shifted on his stool, and the scraping sound echoed in the concert hall.

Still, the restriction in Kate's throat remained.

Michael stopped playing. Painful silence.

"Katie-girl." Her mother's voice rang out. Scanning the audience, Kate's knees went weak as her mother's face blossomed out of the blur. "*Mom?*"

A shot of excitement tingled through Kate. If Cecelia were standing next to her like she had in the choir loft, Kate wouldn't let her down, she thought. She waved her mother onto the stage. "Come up, Mom." Kate called. "This is the woman who taught me to sing." Kate's words squeezed out through the mic in a thin voice.

Another raging wave from the fans filled the hall as Cecelia was lifted up onto the stage. With Kate's arm around her mother, the clapping silenced.

Michael nodded at Kate in support and began playing again.

Clearing her throat, Kate pushed away her emotions, filled her lungs, and sang the lyrics. She strung the phrase out, warbling each word, sustaining the notes with the perfect trill accented by her distinctive touch of soul. "Too precious to leave behind." Her crystal-clear, final note resonated in the rafters, and Kate brought it home.

CPSIA information can be obtained
at www.ICGtesting.com
Printed in the USA
LVHW112257200721
693273LV00003B/75/J